The Three Hunters

Real estate tycoon Lawrence Honegger wanted to blow apart Legend Mountain in order to make it part of his worldwide real estate expansion.

Vietnam vet Boonie Daniel wanted to keep Legend Mountain undisturbed until he could unearth the billions of dollars in gold bars buried there.

Executive engineer Louisa Palmer wanted to stay close to Legend Mountain until she found the love she sought and the wealth she coveted.

But there was one force far greater—and deadlier—than all their hunger, their greed, their lust. And it was about to turn the treasure hunters into the hunted. . . .

THE LEGEND

Nicholas Condé

PUBLISHER'S NOTE

This novel is a work of fiction. Names, characters, places, and incidents either are the product of the author's imagination or are used fictitiously, and any resemblance to actual persons, living or dead, events, or locales is entirely coincidental.

NAL BOOKS ARE AVAILABLE AT QUANTITY DISCOUNTS
WHEN USED TO PROMOTE PRODUCTS OR SERVICES.
FOR INFORMATION PLEASE WRITE TO PREMIUM MARKETING DIVISION,
NEW AMERICAN LIBRARY, 1633 BROADWAY, NEW YORK, NEW YORK 10019.

SIGNET TRADEMARK REG. U.S. PAT. OFF. AND FOREIGN COUNTRIES
REGISTERED TRADEMARK—MARCA REGISTRADA
HECHO EN CHICAGO, U.S.A.

SIGNET, SIGNET CLASSIC, MENTOR, PLUME, MERIDIAN AND NAL BOOKS are published by New American Library, 1633 Broadway, New York, New York 10019

First Printing, December, 1984

1 2 3 4 5 6 7 8 9

PRINTED IN THE UNITED STATES OF AMERICA

For Elaine Markson

ACKNOWLEDGMENTS

I had the good fortune when I researched this story to be taken warmly into the small community of individuals who still pursue the original American dream of finding wealth in the form of gold. They almost never realize the dream whole, but manage to survive by sifting small particles of it from the ground. No matter how ungenerous fate may be to them, however, I always found their own kindness unstinting. For their help, their companionship, and, most of all, for sharing with me the way to the lost treasure—if I would only look hard enough—I express my gratitude to all. But I must send a greeting and express my special thanks to the legendary "Doc" Rosenkranz, to John Wilburn, and to "Shorty" Minsen—who are all actively looking for, and deserve to find, the Lost Dutchman mine. My sincere thanks, too, to Ken A. Phillips and Arthur W. Bloyd, of the Arizona Department of Mineral Resources, for sharing their expertise.

It should be added here, in case there is any doubt, that the Tewani are not an existing tribe, but the Indian customs and folklore described here are based in fact, and my thanks go to Thomas Slowriver and Alicia Blackbear for their knowledge and insight.

PROLOGUE

The Spirit of the Mountain

Getting too old for this sort of thing.

He hadn't been climbing for more than five, ten minutes, and here he was, huffing and puffing like a played-out plug horse. He looked down, toward where the dirt road ended and the bulldozers were pulled up. Just a hundred feet down, but he felt like the climb had taken everything out of him.

Far below, a 'dozer jockey leaning against his cab looked up and waved. The climber waved back—jaunty as could be, didn't want them to think he might be getting old for the job. He reached to take off his hardhat, and his fingers felt singed by the heat of it. Christ. That's what was doing him in—the goddamn sun. That and the mountain itself. Not just the climbing of it . . . but something about the place.

He snatched off the helmet and stood wondering if this time they could really do the job, build it like in the plans and pictures. He'd wondered that on other construction jobs, true. Things went wrong. But something was different here. Couldn't put his finger on what. Maybe it was just the place.

The mountain.

Or maybe it was just that he was getting old.

He took a breath, slipped the metal helmet back on, and started climbing again.

And then he was there, on the long, wide ledge. The activity below appeared very far away. Three hundred feet, maybe, although he didn't think he'd climbed that much farther.

Goddamn sun. The hat must be cooking his brains. He took it off again, dropped it on the ground, and pulled a pad and a ball-point from his shirt pocket. Walking to one side of the ledge, where the face of the mountain cast a shadow, he began pacing off the length in big strides.

At the other end of the ledge he checked his pad and counted sixteen marks. That's what they'd start with, on this section, anyway. Sixteen holes. That was the number they would pack with explosives when the time came to blast the foundation where the first of the condo towers would rise.

The man stood back from the sheer stone that rose to the next shelf, wondering whether to climb up for a look now or let it wait.

It was hard to be certain of the distance. The sun burned directly into his eyes and he couldn't see anything but the face of the mountain, black against the glare of the sky.

He backed off a little, to see without tilting his head back. A few steps backward. A few more.

Whoa! Just behind him the ledge gave only an extra five feet of width. Carefully testing it with the weight of one foot before he took each step, he walked out onto the rock peninsula. It felt firm beneath him, yet at the edge he looked down and realized that this formation jutted out into the air. Standing at the tip, he had a sensation of flying over the majestic view.

God, yes, a beautiful place to build. Worth all the goddamn trouble and money. You couldn't doubt it, once you'd looked across the desert from here.

Better get to it, then. He turned back to survey the mountain.

Just then the blur passed across his eyes, a streak of white, and he felt something very soft, exquisitely soft, brush against his cheek, near the line of his jaw.

He blinked and looked around, following the direction of the blur . . . but there was nothing. Though, oddly, on his cheek and down along his neck a faint sensual tingling still lingered. He stood for a second, waiting, and looked around once more.

Still there was nothing.

What the hell—a breeze brushing by, maybe. The sooner he finished and got back into the shade, the better.

The flashing whiteness came at him again, this time approaching from his right. And the sound—shit, the *sound*—a piercing high note that drilled into his ears. He made a reflex move to turn, but it had whizzed past and brushed his face again. The touch felt different now, not so soft—stinging. His hand went to his cheek, felt the wetness of his sweat. It was only when he brought his hand down that he saw the line of red across his fingertips, blood, seeping from his cheek as if drawn by the blade of a knife.

He sucked in his breath and muttered a "God damn" and started to look around again, but then the whiteness was there in front of him. It hung in the air, a little above him. He reached out, felt something soft, but when he grabbed for it, his hands came together.

Then it started to expand, and he was almost embraced by it. As it hovered and grew—became all he could see—he felt himself being forced backward. Not by pressure, but by the overwhelming presence of the whiteness.

It was not in his nature to yield; he was strong, a bull of a man, and he had never had to give ground to anyone. "Get the fuck off," he couldn't help shouting, though there was only this blur to curse at.

And then he felt the sharp thing go straight into his left eye blinding it, and the only thing that froze his scream was the sheer paralyzing shock.

He stopped flailing then, hunched over, and did something he hadn't done in forty years. He started to whimper, and then to sob. For he knew he was as lost as a child, and that only someone much bigger and stronger and wiser could save him.

But no one came.

The whiteness swelled, taking up all the space between him and the wider part of the ledge, forcing him backward. He couldn't fight it anymore. He kept moving as he was made to move, until finally there was nothing under him. He heard a cracking sound, and then he fell, screaming at last, his long falling cry magnified as it echoed against a million facets of rock.

BOOK I

The Place That Always Was

CHAPTER 1

Louisa Palmer braked her BMW sharply to a halt in front of the St. Francis Hotel and tossed the keys to the doorman as she dashed inside. Hurrying through the lobby, Lou's leggy blond California-golden good looks drew blatantly appreciative stares from a number of well-dressed men who were checking in and out. One man whom she almost collided with in her rush to the elevators even dared to try the oldest line in the book: "Haven't we met somewhere?" In fact, perhaps they had—he looked like someone she might have shaken hands with a couple of weeks ago when she'd gone to a building-trades convention in Seattle to give a talk on "Women in the Construction Industry." But today Lou had no time to sort out a corny pass from plain politeness. She was already nearly half an hour late for what was probably one of the most important appointments she'd ever had in her life. Giving the man a fleeting brush-off smile, she breezed past and into an elevator through doors that had already started to close.

Normally Lou had no problem with enclosed places, but now, even though there were only two other riders, she felt claustrophobic in the elevator. She was practically jumping out of her skin, wound up tighter than she could remember.

Christ, of all the days! If she had any sense, she would have canceled the appointment, begged off.

But of course that was impossible. You couldn't be a woman invited to have lunch with the chairman of the board of the company where you worked—where for eight years you'd been climbing the ladder, rung by rung, with the men above you stomping on your fingers all the way—and then simply cancel out at the last minute. If she'd slipped under a cable car and lost a leg, by God, she'd have come hopping here anyway. And if, to Lou's mind, what had befallen her just before arriving was actually more painful and damaging than losing a leg—whether or not the wound showed—there had still been no choice but to drag herself here. It was just such a damn shame that life had to play these tricks, build you up to knock you down.

Last night, burning the midnight oil to prepare for the ground-breaking of the Crownway Shopping Mall, Lou had been in her office when the phone rang, and it had been Lawrence Honegger himself. Speaking from aboard his private jet, Honegger had said that he was en route to San Francisco to spend a day. "And I would be very pleased, Louisa, if you would do me the honor of having lunch with me." He told her to be at his penthouse suite in the St. Francis Hotel at one o'clock sharp, adding that he hoped she would regard the meeting as strictly confidential.

It was hard not to let the call go to her head. As founder of one of the world's largest private construction firms, Lawrence Honegger had attained the level of a statesman, dealing directly with the heads of many countries around the globe. Of all the people he could have summoned to lunch—one of the Hearsts or the Bechtels or the mayor of San Francisco—he had chosen her. There had to be something big in the offing.

For a long while after hanging up the phone, Lou had pleasantly mulled the possibilities. Perhaps she was being moved up from project manager into overall management. That would explain the request for confidentiality—the ax might be falling on someone who didn't know yet. Her anticipation was diluted only a little by wondering what she could do with her son if she were transferred to one of the foreign offices. Taking Ben along wasn't completely out of the question—there were good schools abroad. Though considering the disciplinary problems he'd been having lately perhaps he should be sent to one of the New England boarding schools.

But all that could be worked out later. There was really nothing to take the edge off Lou's excitement.

This morning she had come to the office in her most expensive, most understated suit. Charged with the high voltage that comes from expecting wonderful things, she had done twice the usual amount of work and by noon had been thinking of leaving early to walk a bit and enjoy the sunshine before lunch. Then she had taken just one more phone call. . . .

Now she was half an hour late for a man who was legendary for his concern with bringing things in on schedule; she had risked violating his request for confidentiality by having her secretary call ahead to say she had been delayed. Finally—assuming she had not already provoked his wrath to such a degree that he'd changed his mind—whatever career prize Honegger was about to bestow on her, Lou was no longer sure she wanted. And, even if she did, whether she could accept.

▲▲▲

The door to Penthouse A was opened by the Filipino valet, who ushered her into a long living room. Next to a window with a stunning view of the bay, a table glittered with two place settings of china, crystal, and silver. A small cloisonné vase just in front of one place held a single white tea rose. Intimate, Lou thought. For the first time she had the idle notion that Honegger's desire for a secret meeting might arise from motives less than purely professional. But then she dismissed the thought. Honegger had been married to the same woman for eighteen years, and his personal behavior was known to be impeccable.

The valet offered a drink, and Lou asked for a vodka Gibson. She didn't enjoy liquor usually, but today she felt it really might help.

Waiting for the drink, she heard a voice drifting through an open door at the end of the living room, intermittent bursts of rapid French—Honegger, on a transatlantic call.

The valet brought in her cocktail, then walked to the door from which Honegger's voice emerged, gave a discreet signal, and disappeared. Taking a long sip of her drink, Lou drifted to the window to wait.

"Ah, our lovely Louisa!"

Lawrence Honegger burst out of the room and came toward her. She put out her hand, and he grasped it warmly.

"Forgive me for not meeting you at the door, my dear, but I had to take this call from Toulouse—you know we've just won the contract to do that airport expansion. . . ."

"I saw it on the teletype yesterday," Lou said. "Mr. Honegger, I'm terribly sorry I was late, but—"

"Never mind, Lou. You're on time when it counts. Every project you've handled for us came in on schedule. Indeed, if memory serves, you came in early when you topped off the Four Corners Center last year."

Memory served, all right. To be exact, the shopping center had come in just two days ahead, but Honegger had noted it and remembered.

It had been not quite four decades since Lawrence Honegger had arrived with a cargo of "displaced persons" from the war in Europe, yet he still bore the stamp of his continental background. His genteel turns of phrase, along with his accented English, the trimmed Vandyke beard punctuating his chin, and his clothes—a plain dark suit of an English conservative cut, pale blue silk shirt with a stud collar, and pearl-gray shantung tie—had an old-world aura. Lou could never see Honegger without wondering about the truth of his past.

By one account, at the age of fourteen Honegger had been drafted into Hitler's army and distinguished himself with a talent for blowing up Russian supply depots. According to another, at the same age he had joined a small resistance group linked to the American OSS. Landing in this country, he worked first as a janitor, and saved enough of his meager salary to buy large lots of dismantled Quonset huts from war surplus. In the postwar housing shortage, he found ready buyers as soon as the huts were reassembled on cheap tracts of land. As earnings multiplied, he plowed them back to buy larger tracts and build better homes. By the age of thirty-three he headed one of the largest construction firms in the country; ten more years and he was one of the two or three largest builders and developers in the world. Lou wondered sometimes if Honegger wasn't driven to build as an antidote to childhood memories of war's relentless destruction.

Honegger steered her now to the small dining table and held the chair for her as she sat down. "Since we're running a little behind time, I hope you won't mind if we start lunch immediately."

The reference to time made Lou a bit wary. Honegger had made so little of her late arrival, she thought; perhaps he was testing to see how seriously she took the transgression herself.

"I think I do owe you an explanation, Mr. Honegger," she said. "A problem involving my son, Ben, cropped up shortly before I was going to leave to meet you. I received a call from the headmaster at his school, asking me to come at once. I tried to put it off, but he insisted on seeing me immediately."

"I understand," Honegger said, and gave Lou a concerned glance as he spread his napkin. "Your son should come first." He paused. "It must be quite a serious problem. Anything you'd like to talk about?"

Lou was powerfully tempted to unburden herself. She'd been such a rock sitting there in the headmaster's office, but all the time, the headmaster's story had been tearing her apart.

Only this morning, he'd said, the school had discovered that her fourteen-year-old son, her pride and joy, was conducting quite a booming little business lending money to other students. Because the affluent children who attended Chadwick Hall were in the habit of frequently exceeding their allowance, but reluctant to go back to their parents and endure a lecture on irresponsibility, Ben had been able to build a business meeting their needs. Charging rates of twenty percent interest on the first five dollars, and twenty-five percent thereafter, he lent his classmates money. Which was bad enough, except that Ben's method for securing his larger loans consisted of the borrowers writing signed notes about themselves with information they'd sooner die than have their parents know. When one third-form girl had nearly defaulted, Ben had said he might actually send a Xerox copy of her "collateral" to her folks—a letter admitting she'd spent a night with three boys in her parents' bed while they were on a Hawaiian holiday. The girl had apparently considered suicide before pawning her expensive stereo instead. At which point her parents had noticed the stereo missing, asked a few questions, and then called the school.

By the end of the account, it was all Lou could do to beg the headmaster to reconsider his decision to expel Ben. The headmaster had agreed to give her plea some thought on the condition that Lou provide psychological counseling. For the present, he would allow Ben to attend classes. But there was little doubt that in the end Ben would have to leave Chadwick Hall—and under circumstances that would make it difficult to reenroll him anywhere else.

Lou studied the intelligent face of Lawrence Honegger as he waited for an answer to his expression of concern. Should she seek his counsel? You could do worse than to ask the advice of a man who, at Ben's age, had clawed himself out of the chaos of war and then climbed to a pinnacle of success in not much more than a decade. God, there were times she just needed a man's viewpoint, and Matt was never there for her anymore—had even forgotten Ben's last two birthdays.

Lou leaned forward, hesitated . . .

. . . and caught herself just in time.

Great. Tell a man who holds your future in his hands that you've been raising a loan shark! That would give him a dandy insight into your managerial skills!

"It turned out," Lou replied, "that it was a slump in his grades. Some tutoring should fix it."

Lord help her, ambition was still her master.

"Well, good," Honegger said. "You were right to attend to it immediately." He regarded Lou a moment longer, then nodded to the iced crabmeat cocktail the valet had set before her, inviting her to begin. "I'm sure you were curious when I asked you to keep this meeting confidential, but I didn't want to start too many tongues wagging inside the company and put you in any kind of difficult position before I had received your answer."

"Answer?" Lou sat up. "To what?"

Honegger put down his fork and carefully wiped the heavy damask napkin over his mouth and beard. "Lou, since working your way up with us from doing geological reports to actual building supervision, you've been responsible for the construction of an elementary school, a hospital wing, and two shopping centers—fancy parking lots fenced in by stores and pizza parlors. I wonder if you've been impatient to tackle something bigger."

So it *was* a promotion.

And this was the crunch. What were her priorities? Didn't Ben need more of her? Hadn't the trouble at school proved that? Though, Lou thought—negotiating with *herself* now—nothing had been offered yet. All he'd really done was ask if she was discontented. Her reply walked the line.

"Building anything is a challenge, Mr. Honegger, big or small."

"Yes. Though the satisfaction of building a barn, I

would say, is more lasting than that of making a sand castle. Would you agree?"

Lou nodded. What was he getting at?

"And then there are experiences that come almost as close as men will ever come to creation—to playing God. Building a city for example."

What was he driving at? She gave him a sidewise look, and then Honegger said:

"Louisa, I want you to be the project manager for Legend City."

She felt the grip on her fork loosen and pressed her fingers tighter before it could drop with a clatter. Legend City? *Her* project? She was flabbergasted.

Legend City was nothing less than Lawrence Honegger's pet dream, the flagship project of his whole organization. A new city, the most modern, ecologically efficient urban environment, conceived to rise whole and complete in a corner of Arizona that was at present barely populated. Not one building, but dozens. Apartment towers, office buildings, homes, stores, and the whole complex satellite system—roads, schools, theaters, stadia—necessary to support an initial planned population of fifty or sixty thousand. All set down in a landscape that was now just desert and mountain.

When Honegger had announced the idea for his development a few years ago, it had been discounted as either a bit of empty publicity-grabbing or the aberrant overreaching of a man in mid-life who had come to believe there was nothing he couldn't build—a dare to nature and death to stop him. Critics had also pointed out that the site was a dangerous place to build, too near the southern end of the infamous Hurricane Fault, which had caused minor tremors as far north as the Grand Canyon.

Since that time, however, Lou had heard Honegger give speeches at company gatherings, and read interviews with him in *Fortune* and *Barron's* and *The Wall Street Journal*, that made the reasoning behind his dream seem eminently logical. "I do not understand why people believe the plan is audacious," Honegger had told *Time* magazine. "In Brazil, the capital of the country was carved out of the jungle. In the Middle East, metropolises rise where there were barren sands. Why must only underdeveloped countries have bold development, and not the richest country in the world?"

Honegger's determination had kept the project steadily rolling forward, from dream to blueprint. The banks were in line (the project, it was estimated, would cost three to four billion dollars before it was done). A skeptic herself, even Lou had come to revere Honegger's visionary daring.

Legend City . . . *hers!*

As the first wave of shock ebbed, Lou recalled that two weeks ago the *I-Beam*, the company's house journal, had reported that preliminary crews were already on the site, working under the direction of Humphrey Davis. "Hump" Davis was a veteran P.M., best in the business. Lou couldn't begin to compete with him in experience or savvy.

Of course, she realized now, Legend City really was too big for *any* one person to supervise. "I see," she said at last. "You mean you'd like me to work along with Hump Davis—be an associate P.M."

"No, Lou. You'd be taking over." Honegger pushed his food away. "Davis is dead. Killed yesterday afternoon."

"Dead?" Her food tasted suddenly harsh and metallic.

"An accident," Honegger went on grimly, "a fluke. You know what the site is like, don't you?"

"Yes, I know the site," Lou said. Pictures had appeared for years in the *I-Beam,* and more recently in newspapers and magazines. A mountain. The apartment towers and houses of the city were to rise along the slopes of a mountain, with a downtown business area spread out at its base. It was this peak, a striking combination of craggy granite faces and gentler intervening slopes studded with boulders and sculpturelike rock formations, from which the city had taken its name. It was called Legend Mountain.

"Davis was doing preliminary blasting surveys. Apparently he stepped out on a high ledge that gave way . . . ." Honegger shrugged. "Bad luck, that's all. He happened to be standing in the wrong place . . ."

Lou shook her head. "A pro like Hump Davis. How could it happen? He'd know the rock—he wouldn't put his weight on a weak spot."

"Lou, no one can avoid this kind of freak accident. A piece of stone millions of years old suddenly . . . grows tired. You can't know when it will happen. for that matter, there are all kinds of problems this project presents that even some of the most experienced pros may never have faced."

"So why me?" she blurted, rashly betraying her thoughts. Didn't he need someone at the very top of the field?

"Why not you?" Honegger countered. "Unless *you* think it's the wrong choice. in which case—"

Hell, she wasn't going to blow it so fast. "Mr. Honegger," she cut in, "you know very well I'm only asking the question everybody in the company will ask. You're bumping me up over two dozen men who are as qualified as I am—ten times more so, as they see it."

The smile touched Honegger's lips again, appreciation for her feisty candor. "Do you know the origin of this project, Lou? Not just with me, but going back before that?"

She couldn't tell if he meant to answer her question or avoid it. "I know that you picked up the land when the Cabot Corporation went bankrupt."

"Correct. They'd planned to use it for a resort hotel. But the minute I set foot there, I knew it deserved something more, a grandiose concept. Lou, it's a spectacular spot, one of the most magnificent on earth. Once you've spent time there, something happens. You perceive the grandeur of all nature, the miracle of—" He interrupted himself, perhaps aware that he had slipped into mere salesmanship. "I suppose all I'm trying to say," he resumed, "is that I understand how a piece of land can stir up powerful emotions. And it's especially true of this mountain. I don't know of any place in the world that's inspired such an incredible bonanza of dreams, superstitions, myths, and lunatic folklore. In other words, legends—the source of its name. Our name." He leaned across the table, bringing his magnetic force to bear on her. "This all has to do with why I want you, Lou. Unreal as legends are, in this case they create problems as potentially undermining to our success as geological faults. Problems I'm convinced you're especially well equipped to handle."

Lou was ahead of him now. In newspaper reports covering the project since its inception, there had aways been some background on the colorful history of Legend Mountain. Sketchy, bits and pieces, but enough to connect with Honegger's reference to problems. On a reservation not far from the foot of the mountain lived a small tribe of Indians who harbored an ancient religious conviction that the mountain was the home of their principal god. There was a story, too, about a lost gold mine, veins of remarkably rich ore that had been worked hundreds of years ago by Spanish *conquistadores*, then sealed or buried in a landslide. Supposedly one lone prospector had unearthed the mine eighty or a hundred years ago, but had managed to keep its location a secret. There was nothing to substantiate the story; one legend just fed on another. The gold-mine tales had been thoroughly discredited—no mine had even been found for all the treasure-hunting over the years.

"What you're telling me," Lou guessed, "is that since we've shown we're really going ahead with this, resistance is heating up among the local people and the Indians."

"So far, nothing serious," Honegger said. "Among the Tewanis—the Indian tribe—there's no more than a handful who cling to the superstitions, a small circle of elders. The vast majority is less concerned with a vague spiritual claim—they have no actual title to the mountain—than with the jobs and prosperity Legend City could bring. On the community side, we've heard only a little grumbling. The nearest town, Coopersville, is very small. Only a thousand-odd people, Lou. So far, they've shown no animosity."

"Perhaps," Lou speculated, "because they never really believed we'd show up one day and start putting up a city right in the middle of their view. Now that our crews are moving in, a visible target, you think a posse could start to form?"

Honegger chuckled. "Nothing like that, Lou. There's no certainty of community action. However, if it did develop, the delays would push our costs up by millions. That's why I want it nipped in the bud. Why I need someone who can . . . defuse the situation."

So there was her answer. He'd picked her to solve the political problems, not the structural. She wasn't sure she liked it. "How do you think I'll defuse it? Because when they see a pretty woman in charge—'a dumb blonde'—they might be lulled into believing she'll never get the city built?"

"I want you, Lou, because you're good at your job, you know construction. But also because I believe you can be a diplomat, an ambassador of goodwill as well as an earthmover."

She caught his tone, a bit frosty, displeased by her impertinent challenge. Still, she didn't back off. She could afford to be tough, maybe, because she half-hoped the lure would be yanked away from her, and she could sacrifice ambition for Ben's sake.

"I just want to get my diplomatic duties straight, sir. Am I supposed to smile and curtsy my way into the hearts of the local folks? Charm the pants off them? Because I'll be damned if I'll take the job if all you want is to use my skirt as a curtain to hide the bulldozers."

Honegger's eyes flashed, and his bushy eyebrows shot up as if at the ill-mannered outburst of a child in polite company.

"My dear Louisa," he said, and now under the cool surface there was the molten fury of the man who always got his way, "I can hardly ignore the fact that you are a woman, and a very beautiful one. But in Coopersville, and with the Indians, I suspect that will count for as much as a thimble of piss at a beer-drinkers' convention. You won't be able to coast on a smile and a curtsy, as you put it, if people think you're ripping up their paradise or evicting their god from his home. You're going to have to make these people realize that what we're planning will bring enormous economic benefits to the whole region."

She wanted it. To build a city. To be the creator. "To make them see," she said to Honegger, "that we're going to bring them a *real* gold mine."

"There! You see?" Honegger clapped his hands together. "You have the campaign already. So . . . I can assume you accept. I'm sorry to press for a decision now, but we can't leave a vacuum out there."

She hesitated another second, daunted by the magnitude of the decision. It would mean moving her life from a cosmopolitan city to the middle of nowhere—and not for a brief interlude. The project would keep her there for two, three years, maybe longer.

And Ben—what would it mean for him?

Honegger was staring at her intently, waiting.

She couldn't escape the iron grip of her own ambition. Savoring the irony, she gave her answer:

"I'm your man."

CHAPTER 2

From the highway she could see the Arm of God.

Lou hadn't realized she was so close to her destination until she spotted the distinctive landmark rising up out of the desert five or six miles ahead. After two days of driving across the broad expanses between California and the northern corner of Arizona, her interest in the landscape had been worn down to indifference by the glaring sun and the constant monotony of pale colors—flat plains of bleached-out greens and parched browns. Mile after mile of it; you began to feel it would go on forever.

But when she saw the huge rock formation, she sat up. The Arm of God, Lou remembered, was situated in the foothills of Legend Mountain. She recognized it at once, not because she had ever seen it, but because after accepting the job she had dug out all the "backgrounders" on the project compiled since Honegger had first considered buying the land. Analyses of the site never failed to mention the magnificence of the landscape. But the natural stone pillar that Lou saw now on the horizon—called by the Indians the Arm of God—was also a clear warning of the site's principal drawback: the local tribe's feeling that Legend Mountain and its environs were sacred ground.

Now, seeing the rock formation in the distance, Lou thought the written descriptions inadequate. It was phenomenal, no doubt about it—a soaring column of black basalt, tapering toward the top like an obelisk, with a huge boulder seated on the summit. Nature had produced one of its most delicate illusions, for the boulder appeared to be resting so far off center that by all the laws of gravity it should have tumbled down long ago. But there were hollows in the rock that could not be seen from the ground, and the boulder rested at its precise fulcrum, balanced as finely as a feather in a jeweler's scale.

"Hey! Look at that!" Ben hauled himself up from his slumped position in the corner of the front seat.

Hallelujah, Lou thought. Something had finally pulled him out of his sullen lethargy. She had done her damnedest in the early phases of the trip to make it an adventure—taken him through Death Valley and some of the old mining towns, ghost towns now, like Desert Rose and Mineral Wells. But he would have none of it. He would not forgive her for the sudden move that was changing his life so completely.

"Your *job*," he had cried at her the night she told him the news, "that's why we're going. So you can be like Dad and get your picture in the paper and be a big star. And don't tell me how great it's going to be for me, stuck in the middle of some desert. It's hard enough making friends here. What am I going to do out there?"

She had tried to convince him that a change of scene might be for the better—but she knew that Ben's assessment was not without some truth. Both she and Matt were ambitious people, driven too much, perhaps, by the search for the American Grail—the Almighty Buck. This had obviously contributed to the failure of the marriage; they were always too busy for each other. But Lou had never believed she was measuring her success by money; she liked her job, liked doing it well, and thought the rewards were a measure of ability.

Yet, over the past couple of days, during the long quiet hours of driving, she had resolved to reappraise herself, her motives. The sort of trouble Ben had gotten into at school had opened her eyes; it could only be a child's dark mirror image of the world as it had been shown to him.

Now she was anxious to encourage Ben's positive show of interest in the land, keep his attention focused on the stone pillar. "Pretty amazing, isn't it? Can you guess what it's called?"

"Called?" Ben asked. "It's just a rock. Do they name the rocks out here?"

"This one they do," Lou said. "As a matter of fact, it has two names. Take a good look at it—you might be able to figure it out."

Ben squinted and cocked his head. "Looks like some kind of tool, like a . . . a hammer."

"You got it," Lou said. "One of the pioneers who first lived around here was a trader named Carpenter, so the name the settlers gave those rocks was Carpenter's Hammer."

"Like Plymouth Rock," Ben said. "What's the other name?"

She hesitated. For some reason, she felt oddly reluctant to tell him. Maybe because it was a reminder of something negative about the job, the problems. Or maybe because she didn't like talking about local superstitions.

"Well . . . ?" Ben prodded her.

Better not make *too* much of it, though. "It's the Indian name," Lou told him. "The Arm of God."

Ben stared at the rock. "Yeah, I can see how it looks like that . . . like God poking right up through the earth and giving me a big 'Fuck you.' 'Cause I have to live here."

The tensions accumulated during the long drive suddenly boiled over. "All right, Ben, that's enough! I've been taking this from you for the last couple of days—the filthy language, putting everything down. I was hoping that this time together would give us a chance to settle some things, start off in a new place on the right foot. Okay, it didn't work out that way because you're mad at me, and you want to let me know it. I've let you get it out because . . . because part of me can't blame you. But we're here now. And I've got a job to do. It's going to be hard enough without having you for an enemy. I'm going to be alone too, you know. And I'm going to need at least one friend. . . ."

She was spent. She wasn't quite sure why it was the bad language that had finally set her off—she'd let it go often enough.

He answered her with silence, and kept his face turned away to look through the window.

She tried to think of something to bridge the gap, and then gave up. It was terrible to feel that she was a failure as a mother, but she did. Her only consolation was the knowledge that Matt would have been no parent at all.

There were a few miles of silence, and still the basalt column seemed hardly nearer than before. The landmark she had estimated as five or six miles away must have been closer to ten or twelve. Distances were deceptive out here—so much open space, so few reference points.

The strangest thing was that she didn't see the mountain. If the Arm of God was in the foothills, then the mountain must be right behind it. Yet as a backdrop Lou saw nothing but a shimmering silver curtain of haze. It was there, of course, *had* to be there, but it was lost in some effect of the desert's heat and glare, a mirage in reverse.

"I'm sorry, Mom," Ben murmured. "For screwing up at school and everything. . . ."

She glanced over at him, caressed the silky hair at the back of his neck. "I apologize, too. I know it's been rough. But if we try now, Ben, this can be good for both of us. Will you give it a chance?"

He turned around and gave her one of those sweet smiles that used to come so easily to him in the good old happy days.

Yes, she thought, it would work out.

And when she gave her attention back to the road, the mountain was right there at the edge of the earth. It was not just a solitary hump in the land, but rather a series of graduated ridges, each marked by sharp outcroppings of rock, that climbed finally toward a central peak with sharper inclines and mammoth faces of sheer stone. The lower reaches, Lou thought, looked as if some gigantic lizard with vertical scales along the spine—an iguana, perhaps—was half-buried in the earth. And the central, steeper part of the peak resembled the shoulders and head of a man.

But her first impression was altered as the road curved slightly and she saw the mountain from a new perspective. It had changed its aspect entirely, lost the shapes and angles that had reminded her of living things, and now looked much simpler and more basic—nothing more than an immense mound of earth and rock. Yet not without a certain symmetry, like a sort of primitive altar.

Somehow it held the landscape and commanded the attention in a way that, in her experience, few other natural wonders had done. She had been to the Grand Canyon as a teenager on a biking tour, and to Victoria Falls not long after Matt had sold out his first electronics company and had decided to celebrate with a safari. Each was incomparable in its way. Still, this mountain had the same ability to make you catch your breath. Lou slowed the car to a stop and pulled to the side of the road.

"Why are we stopping?" Ben said.

"To take a look." She nodded in the direction of the mountain that lay across the wide flat plain tinted yellow by the low growth of ocotillo. "That's it. That's where we're going to build."

Ben looked, then without a word opened his door and got out. Lou walked around to join him. His face was wrinkled in concentration, one fist propped on his waist.

"What do you think?" she asked.

"I think we shoulda stayed in San Francisco."

For a few more moments they stood by the roadside. The sun was getting lower in the sky, and the changing light gave a golden cast to the sheer rock faces of the mountain. It began to look like a lump of ore sitting on the ground, a nugget of gold for a god to put in his pocket.

"C'mon, Ben," Lou said finally, "the company people are expecting me."

She went back around the car and was reaching for the door when Ben cried out:

"Mom!"

She whirled, thinking that it was a cry for help. But when she turned, he was just pointing up toward the sky.

Alone in the sapphire blue, a large bird circled and swooped. It flew effortlessly, rarely flapping its wings, but spreading them wide to float on the warm desert updrafts. The wingspan seemed tremendous, but with the way distances could be distorted in the emptiness, the bird might be nearer and smaller than she thought.

"Never seen anything like that," Ben said, shading his eyes with his hand. "Whattaya think it is?"

"That size . . . ? I guess it must be an eagle. Now, c'mon. It's still a few miles to Coopersville, and I want to get there before the project office closes."

She was reaching for the car door again when she felt a rush of wind and a sheet of white eclipsed the sun. What the hell was that? Instinctively she leapt back, tripping on the ridge of the roadbed and sliding down the edge of the tarmac onto her knees.

"Mom?" Ben shouted, darting around the car to her side. "Are you okay?"

"I'm all right," she said.

The enormous bird had descended, flapping above them. How had it come so close so quickly? At one moment it had been high in the sky; then suddenly it was almost on top of her.

It swooped once more, this time in a soaring arc over the road, casting a shadow that covered them entirely. For a moment it hovered effortlessly, its wings faintly humming then took flight. Braced on Ben's arm, Lou stood up and stepped onto the road. She realized she was trembling as she brushed herself off.

"Jeeeeezus," Ben let out in a whisper. "That sucker is *big*."

"Quick," Lou said, "get in the car." She rushed to open the door and pushed him in.

"That can't be an eagle," Ben said, craning his head to watch through the windshield for the bird.

"What else could it be, big as that?" Lou said as she turned the key in the ignition. Ben was twisting forward, pressing against the dashboard as he searched the sky. "I don't know, but it's white. All white. And there aren't any white eagles."

"There must be," Lou said. "That's what it is."

She guided the car onto the road and started toward Coopersville. Of course it was an eagle; all the features were familiar. And if there weren't any white eagles, then it was some kind of desert mutant, or else it hadn't been all white.

"There it is, Mom. Look!"

Lou caught sight of it, out ahead of the car, above them.

"See, it's all white," Ben said.

Lou scrunched down in the seat for a better angle, but as she leaned forward the bird fell lower in the sky and seemed to fly toward the car. It appeared—no, it couldn't be—to be aiming straight at her. Almost as if it was taunting her, trying to force her off the road. Unnerved, she slammed on the brakes. The car veered suddenly on the shoulder and skidded. Just in time, she threw the wheel over and regained control.

She had no sooner steadied herself than the shadow of the bird appeared again out in front, above the car, very close.

Ben opened his window and peered up.

"Stay inside, Ben! Close that window!"

"Mom, it's *huge*. God, it's right over us."

"Benjamin, I said close the window!"

Ben obeyed, but turned quickly to search through the rear window for another glimpse of the bird.

Oddly, though, there was no sight of it in the sky behind them. It had gone, evidently flying straight up out of sight.

CHAPTER 3

Coopersville, population 1,247.

Lou looked at the sign as she drove past. The town was like a parody—something out of *Stagecoach* or *High Noon*. It consisted of a few bars, banks, a coffee shop with a white-and-blue neon sign blinking out "Legend Mountain Cafe." Side by side at the center of Main Street stood two gingerbread buildings sporting fresh white paint and ocher trim and six hand-lettered signs hanging on two chains from the rainspout—one dentist, two veterinarians, and a lawyer.

Lou searched her memory, back to her summer on the movie sets, the summer after she'd been struck by polio. Six years old, she had spent three months in the hospital, and after that the doctors said all she needed was plenty of rest and sunshine. The place to recuperate, her father decided, was where he worked. A movie sound technician, Steve Considine was much in demand by production managers for westerns.

By then Lou's mother was long gone, run off with a minor character actor named Jack Thomas. Lou remembered the afternoon, her first day of kindergarten. When the bus dropped her off in front of their West Hollywood house, she ran to the porch and found her father waiting with tears in his eyes. Mommy had gone away, he said, and wasn't coming back.

Her mother had been born Shirley Winkleton, a name hastily exchanged in the casting offices for the more glamorous Gladyce Fleming. Before Lou was born, Gladyce had appeared in one movie—a bit part with Loretta Young in *Ladies Courageous*. From then on the parts had gotten smaller, and it became apparent to everyone that Gladyce Fleming was no movie star.

Years at a stretch passed with no word from her. Once, in high school, Lou had tracked her mother to a seedy hotel in El Segundo, but Gladyce in her alcoholic fog could not quite recall having given birth to a daughter, and had thrown Lou out of her one-room bungalow. That was the last time they had ever met. Lou had been married to Matt two years when the news reached her that Gladyce was dead, buried in a pauper's grave by the city of Los Angeles.

Lou tried to forget her mother, and her father worked hard to make up for the loss. The daily trips to the locations where Steve Considine worked—the Republic back lot in Hollywood, the Twentieth Century-Fox ranch out in the San Fernando Valley, the sprawling MGM complex in Culver City—had been one long vacation. She could still remember Gene Autry taking her for a ride on Champion, sitting on Bill "Hopalong Cassidy" Boyd's lap. And listening to the singing of "Leonard Slye"—her father could always get a rise out of the most famous cowboy star of his day by ribbing him about his real name. "Hey, Leonard," he would shout at Roy Rogers. "Leonard Slye. That's some handle for a cowboy."

Her father's voice echoed in her memory as she walked with Ben to the Legend City project office, which occupied a two-story building at the far end of Main Street. The first-floor plate-glass window was unmarked except for a small hand-lettered cardboard sign in the lower-left-hand corner: "Legend City, a Project of Honegger Corp."

The moment she and Ben entered, a six-foot-plus giant of a man came toward them.

"Must be Mrs. Palmer," he said, his voice a deep rumble as he crossed the office with an outstretched hand. "And the young Mr. Palmer."

From the descriptions she'd heard, Lou guessed this was her construction superintendent. He shook Ben's hand first. Lou smiled as he took hers.

"You must be Ralph Tate," she said.

"Why don't you call me Capper?" the big man said. " 'Ralph' was my mother's idea, and I've never been too pleased with it." His nickname, he told Lou, dated from when he worked on blasting crews "capping" charges. Now he was an all-around construction man, and his expertise would be crucial in laying foundations and carving "benches"—flat sites dynamited out of the side of the mountain. Capper Tate was different from most job superintendents. These days, the men running construction sites had advanced degrees in engineering and short corporate haircuts. Capper, on the other hand, had obviously come up through the ranks. He wore frayed work clothes, not three-piece suits, let his salt-and-pepper curls grow long in a frizzy mop, and radiated easygoing charm.

Ben had moved to the back of the office, where a giant model of the Legend City project, complete with miniature people and tiny lights in the buildings' windows, was perched on two sawhorses.

Capper put a hand on Ben's shoulder. "You must be pretty excited coming out here to live."

Ben huddled in on himself and stared down at the floor. "Yeah," he mumbled. "I guess so."

The last thing Lou needed was her family problems spilling over into her work. "Ben," she said quietly, "it wouldn't be so hard to be polite, would it?"

Ben looked up at Capper. "It's a pleasure to meet you, sir." He was exaggerating the role he was expected to play, but Capper answered as if the boy were genuinely interested, pointing out all the details on the model.

He was explaining the blasting techniques for road-building when the front door creaked open and a slender sandy-haired man entered. He was wearing a button-down tattersall shirt, red knit tie, and horn-rimmed glasses. Lou recognized Ted Lundberg immediately; she had seen him on a Chicago-to-San Francisco television hook-up for Honegger executives.

"Lou Palmer, glad to meet you in the flesh. You look even better than you do on TV."

She returned his handshake, reflecting that her first impression of Lundberg still felt right: a good company man—and someone with whom a personality clash was probably inevitable. With his master's degree in engineering and twelve years' seniority in the company, Ted no doubt felt entitled to be the boss—certainly over a woman.

Bored with the scale model of Legend City, Ben came up beside Lou. "Okay if I go check out the town?"

Lou gave her permission but told him not to stray too far.

Capper and Ted showed her around the offices. The secretaries and payroll clerks worked upstairs; the office that would be hers was at the back of the main floor. When they glanced in, Lou saw that papers and files were scattered over the desk and piled on an old Chesterfield couch in the corner.

"Sorry it's not cleaned up yet," Capper said. "Didn't have a whole lot of time, I mean with Hump . . . the accident . . ." He paused, barely hiding his pained expression.

Lou felt a spasm of guilt—stumbling into a terrific job, right over Humphrey Davis' corpse. "Did you know him well?" she asked.

Capper nodded sadly. "We worked on our first job together in fifty-seven, and six or seven more jobs in the last twenty-five years. Real good man, Hump. . . ." His face tightened, the grimace of a grown man avoiding tears.

"Capper," she said, after a moment, "how did it happen?"

Capper turned, straightened his back, and ran his hands through his curly hair. "Accidents happen," he said, not looking at her. "Hump just got careless, that's all."

Lou studied him a second. There was something disturbing in his tone, but she didn't know quite what.

▲▲▲

Weird, Ben thought. They were sitting in groups of four and five, on the sidewalks, with their turquoise necklaces and silver rings spread out on intricately woven blankets.

He had stopped on Prospector Street in front of a big shop called the Indian Trading Post. The man at the cash register looked different from the Indians in old movies on television. The Indians on TV looked kind of . . . well, poor. And the Indians here talked in their own language—a singsong with little clicks in it.

But the weirdest thing about them was the way they looked at you—almost like they could see right through you. At first they seemed to be staring right at you, and then it was like you weren't even there.

"Well, young fella, gonna do some prospectin'?"

Ben looked around. He was beside a souvenir stand, a shop with its front window tilted up and open to the street, and a counter covered end-to-end with booklets and maps and trinkets. BARNEY COSS, said the sign above the window, TOURS OF LEGEND MOUNTAIN. The man behind the counter had thin silver hair, a bushy gray beard, and a face all marked up like a crumpled paper bag.

"Prospecting?" Ben asked with a laugh. "For what?"

"For gold!" the old man boomed. "What else?"

Ben smiled at the crazy old man. "There's no gold out here."

Barney Coss scowled. "Young fella, don't you know we got a mountain that's just full of gold? You musta seen it comin' into town." He bent toward Ben and squinched up his eyes. "There's an old mine up there, boy, got tons of gold in it, called the Lost Russian."

"Sure there is," Ben said sarcastically. Leaning over the counter, he added in a low voice, "But if you'd like to buy something real valuable, there's this bridge in San Francisco called the Golden Gate, and I can get it for you cheap."

"So you don't believe me, huh? Well, listen here, I

knew the old Russian himself, the one who found the mine a long time ago. I knew him *personally*."

Ben cast an appraising glance at Barney Coss. Just an old man selling souvenir junk. Maps and tools to sucker the tourists.

"If somebody found it, then why's it called the *Lost* Russian?"

"Nobody knows where it is, that's why. 'Cause the Russian kept it a secret. We got a saying out here: lost mines never die, they're just never found. But the Lost Russian's out there, all right, I *saw* the gold from it, and people still go searchin'. They come from all over the world."

Maybe this old man wasn't so stupid after all, Ben thought. If he was telling the truth, maybe there was an old mine. "So you say you knew him, huh? This old Russian."

"Sure did," Barney Coss said, holding out a pamphlet. "Here's a little story for you, tell you all about him. And I have something else you might like." He reached under the counter and brought up a closed fist. Slowly, finger by finger, he opened it to reveal a glistening chunk of rock. "This here is a piece of gold. I only got a few of'em, but you can buy this one if you like."

"Yeah?" Ben reached across the counter and took the nugget. It was about the size of a hockey puck, and the surface glittered yellow with specks of green. "This isn't gold," he said after examining it. "It looks like it's painted."

"Now, just a minute here, you can cut right into that"—he snatched the nugget from Ben's hand and scraped a corner off—"and it's gold on the inside, too. Y'see?"

The inside glittered yellow too. "I'll give you a buck for it," Ben said.

"Young fella, this here piece must be worth at least fifty dollars, what with gold going for a few hundred an ounce, and there's maybe an eighth of an ounce right here in this nugget, but you never know till you melt it down, so . . ." The old man thought a moment. "So I'll let you have it for a sawbuck."

"How much is that?"

"A tenner."

Ben took the nugget in his hand again. He had no idea what gold was actually worth, and this thing probably wasn't gold anyway. "Ten, huh? I'll give you two for it." Always bargain, his father had taught him.

"Tell you what," said Coss. "I'll split the difference at . . . six-fifty. Last offer."

Just then Lou came up behind Ben, putting a hand on his shoulder. "Ready to go?" she asked. "We can check into the hotel now."

"Wait, Mom, I want to buy this gold."

Lou took the rock and examined it. "Gold? Sorry to disappoint you, Ben, but this is iron pyrite, what they call fool's gold."

Barney Coss laughed, a deep-throated cackle. "Is that right, ma'am? Well, it makes fools of us all, don't it? And I'm an old fool myself. But it does come from the Lost Russian, and I was going to let the boy have it for practically nothin', a little souvenir of your trip."

Ben grinned at the old man. "A buck and a half," he said. "Last offer."

Barney Coss hesitated and squinted at the boy. "Sold," he said, and then reached for a bag.

Capper met them at the car and carried their bags to the hotel. The Coopersville Inn was anything but luxurious, its lobby decorations done up in a style Lou immediately dubbed Western Cute—stagecoach wheels on the walls and ceiling, kerosene-lamp fixtures with flickering bulbs. But they would have to stay for only one night; Capper had arranged for Lou to see several rental houses the next day.

They had reached the main door of the hotel when a battered green pickup truck screeched onto Main Street and careened into a parking space at full speed, slamming to a halt inches from the curb.

"There's one of our problems," Capper said, nodding to the man who stepped out of the truck. He wore mud-spattered green khakis resembling army fatigues and a peaked hat tilted low on his forehead. His long brown hair, streaked auburn and blond and white from the sun, flew off in all directions, as though it hadn't been washed in a long time.

When he noticed he was being scrutinized, he stopped and stared back menacingly. Under brows so heavy they seemed to cast shadows on his cheeks, his eyes were an eerie dark blue. When for a moment his glare settled on Lou, their eyes locked and she felt a chill. Then, without a word, the man turned and walked off into the dusk.

"Who is he?" Lou asked.

"A squatter. Vietnam vet named Daniels. The other squatters are already gone, but this guy has built himself a shack up on the mountain and he says he's never going to leave."

"He's got a great truck," Ben said.

"Caper," Lou said, "why haven't we moved him out?"

"We've got a court order for him to leave. But Daniels says the mountain is his, not ours. Eventually, I guess we'll have to haul him down by force."

"There must be another way," Lou said, the man's eyes still in her mind.

"I wouldn't count on it," Capper replied, and they strode into the hotel.

▲▲▲

Wow, Ben thought. Millions. It had to be at least two or three. Maybe more.

Perched cross-legged on the bed in his hotel, Ben read with growing fascination from the brochure given to him by the man at the souvenir stand. According to the pamphlet, some guy who'd come out here from Russia a hundred years ago had found a gold mine but kept it a secret, died without ever telling anybody where it was. The problem, as Ben saw it, wasn't that the mine wasn't there. The tourists just never stayed long enough; they searched for a couple of weeks and went home. The way his mother was talking, though, he was going to be stuck out here for at least a year or two, maybe longer. Plenty of time to study the whole proposition, learn more about this Russian guy, and figure out where the mine was.

Tons of gold, millions of dollars.

With that kind of money he could do anything. Get a Porsche or maybe even a Ferrari that would make all the girls want to go with him. Best of all, if he had all that money, his mom wouldn't have to work. Maybe then she and Dad could even get back together. Wasn't it money, after all, that had caused all the problems in the first place? Maybe if he could make them both rich . . .

The door between the two rooms opened and his mother came in. She had a towel wrapped around her head like a turban and was wearing a long yellow bathrobe.

"Come on, Ben, time to get some sleep."

"Why've you got that gunk all over your face?" he said.

"Because the air's so dry out here that without it my skin'll turn into Shredded Wheat. Now, lights out."

"Just let me finish this," Ben pleaded.

Lou glanced at the brochure. "What is it?"

"It's this history about the gold mine out in the mountain. Some foreign guy found it a hundred years ago and it's been lost ever since. I'm gonna find it."

"Oh, are you?" Lou said lightly.

Ben recognized the smile she gave him—the one that said he was still a kid and there were things kids didn't understand.

"Sure," he said defiantly. "Why shouldn't I—if I look long enough?"

"If it's been there a hundred years, a lot of people have looked. Why didn't they find it?"

"I don't know," Ben murmured, and looked down at the map in the brochure. There were dozens of little mountains in the range, with names like Miner's Peak and Mule's Roost and Tewani Ridge. "Look how big it is, Mom. You could spend years tracking around up there. It says here prospectors got lost and died. But if you went about it scientifically, if you had a plan . . . It's got to be there somewhere!"

Lou sat down on the edge of the bed. Ben saw it coming: one of her big lectures on *reality*, all the things that kids didn't know about.

"Ben," she said, "people love to believe in dreams.

Things like lost mines and buried treasure. It's just sort of a trick we play on ourselves. So the tourists come and buy souvenirs and go up on the mountain and spend a couple of days camping out and digging here and there . . . but it's just another adventure story, like those Hardy Boys books you used to read. It's okay if you want to have fun sometime to go hiking and pretending you're a prospector. Just don't go swallowing that fish story whole." Lou pulled back the bedspread. "Okay now, lights out."

Ben had been pondering. "I still don't see how a story can hang on for so long if there's nothing to it."

"It's business, Ben. People around here keep the story going because it helps them make a living. Like that man who tried to sell you a *real* gold nugget for ten dollars. There must be hundreds of people who go for that malarkey." Lou stood up from the bed and tucked the covers around him.

After she was gone, Ben lay awake. He knew all about how people could be fooled. But somehow the story stayed in his mind. The mine was there. He was *sure*.

It was there, and anybody who really looked hard enough would find it.

CHAPTER 4

The morning started badly.

Dropping Ben off at Pioneer Valley Regional High School, Lou realized how difficult his adjustment would be. The school was a sprawling complex of square modern buildings surrounded by acres of asphalt parking lot. The total enrollment was probably in the thousands, and making friends wouldn't be easy. Among the crush of students, moreover, many were Indians, easily identifiable by their tawny skin and blue-black hair. They wore the same uniform as the others, workshirts or sloganed T-shirts—"Will Rogers Never Met General Custer," one said—but they added one more difference to a place already daunting.

Feeling a pang of protective concern, she had left Ben with a few words about how being anywhere new was hard, then had gone off to see the first three houses on the list of rentals Capper had given her, all uniformly depressing.

The fourth house made her day.

It was smallish and by no means luxurious, but had some charm. Modeled on the old Spanish-mission style, the adobe looked freshly whitewashed. There was a graceful promenade of shaded arches extending from the flat roof to run across the front and along both sides. But what entranced Lou most, as she followed the walkway of the terra-cotta tiles around to the back of the house, was the view.

Legend Mountain.

It sat on the far horizon, across a flat expanse of several miles. The vista was completely unobstructed except for the low outlines of desert scrub. Lou let herself into the house through the unlocked rear door. The house had enough space—a room for Ben, another for her, and a third bedroom she could use for an office. Two of the bedrooms lay to one side of the large central living room, separated by a hallway, and on the far side were the kitchen and the office. Adding to the appeal was a basic supply of furniture: beds, tables, chairs, even an old carved sideboard. With a few personal items from San Francisco, the decor might come together into something simple but cozy.

Home. Yes, it could be that.

At the end of the tour Lou paused in the living room. She was struck by how carefully, even lovingly, everything had been maintained—the floors and furniture oiled, the windowsills mended and freshly painted. Why, she wondered, should a house so painstakingly preserved be left standing empty? Either it would be lived in or sold. Or else, like the others she'd seen, simply left to deteriorate.

Whatever the reason, it was her good luck.

She was about to leave and call Capper for the name of the owner when she caught sight of an uneven spot in the planking of the floor, in the corner near the fireplace. Looking closer, she saw that the uneven boards formed a square. A section that had rotted, perhaps, and been replaced. Bending down, she saw that the wooden square seemed to be of the same texture and grain as the rest of the floor. It was a trapdoor, of all things, a trapdoor into the basement.

She remembered reading—or had she seen it in a movie?—how early settlers in the West had dug basements as escape hatches in the case of Indian attack. Women and children downstairs, while the men fought marauding redskins.

Curiosity got the better of her. She went into the kitchen, found a putty knife in a drawer under the sink, and returned to pry up the door. It gave way easily, and she peered into the musty dank hole. Probably hasn't been opened in years, she thought, maybe since the last Indian attack. Without a flashlight she couldn't make out what was down there, which was just as well, since the mushroomy damp smell was overpowering. She dropped the door back into the open spot on the floor and tamped it tight with her heel.

Leaving by the back door, she headed for her car, but stopped again to look at the mountain. In only a short couple of minutes it had changed, the morning light playing new tricks with its craggy facade. There was something about it, that distant shape—the eye swung toward it like a compass needle seeking true north. But of course it *was* the magnetic center of her life, for now and the immediate future. Right out there where she could watch it, keep an eye on it.

Keep an eye on it? Why was she thinking about the mountain as though it were alive, something that could be dangerous if not kept under guard?

Pulling herself away from the hypnotic hold of the view, she imagined herself folded into her sofa in front of some blazing logs in the quaint fireplace. Then she went to find out who she'd have to talk to about a lease.

▲▲▲

A carved wooden sign hung suspended high between the tall twin posts. No words on it, only a symbol, one diamond set inside another: ◈. It had to be the place she was looking for, the Double Diamond Ranch. She swung her car between the posts onto a road that climbed a grassy hill.

Mercy Roy—the name had an old-fashioned ring, an echo of pioneer times. Ted Lundberg had given Lou the name when she called the office from a gas station to find out who owned the adobe house. "She's a tough customer," Ted had cautioned after volunteering to call ahead for Lou, adding that the woman was also the Honegger Corporation's landlord, owner of the building that housed the Legend City project office. "She'll drive a hard bargain on the rent."

As the access road crested the grassy slope, Lou looked down into a bowl of land isolated by gently rolling hills. At the center was the main house of the Double Diamond. A large U-shaped adobe, it embraced a lush garden and swimming pool. Its two stories and jutting wings came together at different angles, vaguely reminiscent of Pueblo dwellings Lou had seen in pictures. Off to one side were a few sheds, a garage, and a stable abutting a corral where several horses ran loose.

Lou continued down to where the driveway ended in a circle of gravel. The entrance to the house was a massive pair of wooden doors, each carved with the double-diamond symbol.

She had to hunt a few seconds to find a bell or knocker. Finally she gambled on a large square of polished wood set into the adobe frame. When she pressed it she heard a chime ring faintly somewhere within.

No one came. She rang again.

Of course, she thought, she should have called ahead herself to make sure Mercy Roy was at home. The sleepy pace of Coopersville had lulled her into the foolish assumption that local people would always be at home because they had nowhere exciting to go. She'd have to shake her city-slicker prejudices.

She started searching the grounds. On a place this size, the owner might be anywhere.

It was several minutes before she spotted the solitary man in a cowboy hat working behind the stable, crouched in front of some sort of wooden frame. A tanned animal hide was stretched across the top, and the man was cutting long thin strips of leather with a hunting knife.

"Excuse me," Lou said, walking up, "I'm looking for Miss Roy."

The cowboy didn't speak, didn't turn, gave no sign of hearing. Perhaps he was deaf, Lou thought.

"Is Miss Roy here?" she asked again, more insistently.

Now the man tilted his face up slowly. Lou stopped speaking the second she saw his eyes, hard glittering black and brimming with violence. Was he an Indian? His skin was dark and the flesh of his cheeks lined like naked earth after a long drought. His sullen gaze lingered on her, and she shrank back. Then he said:

"Can't you see?" He gave his head a slight switch in the direction over his shoulder, and resumed his task.

Lou, irritated, followed the direction of his nod toward the fields behind the barn. At first she saw nothing. Then, in a cleft between the hills, she picked out a light tan horse, a palomino, just galloping into view.

The horse came toward her so fast that even in its

looping path it had covered most of the wide field, and Lou could make out the woman's features, her long blond hair streaming out behind her in the wind, a parallel with the animal's tail. From the way the woman kept spurring her horse, leaning athletically over its neck like a jockey, she was obviously young and strong.

About fifty yards from the stable, the rider slowed her mount to a trot. Lou walked over to introduce herself.

She had to conceal her shock as the horse came near. Mercy Roy was not young at all. The hair Lou had taken for blond was actually silvery white, and deeply etched crow's-feet bracketed the woman's eyes. Time, in concert with the sun, had turned her forehead into a crosshatch of wrinkles. And yet Lou was hard put to guess the woman's age. The skin of her cheeks was smooth and shiny, drawn tight over the cheekbones, and the eyes, now revealed as light gray, sparkled with vigor and intelligence. Her body was taut and erect, her strong legs gripping the saddle. Mercy Roy might be sixty . . . or eighty.

"Hi," Lou called out, putting as much warmth into the greeting as she could, hoping to manage a better exchange than with the hired hand. "Are you Miss Roy?"

"The one and only," the rider said. She reined up and dismounted, easily swinging her leg over the horse.

"I'm Louisa Palmer. I work for the—"

"No need to tell me, hon'. You're the boss lady for this miracle that's going to happen over on our mountain. Glad to meet you." Mercy Roy stuck out her hand.

The grip Lou felt was warm and sure. It conveyed warmth and sincerity, which made the hostility from the cowboy even more puzzling.

"By the way," the older woman said as she released Lou's hand, "out here we don't hold much with being Missed and Mistered and—what's that new one the ladies got nowadays?—Mizzed. Plain talk's what we like. You can start by just calling me Mercy." She paused to size Lou up. "You've come about the house. . . ."

Lou told her yes, she liked the place and wanted to rent it.

Mercy Roy looked at her silently for another moment. It wasn't just a landlady's careful inspection of a prospective tenant. It seemed almost as if the old woman was wondering where they might have met somewhere in the past. Abruptly Mercy Roy spun toward her horse and slapped it on the rump. The horse trotted past her toward the stable.

"You've got your horse pretty well trained," Lou said.

"*He* did the training," Mercy replied, bobbing her head toward the cowboy, who was uncinching the horse's saddle. "He's got the gift for it."

"Then I can see why you keep him around."

A mistake, Lou realized too late. She hadn't meant to say anything about the unpleasant reception the man had given her.

Now Mercy was scrutinizing her again. "Don't take it personally, Lou," she said as she started toward the house, "if my wrangler seems mad at the whole damn world. Because Peter—his name's Peter White Lightning—he's a half-breed, and that's never been a good thing to be around here."

"I knew there were problems with that once," Lou said, "but I didn't think people still—"

Mercy cut in with what struck Lou as extraordinary

vehemence. "Some folks got narrow ideas about mixing the races. They never liked it and they still don't. That's how people are. Ever read about those kids over in Saigon, the ones our soldiers left? I saw in the paper a while back where we flew fifty, a hundred over here to give 'em homes, but my God, there's still thousands of 'em back there running around with no shoes, eating garbage. Half-breeds, see, same as here. Nobody wants 'em. Like Peter. He's got no place to belong. Not with Indians, not with whites. It makes a man mad."

Arriving at the back of the house, Mercy thrust the door open and marched briskly inside. Almost, Lou thought, as if she were more than a little angry herself.

▲▲▲

The lizard chased the deer, and the deer chased the lizard. The bowl turned around and around, the animals doomed to a futile eternal race.

"A vision of life," Mercy said, "as seen by the Tewanis."

The pottery bowl on the fireplace had been crafted with impressive delicacy. The two vivid images were painted on the surface, a gaping-mouthed lizard showing two sharp fangs, and a slender deer, its four legs in figurative motion. Gently Mercy Roy spun the bowl, and as it rotated, the two animals chased each other around and around.

Since they had entered the house, Mercy seemed to be making an effort to strike up an acquaintance, avoiding the business of the lease. Lou liked Mercy; the woman had an almost maternal warmth.

They stood at the fireplace in the house's vast living room. Colorful objects filled every corner, covered every surface. Indian baskets, Indian pottery, Indian rugs on the floor. Ledges built directly into the adobe walls held pottery and rows of old photographs and ancient settlers' tools—a scythe, a prospector's pickax.

"For the Tewanis," Mercy said, spinning the bowl again, "the deer symbolizes all that is good in life. It has a gentle nature, and it also serves man—providing nourishment with meat, and warmth and shelter with its skins. And this"—she pointed to the other animal—"is the gila monster, the poisonous desert lizard. It stands for everything evil in life, an animal that can endure the most scorching rays of the sun, as if it was born right out of hellfire."

"So that's part of the legend too," Lou said.

"Sort of," Mercy answered, smoothing a palm over the buckskin skirt she had changed into. "According to the oldest Tewani myth, the gila monster was created when one of the gods tried to steal the gold owned by Elder Brother—"

"The mountain god," Lou said.

Mercy nodded. "In the Tewani myth the gold was safe as long as Elder Brother kept it. To everyone else it was poison. There was one god, Flint, who couldn't resist its beauty and tried to carry it away. But as soon as Flint stepped off the mountain with it, he shattered into as many pieces as there were lumps of gold. And each fragment became a living thing—the gila. Marvelous, isn't it? The way the Tewanis see it now, the lizard hides under rocks, waiting to kill anyone who comes poking around for Elder Brother's gold."

The thought of poisonous animals lurking around where she was going to build made Lou queasy.

"The bowl," Mercy went on, spinning it once again, "is the Tewanis' view of life in action—the rapacious and the evil constantly pursuing the gentle and the good." Mercy flashed Lou a twinkling glance. "That *is* a good one for you to know, isn't it?"

Was Mercy delivering a subtle message—about evil developers chasing a gentle people from their sacred land? Lou fought her temptation to be defensive; handled correctly, Mercy Roy could be an ally. At the moment, she might be content to make a little money from the Legend City project, renting office space and houses, but there were signs that she was less than enthusiastic about the Honegger Corporation's presence.

"Well, Louisa, let me get you a lease," Mercy said finally. While the old woman rummaged through her desk, Lou looked at the old tintypes and framed newspaper clippings propped against the wall—Indians in ceremonial dress, pictures of Coopersville in frontier days, a bearded settler standing with some Indians in a village of earthen houses. She guessed it might be all one collection gathered from some local attic, shrewdly picked up before museums and galleries had recognized the value of such material.

One newspaper clipping caught her eye—the photograph of the bearded settler. The article was headlined OLD PROSPECTOR TAKES SECRET WITH HIM. An obituary.

"Is this the old Russian," Lou said, "the one who found the gold mine?"

Mercy smiled. "Yes. Alexander Karalyevski. The one who's *supposed* to have found it."

Lou nodded. Of course that was what she'd meant to say. But the fable had such instant appeal, you fell into taking it for gospel.

"Where'd you get all this stuff?" Lou asked.

"Bought it, scrounged it up here and there," Mercy said, gesturing along the wall of tools and pottery and tintypes. "I'm an old pack rat, and ever since I came out here, I've been fond of that Lost Russian story, so I collect bits and pieces."

She showed Lou other pictures of Karalyevski—on Main Street in Coopersville, standing in front of the mountain with his pickax and shovel—and other souvenirs of the local legend. Mercy was a pack rat, all right, but Lou thought she might have another motive, too. Maybe she collected clues to the location of the mine because she hoped to find it herself.

"Mercy, do you think it might really be there, a lost mine full of Elder Brother's gold?"

Mercy chuckled. "Oh, dear," she said, "it does make such a pretty story, doesn't it? I hate the tacky tourist part of it, though—selling hot dogs, and rocks painted gold, and phony maps. I think there's something about stories like the Russian's that ought to be . . . I don't know, kept pure, not dirtied by being used as a gimmick to cheat people out of their money, or made the excuse for a circus." She turned to the pictures on the wall. "But do I think it's true?" She turned back to Lou. "I think it's just that people need to believe in something. You've got to let people have dreams."

Jesus, this old woman was a puzzling character. It seemed she regarded herself, as a keeper of the flame. She had obviously been collecting her artifacts for a long time. But what had started her? When and where had she come from? Although Mercy talked the folksy lingo of the region, Lou detected a faint twist in it, an underlying accent. She couldn't quite figure what it was, but it carried a nuance of sophistication at odds with everything else about the woman.

Mercy produced a standard printed lease.

"I guess the only thing left," Lou said after flipping through it, "is the rent."

"Tell me what seems reasonable to you."

Lou was caught off guard. Hadn't Ted pegged Mercy as a tough negotiator? Lou tried to be fair. "How about two years at five thousand per year?"

"Two years?" Mercy asked doubtfully. "That's a long time. I wouldn't want you to be tied to something that doesn't work out. I think maybe you'd be better off just taking it on a month-to-month basis."

"Mercy, I get the feeling you don't think I'm going to last here."

Mercy gave a small shrug. "You must know there's been people before who wanted to use that mountain."

"Yes, I know. The last owners went bankrupt. But that was a different company, different management. The Honegger Corporation does what it sets out to do."

"Maybe," Mercy said, "but whatever's different this time, that mountain hasn't changed." She plucked the lease from Lou's hand. Leaning over the desk, she pulled a ball-point pen from a wooden caddy, wrote in the rental terms, and signed her name to the bottom.

Lou took the pen, troubled by Mercy's remark. "What are you trying to say?"

"Just that the mountain's a special place. It's meant a lot of things to a lot of people over a long, long time. I don't think you can be a hundred percent sure of taming it to be used just the way you want."

"Are you trying to frighten me?" Lou asked dryly. "Steering me off with warnings about the god who lives up there, all the bad things he does to people who don't leave him in peace?"

Mercy shook her head. "No, Lou, I suppose it's just . . ." She trailed off, and her gaze drifted away to look through the double doors. Legend Mountain was distantly visible, shimmering beyond the transparent curtain of the desert heat. "Maybe it's just that I can't help feeling that old mountain's got a way of taking care of itself."

Anxious to change the subject, Lou bent over and signed the lease. "It's a beautiful house," she said, "and I'm glad to have it. Did you know it has a trapdoor in the living room?"

Mercy's eyes fluttered for a second. "Yes, but of course that basement's all caved in now, not much use for anything."

She slipped one copy of the lease into a drawer, put the other one in an envelope and handed it to Lou. "I'm happy to have you as a tenant, Louisa, and if I can do anything for you, let me know."

They started for the front door. "Even if it means helping to get my city built?" Lou said.

Mercy stopped. "Why, certainly," she said sincerely.

Lou hesitated. Would she really help? "I guess what I need is to get the town behind Legend City."

"Oh, you already got some folks behind you," Mercy said.

"But not everybody," Lou said. "Maybe you could help me gather them together, see if we can't talk over our disagreements."

Mercy considered the idea. "We hold a town meeting once a month," she said, "down at the church. Big crowd, sometimes. How about Monday night, eight o'clock?"

Lou said that would be fine, just fine.

▲▲▲

On her way into town, Lou couldn't stop thinking about Mercy Roy. That accent of hers—where was it from, and what had brought Mercy west? From the sound of it, she had come as a very young woman and, to judge from the figure she cut even at this age, must have been extremely beautiful. Why had she ended up alone?

At the office Lou asked the payroll manager, a local woman, if she knew Mercy Roy. It turned out that Mercy was quite a local character, the subject of much conversation among the people of Coopersville. By all accounts, Mercy had gotten off a train in Phoenix sometime back in the late 1920's, a young girl from Boston looking to buy land. So her accent, Lou realized, was a vestige of Back Bay.

"My dad told me she was real beautiful then," the payroll manager said. "He had a crush on her something fierce, all the men in town did. Even tried courting her, but she wouldn't have none of 'em."

No one had ever been too clear on why the woman had left her family and traveled west. The story was that Mercy, who supposedly came from a wealthy family, could have lived anywhere, but didn't fit in back East—too much of an oddball. And there were rumors of an unhappy love affair, a broken heart Mercy had hoped to mend by running away.

An elusive figure, cunningly evasive and full of contradictions, Mercy would not be easy to know. But Lou had a feeling it would be worth the effort.

CHAPTER 5

The Jeep sped through the gate in the long chain-link fence that surrounded the equipment and supplies depot, and Capper braked to a stop. Lou stepped out and stood for a moment. Like an actor walking out before an audience, any terrors she had felt about her first day on the site vanished instantly. This was her stage; she loved it.

It always struck her as rather phenomenal that she had come by sheer happenstance to this unlikely career. If the marriage had worked, for one thing, she might never have gotten a job in the first place. Even before the divorce from Matt, when she needed to be kept busy, she had analyzed her employable qualities and had feared it might come down to her physical appearance. Model, actress, sales rep with a gleaming smile—she had the looks for any of those. Yet she rejected her beauty as something to be valued, a feeling that came perhaps from knowing how much she looked like her mother, a woman who had been cruel and uncaring. When she thought back over her college education, however, it was hard to find any career for which she was specially prepared. The only courses she'd taken outside the standard liberal-arts curriculum were all in geology. Why she had been drawn to a science dealing with the earth's crust and the formation and development of its layers, she didn't know, but it gave her the only edge that might distinguish her in the job market. Finally she had landed a position as assistant to one of the staff geologists with the Honegger Corporation. She proved to have a particular bent for grappling with details, and by her third year at Honegger, which coincided with the divorce, she had been made an assistant project manager. A year and a half later she was jumped up to full authority. She was the first woman in the Honegger Corporation to be raised to the position.

From the time she had started showing up on construction sites, the hardhats would stop to ogle her and let loose a barrage of wolf whistles. She took it in stride, smiling, trading wisecracks. But when she walked on her first site carrying the responsibility of full project manager, it occurred to her that there was a real cost in lost labor each time the men stopped to whistle and make jokes—a cost, however modest, that no male P.M. would have to account for. That day, as soon as the whistles went up, Lou strode directly over to one of the more muscular men standing by a cement mixer.

"What's your name?" she asked him.

"Jack," he answered, smiling, pleased that she wanted to know. "Jack Benaky."

"What does it mean when you whistle like that?" she said mildly.

The big bozo smiled. "Lady, don't tell me you don't know—"

"I might. But I want to make sure. Tell me."

"Well . . ." The hardhat glanced slyly at other workers,

who were listening. "It means we think you're a knockout."

"Then do it again," Lou said. "Good and loud. Right to my face."

Now the hardhat perceived that the dare arose from indignation, not vanity. But there was too much at stake to back down. He ran his tongue over his lips and then blew the classic whistle up and down the scale.

Before he could hit the low note, Lou had scooped a handful of cement straight out of the mixer and jammed it into the puckered hole in his mouth. The muscled worker gaped for a moment while all the men around him burst into laughter. Then his hand flew up to swat Lou. But he stopped himself.

"You see, I don't completely agree," Lou said. "Your swell compliment is only half the story. What comes across to me is that you think I'd make a great fuck, and you're letting me know that you wouldn't mind trying, you and all your friends." Her glare swept over the ring of men surrounding her. "Well, you're here to raise up a building, and I'm here to see it gets done right, on time, as per contract. Nothing to do with sex. I can't stop you from thinking about it, but even that you can do on your own goddamn time. So when I walk on a site, you keep working—got that? Or it won't be me who gets fucked."

The union rep had come to her office the next day and lodged a protest, but he had a hard time keeping a straight face when he confessed to Lou that the story was all over every site on the West Coast. A week later a box was delivered to her office from Gump's, and when she opened it Lou found a miniature gold whistle on a chain. "From now on, you do the whistling," said the message on the card, and it was signed "Jack B. and Friends."

That was the last time she'd had a problem. They still looked, of course—nothing she could do about that. But they didn't stop and give her leering stares; they stole inoffensive glances while they went on working.

To this day, Lou wore the whistle all the time. It had become a tradition for her to blow it whenever one of her projects was topped off, and then, only then, for all the men on the site to whistle back.

▲▲▲

As she stood in the depot now, Lou caught the looks from men who were loading materials onto flatbed trucks to be moved out to new roadbeds being laid, and from drivers waiting until loading was completed.

Then she heard a wolf-whistle. She swung around, looking for the offender.

"Hi, gorgeous!"

It was Jack Benaky, the one worker in the Northern Hemisphere she was ready to grant a full pardon. "Once," she said, cocking a warning finger at him. "I'll let you get away with that just once."

He laughed as he sidled closer. "Heard you were on this one, Lou. I've already got the men squared away for you. Anybody acts up, I'll set them straight for ya."

"You know I can handle it myself," she said. "But I'm glad you're on the job, anyway."

"Wish I could say the same," the big man remarked.

"Oh? What's wrong?"

The hesitation was barely noticeable. "Nothing, really. It's just . . . a strange place."

There was an awkward pause; then he pointed to the gold charm around her neck. "Still got it, I see."

Lou pressed a hand over the whistle. "Never without it."

They agreed to have a drink together some evening and Lou continued toward the on-site office trailer. Then she saw a knot of about fifteen men lounging in a space between a couple of parked road-graders. Breaks were allowed, of course. But it was not yet ten in the morning, and this group had the look of laying off the job a little.

Lou reached into the Jeep and pick up the hard hat with *Palmer* stenciled across the front. Setting it firmly on her head, she approached the group of men. "Hi, I'm Lou Palmer, the—"

"We know who you are," one of the men said flatly.

Lou paused. She had the feeling this was *the* test—there always had to be one, to find out if she could control the men, and how well.

"I didn't know we were working on elephant time this morning," she said.

A couple of men smiled nervously. One replied, "It's just a break, ma'am."

"Then I can assume," Lou said, "you've all seen the worksheets and know where you should be. You're not just waiting for the pony express to bring the news."

The workers glanced around at each other uncomfortably. Then one stepped forward, a beanpole of a man with steelframe glasses and a deeply tanned bald spot on the crown of his head. "Miss Palmer—"

"Lou," she interrupted.

The man nodded and went on. "I'm Paul Kirk, blasting foreman. I've already had this crew up on the mountain . . . and I ordered them down for a rest."

"I see," Lou said, and for a moment she and Kirk studied each other carefully. She liked the look of him, and decided instantly it would be wrong to challenge him. Yet she also realized he was holding something back. The men could have taken their rest where they were working, refreshments brought up to them. Coming down off the mountain only to ascend it again added to lost time, and the foreman would be aware of that.

"Okay, Paul," Lou said, "thanks for explaining."

Capper walked up now. "Met Paul, I see. He's been taking core samples up in Sector Four. How's it going, Paul?"

"Fine, Cap," Kirk said, a little too quickly. "We're heading back up now."

End of crisis. Lou started away, but then she saw that Kirk had grabbed Capper and held him back for a huddle. Capper came over to her in a minute.

"What was that all about?" she asked.

"Nothing serious," he said. "It'll work itself out."

She couldn't let it go by. "Don't treat me like that, Capper. I'm not a little petunia who has to be protected. Whatever happens on this site is my business, and if I ask about it, you answer. Now, what's the problem?"

"That crew is working just below where Davis was when he . . . when it happened. The place makes them a little edgy."

"They think there may be some other unsafe areas . . ."

Capper pushed his helmet up off his brow. "It isn't exactly that, Lou. They're just . . . well, a bit spooked."

She didn't quite get what he was trying to tell her. "Cap, a whole crew came down off their job. That represents a pretty sizable loss in good time—and you tell me it's because they were *spooked?* What the hell are we talking about here?"

"Easy, Lou. A man died up there a few days ago. Having Davis' death hanging over 'em—his ghost, so to speak—makes it harder not to get shook up when other things are a little strange."

"What things?"

"There was a big wind started blowing when they were up there. Wasn't coming through anywhere but right where they were working—"

"Cap, you oughta know that anytime you've got drafts blowing around a piece of rock like this, there's bound to be some weird wind patterns."

"Sure, Lou. They know it too. But coming through those rocks, it makes an eerie noise. You put that together with what happened to Davis, and those Indian legends about the mountain—"

"Oh, Jesus," Lou cut in. "Is that what's going on? They've really got the idea that this Indian god—Elder Brother, isn't that it?—blew Hump off the mountain, and they're next?"

"No, it's not that, Lou. Of course not. Just go a bit easy for another day or two, let the men get used to it here. Hell, you see the place. We're not clearing an acre of downtown somewhere and sinking a foundation. Here it's . . . well, there's just something about this mountain . . ."

Lou thought it over. Go easy? Give the legend some room? Rumors and concrete didn't mix. She'd have to get the men over this mood, or it would only cause more trouble.

"C'mon, Capper," she said, starting across the depot. "Time for inspection. We'll start with Sector Four. I'll take that crew back up there and put 'em to work."

Capper opened his mouth as if to say something, but then clamped it shut as Lou whirled away, obviously determined to run the show her way.

While the crew rode in half-track vehicles that could handle the rough terrain, Lou decided to climb the last stretch on foot. It would give her a better feel for the topography and allow her a close look at some of the rock formations. Analyzing the "skin" of the mountain would be useful in understanding the problems the crews were up against. Capper insisted on staying with her.

Periodically as they climbed, Lou paused to look at the large boulders that protruded from the surface, or stooped to examine the smaller stones on the ground. At one point, noticing some large chunks of whitish quartzite lying on the surface near a group of boulders, she went over and was about to pick one up when Capper suddenly ran up behind her, grabbed her arm, and yanked her away with a force that seemed almost brutal.

She spun on him, livid. "What the hell do you—?"

"Sorry to be so rough," he said quickly. "But I had to move fast." He pointed to a shadow under the curve of the nearest boulder. "You were a little too near that thing for comfort."

For a moment Lou saw nothing but the dark crescent of the shadow. When her eyes adjusted and the little specks of color became visible, yellow and orange, she could pick out the beaded black scales, and the eyes, and finally the whole form of the thing sheltering under the rock. A puffy wedge, about a foot and a half from the snout of its ugly snakelike head to the point of its fat tail. A lizard like the one she'd seen crudely represented on Mercy's bowl—a gila monster. Lou exhaled slowly with relief as it waddled away to another shadow.

"Know about those things?" Capper asked.

She stared at it a moment before answering, overcome by the feeling that the eyes, two little shining black pinpoints like drops of black blood, were focused on her. "I know they're poisonous," she said at last.

Capper nodded. "Slow, though. The only time they'll get ya is if you're right near 'em, like if you're dumb enough to stick your hand right under a rock where they're takin' a siesta. But then *watch out*. Once they bite on, so I'm told, they don't ever let go. You can cut 'em in half—kill 'em—and that head'll hang on until it's pried off, clamped right in there, pumpin' its—"

"Okay, Cap," Lou interrupted queasily. "I'll keep my rock collecting to a minimum. Meanwhile, what do we do about that?" She gestured to the lizard.

"No point killing it. There's plenty more on the mountain, they seem to like it here. But there's no danger as long as we're careful." Capper looked toward Lou's arm, where she had been massaging it. "You okay now?"

"Yeah," she said. "Thanks." For another few seconds she gazed away at the two pinpoints of black light gleaming in the shadow, and thought of the myth Mercy had told her. For the spirit of evil, she thought as she resumed climbing, the Indians couldn't have picked a better symbol.

CHAPTER 6

On the next ledge, Kirk's men were already at their tasks.

"There's no wind now," Capper said. "But when it's blowing, Lou, it's one of the eeriest fucking sounds—" He caught himself, and gave her a sheepish look.

"That's all right, Cap," she said. "But let's not talk about what's eerie or spooky. It's our job to squelch that stuff, not play it up." She took one more glance around and suddenly recalled something he'd mentioned earlier. "Isn't this where it happened—Davis' accident?"

Capper tilted his head back and looked at a ledge farther up. "There."

"What was he doing?"

"Just getting the big picture, Lou. That's where one of the apartment towers is supposed to go."

"Well, then," Lou said after a second, "I guess I ought to take a look too."

Capper sighed. clearly not looking forward to more climbing. It was past eleven now, and the sun was getting fierce.

Lou smiled. "That's all right, Cap. I'd rather you stayed here to keep things rolling along."

The mountainside was steep, but nowhere perilous; a path could always be found through clefts in the jagged rocks. A couple of times she paused and looked back at the increasingly spectacular view. Off in the distance, Coopersville seemed like some hobbyist's quirky creation—a village constructed on the head of a pin—and the road leading back to it a dwindling thread in the giant fabric of the desert.

When she reached the ledge, she was pounded by a sudden blast of wind so strong that it knocked her back on her heels. She braced herself against it, and in a moment it faded to a strong breeze. It struck her that someone unprepared for such a strong gust of wind, venturing too near the brink, might be swept right off the mountain. Could that be what had happened to Davis?

No. Men didn't get puffed off mountains like birthday candles being blown out; not a man who'd walked a lot of high steel in his time—though the winds tore at you there, too. Still, it was strange to think of an experienced man like Davis getting caught like that. She had to see for herself.

Moving to the rim of the ledge, Lou sighted along it and instantly spotted the point where the rock had broken off. The ledge started curving outward to form a promontory, then ended abruptly, leaving a new face of stone, not yet smoothed and bleached by the elements. Darker, rougher, the place looked to Lou something like a bone hacked off brutally by a butcher's clever. She made her way along the ledge to the point of the break, and then, lowering herself onto her knees, moved closer to the brink. Lying down on her stomach, she put her head over the edge to examine the strata of the rock.

She took a good long look. Then she heard the sound

somewhere behind and above her, a sort of wheezing moan. She thought for just a second that Capper might have followed her up, and she pivoted on her knees.

No one. She was alone on the ledge. But the eerie moaning continued. The wind, of course. As she stood listening, it changed. The pitch rose higher. Lifting her eyes, Lou scanned the heights above her.

The sound grew louder and more discordant. Lou thought of what Capper had said. Spooky, yes. But more. It reached into you somehow. The phenomenon was not unknown—winds that grated on you. There was that moaning wind the Austrians talked about, the *fohn*, that was said to drive the vulnerable to suicide. And the hot Santa Anas that stretched your nerves.

So, okay, the men working this part of the slope could get nervous from the wind. But as the towers started going up and the face of the mountain changed, there would be no more little spaces for the air to whistle through, and the unsettling wind effects would disappear.

But could she explain as easily the way Hump Davis had died?

▲▲▲

It was almost two o'clock when they returned to the main equipment depot, where a commissary had been set up in an open shed. They were late for the regular hot lunch, so they got turkey sandwiches and sodas and sat down at one of the benches.

"Was it just an accident, Cap?" Lou asked. "Is that what *you* think?"

The big man stopped chewing for just a second. "Got no good reason to think different."

"No? A crackerjack like Hump Davis plants himself on a piece of rock that's ready to give way—"

"He was a hardhat, Lou, not a mountain climber. He didn't know the terrain."

"He knew how to watch his step in high places," she said. "That was his business too. That's part of why the men are spooked, isn't it? They think Davis was killed—"

"No, Lou!" Capper said forcefully, and put down his unfinished sandwich. "It's bad anytime a man goes down like this. It's just a little worse here because it happened so early, and because . . . of all the other shit in the background. It gets the men thinking about jinxes, churns up superstition. But nobody's talkin' about murder. We've got to get it behind us, that's all, fast as possible. Honegger's right about that."

"Honegger? Did he say Hump's death should just be . . . brushed off?"

"No," Capper insisted again. "He just wants to move on quickly."

Was there a hint of a cover-up? Lou leaned closer across the table. "I took a good look at that fracture up there, Cap. That rock is pre-Cambrian granite laced with quartz. A pyramid of elephants should have been able to stand right where Davis was without that overhang cracking off."

Capper stared at her intently, then shook his head. "He was up there alone, Lou. And nobody could've known he'd go and stand right there."

"But somebody might have figured that sooner or later one of the men would arrive at that spot. So it was weakened, left as a kind of booby trap."

"By somebody who wanted to stop the project, you mean—get the jinx talk started?"

"I don't know. I looked for chisel marks, drill holes,

anything that might have weakened it. Didn't see a thing, not a sign of any tampering."

Capper's wide brow furrowed. "So what are you saying Lou?"

She shrugged, then let out a short weary laugh. "I don't know. Maybe that there was something heavier up there than a pyramid of elephants. It looks like a clean pressure break that just . . . never should have happened."

"A freak accident," Capper said again, and Lou decided to let it go.

CHAPTER 7

Ben had no choice. He had to sit next to the Indian.

By the time he had figured out which school bus took the Coopersville route, and then run to the far end of the school's enormous parking lot, the bus was almost full. He walked up the aisle, hoping someone might shift over and make room, but no one did. No one even noticed him.

But why should he expect anything else? He'd been pretty much ignored all day except for the other kids whispering about him—"There's the new kid from the big city"—and occasionally one or two ambling up to ask "What's your name?" or "What sports do you play?" before drifting away again. Now, on the bus, they were all too busy chattering about upcoming parties and club meetings to give him so much as a nod.

At last Ben spotted a free seat on the aisle all the way at the rear. He hurried back and was about to plop down, when, seeing the boy seated at the window, he pulled up short.

It was the Indian kid. Wasn't anything better than being paired off with *him?*

But after a moment's hesitation Ben realized it was

too late to walk away. It was either sit or stand all the way to Coopersville. He slid into the seat. The Indian stared obliviously out the window.

Ben had seen him first in the cafeteria line, standing alone. Another outsider. No wonder, Ben had thought. The guy was so strange-looking, dressed like Cochise or whoever that chief was in *Broken Arrow*, with animal-hide pants and a beaded headband with a white feather and some kind of homemade shirt. Ben had heard the other kids joking meanly about Jesse—that was the Indian's name, Ben remembered, Jesse Silvertrees. A girl in a cheerleader's uniform had made fun of the feather, snickering, "Him big brave." An Indian girl had said, without laughing, "They say he's got the power."

What power? Whatever it was, Ben thought now, he didn't want the rest of the kids thinking that he was friends with the Indian, that they were *both* weird.

As the bus got under way, Ben pretended to stare silently out the window like the Indian. But all the time, Ben kept studying him. It was easy to understand why the girls seemed to find Jesse Silvertrees both ridiculous and fascinating. His appearance was so striking he could have been called beautiful. His hair was the shiny glowing black of a panther's fur and hung straight down to his shoulders. His dark eyebrows fell at right angles to his long eagle's-beak nose, and with his high cheekbones the sunlight turned his eyes into dark hollows.

By the time the bus crossed the town line on the far side of Coopersville, Ben and Jesse were the only passengers left. During the whole ride, the Indian hadn't budged, had continued to gaze rigidly through the window. To keep himself from staring, Ben dug into his pocket for the gold nugget he had bought from Barney Coss and nervously toyed with it.

Finally the bus slowed and the Indian rose. As he slipped past into the aisle, Ben noticed him sneaking a glance at the piece of gilded rock.

"It comes from the mine in the mountain," Ben said impulsively as the Indian boy headed for the door. "It's from the lost mine."

The Indian halted in his tracks and revolved slowly. "No, white boy," he said as he faced Ben squarely. "That is not Elder Brother's gold in your hand. If it was . . . you would be dead."

Ben gulped. What kind of thing was that to say? Dead? *Whose* gold? But he couldn't ask, didn't even have a chance to look in the Indian's face for hints it was just a put-on. The Indian had already turned away and walked down to the door. A moment later the bus stopped.

Ben watched as Jesse Silvertrees stepped out onto the roadside and moved along the shoulder to where an unsaddled horse was grazing, a black-and-white pinto pony with a silver streak on its mane. At the Indian's approach, the horse raised its head and whinnied loudly. In one upward gliding motion, as if a string had been pulled from his shoulders, the Indian climbed up on the pony's back. Incredible, Ben thought; the horse had actually been trained to be waiting every day.

Pulling up on the plain rope that was looped slackly around the pony's neck, the Indian gave a light whisking of the halter's end against the pony's flank, and immediately they rode out into the desert. Moving away, the pony and rider gathered speed until it looked to Ben as if they were sailing, the animal's hooves appearing to float above the ground.

The kid might be weird, Ben thought, but he sure as hell knew how to ride. Turning to look through the rear window as the bus drove off, Ben watched the Indian racing away, his black hair streaming in the wind like a flag against the sky.

▲▲▲

One of the company's hardhats met Ben at the Coopersville Inn and drove him with the luggage out to the adobe house. His mother was waiting in the driveway.

"How was school?" she said.

There was no point, Ben figured, in complaining. What could she do about it? "Fine," he said. Heaving his suitcase from the car, he paused to look at the house. "Not bad."

After showing him to his bedroom, his mother hovered in the doorway until he pronounced the room "great"; then she went to make what she called a "housewarming dinner" of his favorites—pizzaburgers and mashed potatoes.

Ben quickly unpacked and took his first good look around. His room was okay. It had a smaller closet than his old room back in San Francisco, but he liked the funkiness of the adobe walls and wood-beamed ceilings. A wide low window made the room airy and bright.

It was then he noticed it, filling the view outside. It felt like you were practically on top of it. He went out along the hall to the door that led to the back patio, and crossed the yard to lean on the slatboard fence. The land was clear the whole way out to the mountain.

Ben leaned on the fence and gazed out at the thing, the big mound above the earth, and the black column they had seen from the road, the Arm of God. It was all lit up orange by the lowering sun, as it had been the day they arrived. What had the Indian said? *If you had Elder Brother's gold in your hand, you would be dead.*

But if that was true, how had that Russian guy lived to be so old? He'd touched it. . . .

Maybe.

With the sun positioned over the mountain, Ben imagined he could make out shapes in the craggy peaks—a sphinx, with eyes and nose and big yawning mouth, some kind of animal. That mountain—all those stories, the gold . . .

His thoughts were interrupted by his mother calling him to dinner. As he headed toward the house, Ben thought he knew just who to ask about those stories. The only problem would be getting the Indian to answer.

▲▲▲

At dinner, Lou tried to find out more about Ben's first day at school, but he communicated little. Everything was "fine." The kids were "okay." When he excused himself at last to do his homework, she could only hope it was a sign that he wasn't too upset. Poor kid, she thought. She understood how hard it must have been for him, but he wrapped himself up. *Tough it out.* His father's lesson, drummed into the boy's head like a catechism.

By the time she finished doing the dishes, it had grown dark out. She moved into the living room to look at the sunset. Against a sky tinted a pale blue-gray-red, the mountain made a beautiful sculptured silhouette. Beautiful, she thought, and perhaps dangerous. She couldn't stop Hump Davis' death from batting around in her consciousness. A *careful man . . . accidents happen.* Just a collapsing edge of rock.

Or was it something else, someone else?

The phone rang, Capper checking to see if everything was all right with the house, and almost as soon as Lou hung up, she was delighted by a surprise call from Marge Willis, a San Francisco friend who'd gotten the number from the main office. By the time she got off the phone with Marge, Lou was tired. Yet, still a little edgy—still thinking of Hump Davis—she sought some distraction, and after kindling some logs in the fireplace, she glanced toward the television set. Not a normal recreation for her, but she felt too keyed up to sleep.

Turning on the old Zenith in the corner, she flipped the tuner until, seeing Humphrey Bogart's grizzled face, she laughed right out loud. Perfect: the late movie on the local NBC channel was *Treasure of the Sierra Madre*.

"Beat it," Bogart was saying to the Mexican kid. "I'm not buying any lottery tickets."

The search for gold, Lou thought, as timeless as an Indian myth or an old Hollywood melodrama. She had seen the movie several times, had even driven once to a Bogart festival at a revival house across the bay to catch it on a double bill with *The African Queen*.

She settled into an easy chair next to the fireplace to watch. Bogart and Walter Huston were going off to find the gold, loading their burros with supplies.

"Gold's a devilish sort of thing anyway," Huston was saying. "When you reach twenty-five thousand, you'd want to make it fifty, a hundred, and so on. Like at roulette . . . just one more turn . . . always one more. You lose your sense of values, and your character changes entirely. Your soul stops being the same as it was before."

Drowsy as she was, Lou stayed up to watch. It was such a wonderful old story, the trek up the mountain,

Fred C. Dobbs starting to doubt his partners and slowly going crazy. Now he was falling into a squabble with his third partner, Ted Lundberg, who was wearing his Honegger Corporation hard hat.

"Glad to meet you in the flesh," Ted was saying as he walked toward Bogey and Huston. "Accidents happen," Bogey shouted as they raced down the mountain to an Indian reservation, where Huston lay in his hammock under a tree, being fed fruit by a beautiful Indian girl, while Ted lay sick on the ground next to him. Bogey walked by and said, "The Indians have rights too," and Huston was saying, "Gold, my young man, that's what it makes of us. Lots of guys go nutty with it. All the time, murder's lurking about."

Ted was trying to talk again, but now his lips were too dry, and he was clawing at Huston's hammock for attention, gasping for air and unable to get a word out. The old man and the Indian girl ignored him, and while they went on eating, Ted's skin started to crack from the heat. Frantic, he waved his arms, choking. . . .

Suddenly Lou was next to him. She thought she could save him, but when her hand touched his face, his flesh softened, came away in her fingers. . . .

A bell rang in Lou's subconscious: Ted Lundberg? With Bogart?

She jerked awake, tautly gripping the arms of the chair. For a moment she sat, not moving, just breathing in and out, calming herself. On the screen in front of her the gold dust was blowing away into the wind and the old prospector played by Huston was saying, "Well, good luck."

Lou walked over and flicked off the set. God, it had been horrible, Ted choking, dying. But given the fact that she really didn't like Ted Lundberg, combined with all that nervous talk at the site, on top of Mercy Roy's Indian legends . . . well, it was no wonder she'd had a nightmare.

No wonder at all, she told herself as she headed for bed.

CHAPTER 8

Coopersville had turned out in force for the town meeting, as Mercy Roy had predicted, to meet the woman who was going to change their town. Cars and trucks jostled for parking places. As Lou walked up to the Church of the Holy Redeemer, the groups gathered by the door were gabbing about cattle prices and the shortage of rain.

Lou had started for the steps when off to one side a flash of light speared the darkness. It took a moment for her eyes to adjust, and then she noticed the figures seated on the lawn.

They were in a circle, passing a long object that was faintly glowing at the tip. Indians—but unlike any she had seen in town. They were twelve old men with movie-craggy faces and movie-Indian costumes, feathered headdresses and leather capes tied with criss-crossed thongs. The glowing object was a pipe.

But this was no movie, the Tewanis weren't actors, and what in God's name were they doing here?

"'Evenin', Lou. You certainly draw a crowd."

Lou turned. It was Mercy Roy.

"Hi, Mercy." Lou lowered her voice and nodded toward the circle of old Indians. "Who are they?"

The twelve old men, Mercy explained, were the *hati'i na'antan,* the hereditary elders of the Tewani tribe.

"Here to protest?" Lou asked.

"No, I don't figure they'll be joining us," Mercy said.

"Then why are they here?"

"Just making themselves known, I guess."

Ted Lundberg came across the culvert. He was wearing his standard attire—button-down shirt and solid-colored tie. Mercy and Ted had met when the office lease was signed, and after greeting him, Mercy excused herself with a wave of her hand.

"Look at those poor old guys," Ted said when Mercy had left. "Aren't they pathetic?" He deepened his voice dramatically. "Indian heap big power, stoppem mountain city."

"Talk a little louder," Lou said, irritated, "and you'll make us some enemies we don't need." For all his engineering skills, she thought, Ted could be remarkably stupid.

"Oh, Lou, really—"

"Let's go inside." She walked up the church steps.

Ted went in, but Lou paused to glance over her shoulder at the twelve old men. What would they say, she wondered, if they did decide to speak?

She continued up the steps and was into the entryway when she noticed several people outside pointing and whispering. Turning to her left, she saw what they were gesturing at: the squatter Capper had identified in town—Daniels, the Vietnam vet. Lou might not have recognized the face in the dusk, but his clothes marked him again as a foreigner—army khakis, flak jacket, peaked army hat.

She kept looking at him, but for a moment he pretended to ignore her, despite the fact that he was three feet away and obviously holding her attention. Then, quickly, he put on a beaming smile. Against her will Lou found it both upsetting and charming. Charming because it was momentarily winsome, and yet upsetting because it was provocative—because behind the smile she felt he was taunting her.

"So you're here to tell them," he said, "how your city will make everything wonderful."

"Now, look, Mr. Daniels—"

"Oh," he said, "you know my name."

"Mr. Daniels, let's be reasonable. You're living on property that's—"

"That's mine," he cut her off. "And I'm not moving."

With that he continued past her down the steps. She watched him for a second, his broad shoulders rocking from side to side as he walked away. He wasn't staying for the meeting.

She didn't know whether to be relieved or disappointed.

▲▲▲

She sat on the dais between Mercy Roy and the town fathers. Mercy obviously played an unofficial role in town life; virtually everyone had shaken her hand and said hello as they passed. This was a tight-knit family, Lou realized, what you would expect from the parochialism of small-town life.

Yet somehow Lou sensed that they were bound by more than familial ties, as though they shared some unspoken knowledge. Several people stood and talked, Mercy calling on them by name—a hardware-store owner, a rancher, the woman who owned the Legend Mountain Café. But strangely, their short speeches conveyed neither anger at nor enthusiasm for Legend City.

Only one speaker expressed a strong opinion—Barney Coss, the souvenir-stand owner who had tried to bilk Ben. Ted, sitting behind Lou, reported that Coss, who also ran tours on the mountain, owned a piece of land Honegger had been trying to buy. "Honegger thinks Coss is holding out for more money," Ted said, "but the old coot says he'll never sell."

From Coss's pronouncement to the crowd, Lou could believe it. "I think the whole damn thing's a bunion on the ass," he said. "We've been gettin' along fine without no new city."

But even Coss's outrage brought only polite titters from the crowd. Where were the complaints? Where was the local furor Honegger had warned her about? Lou searched the mural of faces, the friendly folks of Coopersville.

All so attentive, so earnest. So silent.

Then Mercy introduced Lou to speak, and she stood. What could she add? She had planned a forceful speech, but what was the point? She spoke briefiy about herself and her plans for Legend City, making a pitch for civic cooperation.

And then Mercy adjourned the meeting. "We've heard Lou and she's heard us, and now I think the best thing is for us to go away and, as our Indian friends say, smoke on it."

Dutifully the crowd started filing out. Suddenly from a back pew a shriek erupted. "Friends?" a woman yowled. "You calling them Indians our friends?"

Everyone stopped moving and stared at the woman. who had unkempt gray hair and wild eyes.

She screamed again. "Them redskins ain't nobody's friends. They're nothin' but killers."

Several people exchanged wordless sympathetic glances and soothingly gathered around the woman, trying to lead her from the church. But she broke loose, and bursting up to the dais, grabbed Lou's arm.

For a moment she stared into Lou's face. "Killers! You mark my words! They killed my Hal and they'll kill you too!"

Then she was wrested away by two couples who escorted her out a side door.

Mercy came up to Lou. "She's a sad woman. Don't pay her no mind."

"Who is she?"

"Dora Parmalee. Her husband, Hal, ran the A&P over in Keenesville, and he spent a lot of his spare time prospecting. One weekend he was up on the mountain and he didn't come back. They found him with an ax in his skull. Dora's been raging at the Indians ever since."

"What makes her blame the Indians?"

"No good reason. Hal just ran into some low-life drifters, that's all."

As Lou followed Mercy out and said good night, she saw the Indians again, still sitting in the darkness on the church lawn and passing their pipe. They hardly looked like killers, she thought.

She was on her way down the steps when Capper and Ted walked up and told her she had handled the residents of Coopersville very well.

Perhaps, Lou thought, but somehow she had the distinct impression that it was exactly the other way around.

CHAPTER 9

Today it was the same as always. When Ben and Jesse Silvertrees got off the bus, the pinto was grazing at the roadside, and without a word or a gesture to Ben, the Indian walked toward it and grabbed the rope halter.

Except for that one creepy remark a few days ago about the gold being deadly, Jesse Silvertrees had ignored Ben completely. In school, every time Ben had tried to offer some little friendly glance or smile, Jesse had looked away. What was worse, since moving from the hotel to the house, Ben had been getting on and off the bus at the same stop as the Indian. Still, whenever they met, not a word passed between them. Ben would say, "Hi, Jesse," or "Great horse"—and the Indian would snub him. Each time, Ben would decide he ought to cool it; the kid was a weirdo, and hooking up with him would only make everybody else in school think he was equally weird.

Yet there was a lure about Jesse Silvertrees. Ben didn't quite know what it meant when the other kids said Jesse had "the power," but he sensed that Jesse *was* special, and not just because of how he looked and dressed.

And there was another reason Ben persisted in trying to get the Indian's attention. Jesse had to know something about the gold. All that stuff about dying if you touched it—that was nothing more than a scare tactic to stop Ben from looking. That was why, no matter how much Jesse snubbed him, Ben wouldn't stop trying to get through.

"You know," he shouted as the Indian walked away from him, "it wouldn't kill you, Jesse. Like to just say something. You know my name, we're in the same history class. You could say 'Hi' or something. You could be a little bit human, even if you have to *fake* it."

The Indian never turned around. His long legs swung over the pinto's bare back in one gracefully fluid motion, and with a swish of the rope he prodded the horse into a trot. There was something about the animal's leisurely gait that particularly stung Ben, especially combined with the Indian's posture as he rode off, his back straight and hard as a wall.

"It wouldn't kill you!" Ben screamed, so hard his throat hurt. "Like maybe you'd even learn something, you know. Like maybe it wouldn't be so bad to have a friend. . . ." His voice gave out as he saw the horse continuing away.

"Creep," Ben muttered. His eyes were watering slightly as he started to trudge the quarter-mile to his house. That was it; the hell with Jesse Silverfuck.

Then he heard the drum of the horse's hooves coming up behind him. He wiped his hand over his eyes, but kept his head down. His turn now. He'd gotten through to the Indian. Okay, now let him have a taste of his own medicine.

The pinto came up alongside and slowed to a walk.

Ben waited for the Indian to speak, but no word came from above. Finally Ben had to stop and look up.

Still the Indian said nothing. But he leaned over and extended a lean muscular arm, and it was clear he was offering Ben help to climb up behind him on the horse.

Ben hesitated, but he couldn't play hard to get, after all. His own arm shot up and he felt himself being hoisted up to sit astride the horse's flank. The horse jumped instantly into a gallop, and Ben threw his arms around the Indian to keep from falling. Scared, and thrilled, he hung on as the horse raced away.

Twenty minutes later they were near the base of the mountain, though on the opposite side from the construction depot. Jesse reined the horse to a halt and tilted his head to stare up the mountainside. Ben followed his gaze. It was a beautiful spot. When you looked long enough, you could find super shapes and colors in the crevices. For several minutes they sat silently, hearing only the wind blowing through the rocks and the gradually softened heaving of the horse. Ben wanted to speak, but felt it would be a mistake. With Jesse Silvertrees, silence went further.

At last the Indian spoke. "This is a beautiful place," he said.

"It sure is," Ben said.

"Do you know it's the home of a god?"

"Yeah, I read that in one of the tourist bro—"

"What you read" Jesse interrupted, his eyes fixed on the mountain "is that Indians have strange beliefs. A story written for the tourists. But you did not read what I am telling you now. So listen: this mountain *is* the home of Elder Brother."

Ben nodded, being agreeable.

Jesse seemed to detect a lack of sincerity. "You want

to be my friend, but all you know about me is what you see in those pamphlets they pass out on the street. You have no respect for what I believe. That's how white people want to be friends."

"Look," Ben said, "everybody's got a right to their opinion, but if I don't believe—"

"Believe what you want, but don't destroy the home of our god." There was a pause. Then Jesse half-turned so he could see Ben from the corner of his eye. "Your mother is the one who runs the company."

Ben felt a sudden flutter of panic. Jesse sure acted a little crazy. How far would he go to protect his mountain—or the Indians' gold? "Look, it's her job. I mean, nobody wants to hurt anybody."

"Good. Because too many people are going to get hurt . . . unless she stops."

"Jesse, there's no way you can get her to stop. You've got to realize—"

"No, *you* have to realize: Elder Brother will never give up his home. You tell that to your mother." Jesse pulled the reins in and leaned forward as if to ride. At the last moment, he turned and added, "And he's not giving up his gold."

As if everything had been settled, Jesse urged the pinto around, gave it a sharp switch on the flanks with the halter, and began riding hell-for-leather away from the mountain. Ben had to wonder whom Jesse's threats were really meant for, but one thing was clear: Jesse knew a lot about the mountain, maybe even where the gold was.

In twenty minutes they were back where the bus had let them off. Ben jumped from the horse. "Jesse, I want to be . . . I mean, well, I think we both need friends. But you've got to try to see things the way they are. My mom gets paid a lot to do her job, and the company she works for is spending a lot on this city. You're not going to change anything by telling her there's a god on that mountain."

"Does she think there's no reason to be afraid of a god?"

Exasperated, Ben burst out, "People just don't buy that crap, Jesse."

Jesse looked at him coldly for a moment. "Can you go with me," he asked finally, "this Friday night?"

"Go where?"

"To the mountain. We'll make a camp there, and stay through the night so you can see for yourself."

What could be on the mountain, Ben wondered, that would convince him a god lived there? You couldn't see a god, could you? And then his heart raced as he guessed it must be the sacred gold. "See what?" he asked excitedly.

Jesse merely smiled, and then without a word spurred his horse and rode off.

Jesse really was crazy, Ben thought as he watched the horse fade away behind a plume of dust. But maybe he was crazy enough to show him the gold.

CHAPTER 10

Barney Coss lived on a piece of land near the foot of Legend Mountain. He had begun squatting on a few acres in 1932, only twenty years after Arizona had become the forty-eighth state. The land had been considered worthless then, and he had been able to buy another hundred acres for the lordly sum of a hundred and fifty dollars. His property now encompassed a strip that ran from the state road to the foot of the mountain.

When he had first planned to develop Legend City, Lawrence Honegger had thought there would be no trouble acquiring the old prospector's tract. But to Honegger's amazement, a first offer of fifty thousand dollars had been turned down flat. He had made several offers since, the most recent rising to just under a million dollars.

All the same, Barney Coss's reply had never altered: "Not inter'sted."

There were only two other routes for access to Legend City. Either the roads would have to run clear around the foot of the mountain from the other side, adding millions in costs, or through Tewani land. Just this morning Ted had told her that the tribal elders, the *hati'i na'antan,* were adamantly opposed to any sale, but there might be others in the tribe who could act with authority.

"There's a doctor named Loftway who speaks for a dissident group. They don't want to kill all the traditions, but they want to move a little more into the twentieth century. Loftway's willing to sell us enough of the reservation land to put a nice system of four-laners into Legend. There's only one little problem."

"What's that?"

"His asking price for the land starts at eleven million dollars."

Lou had to try Barney Coss again. She pulled her car up beside the opening in the listing slat fence surrounding Coss's wooden hut and got out. For a moment she paused and looked across the desert. From here the view was not so different from the one at her own house. The mountain. Wherever you went, it seemed, the mountain dominated.

"Whatcha want, lady? Like me to take you on a tour out to look for the mine?"

The question came at Lou in a phlegmy croak. She turned from the mountain to see Barney Coss in his yard, the very picture of the grizzled prospector, with his stiff overalls and stained, collapsed Stetson and three-day growth of stubble.

"No, thanks, Mr. Coss," Lou replied as she walked toward him. "I'm not thinking of buying any of those solid-gold nuggets, either."

He chuckled, taking it lightly. "No offense meant there, you know. Just tryin' to make a dollar."

"That's sort of what I wanted to talk to you about, Mr. Coss."

"Oh yeah?" Coss cocked his head dubiously. "Well,

I'm glad to hear that, lady. Because the moment I set eyes on ya, I was afraid you'd come out here to blow some more air at me about how I ought to sell my property."

Lou acknowledged the old codger's shrewdness with a nod. "You'll listen at least, won't you?"

"Me? Why, sure. Listenin' is one of the things I'm best at. Listenin' champeen of the whole Mojave County, that's me. You can talk the whole day and into next winter, and I'll listen." He gave a slow, deliberate shake of his head. "But I won't sell."

Lou let out a sigh of exasperation, which seemed to affect Coss, because instantly he gave her arm a conciliatory tap. "Hot out here," he said. "Got some beer and Cokes in the icebox. Why don'tcha come inside?"

Directly over the threshold, Lou found herself in a small front area that was devoted to his tourist business. There was a ticket booth of the kind a child might build, three pieces of wooden siding hammered together so they would support each other and leave room for someone to stand within. Uneven lettering brush-painted across the front read "Mining Tours. All Day $25. Haff Day $10." A pair of glass display cases contained a number of pieces of prospectors' paraphernalia laid out on shelves. Lou browsed the cases for a minute while Barney stood back, seemingly pleased by her interest. She saw that each item was accompanied by a handwritten note explaining its function. "Pan for panning," read one. "Canteen—a prospector's best friend," read another. On one shelf, a minuscule pile of shiny particles lay on a square of toilet tissue. "Gold dust," said the nearby card, "the what-for of it all." In a corner beside the cases, there was also a jerry-built wooden rack stuffed with mimeographed pamphlets being offered for sale, as a sign tacked to it declared, for "One buck each." Though there were pamphlets with different-colored covers, Lou found on scanning them that all bore the same hand-lettered title: *The Story of the Lost Russian Mine*. A subtitle line advertised it as "A Tale of Love and Adventure" and gave the author as "Mr. Barnett Coss." The final touches to Barney's makeshift "museum" were added by various bits of western memorabilia that had been tacked up around the walls, "wanted" posters, clippings from old newspapers, photographs, and prospectors' axioms—perhaps also authored by Barney—painted on squares of cardboard. "A FOOL AND HIS GOLD NEVER GOT TOGETHER IN THE FIRST PLACE," said one. And the best: THERE'S NO SUCH THING AS THE GOLDEN RULE, THERE'S JUST THE RULE OF GOLD."

"Interesting display you've got here," Lou said, already crafting a strategy for persuading the old man to sell. "I hope a lot of people have gotten a chance to see it."

"There's been times," Coss said vaguely.

"But not so much anymore," Lou observed.

Coss paused to study her. "No, not so much," he admitted then. Shortly he added, "What's it to you?"

Lou decided the direct approach would work best. "All right, Mr. Coss, let's talk turkey. You know my company would like to buy your land, and you know why. It's also pretty clear to me that I can keep pushing my price up, and that won't accomplish squat. So I've got to offer something besides money that could win you over."

Barney nodded, and then chortled. "Too old for sex, if that's what you're thinkin'—pretty as y'are."

Lou had to smile. "No, Mr. Coss, that's not what I was thinking."

"Well, that would cover the bases, wouldn't it? Sex and money, that's all that ever made the world spin."

"And love . . . ?"

"What's love got to do with it?" Coss said suspiciously.

Lou paused and looked around again. "Seems to me you love the history of the mountain, that it means so much you want to share it with as many people as you can."

"Guess there's somethin' to that."

"So here's my offer. If you'll sell a right-of-way across your land, we'll build you a real museum, move all of this stuff over there. It'll stand next to the road so that every car driving in and out of Legend City will see it—thousands of people every day, Barney. And it'll be yours, you'll run it, meet all the people, tell them your stories. . . ." Lou stopped to let it sink in.

The old man regarded her gravely, running one hand over his stubbly chin. Then a smile trickled out of his cracked lips. "You're a clever one, darlin'. That might've done it, if anything. But it's still no soap."

There was no hope of swaying Coss, Lou realized, yet she was puzzled. No longer concerned with being diplomatic, she vented her thoughts impatiently. "I don't get it, Barney. You've built your whole life around finding gold. You never did, but now you've got the chance at a fortune anyway—and you don't want it. Why the hell did you give up everything to search for that gold if it wasn't to be rich?"

"Beats me," Coss came back immediately. "I wondered about it when I did it . . . and I wonder about it to this day. Would you like that beer now?"

His answer intrigued Lou. The drink had been offered, she guessed, because Coss wanted to talk more, because he had spent a lot of silent time alone with the question and now wanted to think aloud in company. Finding an answer, perhaps, would open him to selling.

A cold drink would be welcome, she said, and they went into the living area of the hut. Coss took a bottle of beer from the refrigerator, twisted the cap off with his hand, then handed Lou the bottle and a coffee mug he pulled from a porcelain sink in the corner. The rim of the mug was still tinged with a brown ring of dried coffee. Lou drank from it, though, while Coss settled himself in a molded orange polystyrene chair that looked like it had come from an airport waiting lounge.

"All I can tell ya is I know when the idea started. It was the day I saw Karalyevski."

Lou lowered the bottle, startled by the mention of the old Russian himself. Having heard so much about him in the context of legend and rumor, she'd come to think of the Russian as a mythical creature. To hear someone speaking of having met him was incredible. Then it struck her that, of course, it was quite likely, given Barney's age, that he could have crossed paths with Karalyevski.

Barney went on. "I was just a little kid then. Don't think I was more'n seven or eight. I was standing outside my father's forge one day—he was a smithy, y'know—and up comes this old gent leading a coupla mules. I don't know what I was doin', just suckin' my thumb mebbe, but all of a sudden this great big shadow fell over me, and I looked up and there he was. A big man. To me he looked as tall as the sky. I knew right off it was him. Maybe it was the beard, or the mules with all the prospectin' stuff on it, but I just knew—though I'd never seen him before. Well, he'd come around because he needed to have one of his mules shod. My father took on to do it right then, and meanwhile the

Russian sat down on a stool and waited. Now, you picture this, lady . . ." Coss leaned toward Lou. "There's this man, just sittin' and waitin' . . . and while he was there at my father's shop, the people in town start to come 'round. First one or two, folks from the nearby houses. But then the word starts to get around, and one by one, two by two, the crowd grows. They don't come up to him, they don't say nothin', they just bunch together across the other side of the street and look at him. They stand there all the time he's waiting, and he sits fiddling with some straw from the ground, until his mule's done. Then he gets up and he pays my father, and as he's leadin' his animal away, he passes me and he stops. He reaches down into his pocket, pulls out a twenty-dollar gold piece, and he pats me on the head and hands me that golden eagle. Then he walks away. The crowd starts to drift after him, but at the end of the street, right near my father's place, he turns around and he gives 'em a look, and that whole mass of people stops dead. By then, see, there'd already been a case where some hooligans tried to follow the Russian and beat his secret out of him, and he'd killed the three of 'em and got off on self-defense. So they didn't follow anymore, they just stood and watched until he'd disappeared out of town. I never saw him but that once. . . ."

There was a silence as Barney stared off into a corner, reliving the moment. Then he turned back to Lou. "But it wasn't the gold that got me that day. It was seein' him—the kind of power he had over people because of who he was, what he knew. To look at him, there was nothin' to envy. He didn't look rich, didn't have fancy clothes or nothin'. But he had that secret, and everybody knew he had it . . . and that's what made him like a king." Coss tossed up his hands. "So I guess that was what done it to me. I wanted that secret too. I wanted it that day, and soon as I could, I went lookin' for it. And I still want it—though I've cut loose from thinkin' I'll ever find it."

It was significant, Lou thought, that the piece of gold Barney had been given in his recollection was not a nugget, but a coin. "So you've decided," she said, "that there never was a mine."

Barney reared back as though at an insult. "Oh, Lord, no! It's there, lady. I never had no doubt 'bout that. I can just *feel* that infernal thing givin' off rays like a radiator sends out heat. But I've looked and looked over just about every inch of that mountain, and I still haven't cracked through. So I've had to throw in the towel. It's just too well hid to be found. Even Karalyevski wouldn'ta found it if he hadn't been told."

"Told?"

"Oh, sure."

"Who told him?"

"You never heard that story? Oh, that's a humdinger. You see, there was this—" Abruptly he stopped. "But, shoot, why'm I givin' this away for nothin'? You want that story, it'll cost you a buck." He rose, walked to the front of the hut, and plucked a pamphlet from the rack. "It's all wrote down in my book. You want the story, buy a copy."

Lou followed him, shaking her head in bemusement. While the old prospector could turn up his nose at the fortune offered for his land, he was hanging on to his story for the sake of earning a dollar. "Sure, I'll buy a book, Barney. I'd buy a million of them."

"Only takes one to tell the story."

Lou took her wallet from the pocket of her jeans, pulled out a dollar, and exchanged it for the booklet.

"Barney, you know when I walk out the door today, there won't be any more offers. We've got to get on with the project, make other plans. You say no here and now, and that's final."

"Be a relief, ma'am."

"You won't have any regrets later?"

"Why should I? Got what I want now. To be near the mountain, close enough to feel the mine if not to own it. And I reckon it needs someone like me to be here, y'know, kinda feedin' the legend . . . the ol' prospector. Not too many dreams like this around anymore. Keepin' it alive . . . well, to me that's a little bit like keepin' part of this country alive. . . ."

The old man walked her out to the car. Before getting in, Lou put out her hand and Barney shook it. She had the curious feeling that without any money changing hands, some kind of bargain had been struck. Almost as if by not pursuing his land she was promising to share his crazy dream.

▲▲▲

Lou was undressing for bed that night when she came across the booklet she had folded up and stuck into a pocket of her jeans. She dropped it on the nightstand, something to read as she drowsed off. After she had showered and slipped naked beneath the sheets, forgoing a nightgown because it was unusually humid, she picked up the pamphlet.

Barney Coss's prose was rough and repetitive—"This is a really true story, and that's the truth," his introduction began—but as Lou made her way through the facts, she was swept up rather than being lulled to sleep. For all his crude style and grammatical errors, Barney made the story come alive, conveyed a sense of almost being an eyewitness to what he reported.

Karalyevski, he wrote, had come from Russia sometime in the 1880's. Why he, a onetime soldier in the czar's imperial army, had chosen to immigrate to Arizona, of all places, no one could be sure. His exodus from Russia had probably been inspired by the general wave of immigration that was then bringing hordes of Europeans to the American shores. Perhaps, on arriving, he had come across some newspaper stories about various gold strikes in the West and had decided to try his hand.

For many years he had prospected without success, until he had come to Legend Mountain, attracted by the rumors of a lost Spanish mine. As early as the fifteenth century the Spanish had filtered up from Mexico and begun mining in the Southwest, enslaving vast numbers of Indians to do the work. Old records documented the existence of a mine at Legend Mountain in the 1500's, worked by Tewani under a Spanish garrison commanded by a Major Arcadio Altavela. The Altavela mine was especially rich. The records showed that millions of gold pesos per year—sums equivalent to millions of dollars even *then*—had been extracted from the lode and shipped to the Spanish monarchy. Then, in 1586, a wildfire rebellion of Tewani slaves erupted at the mine, and Spanish troops were unable to contain the revolt. Ordering the mine sealed, to be hidden against a time when he could return with more soldiers to smother the uprising, Major Altavela loaded his caravan of mules with as much gold as they could carry and set out for Mexico.

But Altavela and his men had been overtaken by the

Indians and slaughtered along with their animals. Their gold was left in the saddlebags of the dead mules. Over the next two hundred years, prospectors drawn to Legend Mountain by the story of the Altavela mine would occasionally turn up a heap of ore or a smelted bar of gold in the vicinity of the massacre—residue from the saddlebags, which had long since deteriorated.

According to Coss's pamphlet, Karalyevski had lived alone on the mountain and looked for the mine for years without success. Then, on a trip to the Tewani village to barter for food, he had become attracted to an Indian girl named Yo-tee-a. Several months after meeting the girl, Karalyevski had asked her father, one of the *hati'i na'antan*, for permission to marry. When the request was denied, Yo-tee-a renounced her loyalty to the tribe and ran away to live on the mountain with the Russian prospector. Within a few days, however, a party of Tewani warriors set out to reclaim Yo-tee-a. Fleeing the mountain, Karalyevski followed a separate trail from his young wife in an attempt to draw the pursuers away from her. But, expert trackers that they were, the Tewani caught up with Yo-tee-a. Exercising their harsh Indian justice, they had neither killed her nor reclaimed her; they merely cut out her tongue and left her to bleed to death. A day later, Karalyevski found her, still alive, though too far gone to save. He brought her back to his cabin, and the next morning a couple of other prospectors passing by saw the Russian digging a grave in the land nearby.

It had been assumed that the savage punishment administered to Yo-tee-a was in retribution for renouncing her loyalty to the tribe. But as time passed, and Karalyevski was seen to emerge from the mountain with cargoes of gold, the assumption changed: the Indian girl's tongue must have been cut from her head for the crime of telling her lover the location of the sacred Indian gold. What no one could figure out was why the Indians who had mutilated the girl had not also murdered Karalyevski to protect their secret. Unless, of course, there was no secret, but simply random findings from small claims or the remains of the Altavela party. When the Russian died in 1927, he was still living modestly on his small patch of land near the mountain. If he had found a vast sum of gold, he had never spent it.

Lou closed the small booklet and turned out the light.

Lying back on the pillow, she thought about what she had read. A tall stranger from a foreign place, a beautiful young girl, an old mine buried in an uprising of the oppressed. It was easy to understand how the story had taken root. But of course the mine didn't exist. It was only a charming tale of the Old West.

CHAPTER 11

"We're ready to start," Capper said as Lou got out of her car, "all except for Benaky."

"Where is he?" she said impatiently. She had come to the site for an eight-A.M. foremen's meeting.

"He was here early, got his coffee, and went for a hike. Wanted to see the mountain by sunrise—as if he didn't see enough of it. Should be back any minute."

By eight-thirty Benaky still hadn't shown up. "I guess we'd better go looking," Capper said.

They worked their way up the slope quicky. The men said Benaky had gone to the first ridge to take in the view to the north and west, a spectacular uninterrupted vista of desert that in the morning light looked like a Frederic Remington painting—hazy golds and browns speckled with green cactus, purplish lead-colored clouds on the far horizon, the red berries and thorned purple flowers of the deadly nightshade. On most days the men took their work breaks and lunch in the same spot—an area of the ledge where the mountain offered a sun-shielded cavity from which to admire the glorious setting.

At the ridge Benaky was nowhere in sight.

"Jack?" Capper hollered, cupping his hands around his mouth. "Jack . . . where the hell are you?"

His voice echoed back to him. Nothing stirred on the ridge. The bulldozers sat idle like giant snoozing insects.

"He's not here," Lou said, and started walking along the bulldozer's path. A quarter-mile of roadbed had been dug. She stopped when she saw fresh footprints in the soft earth churned up by the machines.

"He was here," she said, and pointed to the plastic top of a coffee container.

"Must've gone down to the edge for a better look," Capper said.

They followed the footprints with growing uneasiness. The impressions in the earth were getting farther and farther apart, as if Benaky had broken into a run. At the far side of the ridge they stopped. The footprints ended at the ledge. There was not a sharp fallaway, only a steep slope leading down toward a ravine. But there was no sign of anyone on the incline.

Lou called down. "Benaky? Jack . . . you there?"

No reply.

Tentatively Lou started to creep down, leaning into the steep grade to brake herself.

She had moved down only a couple of yards when she came to the hollow in the hillside, invisible from above. Looking into it, she gagged.

Capper, following behind her, saw it too. He turned away, and in a second Lou heard his retching coming from behind the nearest boulder.

The entire top of Benaky's head had been shredded, nearly torn off. From the peak of the forehead to the nape of the neck there was barely a remnant of scalp, only a series of parallel marks and bits of flesh where something had ripped across Benaky's skull with savage force, tearing into the bone. Along the back of the neck, or what remained of it, long deep slashes were still oozing blood in the morning heat.

But most horrifying of all was Benaky's face. The skin had been peeled from his cheekbones, leaving only staring, bloodied eyes, wide open in terror-stricken agony. His jaw was gaping so that even in death he still seemed to be letting out an anguished cry.

It looked like something an animal had done, but there were no animal tracks on the path, nor around the spot where Benaky had fallen. None anywhere. Lou would have been tempted to conclude that Jack had been running from a human pursuer whose incriminating footprints had been covered.

But she could not conceive of any human being doing what had been done to Jack.

BOOK II

Chant of the White Eagle

CHAPTER 12

Jinx.

The word spread all over the site now; it was the only thing the men could talk about. You lose one man on a job—that happens. But two men in the space of a month?

The county coroner had ascribed Jack's death to an animal attack—some kind of fox, he said, a kit or a gray. But Lou couldn't help thinking of that woman at the town meeting—what was her name? Parmalee, Dora Parmalee—and her rage at the Indians over the murder of her husband.

On Monday a crane operator who had arrived only the previous week called his wife in Tucson to say forget about coming out here, he didn't want to stay on this job a minute longer. The next day four of the men from the road-building crew abruptly quit.

Jinx.

That kind of talk had to be stopped quickly, Lou knew. If she allowed too much lag, more men might leave, and replacing skilled workers took time.

Arriving at the office Thursday morning, she spotted a familiar figure across the street, a man on a ladder with a can of paint. For a moment she had trouble placing who he was, and then, as he turned, she caught sight of his face.

It was Mercy Roy's cowboy, the rude one she had seen by the barn. Half-breed, she recalled. He glanced over at her with the same surly expression he had given her at Mercy's ranch, then returned to stirring his paint. No point in trying to be friendly, Lou thought. Continuing toward the office, she noticed four "Wet Paint" signs, one right after the other. The handyman had apparently been at work for some time; starting in the middle of the row, he had repainted every storefront.

And of the four storefronts, three were empty.

Mercy Roy came around a corner, a bundle of papers under her arm and a small potted cactus plant in her hand. " 'Morning, Lou," she said. "I heard about what happened to that foreman. Awful sad." Mercy paused. "No matter how folks in town feel about your project, they hate to hear about a thing like that."

"It shouldn't have happened," Lou said. "I keep feeling it was somehow my fault."

"Oh, dear, you mustn't feel that way."

"The men on the site are talking about a jinx," Lou said.

But Mercy appeared not to hear her. She had set down her potted cactus and bundle of papers and was looking at the storefront behind Lou, appraising the paint job.

"You own this building too?" Lou asked.

Mercy nodded.

"Expecting new tenants?"

"Not right away," said Mercy. "It's just that I like to keep the town looking spruced up. What with all the dust and heat, we've got to keep painting."

"I can see that," Lou said. "How many buildings do you own?"

"Oh, a few."

Lou had the feeling that "a few" meant more than even those the handyman was painting. Owning a substantial chunk of the local real estate probably figured in the influence Mercy seemed to wield.

"At the town meeting," Lou said, "you mentioned that you'd 'smoke on it' before deciding whether to get behind Legend City. You know, all these empty offices will rent out pretty fast when we're finished."

Mercy smiled at Lou's canny tack. "What more can I do . . . ?"

"I've been to see Barney Coss, but he's never going to sell his land. Now, if we're not going to build access roads halfway across the county, I need to open negotiations with the Tewani. Maybe you can suggest a way to convince them that Legend City would help them, too."

Mercy stepped back, dismayed. "Lou, you really believe your own line, don't you? You think this city would be good for the Tewani?"

"I think growth is good for everybody."

Mercy studied her for a moment. "Well, I suppose they deserve a chance to decide for themselves. I could introduce you to the tribal elders; I've known them for years. They're called the *hati'i na'antan*. They're the ones you'll have to see. The *hati'i* can get you the permission that counts."

"And whose permission is that?" Lou asked.

"Elder Brother's."

Lou looked at the old woman. She sounded perfectly serious. "C'mon, Mercy. You don't mean to tell me *you* believe—"

"Wait a minute, Lou. *They* believe, and that's what counts. For them, the mountain is the god's home, and it'll be Elder Brother's decision whether or not, for the sake of the tribe, he wants to . . . well, I guess you could say, to sublet."

What a cagey old woman, Lou thought. It was still difficult to tell where she stood, and she had no intention of making herself clear.

"You know, Mercy," Lou said impulsively, "we've already lost two men on this job. And about the Tewani, I was wondering . . ."

"Yes, *what* were you wondering?"

Lou hesitated. Talking about the Indians had taken her mind back to Jack Benaky, and swiftly, without consciously making the connections, she was sorting through the incongruities—an unprovoked animal attack, the absence of tracks. And Dora Parmalee: *They killed my Hal and they'll kill you, too.*

Tentatively Lou said, "Only that the way my man Benaky died, with his scalp torn off . . ."

Mercy's jaw tightened and her face colored, all warmth gone. "Louisa, if I catch the drift of what you're saying, then you've been watching too many old movies." She paused, letting the full force of her anger bear down on Lou. "You may think," she continued, "that we are still on the frontier out here, under siege by Indian warriors. And you may think the Indians still scalp their enemies. I imagine many people believe such things, but they're wrong!"

"Mercy, I didn't mean—"

"Yes, Louisa, I'm afraid you did." She bent down to pick up her cactus and papers. "If you want to negotiate with the Tewani, that sort of speculation will get you nowhere. They're peaceful people. They wouldn't kill anyone."

"I'm very sorry," Lou said. "You're right, of course."

Mercy's face softened. "I'll talk to some of the tribe and see if I can't arrange something."

Lou watched her walk down the street to where her handyman was painting the porch trim in front of another empty store. Yes, Mercy Roy was right, it had been ridiculous to blame the Tewani for Jack Benaky's death.

Yet, as Lou headed for the office, the image of his face, what had been left of his face, remained in her mind.

▲▲▲

"Who's there?" called out a quavering voice.

"Mrs. Parmalee, it's Louisa Palmer, from the Legend City project."

Dora Parmalee lived in an old brick-and-clapboard house on the western edge of town. The ranch surrounding it was run down—a brown barn with a sagging roof, an unused corral. Waiting outside, Lou heard shuffling footsteps, and then the door opened. Dora Parmalee stood tentatively, one hand on the knob, the other in her flowered-apron pocket, staring through rheumy blinking eyes. After a second she invited Lou in and offered her a chair at the enameled white kitchen table.

Lou had spent the morning brooding about Jack Benaky's death, and by midafternoon had decided she wanted to hear directly from Dora Parmalee about how her husband had died.

"Mrs. Parmalee, I'm sorry to bother you," she said as she sat down. "I know this is a painful subject, but I've been thinking what you said the other night—about the Indians and your husband."

"They killed him."

Lou waited for her to say more.

"You think I'm going to start screaming," the woman went on, "like I did the other night. They told you I was crazy, right?"

"No," Lou said, "not exactly."

"I'm *not* crazy, but sometimes I get so mad. I hear them talking about the Indians being our friends and all, and I go over the edge. But I ain't crazy."

"Most people," Lou said, "seem to think the Indians are anything but violent. Mercy Roy tells me—"

"Hah!" Dora Parmalee snorted. "Mercy Roy, what do you expect from her? She's been suckin' up to those damned Indians ever since she came out here. 'Course she's going to spout off how they're our friends. But they ain't. They don't want nobody finding that gold up there, and they'll kill anybody who gets near it." She looked down at the floor. "Like they did my Hal."

"Are you sure that's what happened to your husband?"

"Sure as I'm livin' and breathin'. Hal checked out all those stories about the old Russian, and he said he could find the mine and we could stop worrying about our mortgage and puttin' the boys through college—still got my youngest down at State. So Hal went . . . and then one day he didn't come back. Remember it like it was yesterday."

From what Dora said, Lou thought, money had been tight for the Parmalees. Her husband had been vulnerable to the fevered pursuit of riches. Could he have found the gold?

Lou looked sympathetically at the drooping woman. "Mrs. Parmalee, you may not have proof of who killed your husband. But do you honestly think he could have found the mine?"

Dora gaveled a fist on the table. "All I know is he packed his climbing gear in the car that night, said he was going up to the mountain and I should wait for him, not go to sleep, 'cause we were going to be rich."

Lou stood and apologized again for intruding. On the way back to her car, she wondered what Hal Parmalee could have meant when he left his wife for the last time with a promise of imminent riches.

It certainly sounded like the promise of a man who had found a gold mine.

▲▲▲

Lou was working in her study at home when Ben, in his pajamas, ready for bed, came into the doorway. "I've been asked to go camping," he said.

Lou looked up and smiled. "Oh? That's nice. Who invited you?"

"A kid at school," Ben said, adding after a moment, "His name's Jesse Silvertrees."

"Interesting name," Lou observed, laying down her pen. "Sounds Indian."

Ben came into the room. "Jesse's a Tewani. And he's got a horse. He took me for a ride today. It's one of those black-and-white horses, I forget what they're called . . ."

"Pinto," Lou supplied. It pleased her to see Ben excited about something.

"The horse meets Jesse at the bus stop every day," Ben went on. "It's amazing, Mom. The horse just seems to know when to be there. Brings Jesse in the morning, too, then goes off by itself."

Lou nodded appreciatively. "People out here learn to train their animals. Maybe your friend could show you—"

"It's not just training, Mom," Ben cut in. "Not with Jesse. It's something else. The kids at school say Jesse has . . ."

Suddenly he broke off.

"Has what?" Lou prompted.

"Just . . . he knows how to do certain things," Ben said. "Anyway, he wants me to go camping with him over the weekend."

"Camping," Lou repeated, mulling it. She wanted to encourage the friendship if possible. "I suppose that would be all right, if it's somewhere around here . . . somewhere he knows well."

"Oh, it is," Ben said quickly. "Jesse knows the mountain real well."

There was a thump in her chest like a door slamming. "Oh, no, Ben," Lou declared. "Not up there. I couldn't allow—"

"But I went there yesterday with Jesse. We went on his horse. It was beaut—"

"*No!*" Lou erupted in a shout, though she was only half aware of her own voice as the image of Jack Benaky's bloodied head rose into her mind, and the memory of Dora Parmalee talking about her slaughtered husband. "It's too dangerous up there, Ben. I refuse to let you go there alone."

"I won't be alone. I'll be with—"

An Indian, she nearly screamed—though with Mercy's acid reproof still etched in her memory, she managed to hold the accusation back. "You're not going," she shouted, "and that's final!"

Ben glared at her resentfully and then whirled away. But at the door he turned back. "I was only doing it for you," he bawled. "Jesse wanted me to see, so I'd believe."

"Believe what?" Lou said, rising slowly to come around the desk.

Ben gripped the doorframe, as if tempted to run, but reluctant to retreat. "That . . . that you shouldn't build on the mountain."

Lou advanced closer to Ben. "Who is this boy Jesse?"

"He's my friend. The only friend I've got in this shitty place! And if you won't let him help you, then it'll serve you right!" He broke from the doorway to run down the hall to his room. Lou heard the door close with a furious slam.

For all her eagerness to have the answers, she decided it would be best to let Ben sleep off his anger before approaching him. Picking up the pen, she went back to checking a supply inventory.

But again and again she lost her place among the rows of figures. What was Ben's last zinger supposed to mean? she kept wondering. What would serve her right?

And who was this kid who had things to show Ben that would make him "believe"?

▲▲▲

The phone was ringing when she came out of the shower.

"Louisa?"

The cultured Austrian accent came through a crackle of static. He was calling from overseas, she guessed, or maybe from aboard his plane.

"Hello, Mr. Honegger."

"Lou, I thought we'd better confer a bit about this new incident."

"Incident?"

"The Benaky thing."

"That wasn't an incident," she put in sharply, "or a thing. It was a death, Mr. Honegger, and a rather ghastly one."

"Yes," he said simply. "Of course. My daily reports indicate there's been some crew turnover. Are you managing to contain it now?"

"I'm replacing every lost man," she replied. "But it's not easy. At the moment, we're not high on anybody's list of wonderful work opportunities. The men are talking about this place as jinxed, Mr. Honegger. The only thing to do is let it blow over. If we go on and the safety record stays green for a while, that should fix it."

"I see," Honegger said in a way that made quite clear he was displeased with what he saw. "Tell me, Lou, are you also feeling . . . jinxed?"

She tried not to hesitate. "No. But I think we have to give the men room to work out their feelings."

"No," Honegger commanded flatly. "That is precisely what must *not* be done. We cannot have this superstitious emotionality. In view of the situation, Lou, we must bear down with more . . . determination. Do you understand me, Lou?"

"So your advice," she said, unable to keep the edge out of her voice, "would be to move faster—like racing past an ugly accident on the road?"

There was a silence.

"Louisa, I am a businessman, not a priest. The crews can get their sympathy elsewhere, and they are welcome to it. But we cannot have anything that stops us. A lost day costs us more than two hundred thousand dollars."

"I'm not talking about stopping anything!" Lou insisted. "But the men—"

"No buts, Lou." He was practically bellowing. "Forward. If you cannot do it, then obviously I need someone tougher."

A man, he meant. This might be why he had chosen her: to gain extra leverage. Pressure a man with bringing in someone tougher, and he might have the pride to step down without feeling his whole identity threatened. She'd always be easy tinder, though, and Honegger knew it. She'd always have to prove she could be as tough as any man.

"Bring in someone else if you want," she said. "But no one can get this job done any faster than I can."

"Good, Lou, good," Honegger crowed across the clouds. "I was hoping you'd say that. It's what I called to hear."

After the call she started drying her hair so furiously that it hurt. But she had to ask herself if Honegger wasn't right. Maybe the best solution was to move on quickly, without looking back.

Why *should* she have to feel bad if she got tough, gave orders? It was a job. Maybe she'd been too easy, as Honegger said, tolerating the jinx talk because of a couple of accidents. Too easy about other things, too. Like that squatter on the mountain, the vet. The crews were moving up toward the plateau where he'd built a small cabin, and still he was there, ignoring the official orders to vacate that were sent to his post-office box in town. Capper had talked about sending the police in to haul him down, but Lou had said to give it time, he'd have to leave eventually. . . .

A man would have confronted it, though. Might have been more on top of a lot of things—looked personally into a worker's death, for example, when the official explanation was unsatisfying. It was time, Lou thought, that she really rolled up her sleeves.

She thought of the sign she'd seen in a successful bakery in San Francisco, owned and run by a woman. A little plaque next to the cash register always gave Lou a smile. "A tough man is a tough man, but a tough woman is a bitch."

So be it, Lou thought.

CHAPTER 13

The office of the sheriff looked like it must have stood on Coopersville's Main Street back when there were wooden sidewalks and hitching posts and no asphalt paving. For Lou, the one-story brick building immediately conjured the memory of "the hoosegow" referred to by bit players in the Republic westerns her father had worked on. When she pushed open the front door, it jangled a small bell on a piece of springy metal affixed to the lintel.

The small front room contained two desks, a table devoted to some CB gear, and a filing cabinet atop which sat a hot plate. Both desks were empty. Lou looked through an open door that led down a short corridor to a pair of holding cells. In one of them a man stretched out on the lower tier of a bunk bed was snoring loudly. Lou turned just as the street door opened and Sheriff Woody Hartnett came in carrying a Mr. Coffee machine.

"Hi there, Miz Palmer," he greeted her heartily. "Sorry if I kept ya—"

"I just got here, Sheriff," she said. Mercy had introduced Hartnett to Lou at the town meeting, and she had seen him again when he brought the coroner to the ravine where Benaky had died. Like the coroner, the sheriff blamed Jack's death on an animal attack.

"What brings you here?" the sheriff asked as he installed the machine on the filing cabinet next to the hot plate. "Come on in and we'll chat."

Lou was suddenly sorry she'd come. After settling down at her desk that morning, she had spent half an hour accomplishing nothing. All she could do was brood about what Dora Parmalee had told her. Suppose Jack Benaky's death was murder? Or Hump's? But now, confronted with the need to explain herself, she could only think of the way Mercy had reacted to the suggestion that Benaky's death was anything but bad luck in the form of a mean animal. To leave now, however, would be as awkward as to stay, and she followed Hartnett through a door into his office.

She was surprised, as soon as the door swung back, to hear a stunning soprano voice singing an operatic aria. Glancing around, she spotted a single-unit stereo, and propped against it a half-dozen tattered cardboard LP jackets. In front was the sleeve for Callas' recording of *Norma*, currently playing.

Hartnett followed her gaze. "If it bothers you, I'll shut it off. I leave it goin' all the time otherwise. Relaxes me somehow. . . ." He was lost for a moment, staring pensively at the wooden speaker in a corner as Callas hit a high note. "Ain't she got a voice, though," he said finally. "Someday before I die, I'd like to see that woman onstage."

Lou debated whether to tell the sheriff he was already too late for that one. "Leave it on," she said. "I like opera too."

"Now, what was it you wanted?" Hartnett positioned

an extra chair in front of his desk and went around to take his own chair. As if to emphasize his readiness to listen, he took off his rose-tinted aviator glasses.

It was the first time his gray eyes had been exposed to her, and Lou was encouraged by a shrewd intensity she saw there. Maybe he wouldn't laugh her off.

"Sheriff, you're aware that I'm responsible for overseeing the interests of a great many men, and one of my main concerns is protecting their safety. Our work is dangerous enough as it is. . . . I want to be a hundred percent certain that I'm not exposing them to any . . . unnecessary risks."

The sheriff nodded attentively, and left Lou to make her point.

"I wanted to be sure that absolutely nothing is being overlooked. . . ."

"Overlooked?" Hartnett murmured. "In what respect?"

"Are you convinced that the coroner gave you an accurate assessment of how Jack Benaky was killed?"

The springs of the sheriff's chair creaked as he tilted slowly away from his desk. "Doc Cherney's been doin' that job a long time, Miz Palmer, I wouldn't know who else'd give a better opinion."

"I don't mean to suggest there was anything deliberately misleading," she said. "But I had a talk with Dora Parmalee—"

"Miz Palmer," the sheriff interrupted coolly, "Hal Parmalee was killed four years ago. You're not tryin' to tell me that the same drifters who did in Hal could've got your man, too?"

"No Sheriff. In fact according to Mrs. Parmalee, it wasn't drifters who committed the murder."

"Oh, yes . . . oh, yes," Hartnett said in a weary

singsong. "We all know well enough what Dora thinks. We've been hearin' it for years."

"That doesn't necessarily mean it should be ignored," Lou remarked tartly.

The sheriff picked up his rose-tinted sunglasses and fiddled with them, clicking the earpieces up and down. "So what is it you'd like me to do, Miz Palmer? Bring in a few Indians and put 'em through the wringer? That gonna make you feel better?"

"No!" Lou shot back. Dropping her head and letting her long blond hair curtain her face, she gathered her composure. Christ, why did it have to come down to this, a matter of persecution? She brought her head up again. "Of course I don't want that, Sheriff. But I don't see why there shouldn't be some further investigation."

The sheriff's face reddened slightly. Abruptly he slipped the glasses over his eyes. Then he leaked a smile. "Can't blame you, I suppose. You don't really know how far back it goes. You sashay in here one day, and to you it's just a place to do your job, put up your city. But around here, Miz Palmer, we've all lived with that mountain a long time. We know it's got a dozen ways of killin' people. It's got the wildcats, and the gilas, and the rocks that tumble outta nowhere—and then, of course, it's got the legends. They got the power to kill, too. Like that one about the gold, bringin' people here that never shoulda come, turning 'em into victims for other people who've gone crazy lookin' for what they can't find. We've seen it happen over and over again, and maybe that's why we ain't so shook up now. I know that may look to you like we're just a town full of coldhearted folks. But by now we just think we oughta know when it's murder . . . and when it's something else."

It didn't sink in easily. The sheriff was talking about the mountain as if it were a battleground littered with bodies. "Over and over," he'd said.

"How many people *have* been killed on the mountain?" she asked.

"Well, I've been workin' in this office more'n thirty years, Miz Palmer. Nineteen as sheriff, and a deputy before then. In that time alone I'd say it's . . . oh forty, forty-one. And before that, gosh, twice as many more."

Lou shook her head. Just since 1950, an average of more than one a year. "I've never seen anything about it. In the news, I mean."

"Why should you? Most who died up there was no-account loners lookin' for the gold. Not all, mind you. Had a big important surgeon from Denver some years back—my first big case. Used to come in here once a month in his own *helio*copter. It was his hobby, see, lookin' for the Lost Russian, the way some'd go raftin' on rapids or exploring caves. Adventure, y'know. But one time he went in, and that was it. His chopper stood there empty a few days, and then we sent in the search party. Found him with his eyes shot out. Never did find the killer. That one made the news in Denver, I know, but you wouldn'ta seen it anywhere else." The sheriff gestured to a file cabinet across the office. "You can read the cases, if you want. They're all in there."

The opera recording ended. The sound of the needle sliding over the empty band came through the speaker with a sound like an urgent whisper.

"Yes," Lou said. "Since you're offering, Sheriff, I think I would like to look at those files."

"Help yourself."

The automatic changer dropped a new record into place and it began to play. After a second Lou recognized it as Puccini: *The Girl of the Golden West*.

▲▲▲

For nearly three hours she sat at the oak table in a corner of the office and read through the stack of files the sheriff had set in front of her. There were some news clippings going back to near the turn of the century that covered cases of the time, prospectors who had come in search of the famous Lost Russian mine and were then found dead—shot, or stabbed, or killed by pickaxes . . . or flayed by wild animals. Occasionally the killers were apprehended, other prospectors driven to kill by arguments over claims, the jealous lust for ground that turned out to be worthless anyway.

The first actual case files dated from the 1930's. Most of these involved prospectors too. There were also three involving young couples who had probably been driven to believe in the mountain's improbable dream by a time of depression when they thought they could do no worse. One couple had been found murdered, another had seemingly died in a fall, a third had succumbed simply to exposure and starvation.

During the war years, only two deaths had been investigated. One of these was a prospector who appeared to have been killed by animals; the other, a young woman naturalist who'd gone into the mountain to sketch wildlife, had been found with her skull crushed.

After the war the parade of death quickened again. Lone men, mostly, searching for the gold, had fallen victim to other anonymous prospectors protecting their territory from trespass.

In the late fifties, though, there was the case of a

family of seven, two adults and their five children, who had parked their vacation trailer at the base of the mountain, then gone off camping, perhaps taking the children on the adventure of searching for the mine. The entire family had been found hacked to death. The file supplied comprehensive reports on the progress of the investigation. A simpleminded young man from Oregon, found in possession of bloodstained clothing belonging to the victims, had been arrested and charged. Claiming to have found the victims already dead, he had gone to the Arizona gallows still crying out his innocence.

In the file on Hal Parmalee, Lou found nothing either to contradict Dora or cast doubt on the conclusions that had been reached by the local authorities. His death had indeed been gruesome, but after reading of so many other bloody killings over the years, she was prepared to accept that there were faceless, unscrupulous men jealously guarding an empty dream and taking the lives of anyone who threatened to deprive them of it.

To Lou, however, the most chilling case was the murder of the Cabot brothers. Sons of the developer who had planned in the early seventies to build a resort on the mountain, they had been supervising the advance survey. When both climbed to the summit for a weekend exercise and then failed to reappear, one of their team had gone after them. The older of the two brothers had been found with his head—as stated in the medical report included in the file—"torn off." The head itself was never found. Nor was the younger brother. Their father had come to the mountain himself to conduct a search that ran on for weeks, then months. The terrain of the mountain was crisscrossed with endless gullies and ledges, and the elder Cabot had sworn he would not leave until he had covered them all.

Reading this, Lou suddenly realized that it might well be this obsessive search and the consequent neglect of business that had contributed to the bankruptcy of the Cabot Corporation.

And that Honegger's title to the land—and thus, in a sense, her job—stemmed from the bloody tragedy.

▲▲▲

She handed the files back to the sheriff.

"I understand a lot more now," she said. "Reading a history like this, I have to agree—the legend itself has the power to kill. The people who believe in the gold will do anything . . . because they've got to be half-mad in the first place."

"That's how it works, missus. You've got it."

Lou thanked Hartnett again and walked to the door. But there she turned.

"Sheriff, that gold-mine story's lasted such a long time. Did you ever think there might be some truth in it?"

"The Lost Russian?" Hartnett laughed loudly and nodded toward the stereo, where *Traviata* was playing. "Oh, goodness, Miz Palmer, that story's about as real as the plots of them operas."

▲▲▲

She saw the smoke first, a wisp of faint gray drifting into the sky from the chimney of the shack across the meadow. The field of grass stretched before her, inviting, serene—a rare flourishing of green in the arid landscape. Wildflowers and ocotillo dotted the meadow. From here the mountain offered a fabulous vista, north toward the jagged range she had climbed, and east to the towering Arm of God. She could understand why the vet would cling to this place.

But it was time for her to get him out. The project was advancing, crews moving closer and closer. Already Daniels had been allowed to stay too long.

She had assumed Daniels' hut would be primitive. In the shape of an elongated T, it had two tiny canvas-covered windows on the front of the stem and a latticed door jerry-rigged on the side. A crooked tin chimney leapt up at the rear.

Lou crossed the meadow and knocked at the door. It opened, and the vet stood in the half-shadow beyond the threshold, naked to the waist.

"Hello," she said.

Daniels nodded. His steady glare registered now as more brooding than mean, not so much unfriendly as simply wary.

"Mr. Daniels, I think we have to talk."

Daniels shrugged. "What the fuck do we have to talk about?"

She flinched. This was going to be as difficult as Capper had warned. "Mr. Daniels, I can see why you like it here. I know it's hard for you to leave. But our project needs—"

"I don't give a fuck about your project," he said quietly.

The timbre of his voice unnerved her, deep and gravelly. And now, as she looked at his face, she noticed the sinewy lines around his eyes and the taut string of muscle in his neck. There was something coiled in this man; he could explode at any moment. She decided to tread lightly. "Mr. Daniels, this is Honegger Corporation property. I'd like to make it as easy as possible for you, we'll be glad to help you move your things and—"

"Lady, you're not the first one to tell me I'm moving. A couple of years ago some other guy gave me the same invitation, and I'm still here."

"Of course," Lou said, "that would have been someone from the Cabot Corporation."

"I didn't get his name. I just told him what I'm going to tell you. Get the hell off my land."

Lou shifted her pose, tilting her head. "Mr. Daniels, why be difficult?" she tried sweetly, forcing herself to smile. "What can you do here you couldn't do some other place?"

"Look for gold," he said evenly.

"By now you ought to know it isn't here, and we could make it worth your while to—"

Unexpectedly he returned her smile. "You're a very pretty lady."

He was a pretty good strategist himself, Lou thought, disarmed.

But then he went on. "Oh, you're pretty, all right, you're so pretty I'll bet you *know* how damn good-lookin' you are. You think you can come on to me, and I'll just move on out. You can forget *that*, lady, and you can forget trying to move me. And the next time you walk onto my land uninvited, you might get hurt. Now, move. Go back where you came from."

Lou's rage broke through. This arrogant bastard was going to get off the mountain if she had to blast him out, if she had to call in the cops and have him bodily hauled down—

Then she realized how foolish she was. She saw his army khaki pants, and the black boots, and the intense bitter look in his eyes. She remembered all those Vietnam vets she had seen on television. The ones who slept with knives under their pillows, the ones who lived with so much rage inside that they worried about killing their own wives and children. The ones whose nightmares sent them screaming into the night to take their own lives.

Go easy, she said to herself.

"Mr. Daniels, I'm only trying to help you. For your own safety, you'll have to move. We're clearing the mountain of *everybody*, all the prospectors and tourists, because we're going to be blasting up here. Unless you accept the facts, we're all going to have a serious problem."

Daniels glanced away and let out a quick, dismissive laugh. "Oh, I don't think so," he said evenly. "I don't think there's going to be any problem at all."

Her composure broke. She heard her own voice cracking. "Mr. Daniels, you're not giving me a chance, you're not even listening to me. Stop and think about what you're doing."

"You did your job, you delivered your message. There's nothing more to talk about."

With that, barely giving her another look, he turned and closed the door.

Damn him, she thought as she whirled and stalked back across the meadow. Damn his stupid arrogance. Maybe he had suffered in Vietnam, and maybe he was suffering now. But his unreasoning defiance would only get him into bad trouble. Where else, she wondered, might his mindless defiance have already led him?

Was it impossible that he had killed a man—and then tried to make it look like an Indian scalping?

CHAPTER 14

Under the silver-blue moon the dappled black-and-white pony seemed to be made purely of pools of light and shadow. Still fifty yards away, Ben could see the silhouette of the animal standing in a flat field off to the side of the road. On its back sat Jesse, motionless and erect. Had he been waiting like that the whole time—a figure carved in time, the image of the Indian sentinel searching the horizon for another wagon train? Or was he getting ready to ride away? He had promised to wait until eleven, but Ben had been delayed sneaking out of the house, his mother restlessly moving between her study and bedroom.

Ben was on the verge of shouting to Jesse when the horse raised its head and whinnied. Jesse turned the horse and trotted toward him. "Good," he said simply as they met.

Ben nodded and stared back, trying to hide his amazement. Despite the chill of the desert night, Jesse was bare-chested, covered only partially by a fur vest. His long hair was not gathered behind him as at school, but was worn loose, and flowed from under a beaded headband with two large white feathers stuck into it.

Slung diagonally across his body by its string was a bow. A quiver of arrows and a large pouch of tanned rawhide were secured around his waist by long leather strips. His lower body and thighs were draped with a loincloth, also made of rawhide.

Weird. The word applied to Jesse by the kids in school rose in Ben's mind. Maybe he really was too hooked on this stuff. Suppose he really was nuts? Go up on the mountain with him, and anything could happen. If he was angry enough about the city being built, he might think of striking at the woman in charge by hurting her son, get out his tomahawk and . . .

Jesse extended his hand to grasp Ben's and pull him up onto the horse.

Ben hesitated. Wasn't this what he wanted an adventure?

And to see the gold. . . .

Ben reached up. As Jesse swung him onto the rear flanks of the pony, Ben felt the smooth slippery hide under him and remembered then that Jesse rode bareback. "Hold on to me," Jesse advised. "We will ride very fast. It is important to be there before the crack between the days."

And what did *that* mean? Before midnight, Ben guessed.

Jesse gave the horse a light tap with his heels and it bolted immediately into a gallop. By reflex, Ben flung his arms around Jesse's middle and hung on for dear life.

In less than fifteen minutes they covered the several miles to the base of the mountain. Then, still riding the horse, they started up the lower slopes. In the clear night the full moon cast shadows on the rock formations and boulders through which the pony passed. At first they appeared to be on a haphazard weaving course. But then a couple of times Ben noticed that while wide-open ground led off in one direction, Jesse chose to take a more difficult route, passing through gaps between boulders so narrow that the rock surfaces on both sides scraped painfully at Ben's knees. Each time, Ben clenched his jaw tightly, determined to make not the slightest sound of complaint. Jesse's choice made no sense unless he was actually following a trail of some kind.

Eventually they passed through a crevice and emerged onto a narrow ledge that wound upward. There was no doubt now that Jesse was following a well-worn path. Etched deeply into the rock wall along the inner edge were symbols that had obviously been chiseled there by the Indians: stick-figure representations of animals, squiggly lines to suggest snakes, a crudely drawn lizard. Ben had seen similar patterns in the belts and jewelry the Tewani sold in Coopersville.

The ledge grew narrower. Ben couldn't help feeling scared. Was this some kind of test? Or was it a trap? Maybe Jesse had hinted about the gold, Ben thought, as a come-on.

From the few streetlamps of Coopersville twinkling in the distance and the headlights of an occasional car on the highway, Ben could tell that they had already climbed quite far. He could see, too, that the outer rim of the ledge fell away steeply. He gripped Jesse tighter.

At last they came to a point where the ledge was blocked by a huge boulder.

"Get off now," Jesse said. He offered a hand to steady Ben as he dismounted, then jumped off himself.

Ben surveyed the ledge. It seemed too narrow to camp on safely. If he or Jesse shifted in his blanket roll while sleeping one of them could slip over the edge. Then he noticed the Indian boy crouching by the impassable boulder.

Ben moved up beside him. "What're you doing?" he said.

Jesse did not reply, but went on fiddling with something at the base of the obstacle. Ben bent down to take a closer look just as Jesse gave a decisive tug and held up a large cylindrical stone.

"What's that for?" Ben asked.

Again Jesse remained silent, but a fraction of a second later the boulder gave the answer. With a faint rumble it teetered, pivoted slightly, and then rolled with a surprisingly fluid motion into a declivity in the rock face.

The ledge was no longer impassable. Grabbing up the rope halter, Jesse led the pony forward as Ben trooped behind. Just beyond the boulder, the narrow path opened into a small plateau.

Jesse stopped again. "Help me," he commanded tersely.

Ben had to move alongside Jesse before he saw a length of sturdy weathered tree limb was fixed somehow to provide a lever between the boulder and the cavity where it was resting. As Jesse leaned into the piece of wood, Ben joined him. For a few moments they heaved without result. It was hopeless, Ben thought. How could they move a piece of rock that weighed several tons?

"More," Jesse urged. "Push harder."

Ben strained, gave it everything he had.

He felt the rock yield. Under enough pressure, some critical balance was affected so that the huge weight shifted. With another slight rumble, the boulder moved to block the ledge again.

"We did it!" Ben exclaimed.

Jesse appeared not to hear. He was already walking away toward the center of the plateau.

Trailing after him, Ben became aware of the little heaps of rock, each about waist-high, that dotted the field. Ahead of him he saw Jesse stop to kneel thoughtfully in front of one of the piles of stone. Ben was dying to ask the significance of the rocks, but the way Jesse was kneeling, head bowed, he seemed especially absorbed in some private ritual, so Ben just stood by silently and watched. Anyway, he thought, the Indian hadn't answered any other questions, so what was the use of asking?

At last Jesse rose to his feet. He surprised Ben by volunteering the information that hadn't been asked for. "This is the old burial ground of my people," he said. "There are not many who use it anymore. When they die now, the people want to be buried the white man's way. The blood is taken out of the body, and they are put into boxes, and they go into a cemetery on the reservation. Their families will not go to the trouble of carrying the dead up the mountain. They don't care anymore if the spirit lies with Elder Brother." He glanced down again at the nearest heap of stones. "But I put them here," he added. "Because I know it makes a difference."

"Put who?" Ben said.

"My mother," he answered, "and my father."

Ben could only respond with shocked silence. He'd simply assumed Jesse's parents were alive, since he'd never heard anything to the contrary. Before Ben could muster a word, Jesse started away.

"Come," he called over his shoulder. "From here we go on foot, and there is not much time."

Now they climbed over the side of the mountain. Jesse set a swift pace, and Ben had to push himself to keep up. He was beginning to feel winded when they came over a crest onto a broad, fairly level area of naked stone. Looking around, he saw no slopes rising beyond this point. This had to be the summit.

Excitedly he dropped his pack and skirted the area quickly, gathering the views on every side. From one vantage point he could see the Arm of God not far away. The top was several hundred feet below, yet in the moonlight seemed huge. Ben could almost believe there was a titanic fist rising up toward him, that any moment the clenched fingers would spring open to trap him. Focusing on the pillar of rock, he tried to assure himself that it was not moving, but it seemed to loom in the darkness, closer, ever so slightly closer and closer . . . until Ben felt the first flutter of vertigo. The dizziness would have sent him tumbling forward if he hadn't suddenly forced himself to whirl around and lunge back toward the safe center of the summit.

There, in preparation for a campfire, Jesse had already gathered some dry scrub collected from the sparse growth between cracks in the rock.

"I've got matches," Ben said, going for his knapsack.

"The fire we need tonight is already in the wood," Jesse said, kneeling by the fire site.

And then he did what Ben had always thought before was merely a bullshit test for Boy Scouts trying to earn merit badges. Fitting a thin dry twig to a notch in a piece of split wood, Jesse began to rotate it furiously between his palms. Soon a wisp of smoke curled up, a black skein in the moonlight. Moments later the twig caught fire, and Jesse poked the piece of burning wood into the nest of brush he had built. A high flame leapt upward. Flaring from the center of the bare mountaintop, the flames made no shadow. Rising in the night, where the definition between heaven and horizon was lost, the fire seemed to lick at the very belly of the sky.

Abruptly Jesse plucked up the leather pouch he had removed from around his waist and set on the ground nearby. From within he took four small packets and laid them out on the ground directly in front of him. In the firelight Ben saw that each was made of a shiny green leaf folded over to enclose something.

Now Jesse picked up a packet from one end of the row and unfolded the leaf. Inside was an ocher paste into which he dabbed his fingertips. Ben, who had remained standing, watched as Jesse swiped the paste down across his chest, his fingers spaced so that the colors were laid on in diagonal stripes running from shoulder to breast. Changing hands, he repeated the process to draw the opposite diagonal, all the time keeping his eyes locked on Ben. With the residue still on his fingers, he scored the ocher lines across his cheeks.

Now, Ben thought, Jesse would expect him to put on the "war paint" or whatever it was, and Ben wasn't sure he liked the idea.

But though the Indian boy kept looking at Ben, he didn't speak to him at all, asking nothing of him.

The other pastes were colored green, pale blue, and black. Jesse painted all of them onto his face and chest, a line or two of each. This, Ben knew, was exactly what the Tewani must have looked like in the old days when they went out to do battle. The designs drawn on Jesse's skin were really beautiful. His face had become a vivid mask. Somehow the paint seemed to be a kind of armor. The lines of color caught in the firelight looked like rays that hovered above his skin, a magic aura surrounding him.

Jesse folded up the leaf packets and put them back into his pouch. Then he settled back on his haunches and motioned Ben to seat himself on the opposite side of the fire. He stared at Ben for a long silent moment. "I told you," he said finally, "that I would convince you that this is the home of Elder Brother. You thought I would show you his gold. Now you must decide if you are truly ready. . . ."

"Sure," Ben said, though this whole bit with the paint and the way Jesse was talking was making him nervous. "Why not?"

"Because," said Jesse, "it will take great heart—courage. When I call Elder Brother and he comes, you will be terrified, I promise you. Elder Brother could not have his power if it was not enough to make all men tremble when they stand before him. He could not be the Great Hunter, the Maker of Worlds, if he was not able to shake heaven and earth as easily as you and I would rattle a pebble in our hands. This is what you will see. Are you *sure* you are ready . . . ?"

Ben swallowed hard and nodded. He knew Jesse was deliberately hoking it up. Yet, knowing it was hokum—even being one hundred percent *positive*—didn't make it less scary. As Ben stared at Jesse through the flames between them, the Indian boy, his reddish skin coated by the fire, appeared somehow to be aflame, a form made of dancing light. The carefree sense of merely sharing an adventure was gone now. Something more mysterious was happening here.

Jesse went on: "You must know first the story of the

mountain, of how Elder Brother came to live here. Long ago there was another world, the one that the Tewani call the First World, which Elder Brother had also made. He told the tribe that as long as they kept his Way, the world would be good and they would always be happy. But some did not keep the Way, and the world became corrupted. So Elder Brother picked up a clump of dirt from the ground and flattened the dirt into a circle and he began to dance on this circle, which made it bigger and bigger until it spread out to touch the edges of the sky. It was new and clean, and Elder Brother agreed to take all who had kept the Way to live there. He changed himself into a bird, and the people climbed on his back, and he flew up through a hole in the sky to the Second World. Again he told them that as long as they kept the Way, the world would be good. But then the same thing happened. There were some who didn't listen, and the place was corrupted. So Elder Brother made a new place, and flew the good people up to that one, leaving the bad behind. But it happened again, and again. Always there were people who couldn't keep the Way . . . until Elder Brother became tired and angry. Then he made this mountain as a place to live alone, away from the filth and corruption. Sometimes he would fly alone through a hole in the sky, and if people came to the mountain, he would let them know there was a beautiful new world he had made. But he vowed never to take anyone there until he was sure the Way would be kept. And he put the gold here to test us: as long as there are people who want it, then he knows it is not yet time to take us on to the Fifth World."

Jesse had been gazing into the flames. Now he lifted his eyes to look at Ben. "This is why you must stop the work your mother does. For many years the gold has remained untouched by our people. The time is coming when we will have proved to Elder Brother that we are ready to fly with him. But if the mountain itself is harmed—if we *allow* that to happen—then the hope is gone forever. We will never be taken to the Fifth World, and we will never be happy."

Ben couldn't think what to say. *Okay, I'll make sure you get to the Happy Hunting Ground or the Fifth World or whatever they call it, I'll do it all by myself.* How the hell could he? If Ben was silenced, it was no longer by awe. Something else: pity, maybe. No matter how much Jesse believed he could make the god materialize on this mountaintop, it wasn't about to happen. Not tonight, folks. Ben suddenly felt terribly sorry for the Indian.

"Jesse," he said, "I've tried to explain to you before. I can't stop what's going to happen here. You've just got to accept it, learn to—"

"No!" Jesse bellowed. He reared back from the fire and sprang to his feet. "You are the one who must learn. *You!*" Then, suddenly throwing his arms wide, he tilted his head back and began to shout at the sky, a panting yowling singsong of strange sounds.

Ben had never heard it before, but he guessed this must be a Tewani chant. The call had begun.

It didn't matter that Ben knew there was no Elder Brother. No such thing. He cowered by the fire anyway, and peered up at the sky, waiting for the first glimpse of the god that absolutely didn't exist.

CHAPTER 15

Lou came awake with a start.

She was still propped up against her pillow, the bedside lamp still on, the biography of Teddy Roosevelt she had been trying to get into for weeks lying open across her knees. She had simply nodded off. Yet, awakening, she was aware of an odd tension throughout her body.

Was it a noise that had wakened her—someone breaking into the house?

No, that didn't happen out here. Everyone left their houses unlocked around the clock.

Pushing herself up slowly off the pillow, she inclined her head toward the closed door of her room, listening.

Something *was* different. She could sense it.

Sliding out of bed, she put on her robe and slippers and went out of the bedroom, along the hallway, and into the kitchen. There she turned on the lights, looked around, and checked that the back door was locked. She checked the front door; it was also secure.

Returning to her bedroom, she passed Ben's door. She opened it and looked in. All quiet. Then she noticed that the window was open wide. Too wide, she thought; the room was a trifle on the cold side. She crossed the room and slid the window down, leaving a gap of only a few inches above the sill. Better.

Then she turned to the bed, thinking Ben might need to have the covers tucked in around him.

▲▲▲

"It's Lou Palmer, Sheriff," she said into the phone. "I'm terribly sorry to wake you, but this is an emergency. My son is missing."

"Missing" the sheriff repeated drowsily.

"Well I don't mean he's been kidnapped" Lou explained quickly. "But he's not in his bed and if he's where I think he is, then—"

"Now, hold on," Hartnett jumped in, his voice sounding less murky. "If you know where he is, that's in a whole other ballpark from 'missing.' "

"But it's the mountain," Lou said, the shrill edge of panic tingeing her voice. "He's gone up on the mountain."

"Went up there in the middle of the night? How do you know?"

"A couple of days ago he asked my permission to go camping there this weekend with a friend. It was just after I'd been to see you and read all those files, and . . . well, of course I refused permission. Tonight he must have sneaked out there."

"I see," Hartnett said, though it carried no special conviction. After a moment he added, "So what was it, Miz Palmer, that you were thinkin' I should do about your boy?"

She made an effort to sound reasonable; she needed his help. "Look, Sheriff. He's not safe up there. You ought to know that better than anyone. I want you to . . . to go after him."

There was a pause before the voice came back again, slow and calm. "Miz Palmer, I surely don't mean to make light of a mother's concern. Got kids o' my own. But look at this situation reasonable. Your boy . . . What's his name, by the way?"

"Ben."

"Well, your Ben's gone campin', that's all. Now, I'm lookin' out my bedroom window, and it's a fair enough night, and there ain't nobody gonna freeze to death. I'd guess Ben's a smart kid, too, and strong enough, and assumin' he's up there with someone from around these parts, I imagine they'll be able to handle themselves for one night. Whoever that other boy is, his own folks aren't worried 'cause there's been no one else bustin' into my sleep tonight. Now I know the mountain don't have a pretty history, but I can't see nothing to call an emergency. Your Ben'll sleep tonight in the rough, and tomorrow he'll run out of food or want to see a little TV, and he'll toddle on home."

The pressure of her terror could no longer be contained. "Two men, Sheriff! In the last six weeks two men have been killed on that mountain. Not to mention the dozens of others in your files. Are you telling me that you won't do a thing to help my son? For God's sake, he's up there alone, in danger—"

"Alone?" the sheriff interrupted. "I thought you said he was with another boy."

Suddenly Lou realized what was at the core of her panic. She thought of Ben as being alone because the boy with him might be an enemy, because he was an Indian, and it was the mission of his tribe to protect the mountain from interlopers. Was it prejudice, or was she being rational?

"Yes," she murmured, in retreat from herself as well

as the sheriff's interrogation. "Yes, he is . . . with someone. . . ."

Hartnett let out a self-satisfied grunt. "Who's the other boy? Guess I oughta make a note of it."

"His name is Jesse Silvertrees."

"Indian name, ain't it?"

"Yes," Lou said. "He's a Tewani."

"Well, there, y'see now? Your Ben couldn't be in better hands. Those Tewani know everything there is to know about how to get around on that mountain."

She gripped the phone as the sheriff told her there really wasn't a thing he could do tonight. Ben was going to be fine, but in the morning, if Lou was still concerned, a chopper could be called in from State Police to do a flyover, pinpoint the boys' position, and make sure they were well.

"There'll be no need for that, Sheriff," Lou sighed in defeat. "By morning I'll have some of my crews doing overtime up there. I can have them do a search."

Before Hartnett could reply, she dropped the receiver into its cradle.

For a moment she lingered by the phone. Should she try Capper? Some of the men could be organized tonight. Within an hour or two they could be combing the mountain . . .

Of course the sheriff was right, she realized now. What was the point? It would be almost dawn before anything could be accomplished. What choice was there but to wait for daylight?

Lou walked across the living room, opened one of the patio doors, and stepped outside. Warming herself against the chill, she folded her arms across her breasts and stood facing the mountain. Under the full moon, the distant cone seemed to rise gently from the flat surface of the desert, like the bud of some monstrous flower just beginning to break through the ground.

There was every reason to expect he would be fine, she told herself. He had gone camping, that was all. With an Indian boy.

▲▲▲

Ben didn't know where the cloud had come from.

One minute there had been nothing in the sky but the white round moon, and suddenly the wispy shadow floated over half of it, making it look like a heavy-lidded suspicious eye.

Funny, too, but the way the smoke curled up from the fire in a high sinuous column, it appeared to climb straight up all the way to the blot on the moon, to blend with it. An illusion, sure, he knew it. Smoke would be dissipated long before it ever got that high. But in the darkness, distinctions were lost. It really looked like the cloud had been made by the smoke.

Ben was watching it, partly because he couldn't watch Jesse anymore. The chant had been going on *forever*—fifteen minutes, anyway, maybe longer. Ben was embarrassed. The longer it went on, the more stupid it seemed for Jesse to be doing this routine by himself under the moonlight. Head thrown back, eyes squinched shut, he stood with his legs parted and bent at the knees in a half-crouch as he chanted. The tendons of his neck stood out, and a coating of sweat over his body glistened like copper in the firelight.

The adventure had worn thin, but there was no getting out of it now. Ben only wished that Jesse would call it quits pretty soon so they could both get into their blanket rolls and go to sleep.

A few more clouds had gathered, Ben saw. Slowly they drifted across the moon, and the night dimmed.

Attuned to the change in the light, Jesse opened his eyes, and for the first time, he paused in his chant. Glancing at him, Ben saw a smile break across his face.

Was it over? Perhaps Jesse was content to call the few clouds a sign from Elder Brother. . . .

Now the Indian boy began to dance. Still in his splayfooted crouch, he began to circle around the fire, moving sideways at first, his moccasins sliding over the ground. Then he began to hop and stomp, the soles of his feet drumming against the ground like the rhythmic beat of a tom-tom.

Caught up by the growing ferocity of Jesse's chant, Ben found all at once that he couldn't tear his eyes from Jesse. It was only when the Indian boy halted suddenly, planted his feet, and thrust his hands upward as if reaching to accept a gift, that Ben looked up and saw that the sky had filled with massive gray clouds that churned and rolled over one another like waves in a storm on an upside-down sea.

"Ahah!" Jesse shouted triumphantly. "You see . . . you see!"

It was less a question than a dare, a challenge issued to himself—or to a spirit in the clouds. Ben stared at the clouds thickening and tumbling and fragmenting above him. Looking up, he felt as though he was suspended under an impending avalanche of black snow.

Then a single brilliant lightning bolt streaked across the sky, shooting like a dart through all the clouds. Ben threw a terrified glance at Jesse. He wanted to run now, but it would mean breaking any ties to the Indian. Yet it would be crazy to stay. How or why this electrical storm had come upon them at this moment, Ben didn't know—didn't *want* to know. But if there was going to be more lightning, then any dummy knew the craziest place to be was on this unsheltered mountaintop.

But Jesse remained frozen, his arms stretched upward, as though ready to grasp the lightning itself when it came.

"Jesse!" Ben screamed. "We'd better—"

His words were drowned in a boom of thunder.

The lightning began to shoot down from the sky to the earth, advancing steadily across the ridges of the mountain like gigantic jagged needles.

Ben jumped up. "We can't stay here," he shrieked.

But Jesse paid no attention. The Indian's black eyes, crackling with the reflection of the lightning and the flames of the campfire, looked to Ben like small round windows through which he could see a holocaust inside Jesse's head. Ben seized him as if trying to rouse him from a stupor.

With a raucous, cawing laugh, Jesse shouted at the heavens: "So! You have heard me. Me! You came for *me!*"

Now, finally, he broke from his stance and started to jump around, leaping and spinning, while his fists pumped the air. This wasn't part of the dance, Ben realized after a second. This was pure celebration. Jesse was thrilled at his own accomplishment. The storm was *not* coincidence. It had been summoned, called up with a chant.

Jesse was still laughing and whirling as the rain came down, a torrential downpour dumped as suddenly from the sky as if a sluice gate had been opened. Jesse turned his face to the sky again and opened his mouth, drinking the rain as though it had been made only to slake his thirst.

"Me. . . . *Me!*" he screamed through the deluge. "You made this storm for—"

The sky, the air, the whole mountain flared and sizzled as a bolt of blue-white lightning crashed down, and simultaneously a clap of thunder exploded with such ear-splitting force that it sounded to Ben as though the world, the whole universe had cracked apart. His ears rang, and in the electrified air he could feel the hair on his head actually standing up.

Ben let out a wordless wail of terror and turned to Jesse for help. But what he saw only made the sick feeling in his stomach swell. Jesse was staring up at the sky, his legs bending slowly beneath him as he sank to his knees. In a gesture that suggested both a plea of supplication and an attempt to ward off an attack, his hands extended in front of him, palms turned outward. Jesse was again muttering strange words from the Tewani language, but now in a meek, apologetic tone.

Ben thought he understood what had happened. Jesse had somehow insulted Elder Brother—by taking too much credit for the storm, perhaps—and the god was setting the record straight with a show of force.

And the show wasn't over. Another spark crossed the gap between earth and sky. Another and another, shooting down all around, as if to fence them in. The rain was falling so heavily now that there seemed to be more water than air. Ben felt submerged, and the huge drops pelting down on his skull were becoming painful.

"Jesse! Get up, let's go! We gotta get out of here!"

Jesse remained kneeling on the ground, gazing skyward.

Ben hooked his hands under Jesse's arms and tried pulling him to his feet. "We'll be killed—"

"No!" There was a quaver in the Indian boy's voice,

but it did not undercut the tone of resolve. "We must stay. We are safe here—*here* more than anywhere. He is with us here. *He* is the storm."

Ben looked around wildly. He could already see gullies everywhere that had been transformed into streams rushing down the mountainside, washing away footings.

"Oh, God, Jesse, please, please . . ." Ben whined. "I don't want to die."

Jesse turned to him slowly. "Then stay," he declared, shouting to be heard above the drumming rain and the thunder and the gurgling rush of water everywhere. Then he patted the ground next to him. "Kneel here beside me!"

Ben hesitated. Could he rescue himself without Jesse to guide him? Which way should he go? Without thinking, he started to run, leaving everything behind—knapsack, blanket roll, supplies—and headed blindly over the rim toward the downward slope. His feet slid over the rocky cap of the summit, slick with water; and where he had to cross a muddy rill, his legs were suddenly washed out from under him. The rush of water propelled him over a stretch of smooth slope before it leveled off for a few yards and he was able to stand.

The lightning flashed again, but the bolt struck farther along the ridge, and Ben ran on. The brief illumination showed him where the mountain sheared away precipitously and where he could proceed safely.

Then the lightning struck closer. Panicking again, he started to move faster, running—though the grade was so steep that when he felt himself going too fast he tried to stop and *couldn't*. Losing balance, he fell forward and plunged headfirst over the mud-coated rock.

For a few seconds he thought he was going to careen

into a boulder, have his skull dashed and his brains smeared all over the rock.

Then suddenly all the bumpy friction that was tearing at his stomach and hands as he slid downward disappeared. The sensation was momentarily pleasant, like flying. Then he realized something terrible was happening. He had gone sliding right over a brink of rock.

And now he was falling.

Falling. . . .

▲▲▲

Lou got up and went to the window. The mountain was still faintly visible, shrouded in a corona of dense clouds.

As she watched, the bolus of cloud seemed to light up from within, as though a flashbulb had gone off deep in the recesses of a smoky room. It looked odd to Lou, because she didn't see the lightning shoot down to earth. The mountain lit up again, but this time the enormous spark was there, snapping between sky and ground. Several more followed, all striking around the mountain. Thunder cracked and echoed across the desert like the boom of artillery from a battleground.

"Oh, my God," she murmured softly.

In the next second she heard the rain on the roof, not yet solid driving sheets but the first few droplets blown ahead of the storm on the breeze. She could see, though, that a heavy curtain of rain was moving rapidly toward the house.

She glanced anxiously toward the phone. Who would help her with a rescue party! Not the sheriff; his desire to wait until morning was not going to be changed by having to conduct a search under *these* conditions.

Abruptly the roof was hit by the loud persistent drumming of the deluge.

Capper! She grabbed up the phone . . .

. . . and slammed it down again without dialing. What could she reasonably ask him to do at this point? Haul a couple of dozen men out of bed to go clambering around the mountain looking for her son in a blinding rainstorm? He'd say to sit it out—the only reasonable thing to do. Though no doubt he'd be kind enough to come over and hold her hand. . . .

Shit, she wasn't even *allowed* to accept that kind of sympathy. Let a woman show her helplessness in any situation, and the men she commanded would never again be as ready to obey her orders. She couldn't cry on Capper's shoulder tonight and turn back into his boss in the morning.

But, Christ, she had to do *something!*

She stood for a minute, giving herself every responsible command she'd have given someone else in the same crisis.

Then she ran to the bedroom, and without taking time to remove her nightgown, threw on a denim workshirt and jeans and slipped into a pair of sneakers.

The phone started to ring when she was in front of the closet pulling out the old waterproof sailing jacket Matt had given her.

It was Hartnett. Unable to sleep after her call, he'd contacted the state police in Kingman. "Soon as this weather lets up, they'll be able to send in a chopper. Meantime, Miz Palmer, I just wanted you to know everything possible is gonna be done."

He was obviously overcome with guilt now for his earlier unresponsiveness. Lou was not inclined to let him off the hook.

"I don't want to hear what's *going* to be done, Sheriff. Tell me what's being done now!"

He coughed, loosening his throat. "Miz Palmer, a chopper can't fly safely in this storm. And it ain't gonna help no one to send more men climbin' up old Legend right now. I'd say the visibility's right down near zero. Now, I want you to know you've got my support and my sympathy. But our best bet is still waitin'. It's tough, I know. But I expect those boys saw the storm comin' on, and they've got enough horse sense to find a good spot to sit it out until—"

"Sheriff, that mountain is caked with clay. Whole pieces of it could losen up, and if they do, it won't matter where my son and that Indian boy are 'sitting it out.' They could be buried within seconds under tons of mud."

"Holy shit," the sheriff said in a hush. "I just wasn't thinking. But as long as he's with that Indian kid, I'd bet my boots they'll come through okay. Specially if the conditions are as dangerous as you say, we just can't send out more people. It still comes down to waitin' and prayin'. I swear to ya, though, soon as it's reasonable, we'll get out to Legend with some lights and—"

"When it gets to that point, Sheriff," Lou erupted in a shout, "I won't need your damn help. One way or another, it'll be too late." She banged down the phone, cursing him, and raced straight out of the house.

It was like diving into a pool. The sky was sending down sheets of rain so heavy she felt smothered. Reaching her car, she shivered the water out of her hair, then turned the key in the ignition. The engine turned over but wouldn't catch. She pumped a bit more gas and tried again. The engine shuddered and caught. She revved up to a roar, then threw the shift into gear.

Wheeling out onto the road, she floored the accelerator and drove hell-bent toward Legend Mountain.

The windshield was awash with water, blurring everything. The curtain of rain in front of the car was so thick that there seemed to be a wall of silver reflecting the headlights at her, cutting off vision beyond ten or twelve feet. The job of steering occupied her concentration so totally that she hardly gave any thought to what she intended to do when she reached her destination.

The curve came on fast. She was into it before she could see that the dotted white lines down the middle of the road were no longer in front of her, but peeling away rapidly to the left.

She threw the wheel over hard, too hard, and the car went into a spin, planing over the watered surface of the road like a hockey puck gliding over ice. The car made a complete circle, then a second, while Lou pumped the brakes frantically and tried to bring the wheel in line with the direction of the skid.

The rotation stopped, and the car lurched forward, but it was off the road now, and when at last Lou brought it to a halt, it tilted down at a precarious angle.

She sprang out into the rain to inspect the situation. The BMW was five or six feet off the road, headed down the slope of a gully, though mercifully it had stopped short of the bottom, where a stream of muddy water eddied around knee-high rocks.

She got back behind the wheel and tried to reverse out of the gully, though she knew it was hopeless. The slope was viscous mud, and the spinning wheels only dug in deeper.

Climbing out of the car again, her will whipped by the same animal instinct that had driven her out into the wild night, she started slogging on foot along the road, continuing in the same direction. Toward the mountain.

The water went on cascading from the sky, dripping into her eyes until they stung. Step after step she pushed on through the ankle-deep water on the flooded highway. She could feel the effort taking a toll on her legs. The muscles in her thighs began to ache terribly, her ankles grew numb.

Finally she was forced to rest. She stopped to look back over her shoulder, and stifled a moan of despair. She could still faintly see the glow of the brake lights and parking lights she had forgotten to switch off. Then she swiveled in the direction of the house—where, at least, she thought the house *might* be. She had purposely left on the driveway floodlights, thinking they might serve as a beacon.

Faintly Lou picked out the pinprick of murky brightness deep in the heart of the storm. Not really that far away—if indeed it was the lights of the house.

She spun around again to face in the opposite direction, and waited for the next flash of lightning. When it came a few moments later, she could see the mountain. Miles beyond her. She would never make it.

Resigned, she started walking back toward the house, heading for that faint star in the night, light-years away.

CHAPTER 16

The thunder woke her again. An unusual thunder, a rapid steady stream of hollow booms. Lifting her head, Lou looked out through the glass patio slider. Visible on the horizon was the pale lavender fringe of dawn and the grayish outline of the mountain. Remnant drops of rain pattered lightly onto the roof from the ironwood tree beside the house. The storm was over.

And the thunder was someone pounding urgently on the door.

She pulled herself drowsily out of the chair. After returning to the house, she had shucked off all her sodden clothes, chased the chill from her body with a hot shower, and wrapped herself in a blanket. Then she had curled up in a living-room chair positioned directly in front of the glass door so that she could maintain her vigil. But sleep had taken her prisoner.

The pounding quickened, demanding to be answered.

Lou ran halfway to the front door before she became aware that she was still robed in nothing but the blanket. The knocking was getting louder, more insistent. The sheriff, she guessed, rousing her for a search party.

She'd let him in, then get dressed. Clutching the blanket tighter around her, Lou pulled the door open.

Ben lay cradled in a man's arms, his prostrate form encased in a khaki greatcoat, its wool old and tatty but obviously warm.

At the sight of him, she felt such tension flow out of her body that her legs seemed to lose all strength. For a moment she thought she might buckle—or just fall to her knees and give a prayer of thanks.

But the dizziness was virtually knocked out of her by the shock of being rudely jostled aside as the man holding Ben pushed into the house. Lou's grip on the blanket came loose and the blanket slipped down around her shoulders.

"Which way . . . ?" she heard the man say, then a few more words, muffled and indistinct as he kept moving farther along the entranceway.

"What?" She turned slowly from the door, not yet fully awake or recovered from the shock of seeing Ben.

The man stopped and looked back at her. "I said," he repeated in a harsh, impatient tone, "which way to the kid's room?"

Occupied with gathering the blanket, intensely conscious that her breasts had been half-bared, it took Lou another moment to realize that Ben's rescuer was not, after all, a complete stranger. The army-fatigue cap with a peaked brim had kept his face in shadow when he stood outside in the early-morning gloom, but in the hallway there was enough light to recognize him as Daniels, the war vet.

She recalled his brutish treatment of the day before, and fury welled within her; she nearly said: *You can't come charging in here . . .*

Then, of course, she buried it. "That way. . . ." she

said quietly. Clutching the blanket around her, she could only nod along the hall and supply a vague motion with her hand.

Daniels didn't move. She thought he must be ogling her bare shoulders, but then realized her instructions were incomplete, and added, "First door after the bathroom."

Immediately he moved toward the room.

Lou turned to close the front door, but froze with her hand on the knob. Outside, beyond the end of the drive where Daniels had left his truck, a horse stood in the murky light of daybreak, a motionless figure seated on its back.

What should she do? Slam the door—signal banishment of the Indian boy from Ben's life? Or call him into the house? He was only a boy, after all. Shouldn't she talk to him, attempt to bridge the gap?

She hesitated too long; the Indian grabbed the end of the rope halter that dangled from his hands against the horse's flank, wheeled the animal around, and sent him into a gallop.

Only then she found her voice. "Jesse!" she called. "Wait!"

But the horse had faded into the purple mist lingering on the desert floor.

She closed the door, ran to put on her terry robe, and then dashed into Ben's room.

He was stretched out on his bed, Daniels kneeling alongside. The vet's hands were probing along the boy's legs. Lou moved to the head of the bed and looked down at her son, his face turned away on the pillow. She thought he was unconscious, but then he rolled over and his eyes flickered open.

"Hi, Mom," he whispered weakly.

"Hi." She laid her palm on his forehead and felt a fever.

Ben lifted up slightly. "Sorry if I made you—"

Daniels broke in: "Lie still and be quiet."

With obvious care and patience, the vet pressed his fingers lightly around Ben's left ankle, which was bluish and swollen. Then, gripping the foot, he manipulated it from side to side, instantly stopping when Ben groaned.

"What do you think it is?" Lou asked.

Daniels stood. "Got any athletic bandages?" he snapped impatiently, ignoring her question. "You know, the kind basketball and tennis players wrap around their knees?" Lou could only shake her head. "Then take the biggest towel you can find," Daniels said, "and cut it in strips, lengthwise." Lou started toward the bathroom, and his voice arrested her from behind. "First bring a bowl of ice cubes and a couple of washcloths. On the double."

She almost gave him a snide salute. All right, she had to be grateful—but did that mean he had a right to be so goddamn boorish and insensitive?

She returned with the ice and washcloths. Daniels was hunched over an open drawer at Ben's dresser, and Lou's first thought was the mean suspicion that he was hunting for valuables, Ben's pocket money. But then he yanked out a pair of clean pajamas and went back to the bed.

"C'mon, son," he said, sliding one arm under Ben's shoulders, lifting him. "Sit up, let's get that shirt off."

It was another voice entirely: soft, patient, appealing. Lou was astounded that it was the same man. She watched as he helped Ben into his fresh pajama top, all the time maintaining a lulling monologue. "Atta way, son. I know you're stiff . . . just slide that arm in easy. . . ." She couldn't ever recall seeing a man handle a child with such patience.

Then he noticed Lou watching. "Dammit, lady, I thought I told you to cut up a towel. You're pissing away time."

She scampered out of the room, then felt foolish and demeaned by her own reflex. But she went to the cupboard where she kept linens and towels and rummaged inside. *The biggest towel you can find*, he had said. Now she saw the biggest she had was an expensive color-printed beach towel, a fifty-dollar luxury from Magnin's to which she'd treated herself last summer. Surely a regular bath towel would do instead. . . .

She couldn't shake off his effect. *The biggest*. Those were the orders. Maybe it would make a difference. Lou grabbed up the beach towel. Feeling stupid and driven and furious all over again, she went to her bedroom and cut the towel into strips with her sewing scissors.

When she got back to Ben's room, Daniels was seated on the floor beside the bed, holding a compress of ice cubes against the ankle.

"Got a few safety pins?" he asked as Lou walked up to the bed.

"I think, in my sewing bas—"

"Get 'em. Paper clips or hairpins'll do if you can't find the safety pins. And two stiff straight rods of some kind—rulers, chopsticks, a wooden kitchen spoon, anything like that. C'mon, don't just stand there."

She opened her mouth to say a word or two on courtesy and common decency, but he had already turned away to administer to Ben's ankle.

"But leave the bandage," he said without looking up.

She dropped the towel strips she was absently carrying away.

"Crumb," she muttered as she left. The man made her feel like a parody of the helpless woman, too cowed even to talk back.

He was helping her son, though.

No safety pins in the basket, but she took a wooden shirt hanger from the closet, went to her office, and reaped a handful of paper clips from her desk, then returned to Ben's room.

For a while the vet continued to refresh the compress with ice and apply it to Ben's ankle. Lou stood by brimming with questions—how and where had Ben been found? . . . what was wrong with him? . . . should she call a doctor? But Daniels worked with such concentration she was discouraged from breaking into it. Ben appeared to have lapsed into sleep.

At last Daniels dropped the compress into the ice bowl and wrapped one of the towel strips around the ankle, secured it with an unbent paper clip. He repeated the process with a couple more strips, then broke the wooden hanger in half, laid the two pieces on either side of Ben's ankle, and wound them inside yet more towel to make a splint.

"Keep him off his feet a couple of days. Nothing broken, just a bad sprain and a pulled ligament, but it'll be painful as hell to start. You might want to bring in a doctor to get a prescription for painkiller, but you could save the money. Kids are tough, and yours could probably get by on aspirin. A week from now he'll still be a gimp, but halfway to mended. Three weeks, good as new."

"Do you know how it happened?"

"He took a ten-foot tumble to a ledge and landed

with his foot folded under him. Could've been a lot worse, but the ledge was covered with mud, and that cushioned the fall."

"How did you find him?"

"Didn't. I was led to him. The Indian kid wasn't far behind and heard a call for help. He couldn't get your kid off the ledge by himself, so he went for help. I was the closest help around."

"I'm very grateful to you," Lou said.

Daniels went silent again. There was a subtle change in the man's posture, the tilt of his head, a stiffening of his shoulders. She couldn't imagine why, but he seemed to have taken her appreciation as an insult.

A new surge of resentment for his insolence—even a spark of hatred—went through Lou. She wondered if she could possibly trust Daniels to give responsible diagnosis and treatment of Ben's injury. She watched him for another minute.

"You do that very well," she remarked, fishing.

"I suppose," he replied laconically. "You watch enough medevacs work on guys who've got bones sticking out of their legs like broken matchsticks 'cause they got stitched by a machine gun or stepped on a ponji stick . . . and, yeah, that'll turn you into a pretty fair medic yourself."

The desire to shock and affront was willfully cruel. It was all Lou could do not to throw him out of the house.

Except that his tenderness never faltered. Rising from his knees, the vet took the blanket folded at the foot of the bed and covered Ben. There was even a delicacy in the way he did this, smoothing the counterpane under Ben's chin before tucking it in. Then he turned off the lamp, stooped to pick up the bowl of melted ice, and headed out of the room straight past Lou.

She followed as far as the kitchen doorway, where she paused to observe as he poured the ice water into the sink, dried the bowl, squeezed out the wet washcloths, and hung them over the rack with the dish towels. Then he began opening and closing the cabinets under the counter, searching. She looked on curiously, saying nothing. In a minute he located a teakettle, filled it with water, and put it on the stove. Then he stood back in front of the burner with his arms folded. Lou was tempted to try some repartee about "watched pots," but she guessed it would fly past him without winning a smile or an answer. She just went on watching, puzzled by the vet and by the mix of emotions he inspired. Her fury had not abated, yet it was addled by some softer feelings—sympathy, perhaps. Or was it pity? Lou found it sad that a man with such an obvious capacity for tenderness preferred to show an uglier side of himself.

The kettle began to whistle. Rather than wait for Daniels' rude demand or watch him clatter through her shelves, Lou moved into the kitchen, took out a mug and a tea bag, and clapped it onto the counter beside the stove.

He glanced at the cup. "Only one? Warm drink'd settle you down, you know." His eyes came up to study her face. "You look beat to hell."

She was strangely touched. He had taken notice, expressed concern. The tea, she suspected, had been for her, not himself.

She brought out a second mug and tea bag, and he poured the water from the kettle. In silence they carried the mugs to the kitchen table and sat down. Daniels kept his chair turned to the side and stared down at the floor, self-contained, an island. Lou thought that she probably hadn't sat at a table with anyone so little concerned with social graces since she'd been in kindergarten.

The silence became oppressive; she could practically hear the tea brewing. Finally it was unbearable to her.

"I . . . really don't know how to thank you. . . ."

He looked up sharply. "I don't want a thing from you, not even your precious thanks. If you want to know the honest truth, I'm not exactly thrilled I ended up doing you one of the biggest favors anybody'll ever do you in your whole life. But a kid needed help, and he happened to be yours." He leaned closer across the table. "It still doesn't change a lick how I feel about you and your goddamn company and the way you want to fuck up my life. You understand?"

She took a deep breath and let it out in a sigh. "Mr. Daniels, what's being done with the mountain isn't a personal vendetta against you. I know it means losing things that . . . that are valuable to you. But my firm can make compensation, and you can find the same things somewhere else."

"You think so, huh?"

"Yes, I do."

He gave her another intense appraisal. "You really believe in what you're doing, don't you?"

"Yes. It will fill an important need, and it will help people."

He let out a bitter laugh. "Christ! Will the bastards who want to screw the world never think up a new line? Lady, that was the one I fell for fifteen years ago. And filling that 'important need' helped how many hundreds of thousands of people get their asses blown to shit? But it never changes, does it? The fat cats never come up with a better slogan for making suckers outta the rest of us poor bastards."

Lou opened her mouth to argue, then let it go. Daniels was clearly nursing grudges that had been seeded long before she came along, and there was nothing she could say about Vietnam and the peculiar historical currents of the time that was likely to make him surrender his anger. It was too precious to him, she thought, a fuel that kept him going. She couldn't blame him for feeling as he did, either; she simply felt it was unfair to tar her with the same brush.

They were locked into silence again. Daniels finished his tea but kept sitting over the empty cup. Lou finished hers, too.

"Helped settle me down, all right," she said at last. "Thanks, I'll be able to get some sleep now." She raised her arms in an exaggerated stretch, then rose and brought the mugs to the sink.

Daniels did not take the hint. Lou moved to the nearest window and pushed the chintz curtains aside. "Almost sunrise," she said pointedly. "You should have an easy time getting home. . . ."

"I'm staying."

She turned, confused and alarmed. "What?"

"It'll be another couple of hours before we see how bad the swelling's gonna get. Assuming I'm right about the ankle, it should be okay, but I want to be sure. I'll take off the bandage have a look, then do it up again." Only now he responded to the reluctance in her expression. "Don't have to. It'd just be a good idea . . . long as I'm here."

Lou was stuck for a reply. She was put off by Daniels' presumption, the sullen presence that had taken over her house like an occupying force—"squatted" there, as on his piece of the mountain. And of course his whole manner was disturbing. The fires of violence were stoked so high within him that from across the room she imagined she could feel the heat radiating off his skin. She should tell him to leave.

Still, she believed his intention was wholly unselfish, and she'd seen his knowledge of how to treat Ben's leg well demonstrated.

Daniels' chair scraped backward as she struggled with an answer. "No skin off my ass," he said, starting to rise.

"Okay," she said quickly. "If you think it's best for Ben. . . ."

He settled down again.

Lou gestured toward the living room. "You can rest in there, if you'd like . . . lie down on the sofa."

"This'll be fine."

"There are newspapers and magazines around. Help yourself. . . ."

His curt nod implied he'd help himself if he needed anything. He was staring at the floor again, back on his island.

Lou went to the door, then turned back. She had never felt such a violent clash of emotions. The vet made her think of purging herself in military terms. She wanted to attack that island with a salvo that would decimate it, sink it. And she wanted to land there as a friendly force and civilize it. But neither strategy, she thought, could win.

CHAPTER 17

She went to check Ben and found him peacefully asleep. Returning to her own room, she closed the door and quietly pushed in the button that locked the knob. No sooner had she touched the belt on her robe, however, than she decided against removing it and getting into bed. She wouldn't be able to sleep with Daniels in the house.

It had been a dreadful mistake to permit him to stay. Why hadn't she realized it sooner? Why was she so easily intimidated by him? Perhaps she was overly sympathetic to his expectation of shelter out of guilt—because, ultimately, she was responsible for depriving him of his home. Or was it his references to the war, an experience that had plainly scarred his soul if not his body, that had tapped into her guilt?

But, Jesus, that wasn't *her* fault! She ought to go right back to him now and say she'd changed her mind: it would be wiser if he left. . . .

She couldn't—hated giving him the idea that she was irresolute, vacillating. It might actually do harm later, when it came to resolving the problem of dislodging him from his land.

She paced her room until she began to feel penned up. Then she went out again. Passing by the kitchen door, she saw him still sitting at the table. His eyes were closed, though she sensed he was awake. Even in repose he wore the hard shell.

Suddenly his eyes opened and he caught her at the door.

"Couldn't sleep," she alibied. "Too keyed up. I'm going to do some work." She continued on to her office.

She couldn't relax there, either, though she passed forty minutes typing up some of the biweekly progress report she sent back to headquarters. Twice she interrupted herself to look in on Ben.

The third time she made a trip to Ben's room, Daniels was there. As she entered, he lifted his palm from Ben's forehead. "Seems better," he said softly.

"Yes."

"Another hour and I'll take a look at the leg." He started back to the kitchen.

She didn't want to be isolated again. "Mr. Daniels, would you like some breakfast? I was going to make myself a couple of eggs and some toast."

"Wouldn't mind," he said.

Not even a thank-you.

They went into the kitchen. "How do you like your eggs?" Lou asked as she opened the refrigerator.

"Same as yours'll be okay." He scanned for a breadbox, located it, and took a couple of slices from the package.

"I'm scrambling mine," Lou said. "But if you have a preference, I could—"

"Hard-boiled," he put in.

He noticed her smiling as she filled a pot with water. "That's funny?" he snapped.

She couldn't resist. "In a way," she replied. "Hard-boiled eggs for the hard-boiled man."

"Like yours suit you," he countered as he put the bread into the toaster. "Scrambled . . . for the scrambling career woman."

She darted a look at him. "Touché, Mr. Daniels."

The water came to a boil and she dropped two eggs in for him. He buttered and sliced the toast, and brought the plates to the table as she sat down with her eggs.

"Thank you, Mr. Daniels," she said.

"You've given me enough of the 'Mr. Daniels' shit to make your point," he said, taking his place across from her.

"I don't have a point. I just don't have another name for you." Yet she knew that he had shown another flash of insight. Sure, she had a point. By observing elaborate formality with someone so rude and unpolished, she meant to put him down.

"It's Boonie," he said after a moment, and crunched into a piece of toast. "My folks' idea of a joke, I guess, or some patriotic bullshit. Christened me Boone Daniels—like Daniel Boone, see, only backwards. Crazy fucking name. Never got used to it when I was a kid. I was always Danny . . . till I went to Nam and was stationed down in the delta. After that I couldn't shake 'Boonie.' It fit too well."

"Fit . . . ?"

"Short for 'boondocks,' get it? That was what the 'grunts'—the infantry regulars—called the southern delta in Nam: the boonies. And there I was."

"Oh," Lou said. The war hadn't only molded the person he was, it had named him—as if he had been born in the war, made out of it. What path, she wondered, had brought him from there to the mountain?

"Were you born out here?" she said.

He shook his head.

The man volunteered *nothing*. She had to ask. "Where are you from?"

"Place called Polkville. Nothin' little town in Ohio. Only thing there is an asbestos plant."

"You didn't go home after the war?"

"Oh, I went." He shrugged and smiled thinly. "I guess you could say home didn't come back to me." He got up and brought his plate to the stove.

"They haven't been in the water long enough," Lou remarked.

"They'll do." With a spoon he transferred the eggs from the pot to his plate, then sat down again.

"What brought you here?" Lou persisted. She was getting used to his surliness.

He tapped one of the eggs lightly against the corner of the table and started peeling the shell. A series of small winces rippled over his face. Lou guessed the eggs must still be extremely hot, and that accounted for the little tics of pain.

But when he glanced up at her, she saw a revelation. The pain wasn't on his fingertips, it was there in his eyes, inside him, touched off by her question.

He looked away again and went on peeling the egg, flaking off one tiny chip after another, as slowly and carefully as if it were a relic being redeemed from a buried civilization. When it was done he laid it on the plate. For a minute he stared at the other egg, still in its shell.

"Tell me, Boonie," she said quietly.

"A Tewani I knew in Nam," he said flatly, still staring at the table. "Said it was a nice place."

He paused. She expected him to elaborate—you didn't

move to the middle of the desert simply because another soldier told you it was a nice place to live.

"Somebody who lives on the reservation now?" she prompted.

"Somebody who doesn't live anywhere now," he said gruffly.

"I'm sorry," Lou said. "I guess I'm prying where I'm not wanted."

"Hey, a lot of my friends didn't come back. A lot of people's friends didn't come back."

"I guess that's what war is," Lou said softly.

"That's right, lady. Some people make it and some people don't."

"Your Tewani friend told you about the mountain," she said, "so you moved out here. Wasn't there anything for you in Polkville?"

Still not looking up at her, he let out a short snarling laugh. "Oh, yeah, there was Mom's apple pie and the American flag. There was a whole lot for me there."

"Family?" Lou said. "Friends?"

He laughed bitterly again. "When I got back to the States I went home and watched my dad die because his lungs were so crudded up from working in the asbestos factory. In the end he couldn't breathe enough air to stand and walk across a room. I got a big homecoming from the town, too. Kids marching outside the house with posters. 'Welcome Home, War Criminal.' Shit, if the crap in my dad's lungs hadn't killed him, that would've."

His words shamed her. The country had turned against the war, then against the men who had fought it.

"So what did you do?"

"You got a lot of questions."

"Isn't that natural? I'm just wondering why you came here."

He took a deep breath. It had been a long time, Lou guessed, since he had talked to anyone about his feelings.

"I spent my army savings on a bender," he continued, "and what was left on my dad's funeral. And then I took up where I'd left off. My girl was waiting for me, not like most of 'em, so I got a job selling insurance and . . . and . . ."

He turned away and shook his head.

"And what?" Lou said.

"And none of it worked," he said tonelessly.

"Why?"

"I don't know why. The war had done something to me . . . it did something to a lot of us, messed up our heads . . . made us harder to know, maybe, harder to please. Left us with a lot of bad habits and bad ideas."

"Maybe Polkville wasn't the right place for you," Lou said.

"That's what I thought," he said wearily. "So I moved on. And I met other guys having the same troubles, the same rotten time. I drifted into some vet groups. Me—a protester. I did it all. Sit-ins, letters to congressmen, trying to get us the benefits we were entitled to, anything to show that the country gave a shit about our being in a lousy war and getting wrecked by it. And what did all the noise get us? Ninety seconds on Walter Cronkite every Veterans Day."

Boonie stopped again, but kept staring at the floor, and Lou waited, filled with an intuitive dread of the part that he was holding back.

"I still don't understand why you settled here," she said.

"What's to understand?"

"You were getting involved in something important. You were trying to make a difference."

"Some difference we made," he said with harsh resignation. "I was in a protest at a V.A. hospital 'cause they kept denying that guys with cancer had gotten it from Agent Orange—the crap we used in Nam to take the leaves off the trees. And this friend of mine"—his voice started to rise, and Lou could hear the burgeoning anger—"he got arrested and got his head bashed in. I bailed him out, and you know what he did? He went home to Toledo and took out his old Radom nine-millimeter and bailed himself out once more, for all time." Boonie touched the half-peeled egg on his plate and gave it a spin, then regarded the twirling oval as if it were a small spinning globe, the model of a world bent terribly out of shape. "And then's when it came back to me, when I remembered what Joe Sundown told me about—"

Abruptly he broke off and looked up.

"Joe Sundown?" Lou said. "Your Tewani friend."

"This ain't none of your business," Boonie said. "You're just lookin' to get inside me. You just want a little hook in me, don't you? Get me figured out, and then you'll figure out how to get rid of me."

"No," Lou said. "I only want to know what keeps you here. I'm only trying to understand."

His face registered his confusion and doubt. Whatever his motive for holding so tenaciously to his patch of mountain land, Lou realized that it involved a secret—something he wouldn't trust to a stranger.

He fixed her with a hard gaze for another moment. Then he picked up the shelled egg and took a bite, finishing it, as though it was a plug to stop the flow of truths he might regret. When he was done he pushed his chair back. "I'm not hungry enough for the other one," he said, nodding to the half-shelled egg.

"It'll keep," she said.

He glanced to the window. Outside, the sky had begun lightening to a pale gray-blue. The sun would be up in an hour. "I'll look at that ankle now," he said.

In Ben's room, he turned back the covers and removed the bandages, so gently that Ben didn't wake. Lou watched from the door. After checking the leg, lightly pressing his fingers to the discolored area, he wrapped the bandages again.

"It's good," he told her when they were back in the hallway. "Get painkillers if you want—or an X ray for your peace of mind. But the worst he'll have is two or three weeks of the hobbles, and maybe a sniffle."

He moved to the door and she followed. After the way he'd confided in her, Lou expected some alteration of the atmosphere between them. But the strain was still there, the same note of underlying fury as when he'd arrived. He pulled the back door open and left without a good-bye or backward look.

Until she called lightly, "Thanks again."

Then he halted in the driveway and snapped around in the brisk manner of a soldier executing an about-face. Glaring at her hotly, he declared, "Nothing's changed, lady. Don't go getting the idea it has. We're enemies, on opposite sides. You still want to take all I've got. So you'd best remember this: I fought in one dirty godforsaken war, and when it was over I had shit to show for it. You go to war against me, and I'm gonna make damn sure this time I come out a winner."

He stalked away down the drive and got into his pickup truck, slamming the door with the sound of a grenade exploding. Reversing down the drive with his motor roaring, he peeled rubber as he went off toward the mountain.

Lou stood in the cool morning air and watched until the truck had melted away into the low-lying haze over the desert. She wondered at all the ways life had hardened and wounded Boonie Daniels. His rage was terrifying. She didn't doubt that he was prepared to fight a personal war for the defense of his high ground. But why? What hadn't he told her? What was he really fighting for?

And had the casualties in that war already begun?

▲▲▲

" . . . then, holding the rope, he sorta walked down the cliff, and he tied another rope around me, and then he climbed up again to where it was safe, and hauled me up with the other rope. . . ."

Lou waited until Ben had wound himself down. "I hope you realize how lucky you were. If you hadn't landed on that ledge . . . if you'd fallen the wrong way . . . if there hadn't been someone around to get you up quickly . . ."

"Yeah, it was amazing. But I wouldn't call it luck."

"Oh? What would you call it?"

"Well, after Jesse helped Boonie pull me up and I was so grateful, he said I ought to thank Elder Brother."

Lou shook her head. "I don't want to hear what that boy had to say. It's listening to him that almost got you killed. He's trouble, Ben. You're not to have any further contact with him."

"Jesus, what do you want from me?" Ben exploded. "Back in the city you were always bitching about my friends who smoked dope and didn't have any appreciation for"—he parroted her—"culture, art, nature. Then

I meet someone who has *all* of that, and you tell me he's no good!"

"Don't you think he proved it? Getting you to sneak out and—"

"He didn't prove anything except the truth. He wanted to show me that if you didn't stop working on the mountain . . ." Ben hesitated, then expelled it in a rush. "Then you were in danger—from Elder Brother."

The words shocked her, not as a threat, but in the realization of how much Ben seemed to be in the thrall of the Indian boy.

"He proved it, too," Ben added excitedly.

"Proved it?" Lou demanded. "How?"

"He made the storm."

Lou's alarm grew "Made—?"

"Mom, I saw him do it!" Ben broke in earnestly. "One minute there was nothing—the sky was clear. Then Jesse made a fire and he chanted and danced . . . and then the lightning started and the thunder, and . . . well, you saw."

She paused gauging the strength of his belief by the intensity of the light in his eyes. There was no doubt: Ben truly believed that an Indian boy had put the forces of nature at his beck and call. So how did she deal with that? Belittling Ben's convictions might only harden his rebellion against her.

"Listen, Benjy, I know the Indian customs are colorful and worth preserving. But you mustn't confuse Jesse's need to keep them alive with taking them literally."

"I know what I saw," Ben insisted. "And I know that before it happened, Jesse said he'd *make* it happen. He said he had the power, the *diyi*, and then he proved it."

"Just because a magician tells the audience he's going

to make rabbits come out of a hat doesn't mean he's really done it. It's an illusion, a trick."

Ben laughed sharply. "That storm was a hell of an illusion."

"Suppose he knew it was coming," Lou suggested. "He listened to the weather report."

"No way. He asked me to go up on the mountain almost a week ago. He couldn't know that far ahead—and anyway, there was no storm predicted."

"Then it's something else," Lou said. "He recognized some kind of threatening cloud formations—"

"There were no clouds."

"Then it was the winds," Lou said forcefully. "Ben, did you know that before an electrical storm, if you're anywhere around ants, then you'll see them start walking in a line, single file?"

"Really?"

Lou nodded. "Nobody knows why, but it happens. Well, there might be other ways the Indians have to tell when there's going to be a storm. But one thing is sure: nobody can make one."

"Please, Mom, you've got to leave the mountain alone, or that Indian god—"

"I'll take care of myself, don't worry. But it's also my job to take care of you. And right now, Ben, that means keeping you away from bad influences. You will spend no more time with Jesse Silverstone."

"Trees," Ben muttered. "Silver*trees*."

"Stone, trees, whatever. If you disobey me and see that boy again, I won't have any choice but to send you away to boarding school." Lou stood up. "Have I made myself clear?"

Ben nodded.

She fussed a little with the covers, told him to get some more rest, and walked out.

Only when she reached the living room did she allow herself to crumble. If she had loved Ben well enough, given him the proper feeling of self-worth, then he wouldn't be so sadly vulnerable to Jesse. Ben's belief in Elder Brother reminded her of those kids who joined strange cults because at least there they found kindred spirits, people who accepted them.

For a while she stood by the window and gazed out absently, thinking about her priorities, the job versus her son. Should she ask Honegger to put her back at a desk? It would be the end of advancement, but she'd have more time for Ben.

But how could he possibly believe . . . ?

Perhaps it would help him—and her, too—if she could establish the falsity of Jesse's "proof."

She went to the phone in her office, called information in Phoenix, and got the number for the state meteorological office.

The meteorologist who came on the line was very cooperative: "No, ma'am, we didn't see a thing to indicate that storm was heading our way, not even in the satellite weather patterns."

"But . . . it couldn't come out of *nowhere?*" she said.

"Only in a manner of speaking. Though, of course," he added, "that's pretty common with these desert electricals. They just seem to sweep in sometime with no warning at all."

The words resounded in her brain long after she had hung up. No warning at all.

Yet Jesse had known.

And he had warned her, too, of other storms that could lie ahead.

BOOK III

Riddle of the Hand

CHAPTER 18

The Jeep Renegade took the Old Coopersville Road with ease. Behind the wheel Mercy Roy shifted into low gear and pressed harder on the gas.

"Think you could learn to like desert life?" Mercy said. She had surprised Lou by calling out of the blue that morning to invite her to a meeting with the *hati'i na'antan*, the elders of the Tewani tribe. They were fifteen miles outside of Coopersville now, where the road ended and gave onto a narrow strip of tar-and-patch that stretched into the desert. Here there were no houses or highway markers, only an occasional gas station and grazing cows. "Or when you're done," Mercy added, "will you go back home?"

The mention of home disturbed Lou, emphasizing how alone she felt. "I don't know," she said. "I haven't gotten used to being here yet."

"It must be hard, not having a man to help you raise your boy. How's he taking it?"

Lou was silent a moment. Although she had been wishing lately that there was someone she could turn to for advice, her last encounter with Mercy had left her wondering how much to say—especially anything that might be taken as critical of the Tewani. But considering their confrontation on Main Street, Lou was relieved to find Mercy in a friendly mood. She had not really expected an introduction to the elders, let alone a chaperoned visit to the reservation.

"Ben's made one friend," Lou said finally. "An Indian boy named Jesse Silvertrees. Frankly, he frightens me a little. He dresses up like something out of . . . oh, out of some wild-wild-west rodeo show."

"The way a person dresses shouldn't—"

"Mercy, if you saw the way he looked, you'd understand."

"Well, as it turns out," Mercy said, "I know Jesse, and it's true he might look strange, and I can see as how you might not be used to boys like him, but he's not a troublemaker or anything like that."

"Mercy, he dragged Ben up on the mountain during that terrible storm, and I spent half the night scared witless. He strikes me as a bad influence."

"Lou, Jesse's had . . . well, life has knocked him around. He's an orphan, you know."

"No, I didn't," Lou said quietly.

"His mother and father—she was Chiricahua, he was a Tewani medicine man—they were killed in a car accident when Jesse was nine. Big truck crashed right into them out on Route 63. That can do things to a boy."

Lou felt sympathetic; she, too, had known what it was like to grow up without a parent. "Who takes care of Jesse now?"

"The *hati'i*," Mercy said.

His father a medicine man, Lou thought—maybe that accounted for Jesse's strangeness. "Mercy, he told Ben that *he* caused that storm by doing a rain dance for

Elder Brother. And now he's got Ben all worked up with this superstitious stuff."

Mercy was silent. Was she offended? Had she taken Lou's wariness about Jesse Silvertrees as prejudice against the Tewani?

The Jeep gradually emerged from a dip in the road, and Mercy gunned the engine as they climbed a steep hillock. At the top, she pulled to the side. "I like to stop sometimes and just admire," she said. "I do love this land." She turned and looked earnestly into Lou's face. "I don't mean to meddle, Lou, but anybody can see you're tying yourself up in knots."

"Oh, Mercy, sometimes I look at the decisions I've made . . ." It flooded out of her then, despite herself. "Everything I've done. Leaving my husband. Getting a job. Giving my life over to it. Maybe I should have stayed home and just raised Ben, gotten another kind of job where there wouldn't have been such a temptation to run after success." She turned to face Mercy. "Do you know what a friend said to me? Find another man, get married again. As if you could run down to the store and charge a man on your Visa card." She stared out over the ridge at the vast desert. "Hell, I look at this beautiful place and I think maybe I don't belong here, maybe Legend City doesn't belong here, what am I doing tearing up this land? I don't know what's right anymore, not for me, not for anybody else."

She stopped. What had possessed her? Why had she felt this rush of insecurity, a childish wish that Mercy would take care of her, protect her . . .

. . . *mother* her! Yes, that's what it was. Did she look on Mercy as being able to fill the gap, the emptiness she'd felt ever since coming home that day to find her father crying on the doorstep?

"Don't be so hard on yourself, Lou," Mercy said. "You're doing your best. Things will turn out okay for you and Ben, I'm sure."

For no logical reason, Lou felt better. Mercy's reassurances gave her a much-needed boost of optimism. But hearing Mercy talk about Ben, and feeling the motherliness of her concern, she had to wonder: why had Mercy Roy never had children of her own?

"Mercy, didn't you ever think of getting married, raising a family? The stories people tell—are they true?"

"About running away from an unhappy love affair?" Mercy erupted in a gusty, deep-throated laugh. "I can't imagine how that got started. I came out here because I'm a restless soul, I wanted wide-open spaces. And as for settling down with one man, I'm just not the marrying kind." Mercy glanced at her old-fashioned pendant watch. "Oh, my. We've done enough gabbing. The old men will be expecting us." She switched on the ignition again and gunned the car off along the road.

Lou studied the old woman. She wondered if Mercy's sudden awareness of their appointment was a device to escape her prying. Could restlessness and wanderlust completely account for her presence here? Why would a beautiful woman leave her home thousands of miles away, settle herself in an out-of-the-way town in the middle of the desert, and then spend the rest of her life by herself? Surely some man would have chased her. And could any woman, even Mercy, be so independent that she had no need for companionship?

The picture Mercy Roy gave of herself, Lou thought, had the quaint light of an Old West tintype like the ones she collected—pictures that seemed real enough, unless you looked close.

CHAPTER 19

ATTENTION
YOU ARE NOW ENTERING THE
EXCLUSIVE TEWANI RESERVATION AREA
YOUR ENTRANCE CONSTITUTES CONSENT
TO THE JURISDISTION OF THE TEWANI
TRIBE AND ITS COURTS
—By Order of the Tribal Council—

▲▲▲

"And they mean it," Mercy said as she and Lou rode past the sign erected at the side of the road. "They have their own law, they're a sovereign state."

They had driven far from civilization now. There wasn't a building in sight, only a two-lane dirt road that ran through open land as far as the eye could see. The entire experience confounded Lou's notion about Indian reservations. She'd thought they were like suburban subdivisions, except that instead of neatly tended lawns there would be a chain-link fence, guardhouse, and tumble-down shacks. But wherever Lou looked, the uninterrupted horizon encircled her.

Far off in the distance she could make out two red-clay mounds rising from the desert floor, shaped like cones with the tops sliced off as if by some heavenly scythe.

"First Mesa and Second Mesa," Mercy said, pointing. "That's where the Tewani live. When they were under attack, no enemy could approach without being seen." The Tewani reservation, Mercy added, covered nealy 780,000 acres, more territory than the entire state of Rhode Island.

"I never imagined it was so huge," Lou said.

"Oh, there are a lot of big reservations," Mercy replied. "When the reservations were set up by the government, the Indians got all the land they happened to be living on at that time. The Navajo, who were nomadic, had drifted over a huge area—so that now they have practically the whole northeastern corner of the state. The Tewani always stayed put; this land is where they've been living since the beginning of time."

As the Jeep approached First Mesa, Lou's preconceptions were shattered again. Crossing the state to Coopersville, she had passed the reservation of the Hualapai, a poor tribe with nothing more than a few ramshackle stores and tract houses in disrepair. Reaching the top of the corkscrew road carved into the side of First Mesa, Lou was amazed to see, not broken-down huts, but substantial adobe houses, many with large corrals and well-tended fields. Rectangular panels of gleaming gray solar glass slanted toward the sun on the rooftops. At the crest of the road a small village spread out across the mesa—a central mall covered in glazed tiles, playgrounds, a swimming pool, and a sprawling structure in modern ranch style with a wide circular driveway and a multipeaked roof. A gold-lettered sign on redwood read "Tewani Reservation Clinic."

No sooner had they stepped from the Jeep than Mercy was surrounded by clinging children. They all had stories to tell, and all used a strange word to address her.

"What are they calling you?" Lou asked.

"Da-go-*ta*," Mercy said. "It translates as 'Woman of Many Families.'"

The name gave Lou some idea of how Mercy had survived alone out here. She had developed something beyond friendships; with the Tewani and the townspeople she had found surrogate families.

Lou followed her across the central mall, which was flanked on each side by pedestals with rock formations. "A sun clock and a moon clock," Mercy pointed out. "The Tewani were among the earliest astronomers on the planet." As they reached the end of the mall, some older Tewani strolled out to join the children in greeting her.

"They really love you, don't they?" Lou said.

Mercy shrugged. "I've always been interested in their culture and way of life, and I've done whatever I could to promote good relations with the town. I've been coming out here for fifty-odd years."

She pointed ahead to their destination—a circle of low cramped hogans, eight-sided unpainted clay structures with hide flaps covering roughly cut windows.

Lou was puzzled. "Mercy, aren't the elders the most venerated members of the tribe? Why are they shoved off into the poorest housing?"

"Shoved off?" Mercy echoed. "Our civilized ways can fool us into thinking they're poor just because of how they live . . . but the elders *choose* to live this way, Lou. They keep the traditional way because when they call on Elder Brother, they know he won't have any trouble finding them. They'll be right here, living in the same houses their ancestors lived in."

Lou admired Mercy's sympathy for the Tewani faith. Having been friends with the Indians for so long, she could probably shift between their state of mind and her own as easily as changing clothes.

Mercy stopped just beyond the sun clock. "Wait here. I'll go and—as the Indians say—lay down the blanket."

Sitting on a wooden bench while Mercy walked down the path to the largest hogan, Lou mused on how she might describe this experience to friends in San Francisco or to a fellow project manager. How many executives had negotiated like this—with Indians living in clay huts, and a god who lived on a mountain?

When Mercy emerged through the hide-flapped door of the central hogan, she appeared distracted and lingered on the path.

"Mercy?"

Mercy looked up, giving her head a twist, as though shaking off sleep, and walked toward Lou. "They'll see you," she said.

"But they don't want to see me, do they?" Lou suggested. "You had to convince them."

"No, not at all," Mercy said. "They agreed to consult Elder Brother for advice on your behalf. I should tell you, though, that they expect you to participate in a ceremony."

Lou supposed she could go along. Anything to be diplomatic. Mercy pulled back the door flap and they entered a dark adobe-walled room. Gathered in the center, around an open fire pit dug into the floor, were the twelve old men sitting with their legs folded in front of them. Mercy gestured to two clay stools draped with intricately woven rugs. Lou took her place in the circle and Mercy sat beside her. By the light of the fire the faces of the old men seemed like shadowy fright masks.

"You can talk now," Mercy whispered to Lou.

How did she begin? Despite the setting, Lou tried to think of this as just one more city-planning-commission meeting. "I'm honored that you've invited me here today. . . ."

She forged ahead, making her pitch—the opportunities Legend City would bring to the Tewani, the promise for their children of greater integration with the modern world.

When she was done, no one spoke. The fire in the open pit had grown brighter, illuminating the old men's faces. They had reached that stage of indeterminate old age when the exact number of years no longer mattered, their skin wrinkled into so many layers and folds, the crows'-feet around their eyes so deep that it was hard to imagine they had ever been young.

Slowly eleven of the men turned their heads to the eldest of them all. His tiny arms were skin on bone, his gnomish eyes mere pouches of flesh hidden in deep sockets. He stirred not a muscle, but went on gazing in the fire as the other elders waited for him to speak.

A minute passed, perhaps more. Lou threw an impatient glance at Mercy.

Mercy smiled, indicating that Lou should be patient. "His name is White Eagle—it's the name always given to the wisest of the elders. Wait . . . he'll answer you."

Slowly White Eagle lifted a withered hand and his dim watery eyes came alive as if absorbing every particle of light in the shadowy hogan. Then the seeming frailty of his body was overtaken by a magisterial presence of spirit, and suddenly he conveyed an air of regal strength and superiority. In a quavering voice he uttered a single word. It sounded to Lou like "melody."

"*Maa-lo-ti,*" Mercy translated. "It means 'gathering together.' "

A good omen, Lou thought.

Now from baskets at their sides each of the elders produced what appeared to be fancy candlesticks. Peering closer, Lou saw that they were made of wood, not wax. At the top of each stick were green dots arranged in the shape of a face. Lou recognized them as chips of peridot. Bound at the top of each stick by strands of red and yellow yarn were several feathers.

"The talking prayersticks," Mercy explained. "They're used for communicating with Elder Brother."

Lou was fascinated. While all around them the world changed—a world where now scientists explained how the earth was formed without referring to mountain gods, where psychiatrists would understand their beliefs as psychotic delusions—these old men clung to their ancient rituals as though history had stopped, waving feather-decorated sticks and expecting their mountain god to speak.

White Eagle held out his hand, his eyes now fixed on Lou's. The man's intense gaze unnerved her.

She turned to Mercy. "What does he want?"

What am I committing myself to?

But she reached across the fire pit toward White Eagle. The hairs on her arm curled from the flame.

White Eagle guided her arm down next to the fire. For a terrible moment Lou thought he would thrust her fingers directly into the flames, but he merely placed her hand on the dirt. Applying a slight pressure, he smoothed a patch of ground with her palm, then lifted her hand as if to return it. What, Lou thought, could this possibly have to do with negotiating for land?

Now the old man, using the pointed edge of his talking prayerstick, began to carve figures in the dirt as a child draws in the sand.

A mountain.

The figure of a bird.

Seeing the third figure, Lou said to Mercy, "It looks like your brand from the ranch—except for the dot."

"It's . . . it's their way of including me," she said, sounding oddly unsure.

The elder next to White Eagle, who wore a red bandanna, lit a long-stemmed pipe and began passing it. When it reached Lou, the elder beside her said. "Do not smoke, Mrs. Palmer. Pass it along."

His admonition came as a shock. It was the first thing any of the Indians had said in English. Involuntarily Lou smiled—the meek anxious smile of a foreigner.

When the pipe reached White Eagle, he took a deep

puff and effortlessly expelled from his lungs a billowing gray cloud. Then he began to chant: "*Bey-o-cidi ch'alke na'a'ci . . . Ch'alke na'a'ci maa-lo-ti . . . Na'a'ci maa-lo-ti ch'alke.*"

He repeated it several times.

The elder on Lou's left, the one who had passed the pipe, reached out and took her hand. His touch was warm.

"White Eagle has given the prayer of One-Follows-the-Other," he said. "The spirit of One-Follows-the-Other is the spirit of life and death. The spirit of life is Wanderer-in-the-Dark, and the spirit of death is Wanderer-in-the-Light."

Suddenly White Eagle raised his prayerstick and plunged the sharp end into the fire. An even stronger flow of smoke was whipped into the air, rising straight to the roof, the wisps seeming to shoot out in straight lines above. Air vents creating a crosscurrent, Lou thought, looking up. But when she brought her eyes back to the circle, she saw that none of the others had noticed. White Eagle was staring at Mercy, and Mercy at him. A few rapid words were exchanged in the Tewani language.

All the men were leaning forward and putting away their prayersticks. An important moment had come in the ceremony, Lou guessed. White Eagle emptied the ashes from the pipe into a clay cup, then tipped the cup over the drawings in the dirt.

And somehow the old man did a wonderful magic trick. The ashes all blew in a fine stream toward Mercy and Lou, then settled on the ground in a straight line. The next elder, in his turn, also sprinkled ashes over the drawing . . . and again the ashes wafted toward the two women. On and on it went, around the circle—

until a distinct pattern of gray ash lay directly between them.

The smoke had thickened, and Lou felt light-headed in the half-lit darkness. The dense air swirled around her and the shapes of the elders wavered, the smoke acting as a gauzy lens. The effect softened their sagging lined faces, turning them into the faces of younger men. Mercy, too, had suddenly become a spectral figure, the old woman of eighty transformed by the drifting haze into a ravishing girl with hair blazing an auburn red and sparkling eyes, wide and youthful.

Lou had the disturbing sensation of time becoming unmoored, her body floating. She tried to remember why she was here. . . .

The talking prayersticks had all been thrust into the fire, forming a circle on the rim of the pit. The green peridot eyes danced in the light of the flame. Flashes of red and yellow and green seemed to shoot between the sticks, a twelve-sided prism of darting light hovering above the fire.

The elder sitting next to Lou took her hand again. "The mountain is called Acoma," he said gravely. "It is 'the place that always was.' Elder Brother knows that you would bring changes with your city on the mountain, but the mountain is his. And he wants it untouched. You will never build your city."

Lou was chilled by the Indian's pronouncement. She tried to protest, but her mouth was dry as cotton and no sound would emerge. She was disoriented—the smoke, the darkness.

White Eagle spoke abruptly, a fast phrase.

Lou heard the word *Da-go-ta*. It resonated in the airless room, echoes caroming from the walls and inside her head.

Then, in an instant, the thick smoke dissipated. The air was clear.

And Mercy was old again, and ashen, drained of color.

Lou touched the ground at her sides as though to reassure herself it was there.

"Why . . . I don't understand. I only wanted . . ."

She trailed away, knowing she could never change their minds.

Forcing a fast thank-you, she lurched to her feet and fled from the hogan.

▲▲▲

Fresh air. Sunlight. The real world.

Then Mercy was standing beside her. "Are you all right, Lou?"

"I . . . I guess so. But I didn't really get a chance—"

"They heard you, Lou." Mercy started away.

Lou followed alongside. She felt better as she put more distance between herself and the hogan.

This episode, she realized, had been useless. She had come in the hope of convincing the old men, when, in fact, their minds were already made up. The whole interlude—the pretense of consulting their god, the hocus-pocus of the talking prayersticks—had been just a show, like the Hopi snake dances performed for the tourists. Now she would have to seek out the Indian doctor Ted had mentioned, Loftway.

"I have one more stop to make," Mercy said as they passed the sun clock at the end of the mall. "There's a little girl in the clinic I've been visiting."

"I'll go with you," Lou said. "I have someone to see too."

"Oh?" Mercy said.

"Yes. Dr. Loftway."

Mercy nodded knowingly. "Lou, I don't think he can help you. I told you, the permission you need—"

"I know what you told me, Mercy," Lou broke in quietly. "But I still want to see Dr. Loftway. And as far as Elder Brother is concerned . . . I'm just going to have to take my chances."

CHAPTER 20

The Tewani reservation clinic was small, but it had the feeling of a modern urban hospital. Among the names Lou saw listed on the lobby directory were Dr. Black Moon, Dr. Honotafte, and Dr. Tracking Bear. But no Dr. Loftway.

Lou went along with Mercy to the second floor and walked down the main corridor to a door around which huddled a number of Indians—several old men and women and three teenage boys.

"I'll only be a few minutes," Mercy said, entering the girl's room. Lou caught a glimpse of a young girl on the bed, no more than fifteen or sixteen, connected to monitoring equipment that emitted blips of green light from cathode-ray screens. Then the door closed and Lou was left standing uncomfortably alone, facing the solemn Indians.

She was about to start down the hall in search of Dr. Loftway when she noticed the alcove in the wall next to the room, a sort of creche. On the shelf inside was a bowl, and except for the fact that it was somewhat smaller, and the colors brighter, it matched exactly the one she had seen on Mercy's mantel—the lizard chasing the deer. It must be a common piece of Indian pottery, she thought.

A man with a stethoscope around his neck approached and stopped to talk with the family assembled in the hall. He chatted with them a moment and then came over to Lou. "You're a friend of Mercy's . . . ?"

The doctor was in his late thirties, with prematurely graying hair cut short in a contemporary style, not worn long as with many of the Tewani. Under his white doctor's smock he wore a button-down blue shirt and jeans.

Lou explained that she had come out to the reservation with Mercy on business.

"Business?" the doctor repeated. "What sort of business are you in?"

"I work for the Honegger Corporation," Lou replied. "Actually, maybe you can help me. I was hoping to talk to Dr. David Loftway. He's supposed to work here, but his name wasn't listed downstairs."

The man smiled. "Oh yes, my name is there . . ."

"You're Dr. Loftway?"

Lou's glance flicked to the black plastic ID tag pinned on the doctor's smock. The name wasn't Loftway at all.

"It's Lohaftapowe," he said, the last syllable spoken as a soft *a*. My secretary finds it easier to mispronounce my name than to spell it for everybody. My other choice would be to use the English translation—but that might seem a little pompous."

"Oh? What is it?"

"Great Hunting Spirit," the doctor replied with a grin. "I don't think being David Great Hunting Spirit would make things any easier."

Lou was charmed by the man. He had handled her confusion over his name gracefully. "I'm surprised Mercy didn't tell me this girl is your patient," Lou said, then remembered that Mercy had been against her meeting him.

"On the subject of tribal governance," he said, "Mercy and I have some disagreements, especially when it comes to my speaking for the tribe."

Lou explained that Mercy had accompanied her to approach the *hati'i na'antan* about acquiring the tribe's land. The elders had refused and now Lou was hoping the doctor might help.

Lohaftapowe led her to a bank of molded styrene chairs on the opposite wall, where they sat. It was true, he said, that many younger members of the tribe were in favor of selling the land, but he could not guarantee the decision of the *hati'i* could be reversed.

"Of course, no one has ever tried to go against them. Even the young people defer to their judgment. But since I've come back to the reservation they've made me their informal spokesman. Maybe because I'm a doctor, and because I've spent time away during my training, they believe I have a new perspective on the tribe and might be the one to bring some changes."

"But can you really get around the elders?" Lou asked. "Having seen them I can imagine that they still exercise a lot of power."

The doctor half-smiled. "I suppose they did One-Spirit-Follows-the-Other for you? The talking prayer-sticks?"

Lou nodded. "To tell the truth, they really had me for a minute there."

"They've been doing their magic for a long time," the doctor said. "And it *can* be impressive. I still remember when I was a kid, the ceremony where I was accepted into the tribe as a man. The lights from the fire and the prayersticks, the smoke—to a twelve-year-old it was as mystical as anything could be. But for us these ceremonies are like going to Mass. The magic wears off."

"Then you don't believe in Elder Brother?"

"I'm not saying that. But there are lots of ways to interpret the meaning of a god and his power. On the issue of the land, anyway, we might swing a tribal vote to overrule the *hati'i*. It's sensitive, though. I'll need a week or so to sound people out." Lohaftapowe stood up. "I ought to go check on my patient. . . ."

"What's wrong with her?" Lou said, crossing the hall with him.

"Bone cancer," he said softly. "It's terminal." He gestured toward the bowl in the creche. "You can see the family are prepared for the end."

Lou gave him a questioning look. In what way could accepting death be connected with a bowl?

"It's the burial bowl," the doctor said. He started to explain the symbolism of the lizard and the deer, until Lou said she had already been told about it. "Eventually," Lohaftapowe went on, "it'll be part of the funeral ceremony. The bowl will be kept always as a reminder that a lost family member is alive in another world. It's one of the most precious possessions a Tewani can have." As the doctor returned the bowl to its shelf, Lou wondered about the one on Mercy's mantel. Mercy must have been lucky—or paid a great deal—to acquire a ceremonial item of such importance.

"Well," Lohaftapowe said, excusing himself, "I'll call you as soon as I know something more definite." He disappeared into the dying girl's room, the door whooshing closed behind him.

As Lou waited for Mercy, she felt encouraged by her visit to the reservation. The old men wouldn't necessarily have the last word, after all. With a name like David Great Hunting Spirit, the doctor ought to have a pretty good connection to Elder Brother himself.

CHAPTER 21

"He shot at us, Lou," Capper was screaming. "The bastard actually shot at us!"

The call came in on the CB not ten minutes after Lou walked into the office. It was two weeks after Ben's adventure, and until now it had been the best time she'd spent on the project. There hadn't been a hitch. Supplies arrived on time instead of getting hung up on railroad sidings thousands of miles away. The roadbeds pushed steadily forward, with no delays caused by cave-ins or buried shelves of rock.

Her situation with Ben had improved, too. He was less disobedient and rebellious than she could remember at any time since the divorce, and there was no further sign of his friendship developing with Jesse Silvertrees. Because the project was rolling ahead with steady momentum, Lou was able to spend more time with Ben. They had gone to a rodeo down in Bullhead City, to the movies over in Payson, and they had spent all last Sunday at the mining ghost town of Wickenburg. Ben remained fairly quiet when they were together, but she definitely sensed that he appreciated her company.

She didn't think very much about Daniels. Though the fact was that he hadn't simply slipped from her thoughts; she was working *not* to think of him, unwilling to grapple with the dilemma of conscience he represented.

On Monday of this week, Capper had urged Lou to take measures to ensure that work would proceed without resistance. She thought the advice sensible, and on her desk pad had scribbled a note to instruct Honegger's Phoenix law firm to serve Daniels with a final notice to vacate.

But she hadn't made the call—had blocked it completely from her normally acute awareness of priorities.

And now the crunch had come. Capper had moved a three-man crew up the mountain to study the terrain to be prepped for blasting, and Daniels had fired on them.

"Are you there, Lou?" Capper prodded. "I said that crazy man Daniels—"

"I heard you, Cap. Anybody hurt?"

"Phil Giordano fell and skinned his cheek when we were hauling ass outta there. That's about it. Christ, we weren't even near his goddamn shack, just at the edge of the plateau. The bastard came after us. Lou, we can't wait any longer on this. Get the state cops. We've got cause now to have Daniels forcibly removed."

"Cap, you know what it means as soon as we bring in the police. Daniels will try holding them off, and in no time we'll have press crawling all over us."

"For Chrissakes, Lou, you can't think about public relations now. If we don't get rid of that maniac, the project will stop. Our guys aren't going to work with someone taking potshots—"

"Can't you just keep the crews away from there for a while? Concentrate on another sector?"

"What're you saying? You're gonna *leave* that nut case up there?"

"Of course not. But can you see the headlines if we don't go easy—if we call in the cops and they end up in a shooting war with a lone war hero? 'Callous Developer Denies Soldier's Prayer for Peace.' We've enough trouble with the Tewani religious issue, Cap. I've got to see Daniels and try to reason with him."

"Reason," Capper snorted. "You go up there, and that son of a bitch'll blast you out of your socks. He's a fucking psychopath, if you ask me."

"I'm not asking you," she said flatly, then regretted the curtness. "Cap, I've just got to try."

His sigh came audibly through the CB. "Then I'm going with you."

"No, you can't. He's less likely to fly off the handle if I go alone."

"Lou," Capper protested, "it's suicide. You can't—"

"Alone," she announced firmly.

She told Capper to give the men who'd been shot at the rest of the day off and to take any other measures that might keep talk of the incident from spreading all over the site. When she turned from the CB, she found Ted Lundberg standing behind her. He had been monitoring the whole conversation. She started to walk past him, but he caught her by the arm.

"Capper's right, Lou. It's taking too big a chance to go up there alone. I just can't let you—"

"Let me?" Lou erupted, wrenching free of Ted's grasp. "*Let me?*" Her voice rose higher with outrage against his patronizing, protective chauvinism. The office had gone dead quiet, the secretaries all stopping work to observe the flare-up. Lou was aware of the audience, but her anger kept spilling over. "Don't you ever tell me again, don't even *think* of telling me what you'll *let* me do," she shouted. "I'm the P.M. here. I'll decide how to handle emergencies. Have you got that? I'm the boss!"

She was at the wheel of her car, still trembling, before she realized that her explosive reaction couldn't be ascribed wholly to feminist pride and principle. She wasn't shivering with anger so much as fear: she had committed herself to facing Boonie Daniels.

But he was beyond reason. He had declared that himself. There was every chance he'd do exactly what Capper had warned.

Blow her right out of her socks.

▲▲▲

On a narrow lip of rock just beneath the edge of Boonie's plateau, she hunkered down like a trench fighter preparing to go over the top.

Suppose he was waiting for hostile visitors, gun at the ready? He'd have to anticipate that the news would be carried back, and that the police would be brought in. A soldier would have his defenses prepared in advance. As soon as she poked her head up, he might shoot. . . .

She shouted at the top of her voice, "Boonie!"

Her call caromed off a thousand faces of rock and died away.

No answer.

Perhaps he wasn't there. Or was out of earshot, in his cabin reading a book, or taking a nap. Perhaps firing off a few rounds of ammo was not an act he expected to have any consequences. He'd been a soldier, after all, accustomed to shooting without any thought of punishment.

She shouted again. "Boonie . . . it's Lou Palmer! I want to talk to you!"

Still no answer. The only sound in the world was the faint roar of a jet plane.

Well, if he *was* there, at least he'd know who he was shooting at.

She climbed up to the meadow and started toward the shack.

She was still fifty yards away when the door burst open. Framed in the opening stood Boonie, a rifle stock pressed against his cheek, his eye behind a telescopic gun sight. Swinging back rapidly on its hinges, the flat wooden door slammed into the siding of the shack with an explosive *bang*. The sounds and images came at Lou so fast that she was confused, unable to separate them. Was the noise only from the door, or had there also been a rifle report? Had he shot at her?

By reflex she dropped down on one knee.

Now his voice came at her in a hoarse scream. "That's it, lady! Not one fucking step closer. Just turn around and get the hell off my land!"

For several seconds she remained frozen with terror. Never in her life had she faced anyone aiming a gun at her. And this was not just anyone. This was a man with a grievance against her. Grievances against the world.

At last she rose. Slowly. But she didn't turn away. Scared as she was, she couldn't bring herself to yield. Perhaps if he had not sent her scampering around so easily the other night, she would have been more malleable now. But the memory of behaving so spinelessly in the face of his bullying made her unwilling to be stampeded again by his threat.

She took a slow step forward, then another, calling out as she advanced, "Boonie! You've got too much to lose if you hurt me. That'll be the end for you, the end of everything. If we can talk . . . if you'll listen . . . we can find a way—"

The *bang* this time was definitely not from the door. She could even hear the bullet make a whistling zing as it cut through the air three or four feet above her head.

She stopped for only an instant, then continued. She was six or seven yards closer already. Boonie lowered the rifle slightly, as if he had to take the gun sight from his eye to believe what he was seeing.

She kept up the loud patter. "You said you wanted freedom, didn't you? Money to live on? I think my company will agree to—"

The sight was at his eye again before she knew it, and the *crack* of the shot being fired sent such a sickening bolt of fear slicing through her stomach that for a second she imagined it was the bullet—this was what it felt like to be hit. She closed her eyes.

And when she opened her eyes it was done. There was no wound at all. It gave her a giddy sense of invulnerability.

"Keep shooting, Boonie!" she shouted. "One of them's going to hit me. All you have to do is *aim* it at me, for Chrissakes—one clean shot to the head or the heart. And what in God's name will that do for you, asshole?"

She was moving faster now.

And this time when he squeezed off the shot she didn't duck, didn't even flinch, but kept on moving forward. "But if you'll just listen, dammit, we can work it out!"

Ten yards away. And she could see the heat in his eyes, see his arm shuddering with the strangled will to pull the trigger. Jesus, she had never been so scared. With the man shaking like that, it might not matter which way his decision came down, whether he meant to miss her or not.

Two quick shots. They landed two feet in front of her, blasting away two buttercups.

"For God's sake, Boonie, please. I want to help you."

Five yards. She stopped. From here she could look right down the small angry black hole where her death might be hiding.

"*Please*," she said once more. Not shouting now. Quiet. Begging. Not for her life alone, but for his, too.

His trembling gradually ceased. The gun held steady on her. There was a finality in his stance now, the stillness of decision.

Oh, Lord, he wouldn't kill her in cold blood. *Couldn't*.

Though she thought then of his warning, his parable of war, and she remembered that he had been a soldier and must have killed before, and that he had fought in a place and a time where men were driven mad by their duty—and that nothing had happened to him since to heal him. He *could* do it. If he was too tired of fighting, or too bored, too desperate. It would take no more than a tiny twitch of one finger against a curve of metal, and he would no longer have to wrestle with any of it. His statement would be made.

She squeezed her eyes shut. Still refusing to believe he would. But knowing he could . . . and prepared for it.

Then she heard his hissing whisper of self-disgust. ". . . shit . . ."

When she opened her eyes the hand that propped the rifle from beneath was dropping to his side, sinking slowly as if through liquid. Then the rifle, too, fell with the same surreal languor.

"Lady," he said, shaking his head in open bewilderment, "where the fuck did you get your balls?"

She had to smile. "Earned 'em. In my business they give them out for achievement—like the army gives stripes."

He turned into the house. From within Lou heard a *clunk* as he tossed the rifle aside and it struck the wooden floor of the shack. The door had been left open. It was, she guessed, as much of an invitation as she was likely to get.

She entered.

Boonie was leaning over the iron sink in one corner. With one hand he manipulated the handle of a water pump; with the other he was catching water from the tap and sloshing it into his face. The shack was neat and orderly, its metal camp bed covered with a yellowish spread reminiscent of the saffron robes Lou had seen on young Buddhist monks in documentary films about Asia. Maybe Boonie had brought one back as a souvenir. Set on the pine table used for eating was a small open crate with the word "Ammunition" stenciled on the side. Had he been getting ready for a siege of police? She crossed to the table and saw several boxes of bullets and a few rifle magazine clips in the crate. There were also two packs of much-used playing cards, a chain of dog tags, some letters and documents held by a rubber band, a Japanese 35mm camera, and a bunch of snapshots. Lou poked at the pictures, separating them with a fingertip. Boonie in army uniform, his arms around a short swarthy man with coal-black hair; a teenage girl and boy—Boonie, maybe—in graduation gowns.

Before she could look at any more, he came up from behind and swiped the crate off the table. He shoved it under the bed, then came back to stand directly in front of her.

"Okay," he said, "you wanted to talk. I'm listening."

"There's no point in talking if you're not ready to negotiate."

"Great. That's your idea of dealing. I've got to agree in advance to do whatever you say."

"Boonie," she sighed with exasperation, "you're in a no-win situation. You can accept what I've got to offer and walk away with something. Or else force me to send the cops in, and you end up getting carried out of here—dead or alive."

He smiled dreamily. "There is another choice," he said.

"I don't see any," Lou said.

"Well, suppose you don't give me a nickel, but I leave here anyway. I just pack up and go off over the hill, disappear, and nobody sees me anymore. And then you go right on building your roads and towers and what-not. Until one night all your fancy tractors and bulldozers and cranes are sitting around, and suddenly, out of the blue, there's a big ball of flame . . . and they're all gone. Or some guy stringing wires for you somewhere gets picked off by a bullet that comes out of nowhere. Or a charge of dynamite goes off right at the base of one of your beautiful concrete towers, and the whole fucking thing falls over like a dead tree. . . ."

She had some experience now at calling his bluffs. "And how long do you think you could keep that up?" she said dryly.

"How long did the little men in black pajamas tie down our whole goddamn army?"

It would, of course—if he could do it, even keep it up for a little while—cost the company tens of millions in lost time. Not to mention the stigma that would cling to the development for years afterward.

"Look, this isn't getting us anywhere," Lou said reasonably. "Why don't we talk in real terms? Let's say my company accepts that you have certain proprietary privileges by virtue of occupying this land for—what? —four, five years . . ."

"Seven," he said.

"So you're entitled to call it home. As compensation for depriving you of your home, we'll give you . . ." She paused, making a show of careful mental calculation. "Twenty-five thousand dollars."

He smiled down at her and said nothing.

"Thirty-five," she said. "I can't go higher."

He gave a short bitter laugh.

Lou glanced around at the shack, jerry-built out of flotsam and jetsam. "C'mon, what the hell do you expect for this place?" she said tartly.

"Christ, lady, you just don't get it. To look at the outside of you, I'd have to swear God put you together and did nothing wrong. Then I get a hint of what goes on inside your head, and I realize even He ain't perfect—'cause He left out the brains and put in garbage. You're just one more fucking crook."

She glared at him for a second. Then she could contain herself no longer. Her right arm swung up, the open hand arcing around to strike him viciously across the face.

He caught her by the wrist in a tight grip, and held on until her resistance ebbed. Then he flung her hand away. "Now, will you leave me alone?" he muttered.

"No," she answered flatly. "I can't. I've got to get through to you. Because if I don't, everybody loses."

"And if you do, only *I* lose." He turned and moved away.

She went after him. "I'll up the offer. Fifty—"

He spun on her again. "Can't you understand?" he demanded fiercely. "It's not a matter of money."

"What, then?"

"Promises," he snapped. "Promises and dreams."

What dreams, she wondered, what promises kept him here? Hundreds of people searched for gold without giving up their whole lives to stay on a mountainside. Maybe he was searching for some peace with his past that could be reached only in isolation.

"Please, Boonie, give it up. I don't want to see you hurt." She heard her own voice, filled with the ache of concern, and realized it was the first time she had expressed in personal terms her wish to resolve the impasse.

Boonie had noticed too. He cocked his head and studied her, then took a few deliberate steps to return and face her squarely.

"Why do you care?"

It took a second for the words to come. "Because," she said quietly, "you've already been hurt so much."

There was a long silence. It seemed to Lou then that her answer was only a ploy, not the whole truth. In a remote corner of her mind another reason still lay buried, though exactly what it was, her own secret motive, she had no chance to wonder before he was grasping her shoulders with his large hands and pulling her nearer. Then his mouth was on hers, and for an instant she had the cool detached awareness of how surprisingly soft his lips felt.

She did not resist. Thoughts ceased and there was

only sensation. His tongue on hers, the grasp of his strong hands pulling her closer, his tall hard body against hers.

She didn't know when it happened, but her arms were free and around his neck. As they kissed, his long arms slid down her back, hands reaching inside her thighs, pulling her up. She kissed him harder, telling him with her searching tongue that she would do nothing to stop him.

But suddenly he did stop. Pulling his head back, he looked at her questioningly. Asking reasons. Asking permissions.

She gave them silently, her hand softly caressing the side of his face, his neck.

Bluntly he asked, "Is this why you came?"

"I didn't think so," she whispered.

Now he kissed her again, and in the middle of it he lifted her and carried her to the bed. Then he knelt alongside the bed and undressed her, delicately, as if with her, too, there was an injury under the clothes. As her skin was bared, he kissed it, as he inhaled her scent as though from a flower. When she was naked, he started to undress himself, but she stopped him. She wanted to do it for him as he had for her, carefully, lavish with gentleness. For a moment he resisted, but she pushed his hands away and unbuttoned his shirt and slipped it off. He stood up so she could remove his jeans and underwear. Kissing his chest, his hard stomach, stroking him, she failed to notice the scar until he started to climb over her. Then she saw it: a stripe of livid polished tissue that ran down in an uneven crescent from below his left shoulder across his hip bone. At the point where it cut across his chest, the nipple was missing. Stunned at the sight, she sucked in her breath and opened her mouth to ask how . . . *what* . . . had done it.

But as if to avoid the question, he climbed over her quickly, thrust himself inside her, making her gasp until he brought his mouth over hers.

Now the tenderness vanished. He plunged into her deeply, drawing back and then spiking down again, his body pummeling hers, grinding himself over her. She thought once she could feel the smooth band of scar rubbing across her nipple.

She urged him on harder, deeper. Was it just her mind or her voice whispering *yes?* She wasn't sure. But she wanted him to be rough with her now. The scar stayed in her mind and she longed to heal it, as if they could generate the heat to cauterize it, burn it away.

Again and again he rammed down into her, and then she began to feel the stirring of sensations that mushroomed so quickly from a slow confined warmth to a conflagration spreading to the tips of her limbs that it was almost terrifying. Never, she had never felt this before. She didn't want him to stop, yet she knew if he went on, went to the end, she would be destroyed. The burning spread, and she heard herself cry out just before she bit down on his shoulder and clung to him. Then she began to shudder, and his strong hands cupped her buttocks and pulled her up, up, up, up, until it seemed he would split her apart. At that second she exploded, taking him with her. The fire filled her, dissolved her . . . and then billowed away in waves that took forever to disappear.

They separated and lay beside each other, both silent, looking at the roof overhead. After a while she glanced over. Boonie kept turned to the ceiling, one arm flung across his face, shading his eyes.

She looked away again. The mystery of the interlude grew, the farther it receded behind her.

"A fine pair of enemies we make," she remarked at last.

He sprang off the bed and started to dress.

The silence hurt. "Wham-bam," she said acidly. "But not even a 'thank-you-ma'am.' "

He looked sharply at her. "Oh? Was that a favor you did for me, some fucking gift!"

She sat up and started hastily pulling her clothes around her. "No," she said, feeling suddenly small.

He finished dressing and crossed to the door, which was still standing open. Poised within the frame, he stared out across his meadow. On sentry duty.

Clothed again, she went to the mirror that was propped on a shelf above the iron sink. She shook out her blond hair and combed it back with her fingers.

"What happens now?" she asked, gazing into the mirror. A question to herself as well as the angry man who had just made love to her.

"Same as before," his voice came back.

She spun around. "Why?" she cried out. "Jesus, why do you have to make this *nothing?* Boonie, I'm not sorry about it. You gave me something I haven't had for a long time. . . ."

The look he tossed over at her was no less callous than one of his remarks.

"No, dammit," she said harshly, walking toward him, "I don't mean just a good fuck. I mean you . . . you touched me. For just these few minutes, I was nothing but a woman. No job to do, nothing to prove." With a wry little smile she added, "No balls. You reminded me of what I've given up. And I'm grateful, dammit. Like I was grateful for what you did the other night. So why do you have to make it something bad, shut out my feelings . . . and yours? Why must you walk away from the good things that happen between people . . . like some rotten army in retreat, blowing up bridges so no one can follow?"

He turned and moved out of the doorway. "Are you telling me we have a future?" His voice was soft, but the edge of irony still came through.

"I don't know," Lou replied. "But I've always thought that built right into the future, one of the very best things about it, is the way it'll give you answers if you just wait and see."

She was near him again. He gave her a sweet, sad smile, the nicest one yet. Raising a hand to her hair, he smoothed it down, lightly as a breeze.

"Look at you," he said, only slightly above a whisper. "You're nothing short of a princess, even got the gold hair like in the fairy tale. And me? I'm still . . . a 'grunt.' No, lady, on this one there's no need to wait and see."

She huddled against him, and for some time he held his arm around her. Finally he let go and she pulled away.

"But I do care," she said. "It'd tear me up if you pushed things to a confrontation."

"I can't help that, Lou. This is the line I've got to hold. At least until . . . until I find what I'm looking for."

"What *is* it?" she blurted with a desperate tone. "What on earth can you find here that you can't find somewhere else?"

He turned, hiding his face. "The gold," he said softly.

"Oh, Boonie," she sighed.

He turned back to face her. "But I know where it is," he said. "That's why I'm here."

"Boonie, *everybody* thinks they know. But there is no gold. It's a tourist story, a legend, nothing more."

"It's here, Lou." He pulled a chair up to the table and sat down. "I told you I came out here because of a friend of mine. I'll tell you why"—there was a dare in his voice now—"and maybe you'll get the message. His name was Joe Sundown. I used to take sentry duty with him, and we'd talk all night. It was either that or sit there scared shitless. He told me about the Tewani, how they fought for Uncle Sam in the 1800's clearing the Apache off the land. And he told me about the mountain, too—what it meant to the tribe, Elder Brother and his gold, the Lost Russian and all that. He'd get me going every time, I couldn't get enough of those stories, and then he'd pop the balloon and say only a dumb redskin would believe that shit."

"But you believed him," Lou said.

"Never. I thought it was all a crock." Boonie dragged his palm across his forehead, pushing his long hair out of his eyes. "Until one night when we were on the line together and he started goin' again with this stuff . . . and somehow it was different. He said there was a mine, it was *true*, and the route to it was a sacred secret passed down to only one or two members of the tribe in each generation. Joe knew the secret, he said, just like the Russian guy, and after the war he was going to come back and find it. He'd already told me how the gold was supposed to be poison for the Indians to touch, but when I brought that up he said he figured he was entitled to take something out of the ground of the country he was fighting for. After the war we could go dig it up, share it. Not *all* of it, mind you. According to Joe there was too much to take. But he said we'd have enough to take care of us for the rest of our lives." Boonie released a private smile, spread his arms, and pressed his palms against the table. "Then the sun came up, the duty ended, and that was that. Joe didn't bring it up again, and neither did I. I figured it was battle-zone bullshit, and I didn't want to call him on it. So we never mentioned it again. Never. Until . . . the last time."

Boonie shifted in his seat. "It was a routine recky mission, and I was right next to him. Joe took the first round, and he knew he wasn't going to make it. That's when he told me the rest, and he made me take a vow. Get it, he said, and live good, but don't take too much. He said Elder Brother would kill me if I did." Boonie shook his head. "Christ, it's like I can feel his hand on my arm right now, begging me to promise—he believed that *much*. So I took the vow, and it couldn't have been more than thirty seconds later he died. The chopper was just . . . going up . . ."

Lou heard the hitch in his voice. But then his eyes met hers, cool and unmarked by any feeling.

"So at last you believed him," she said, "and you came looking."

"Yeah, finally. Why *not?* After fighting that stinking war, what else have I got? Going home turned out to be a pipe dream and when I wised up, I thought, what the hell, if I'm gonna have a crazy dream, it might as well be this one. I don't even ask myself anymore if I believe it. I just live here and look for that mine. It's the only thing left in this world that I *want* to dream about.

It wasn't a lust for wealth, Lou thought. His pursuit of the gold was no more than a form of renunciation. Having the dream kept him alive. It broke her heart.

"Boonie, you won't find it here. You ought to know that by now. If Joe Sundown had given you a way to the gold, you'd have hit paydirt a long time ago. It's time to forget this dream. Go looking, and you might even find a better one."

He paused, as if pondering the advice. Then once again his features were set in a hard mask of stubbornness. Abruptly he strode to a metal footlocker at the end of the bed and took out a long roll of paper. He brought it to the table and spread it out. "Look at this."

She went to the table. The piece of paper was a map of some kind, meticulously hand-drawn in pencil. In the lower-right corner was a "compass rose" of the kind she remembered seeing on all Matt's sailing charts. On Boonie's map, hundreds of small irregularly shaped patches had been completely shaded in with pencil.

"The west face of the mountain," he explained. "The places I've filled in are the ones I've already checked out." His finger traced a path over the shaded areas, which Lou observed were laid out along fan-shaped spokes that radiated from a number of focal points along the upper edge of the paper.

Lou scanned the map with dismay. From the look of it, Boonie was methodically raking over the mountain inch by inch—*not* following any secret route straight to the gold. The chart was proof of his obsessive delusion. To what extent, Lou wondered, had Boonie been left mentally unbalanced by his war experience?

"That's seven years of searching," Boonie said, nodding over his chart. "I've put in too much time now to give up."

"But at the rate you're going," Lou said, "it'll be another . . . forty or fifty years before you've checked everywhere."

"No, Lou. I don't have to look everywhere. Not with what Joe told me. . . ." For a few moments, the only sound was the tap of his fingers on the map. He was weighing whether to trust her. "He said I'd find the entrance to the mine under the shadow cast by the hand at the time halfway from the brightest light to the final darkness."

At first she believed she must have missed a word. She took in the phrases, but she couldn't assemble them into meanings.

"Is that all?"

He nodded.

Then it came through. Of course, the instructions were opaque. That was why Boonie had looked so long in vain. "But then, he didn't really give you the secret," she said. "He just told you a riddle."

"It's enough," he said.

"How can it be?" she said, exasperated. "How do you expect to find anything by looking under—how does it go?—'the shadow cast by the hand'? That's meaningless unless you know where to stand, which way to face, even before you put out your hand."

"It's nothing to do with *my* hand, Lou. It doesn't mean the hand of the searcher."

"Whose, then?"

"God's."

"And what the hell does *that* mean?"

"A hand is attached to an arm, right?"

She stared at him. Then she got it. "The Arm of God," she murmured. "So the hand is—"

"The boulder on top. You have to look where the shadow of that boulder falls—"

"At a certain time of day, halfway from the brightest light to the final darkness." She paced excitedly around the table. "The brightest light: that could be the time when there are no shadows because the sun is overhead. Noon!"

"I think that's what it means."

"And the final darkness . . . I suppose that would be the last dark moment of the day, midnight."

"Might be. Or else the time when darkness finally descends—sunset."

"One or the other," she allowed. "But that narrows it down to two points on the clock. Six P.M. or whenever sunset is. You have to look at the position of the shadow at either of those times . . ."

"Yeah," Boonie said. "I figured that much out myself."

"But then how can you still believe the riddle? It should have led you straight to the mine."

"No, Lou. Solving the riddle isn't the same as solving the problem. Think of this: the height of the sun varies from day to day, and the sun sets at different times; the whole earth changes its relationship to the sun, depending on the season. That means every single day of the year, the sun stands in a slightly different relation to the Arm of God at either of those two points on the clock. What's more, that piece of rock is so tall, and the boulder on top is so damn huge, that it'll lay down a shadow over a pretty wide area. Sometimes, like on a winter day when the sun follows a low trajectory, there'll be a dark spot on the side of the mountain that covers a thousand square feet. There's no way I can check out that much ground quickly. Remember, the last time that mine was open—assuming the Russian found it—

was sixty years back. In that time the entrance could've been buried under half a dozen rock slides, filled in by mud, the timbers rotted out and the shaft collapsed. So checking each location means digging my ass off, shifting a load of rock, looking for buried timbers. If I haven't found it yet, I'm not surprised. But it doesn't mean there's nothing to the riddle. Any day now, it's gonna put me right on top of that mine."

Lou glanced down at the map. The dark fan-shaped areas made sense now as shadows radiating out from the Arm. She wondered nevertheless if Boonie hadn't been sent on a wild-goose chase by the whispers of a dying man. But unless he discovered that for himself, Boonie would always be the victim of this dream, with no place in his life for a new one.

"You've already covered quite a lot of ground," she observed.

"Most of it," he said. "Seven years is a lot of lookin'."

"So you're nearly finished . . . ?"

"Nearly."

"If you could go on with the search, would you move on peacefully when it's done?"

"Move on?" He laughed. "Lady, I'd *fly* on—'cause I'd be taking a load of gold with me."

"You said before that it might be any day. Did you mean that?"

"Sure I might find it any day. That's always been true."

"But at the outside—to finish checking every place the shadow falls—how much longer would you need?"

"Not long," he replied airily.

"In exact terms, Boonie," she insisted. "I've got to stick to a schedule. It's pretty strict, but I might find some leeway to let you continue . . . if it wasn't very long."

He nodded and pondered. "At the outside? A year. Maybe two."

The fragile bubble of hope popped. "The company couldn't wait that long, Boonie. There are millions at stake."

"Yeah," he said with a smile. "For me, too."

"It doesn't matter what I want. I've got to get you off this land in two weeks. If anyone gets the idea I'm stalling it even that long, I might be fired. Then someone else will come in and get the job done—any way they can."

He rolled up his map. "Well, then," he said, carrying it to the footlocker, "I guess we know where we stand." He dropped it inside and slammed down the lid. Then he stayed by the bed, refusing to look at her.

The moment when they had touched, made love, seemed as distant as his war. Lou went to the door, then turned back.

"I'm glad . . ." she began, and paused to revise her thoughts. "I'm glad you trusted me enough to tell me about Joe."

"Nothing to do with trust, lady. I thought it'd help you understand why I can't be pushed."

"But you didn't worry I might use the secret for myself."

At last he glanced over. "No, lady, I don't worry about you." She thought he meant it nicely until he came to the door and she saw the flinty look in his eye. " 'Cause if you ever tried, I'd be the first to know. And then I'd kill you."

She studied him for another instant, long enough to know that this time he was deadly serious.

She walked out, and away across the meadow. Only when she reached the rim of the plateau did she stop for one more backward look.

He had taken up his sentry post in the doorway. He was watching, she felt, only to make sure that she headed down the mountain instead of going off toward the Arm of God.

CHAPTER 22

"Mrs. Palmer, there's an Indian calling," the secretary said.

Lou picked up the phone in her office.

"Lou, it's David Lohaftapowe."

Had he arranged a tribal vote so quickly? "Good news, I hope."

"Quite the opposite, I'm afraid," he said frostily. "You realize that what your men are doing right now will make it impossible for my tribe to deal with you."

"My men?" Lou said. "Why? What are they—?"

"You don't know that your bulldozers are at this moment right on the edge of our sacred burial ground on the mountain? We never imagined you'd work in that area without informing us."

"My God, David, please believe me I had no idea."

"It should be clear to anyone who's near there. And it was my understanding that your predecessor had not only been told, but it was agreed our burial ground would be left untouched. The least you could have done was give us a chance to clear the remains."

Lou thought back to the reports she'd read. Had there been any mention of an Indian cemetery? No, she was sure. Apparently it had been fudged so that work would go forward. "David, you have my deepest apology. I'll get right up there now and do whatever I can." She paused. "David, I hope you believe that I had no part—"

"I believe you, Lou," he said. "Unfortunately, that may not help."

"I'll get back to you later," she said, already grabbing her keys from the desk.

Capper caught sight of her coming toward him and ran to meet her. Reading her stricken expression, he called out, "What's the matter?"

"There's an Indian burial ground here somewhere, Cap. We've got to stop work immediately."

"Is it . . . so important?" Capper asked tentatively.

"Of course it's important," Lou shot back. "The Tewani want to bury the remains somewhere else."

Capper gave her an uncomprehending look, palms up in a helpless shrug. "Lou, I don't see how they're going to find out, and even if they did—"

She cut him off. "Capper, they already know. They're outraged that we've even come near their sacred ground."

"What's happening to you, Lou? Is this Elder Brother horseshit getting under your skin?"

"Capper," she said heatedly, "the Tewani are entitled to the same respect as anyone else. If you were building in the city near a cemetery you'd get a special permit, and you'd stop excavating if you hit a grave."

Ted Lundberg approached from the far side of the bulldozers. "Problems?" he asked innocently. His manner grated on Lou more than ever.

Capper and Ted exchanged uneasy glances as she told them to stop work. "Lou," Capper said sheepishly when she finished, "I'm sorry. But it may be too—"

Lou exploded. "You've dug it up already! I thought you were only near—"

Ted put in ingenuously, "Well, we saw a few bones."

Lou aimed a searing glance at them. "So you just gave the order to go ahead. You didn't even stop to think—"

Ted interrupted her. "*I* gave the order," he said. "You weren't in the office. Somebody had to take charge, and I *am* the assistant project manager. I didn't think we should care about a bunch of bones."

His self-righteous tone rankled. "You didn't *think*, period. I was in the middle of negotiating with these people for rights-of-way across their land. You've probably blown the deal."

She stalked off toward the bulldozers. They had cleared a quarter-mile of road, piles of dirt and rubble heaped on either side. She kicked at the earth between two of the giant rockmovers. There it was, the evidence, lying at her feet—shards of bone. One had been broken from the side of a skull, a round smooth plate sheared in half, leaving a cavity that had once been the top of an eye socket.

Lou knelt and picked it up. You didn't have to believe in a religion to be sickened by the desecration of a cemetery.

Something had to be done, the damage somehow limited. She told Capper and Ted to use the entire road crew, drag in another crew if necessary, to scour the bulldozed path. If only a few of the graves had been disinterred, others might be untouched. The Indians could then be asked to survey what was left.

The crews were assembled, and she started toward her Jeep. "Idiots," she murmured as she passed Ted and Capper. "I just hope he doesn't take this out on me."

Capper chased after her. "Lou, come on, now, don't let this Elder Brother stuff—"

She whirled. "Not Elder Brother, dammit. Honegger! What do you think he'll say if the Indians get so pissed off they won't sell us their land?"

▲▲▲

They met at the Legend Mountain Café.

She had telephoned David Lohaftapowe, apologizing for damage to the burial ground. Despite much bitterness, he told her, his supporters in the tribe had agreed to keep discussions open. The money was a factor.

"I stopped it as soon as I could," Lou said over the drinks. "I know it was too late, but I detailed the men to gather up all the bones, to be turned over to you for reinterment."

"I appreciate your efforts, Lou. But you'll have to do more. A letter of apology to the tribe . . . and perhaps a sizable donation from your corporation to the clinic."

"Done." She should have broached the idea herself.

Then she opened serious discussion of the land purchase. As delicately as possible, she suggested that nine million dollars was a rather high price for a few dozen acres of scrub desert.

"We fought for seventeen years to gain that land," said Lohaftapowe. "The price will only pay what it has cost us."

"All that was a long time ago, David. Should we have to pay—?"

"I don't think 1973 is very long ao, Lou."

What was he talking about? The reservations had been defined by the government in the 1800's.

Lohaftapowe went on, explaining the land in question had been tied up in the state courts from 1956 to 1973. The tract had belonged to a Tewani woman who, thirty years earlier, had married a white man. An old Arizona law stipulated that Indians who married whites lost their state citizenship and property rights. When the white man divorced the Tewani woman, he claimed title to the land.

When Lohaftapowe finished, Lou gaped in disbelief. "You're telling me that in . . . in 1956, two years after the antisegregation laws, there was still some kind of intermarriage law against Indians."

Lohaftapowe shrugged. "Maybe you're getting some idea of what the Indians have been up against. The law wasn't struck down until 1964. This fellow kept making appeals, and we ended up in state Supreme Court. By then the woman had died, and we were fighting for her children's rights. You see, under the law, they didn't have any rights either. It cost the tribe a lot of money and a lot of anguish."

For all of Lohaftapowe's quiet reserve and dispassionate description of the Tewani's plight, Lou detected a reservoir of anger.

"This all has something to do with your coming back to the reservation."

"Partly," he answered.

"But it's all over now, isn't it? The legal issue is settled."

"Technically," he said.

"What do you mean?"

"The courts still aren't friendly to Indians," he said evenly.

"You're angrier than you sound, I think," Lou said.

The doctor glanced down at his half-eaten meal, the

food on his plate hardly touched at all. "I was in Phoenix today, in divorce court. My wife, who happens not to be an Indian, is doing everything she can to keep my children away from me, and the judge tends to see her side a lot more easily than he sees mine."

"You think you're getting a hard time from the court because you're an Indian?"

"The one thing I've had to learn is that no matter how I dress, no matter where I went to school, no matter that I did my residency in one of the best teaching hospitals in the country—to some people I'm just another Indian."

It was hard to look him in the eye. "I thought all that had ended," she said.

"It hasn't. So you can understand about the land. We owned this land once, all of it. And how did we lose it? By clinging to our pride, counting on Elder Brother to protect us. So now, if we're going to force the elders to sell, we want a good price, and the Honegger Corporation can afford it."

"You've made your position very clear," Lou said. "But there's one thing I don't understand. The Tewani have a comfortable life. The houses, the clinic, the playgrounds . . . It's not as though you're a poor tribe. So for all the bigotry—"

"We've been lucky," Lohaftapowe said, "unlike some of our Indian neighbors. But the Tewani are proud enough to resent charity. Everything we can raise on our own strengthens the tribe."

"Charity?" Lou asked. "Is that how you describe what the federal government—"

"Not the government," Lohaftapowe said. "I'm talking about Mercy."

"Mercy Roy?"

Lohaftapowe seemed confused. "Yes, I thought she'd told you when you were out at the clinic."

"I know she's been friendly with the Tewani."

"She's more than friendly. She's one of our biggest benefactors. How do you think we built that clinic?"

"How much has she given, exactly?"

"It's hard to figure," the doctor said. "The money is funneled through the *hati'i*. But over the years, with the clinic and some scholarships, the community hall and construction of the mall, I suppose Mercy's contributions add up to . . . anywhere from ten to twenty million."

Twenty million? Lou had known Mercy must be well off . . . but was she *that* rich?

"David, do you think all the money came from Mercy?"

"Where else would it come from?"

She had not known the words were coming until she spoke them. "Maybe the elders have the gold. The gold of the Lost Russian mine."

Lohaftapowe nodded with the soothing, paternal charm of a well-practiced bedside manner. "Lou, in the first place, the Tewani couldn't touch the gold if it was there. You know the myth of the gila monster. The gold would be poison to us."

But Lou had barely been listening, her mind running a course all its own. "Maybe Mercy has it," she said.

"And in the *second* place," Lohaftapowe went on, refusing to take her seriously, "the mine isn't there. It's folklore. It's legend. It's a bedtime story."

"David, what if it isn't?"

"If the mine's there," he said ruefully, "then I feel sorry for whoever does find it. What would anybody do with billions of dollars in gold? It would drive the sanest man out of his mind."

Driving home alone, she considered David Lohaftapowe's revelations about Mercy Roy. One of their biggest benefactors, he had said. Mercy's generosity to the Indians added one more to a series of mysteries about her. Now the questions were irresistible.

Why had a beautiful woman broken all ties to family and birthplace to live her life alone?

Why had she chosen this place to come to?

And those stories about an Eastern manufacturing fortune—exactly how large was it?

Or did Mercy have another source of wealth?

It was time, Lou decided, that she applied herself to getting some answers.

▲▲▲

She telephoned Dale Bannerman first thing in the morning.

If it was true that Mercy's fortune had originated in New England, then somewhere there had to be a family trust and a bank to administer it. Without asking any of the secretaries, Lou casually extracted the office rent records from the filing cabinet, carried them to her office, and closed the door.

The checks to Mercy Roy for the office rent and Lou's house had cleared through the Kingman National Bank. Bannerman was the manager. On the pretext that a lost rent check might have gone astray to the wrong bank, she asked Bannerman if there was a corresponding bank, in some other city, on the Roy account.

"Mrs. Palmer, I'd be glad to help you out, but there is the matter of confidentiality, and Mercy's been my customer for many years. Why don't you ask her? That'd be better."

"I tried to call her this morning," Lou said, inventing

a story to cover her real reasons. "She wasn't in, and I'd rather not bother her. I've got my comptroller on the line from San Francisco, and he wants to close out a ledger." She waited a respectable few seconds, then added, "You know, once Legend City starts to grow, we'll be a pretty good account, too."

Under Lou's unsubtle assault, Bannerman's wariness collapsed. He quickly supplied the name of Mercy's Eastern Bank—First Metropolitan Bank of Boston. Lou thanked him, hung up, and immediately reached for the Honegger Corporation directory.

There were Honegger offices in twenty-two cities around the world, ranging from outlying project departments in Singapore and Kuala Lumpur to operating divisions in the financial capitals. The Boston office listed more than fifty employees. Lou needed someone who would be willing to do a small favor for a major project manager, and among the names on the Boston list was Frank Benson, an assistant comptroller for purchasing. She dialed his direct number.

There was no answer.

Of course: it was seven in the morning in Boston, the office hadn't opened yet.

Two hours later, after she had made one round trip to the site and cleared an order for additional housing trailers due in six weeks, she tried Boston again.

Not surprisingly, Benson recognized her name. Her photograph had appeared prominently in the most recent issue of the *I-Beam*, announcing her appointment to Legend City. Benson sounded properly deferential, even pleased that someone so high up in the organization had called for his services. Still, she had to be careful with Benson, who in his junior position would be reluctant to take on any task outside the normal scope of his duties.

Lou began with a routine inquiry on the dependability of certain Boston subcontractors, coating her request with appropriate facts—specialized drilling parts from a Waltham importer, computerized inventory control programs from a high-tech manufacturer on Route 128.

Benson had taken notes and was reading them back, confirming her request, when she added in the lightest tone possible, "Oh, and one more thing, Frank. Could you check on an account at First Metropolitan Bank of Boston? The name is Mercy Roy. See if you can get some idea of how much it's worth, how old it is, and if they know anything about the Roy family."

There was a pause from the other end of the line. "First Metro's a pretty stuffy bank, Lou. Is this information important?"

"She's one of the locals here and we may be doing business with her. I'd like to check her financial condition before we go ahead."

Benson saw her point—a normal practice. "We've used First Metro for letters of credit, and I have a friend over there in the pension department. I can probably pry something loose. It could take some time, though."

No rush, Lou said, and ended the conversation with her thanks.

But returning the rent file to the front office, she felt a little foolish. She had engaged in clandestine research before, but always in the line of work, where scouting the opposition was taken for granted. Lou realized she had gotten carried away.

People could inherit fortunes and give away millions in philanthropy without finding lost gold mines.

CHAPTER 23

There had been no storm until Jesse asked for it. Ben was certain of that, no matter what his mother said.

He didn't want to be sent to boarding school, though, so he stayed away from Jesse and made an effort at finding other friends. But it turned out to be as hard as before—how the hell did you make friends out here, when everybody lived so far apart?—and he decided to forget his mother's orders. The only problem was to apologize to Jesse for avoiding him. The opening finally came two weeks later during a phys-ed class. They were all lingering on the soccer field in their gym shorts and T-shirts, waiting for the coach to show up, when Jesse sauntered over.

"Did you tell her about the mountain?" he asked. "About what you saw?"

It was the chance Ben had been hoping for. "I told her, Jesse, but she said I shouldn't talk about it, she even said not to talk to you anymore. And that's why I haven't." Ben felt the shame of disloyalty flood through him. If Jesse hadn't stood by him that night on the mountain, gone for help, Ben knew that he would have died. "Jesse. I'm really sorry. I'll never do that again. I want to be your friend."

Jesse gazed at him steadily. "If you are my friend, then you can help me. But to help me, you must believe. . . ."

"I do," Ben insisted. "I told my mom how the storm started, that you talked to Elder Brother. She wouldn't believe it, but I do. If you want proof that I'm your friend, I'll do anything. Just ask me."

For another long moment Jesse stared and said nothing. Then slowly he held up his hand, palm outward. At first it looked to Ben like the way a traffic cop gestured cars to stop. It must be some ancient Tewani oath of undying friendship, he thought, and raised his own hand.

"Anything" he repeated in a whisper just before the coach arrived and blew a sharp blast on his whistle.

▲▲▲

The backyard smelled of dust and flowers and the lingering scent of pine cleaner she had used in the kitchen. Beyond the fence, mesquite crackled from the alighting of sparrows and creeping desert mice. A mockingbird chirped, and in the distance there was the faint hoot of an owl.

She sat in a lawn chair and stared at the mountain, as if by looking she could resolve her confusion. There had been another argument at dinner tonight, Ben suddenly imploring her to leave the mountain alone, warning her that she was in danger. When she had charged him with spending time again with Jesse Silvertrees, Ben had not denied it.

What could she do? Whatever she had threatened, she could not ship him off to the care of strangers. She had never quit at anything—well, perhaps the marriage, and sometimes she wondered if she hadn't quit that too soon. But she couldn't give up on trying to raise Ben herself.

Her job, then? Could she keep faith with her son only by giving up her work, the balance of her identity?

The mountain was stark against the midnight sky, surreal amber in the light of the waning moon. She thought about the legend of Elder Brother protecting his gold. He would be a more generous god, she thought, if he would only protect men from their folly of pursuing it.

She got up and walked over to the fence, letting the moonlight play over her. Her thoughts went to Boonie, and the depths he had touched in her. She felt worried and sorry for him, and troubled by the realization that she could not avoid hurting him. He had built his life on a doomed mission, pursuing an insane wisp of grandeur because he couldn't find anything else to believe in. But the legend of the gold had as much substance as the clue in Joe Sundown's riddle—all mere shadows on the ground.

Lou turned back to the house. In her bedroom window a single lamp burned, and the yard was dark. For all the stress between herself and Ben, the house looked so peaceful. As she walked, she noticed her own pale shadow on the ground, as though the light cast through the bedroom window was mocking her thoughts.

She was halfway to the door when she stopped.

The shadow.

Her shadow lay in front of her, elongated toward the rear door.

And *not* cast—her thoughts raced wildly—by the lamp

in the bedroom. In that case the light would have projected across her and thrown the shadow behind.

But she had been coming toward her own moving image, not trailing it.

She glanced over her shoulder.

There was no light, of course, no house for miles around, no cars breaking the still night.

There was no light but the glowing yellow orb in the sky.

The moon!

The revelation seized her.

The moon!

She strode to the fence, whirled around to the house, her eyes darting from her shadow to the sky and back again. Joe Sundown's riddle—the damned riddle of the shadows: if interpreted by the moon instead of the sun, the path of the shadow from the Arm of God would lead to a wholly different part of the mountain, not the slopes so meticulously mapped in Boonie's obsessive preoccupation with the sun. And what else had Sundown said? She rummaged through her unyielding memory. Dammit, she had hardly listened, it had all seemed so pointless, the unhinged ravings of a dying soldier.

Brightest light, she thought. Something about brightest light.

. . . and the final darkness.

That was it, the time between "the brightest light and the final darkness."

Not the space between morning and night, she thought. That would be interpreting the riddle by the sun.

So how did you interpret it by the moon?

She craned her neck and looked at the imperfect

circle in the sky. She remembered the moon clock on the edge of the mall at the reservation, marked into quadrants and days. You could tell the time of the month by the size of the moon. The Indians, Mercy had said, were among the earliest astronomers. How else would they calculate the seasons, the proper planting time for their crops?

So, using the moon, what was the time between the brightest and darkest? The brightest moon was full, the darkest moon was no moon at all.

Of course: the *half*-moon.

Lou started to pace, crossing the yard in lengthening strides. Under a half-moon the shadow would be so pale as to be all but invisible. Unless, that is, you happened to be *searching* for it.

She came to a dead halt, turned to the mountain. Now it grabbed her with an almost physical presence, hurtling her through the barriers of her own imagination. She ran toward the car. She was ready to climb, stand at the Arm of God, and follow its shadow until she found the mine.

Wait! Wrong time. The half-moon was two weeks away.

She was like a dervish now, a possessed spirit, pacing more wildly. Could work on Legend City be delayed for three weeks? Only two weeks remained until Memorial Day, and in the first week of June the east face would be turned into millions of pounds of shattered rock. If the hidden mine lay anywhere near, no one would ever find it after the charges had wrought their damage. It would be a miracle if a large boulder survived, let alone the shaft of a mine.

It was there, by God.

With an excitement that she knew would keep her

from sleep, she turned back to the house, then stopped for one long moment to bask in the moonlight and gaze again at the mountain.

The gold of the Lost Russian.

It was really there.

CHAPTER 24

When the alarm sounded, she practically leapt from the bed. In a fog, she allowed habit to guide her through a shower, breakfast, and getting Ben off to the bus.

During the morning she went through the motions of her job.

And all the while the riddle of the shadows took on palpable life. It became as much a fixture as the gridded map of Legend Mountain on her office wall. Each time she swung to face it, she inevitably thought about moonlight, the Arm of God, gold.

At eleven, Ted called from the small apartment he rented in town. She had not even noticed he was missing, had thought he must be at the site. "I've caught a bug, a chest cold," he said in a clogged, sniffly voice. "I'm too wiped out to move. Do you mind if I just don't come in?"

Lou had no objections; he should of course stay in bed and get well. His absence gave her the excuse she needed for a drive to the site. There was little for her to do there—the road-building ran along almost on schedule—but the basalt column that she had once considered merely an interesting rock formation now beckoned to her like the lights of a port to a boat stranded at sea. She wanted to see it now, imagine where the moon would lay down its shadow.

And she also considered how she might throw a wrench into the steady pace of construction.

Not that she would do any such thing. It was only a thought.

The gold is there, she told herself.

And at the same time, like a top spinning around and around: how could it be there?

▲▲▲

Ted came into the office Tuesday afternoon. Capper had roughed out a preliminary blasting schedule, but it needed the engineer's professional eye and approval. He looked awful, though, tired and dragging his feet, but he stayed long enough to amend the sequence of the blast holes and calculate new depths for several of the charges. Lou told him he ought to go home or see a doctor.

It was just after Ted left that Lou's intercom buzzed. Frank Benson was calling from Boston.

"Your Mercy Roy has a substantial account at First Metro," Benson said. "She's tied into several trusts and has her own fairly large portfolio."

"How much is she worth, Frank?"

"Might be up to fifty million."

"Wow."

"Well, it's one of those old Boston fortunes, been sitting for a long time gathering interest. Hard to track just where it started, because no one in the family has lived here for sixty or seventy years. Somebody said something about a mill up in New Bedford. The history gets a little confusing because of the name change," Benson added.

"Name change?" Lou echoed.

"The original account was opened in the name of A. Royal," Benson explained. "Later it passed to Mercy Royal. A couple of years later, she changed the name on the account. To Roy."

Roy? Royal? Why would Mercy bother with such a small change? Two letters, virtually inconsequential. Well, Mercy *had* been quirky enough to leave a comfortable family in Boston—probably because she had been an odd fish since childhood—and travel west alone in a day when that was high adventure. It followed that she would be quirky enough to arbitrarily change her name.

She asked Benson to search a little further on the history of the fortune, and to call her when he had something new.

Royal to Roy.

Why would anyone bother?

▲▲▲

Ted stayed home on Wednesday. He could barely keep food down, he said, probably the effect of an antibiotic prescribed by the local doctor. On Thursday morning, Honegger's Phoenix lawyer called to report that the eviction papers had again been served on Boonie Daniels—but this time had come back promptly in an envelope, shredded to bits.

Thursday night, she called Ted at his apartment. She wanted to bring him groceries and the current project report if he felt well enough to read. She let the phone ring a dozen times. Had Ted been faking his illness?

Lou grabbed up the project report and walked down

Main Street to the rooming house where he lived. She would slip the report under the door; when he returned, he would know she had been there and gotten wind of his ruse.

At the door she knocked. Again no answer. She was turning back to the hallway when she heard something move inside. At first it sounded like furniture being shoved across the floor.

She put her ear against the door.

It was a voice. Someone moaning.

"Ted?"

The moaning grew louder.

"Ted, is that you?" She banged with her fist.

No one came. She turned and tripped down the steps to the first floor, almost losing her balance. In the back apartment lived the old man who owned the building.

He took his time answering her knock, but finally opened his door a crack and peered out. He wore a tattered bathrobe and was slipping his false teeth into his mouth.

"I'm a friend of Mr. Lundberg's. Upstairs? The man who lives upstairs?"

"I know you," he said. "You was at the town meetin'."

"That's right," she said. "Do you have a key to Mr. Lundberg's apartment?"

"Sick, is he? Didn't look none too good yesterday."

"Yes, hurry, please."

The old man tottered away from the door in his slippers and returned with a chain of keys, fiddling through them as he snailed his way up the steps. At the door he produced one that didn't work, then another. The third key dropped the tumbler with a loud click.

Lou rushed in.

Ted lay on the floor between the bathroom and the

living room. She ran and knelt next to him, taking his hand, which was sweaty and trembling. His eyes had puffed up, swollen at the top of the lids and sunken at the bottom.

This was no bronchial flu. She had to get him out of here, and quick. She reached out to brush the hair from his forehead, and his flesh literally seemed to burn in her hand. She flashed for an instant on a vision of Ted and Bogart, that dream, Ted sick . . .

"Water," Lou said, turning to the old man. "Get him a glass of water."

He ambled to the sink in the kitchen and she could hear the faucet running. But water wouldn't help Ted now. She could call for an ambulance, but it would have to come from Kingman.

Too long a drive. She needed a doctor. Where . . . ?

The Tewani reservation clinic!

The old man had returned with a cup. She held it to Ted's parched lips and poured as much as she could into his mouth.

I'll take him myself, she thought. She pinioned Ted against the wall, her hands under his armpits. He was light, and she managed with a single yank to prop him up on his feet. But there was no hope of his walking down the steps.

She snapped at the old man, "Get him under the arm. We have to take him downstairs." She stopped. "Oh, Christ." Her car was a block away. She rummaged in Ted's pockets, found his key chain. His Volvo had been parked, she remembered, out back in the alley.

Clumsily they pulled him down the steps, his feet slapping against the torn plastic runner the whole way down. The old man took some of the weight off Lou but was useless at guiding Ted through the door. With all her strength, she hoisted Ted up and eased him into the alley. Awkwardly balancing him against the side of the car, she opened the passenger door and poured him in, a collapsed lump of flesh.

She floored the car onto Main Street, scattering passersby and speeding right through the red light in the middle of town.

▲▲▲

Lou sat in an easy chair in the semidarkness, across from the glowing nurses' station. Finally the admitting doctor approached her from the end of the hall. Ted's condition was stable, he said, but they hadn't yet established what caused his collapse.

"Is he going to be all right?"

"I think so," the doctor said. "We've got him on a respirator now. You probably saved his life. Another hour and he wouldn't have made it."

Twenty minutes later Capper blustered out of the elevator. They walked down the hall to Ted's room and stood at the door, peering in. Against the bleached white of the sheet Ted's arms lay pale and gray, his face yellowed to a pall. He looked dead.

Lou put her hand to her mouth, covering a gasp.

Capper wrapped his arm around her and pulled her away from the door.

▲▲▲

It was nearly ten when David Lohaftapowe approached them, untying an operating-room mask from his face. "I think Ted's out of danger," he said.

"David, what caused this?" Lou asked.

"It was the bones," Lohaftapowe said.

Lou and Capper looked at each other blankly.

"The bones from the burial ground," he added.

Now Capper's face twisted into a half-smile. "Now, wait a minute . . ."

Lou stared incredulously at David. Was he trying to say some Indian curse was at work?

"It's a very rare condition," Lohaftapowe said. In the past two years, he continued, the clinic had seen only one other case. It was called coccidiomycosis, popularly known in the west as valley fever. It had been identified in December 1977 after an outbreak following severe winds in the dusty San Joaquin Valley, hence the name. Twenty people had died. The cause was a microscopic organism inhaled by the victim. Not everyone fell prey to it. Several years before the San Joaquin incident, in fact, a group of students had come from a college in New York City to a northern California town to dig in Indian ruins. Sixty of the students—most, but not all—had come down with identical symptoms: fever, chest pains, dry coughs, and muscular aches. None had died.

"A Greek doctor in California," Lohaftapowe said, "finally figured out it came from the bones. Down at the university in Tucson they're working on a vaccine."

His even tone, the soothing matter-of-fact quality of his voice, calmed Lou. "So Ted will be all right . . . ?"

"Ninety-eight percent of the victims recover completely. We've got Ted's lungs functioning now, and his fever's down. It's just a question of how strong his body is, and he looks pretty strong to me."

"But those twenty people who died . . ."

"That's two percent, Lou," David said. "The odds are very much in Ted's favor."

Still, she refused to leave the clinic until assured that Ted has passed the danger point.

Capper urged her to go home. "Lou, don't get yourself all worked up. The doctor said Ted will be fine."

Common sense told Lou he was right. Still, she felt impelled to remain. Ted worked for her, he was her man. He wasn't her favorite, but on a construction job away from home a man had no family. As his boss she felt obliged to stand by.

▲▲▲

It took no great powers of perception to read the disappointment in Lohaftapowe's eyes as he came down the corridor.

Lou pulled herself reluctantly from the chair.

"Lou, Mr. Tate, I'm sorry . . ."

"He's dead," she said, the words catching in her throat. "Jesus Christ, he's dead."

She felt weak and lowered herself onto a couch. David sat and put an arm around her.

"The mountain . . ." she whispered.

Capper's face tensed. "Cut it out, Lou, please. Ted got the short end, the lousy two percent, that's all."

"That mountain god is taking revenge," she muttered. "It was Ted who gave the order, and it's Ted who died."

"Lou, you heard the doc," Capper said. "This is a known medical phenomenon."

David spoke. "There's no explanation but the scientific one, Lou. There is no mountain god."

Lou turned to him. Denying the traditional beliefs of his own tribe seemed almost like a sacrifice he was making for her. She nodded, surrendering to reason.

"I'll stay and help you make arrangements for the

body," Capper said. "You've done enough of that already."

"No, Cap. It's my responsibility."

Another body to be sent home, she thought. Another victim of the mountain.

CHAPTER 25

What kind of person was she becoming?

She went to Phoenix and consigned Ted's body for shipment on the Flying Tiger freighter. She wrote a letter to his sister in Philadelphia, with all the disguised platitudes about how much it had meant to know Ted, to work alongside him. She talked to the San Francisco office about a replacement and she said "it won't be easy" and told them to give her a little time, because it would be hard getting used to the change. . . .

And she didn't really care.

In the hospital, if she had been disoriented, it wasn't because Ted had died. In a moment of shock she had believed the mountain had killed him. But the next day she saw the rational side of it all. The disease, coccidio-whatever-it-was, had killed others. Hadn't she once read of something similar in Egyptian tombs, a medical explanation for the curse of King Tut? David Lohaftapowe himself, a doctor—and an Indian—had dismissed any notion of unnatural causes.

As she drove back from Phoenix on Saturday, the shock of Ted's death receded with the finality of a blackboard swept clean by an eraser.

And her attention again focused single-mindedly on the gold—and on the riddle of the shadow.

She went to Ted's apartment, attending to his belongings. For all the emotion she felt, she might have been the cleaning lady. She filled cartons, packed suitcases, but churned inside with thoughts of gold.

Royal to Roy, two letters. The tiny change still nagged at her.

Clearing out Ted's desk, she glanced out the window at the mountain and felt the challenge: come and get me, it said.

Come if you dare.

▲▲▲

By Sunday she was determined to test her theory.

That night, after Ben was in bed, she went to her study and sat down at the desk. One week until the half-moon, she thought. Did she have to wait that long? There had to be another way to test her theory about the moon's shadow. If the position of the moon could be plotted forward . . .

She remembered sailing trips she had taken with Matt. At night, he would use his sextant and navigation books to fix their position by the stars. She ought to be able to pinpoint the position of the moon now, just as he had.

The idea formed even before she knew it.

Why not call Matt?

True, their relationship had sunk to an all-time low. Their sole common ground consisted of Ben—his problems, his education, visiting rights.

Still, they *had* been friends once, hadn't they?

Worth a try.

She had to look up the number of his marina

apartment, which showed just how far apart they had grown.

"Hi Matt, it's Lou."

"Hello, Lou," he said guardedly. "How are you?"

She said she was fine, the job had turned out to be as fulfilling as expected, and went on to some talk about the custody arrangements for the summer. His guard dropped a little. She bided her time as Matt bragged about his latest successes. Then she said: "I thought you might be able to help me?"

"Oh? How?" He sounded agreeable.

"I need to know a few details about the position of the moon in the night sky."

Matt half-laughed. "Why this concern with phases of the moon?"

"Something to do with the project," she replied. "I just need one little detail. Could you tell me the precise point in the sky where the moon will be in"—she paused, not knowing the right day—"when it's half-full? In a couple of days, I guess."

Good-naturedly Matt got out his lunar tables. He explained that the position of the moon depended on the hour—the time of night. The world, after all, was constantly turning. What time did she want the data for?

Time?

Time?

Lou was stymied. The riddle had given no clue to the hour. But if the Tewani elders, hundreds of years ago, had devised a message clever enough to describe the phases of the moon, would they have left it so vague as to ignore the time? The whole purpose was to fix definitely the location of the Altavela mine. The tribe's wise men would hardly have expected their descendants to follow the moon's shadow every night of the year. Somewhere in the riddle there was an answer.

"Lou?"

"Just a sec, Matt. I have to consult some papers. . . ."

She put down the phone, but stood there thinking. How would the riddle indicate the hour, the minute?

The time halfway from the brightest light to the final darkness.

What if that related not only to the phase of the half-moon but also to the exact moment in a span of twenty-four hours?

But how?

The brightest light would certainly be noon . . . in which case the final darkness could refer to sunset.

No, that wouldn't do. Only a few days a year was the moon visible at sunset.

Could "the final darkness" be midnight?

She ruled that out, too. The sky stayed dark long after midnight.

When, other than sunset and midnight, could you say the darkness was "final"? When was the sky darkest?

It's always darkest . . .

The phrase sprang from memory:

. . . *just before the dawn!* Of course! That was it.

"Final darkness" meant not the onset of darkness, but the last moment of darkness.

Which would be sun*rise*, not sunset.

The midpoint would be the exact moment halfway between noon and sunrise.

She snatched up the phone again. "Matt, what time does the sun rise these days?"

"I thought you were interested in the moon."

"I need this information too."

There was a sighing chuckle from the other end of the line. "What's this all about?"

"I can't tell you," she said. "When's sunrise?"

His sigh this time had no laugh in it, but he obliged and consulted the weather page of the San Francisco *Examiner*. "On daylight-saving time, five-twelve. But that's here. You'd be a couple of minutes earlier, because you're farther east."

"And I'm in a different time zone," she said, thinking aloud.

"Yes, but we're on daylight-saving; I don't think Arizona has it. That would cancel the hour difference."

Lou pulled a pen and legal pad from the desk drawer and scribbled a quick calculation. From noon ("the brightest light") until 5:12 in the morning ("the final darkness") was seventeen hours. The halfway point ("the time halfway from") would be 8:32 P.M. Dark enough for the moon to cast a distinct shadow.

"What day is the half-moon?" she asked.

"Thursday," he said.

"Okay, where would the moon be at eight-thirty-two on Thursday?"

Matt consulted his tables. While she waited, Lou checked her own calculations, considered again the logic of the riddle. It was astonishingly complete—with the double-edged significance of "the time halfway from the brightest light to the final darkness."

If she was right.

Matt reeled off the coordinates of the moon, and she copied them down.

And then realized that she didn't need the numbers at all.

The riddle gave the time and the day; it didn't matter where the moon was. Matt's question had driven her to the interior puzzle within the riddle, and forced her to solve it.

Again he prodded her to explain her strange fascination with lunar positions. "Building a glass tower?" he needled. "To reflect the moon?"

"I can't explain, Matt."

"Oh, c'mon, Lou," he said, obviously irked. "You ask me for a favor and—"

"No, Matt."

There was a pause. She heard him breathing. "All right," he muttered. "Maybe this is moon madness, plain old lunacy. I'll keep that in mind if we ever get back to scrapping about Ben's custody."

A low blow, sparking her ire. "That's totally uncalled for," she shot back. "I don't need—"

"What you don't need," he interrupted, "is any more help from me."

Before she could answer the connection was broken. He had hung up on her.

▲▲▲

She lay in bed, propped against the headboard, with the moon and the mountain in full view. Tomorrow she would drum up an excuse to get some supplies, go up on the mountain . . .

But she wondered if she dared climb alone. Whom could she trust to help? The riddle belonged to Boonie, of course; he had supplied the key. After seven years in that little shack, he deserved the chance to share in her discovery.

But her involvement with Boonie frightened her—a dark passion out of keeping with everything else in her life. She had looked into those eyes where the violence burned as uncontrollably as the fires of war. She didn't doubt he'd meant his warning about looking for gold: *Then I'd kill you*.

When she thought of the dream as his, it seemed a grotesque fantasy, an escape; and she recoiled from pursuing it.

But floating into sleep, she understood that it was too late. The dream—the madness in the soul that came from the very thought of gold—had already become hers as well.

CHAPTER 26

Monday sped by. Shorthanded with Ted gone, Lou had no hope of getting to Kingman for climbing supplies. Late in the afternoon, the mammoth B&C drilling rig arrived, towed by a twelve-axle trailer. It met all of the job's specifications: a self-propelled track-mounted blast-hole drill, rotary type, mounted on its own platform. It weighed a hundred tons.

Forced to pretend interest, Lou drove out to the site at four to watch the drill pull into the depot. In pieces on the trailer, it was a mere pile of steel. Assembled it would be nearly five stories high. There had been a time when it thrilled her to see such a massive piece of equipment.

Not today.

Everyone agreed it was too late in the day to begin drilling, and so Lou shuttled the rig's operators into town. She made a show of talking shop with them—other jobs they had worked on, the careful work necessary to drill the blast holes properly. She bought them drinks at the hotel bar and then bid them good night.

Hurrying out of the bar, she thought: I have to get to that mine before you blow it up.

▲▲▲

But there was dinner to make for Ben. This time she was the one who sat through it uncomfortably.

"You're itchy, Mom," Ben observed.

"Without Ted, I have even more work," she said, adding, "I'll have to go into the office tonight."

"You usually work at home nights," Ben said querulously.

"Too much paper to carry today," she explained.

Ben said nothing more.

After dinner, she finished the dishes in record speed. She went into the living room where Ben was watching a rerun of *Fantasy Island* and reminded him to do his homework.

"Don't wait up for me," she said as she pecked him on the cheek.

As she backed the car around and started down the hill, she had an uneasy feeling that he was watching her.

And that, more than watching, he suspected.

▲▲▲

The moon was already faintly showing in the twilight sky when she reached the site. The men were all at dinner, or out drinking, and in the windows of their trailers at the edge of the area, only a few lights showed.

She left the car at the camp office and walked over to the supply shed. Opening the lock with her key, she went in and yanked the door shut behind her. Immediately she found what she needed: a high-powered torchlight beam, a shovel, and a compass. The torchlight needed batteries, and she quickly located a box of the rechargeable nickel-cadmium type. She considered signing for the supplies—but why leave a record?

She got back into her car. Overhead, the moon was rising.

Darkness was settling as she reached the mountain. Even after four months in the desert, the slow descent of night, its long creep followed by a sudden collapse into pure black, always took her by surprise. She had left herself more than an hour for what in daylight would have been a climb of fifteen minutes. It was now 7:37. But would she make it?

In the dusky twilight the mountain was altogether different. No easy paths were visible, no footholds certain. All she had before her was a narrow cone of yellow from the torchlight. The most direct route to the Arm of God had long since been enshrouded in the wavering shadows of nightfall. Several times she would have sworn she stepped on something alive—and the little gray lizard with orange spots sped full-blown into her mind's eye. Each step, riskier than the last, took her closer to the hidden promontories of the east face, to the sharp drops into ravines lathed smooth by rain. At every touch of her foot, a fresh tumble of rocks was dislodged to clatter away into the darkness. Every poke of the shovel she was using as a probe reminded her of another potential fall into oblivion.

She began to lose her nerve. Alone on the mountain at night: a target for death, not at the hands of a murderous prospector or garden-variety psychopath, but nature itself.

And then the grisly accordion file of Legend Mountain's death toll came into her mind. She had the sensation of footsteps following behind her, the certainty that the clattering rocks had been loosened by someone else's tread.

She stopped and flicked off the light. In confused terror she instantly turned it back on.

"Is someone there?" she cried out impulsively, and whirled the torch beam in a circle.

Emptiness.

Her breath pulsed in uneven spurts. She laid a hand across her chest to steady herself, then shone the light on her watch; forty minutes to go. Even if she reached the Arm of God in time, how was she to follow the shadow? Even if she had known the mountain well enough, she was far too afraid to continue on alone.

But Boonie knew the mountain, knew it well. And nothing frightened him.

▲▲▲

She reached the plateau at ten mintes before eight. The lights inside his cabin glowed reassuringly.

She crossed to the door and knocked boldly.

A moment later the door creaked open.

He appeared with a book held open, cradled in one hand. A pair of round tortoiseshell glasses were balanced on his nose—inappropriately peaceful for his face. He looked almost benign, like a country schoolteacher.

But from the moment he opened the door the electricity was there between them as always. He said nothing, awaiting an explanation.

"Boonie, can you come with me? Right now?"

"What are you doing here?" he asked quizzically.

"I . . . I think I can show you . . ." She paused on the brink of uttering the words, struck suddenly by how far her obsession—*his* obsession—had taken her.

"Show me what?" Boonie said.

She swallowed hard. "How to find the gold."

The hand holding the book dropped slowly to his side, and with his other hand he raised his glasses and propped them on his forehead.

"How?"

Still standing on the cabin threshold she stammered out her interpretation of the riddle—the moon shadow, the double meaning of the clues. But they had to move fast, she said, the moon was almost in position now, there was no time to lose. . . .

As she talked, Boonie's face clouded—in anger or resentment, she thought, at her violation of his quest. Or was it only disappointment and regret that he had devoted seven years to mapping patterns of the sun, to discover in the end that the riddle's true meaning had eluded him, bared by a stranger?

"Boonie, please, we've got barely half an hour. Come with me . . . please!"

He turned from the open door. As if struck dumb by the enormity of her revelation, he glanced around the cabin. He murmured something she couldn't hear, then set the book down on his table of maps and notebooks. He went to the dresser, eased the top drawer open a crack, and stared intently into the mirror.

It occurred to Lou that the idea of actually finding the gold might be too overwhelming for him.

"Boonie!" She had lost her normal voice; it came out in a hoarse cry.

There was a gun in his hand when he turned around—an army-issue .45 automatic. He checked the clip, pushed it back in, then slipped the gun under his belt as if it were nothing, a mild encumbrance. Lou stared at the crenellated grip of the pistol showing above his belt. Carrying a gun for protection made sense, but again she thought of Hartnett's files. If she and Boonie unearthed the mine together, what might he do to keep all the gold himself? It was too late though, to do anything but trust him.

He hurried into his sheepskin jacket and bent quickly over his footlocker. When he straightened he was holding a sort of snub-nosed telescope with a two-lensed eyepiece, rimmed all around by a black shield like an underwater mask.

"Let's move," he said quietly.

▲▲▲

To Boonie the mountain opened up like a level plain. It was his friend; he knew it well. He cautioned Lou to follow close, and he moved unerringly in the darkness, hardly paying attention to the beam of light on the ground. Twice he paused to scan the peaks, bracing the two-lensed scope against his face. It was an Owl-Eye, he said, army surplus, a nightscope he had used in the war.

They crested the jutting ridge beyond his cabin at a few minutes past eight. Boonie lifted the scope to his eyes once again. Across from the ridge Lou could make out the towering Arm of God in the moonlight, but the shadow of the hand was lost in the ripples of rock and dirt below.

"Look," Boonie said, handing her the scope.

It was heavy. She passed Boonie the shovel and gripped the barrel of the lens with both hands. Looking into the eyepiece, she needed a moment to adjust to the landscape on a field of green, but the light-enhancing device brought the rocks into clear definition. The murky shadow of the Arm of God stood as a broad waving form.

Boonie looked at his watch. "Come on," he said. "We're not close enough."

The scope's range extended just short of a mile, but to find where the shadow fell they would have to cross the narrow ravine below. Laboriously they crawled down, and across the sheer sloping face, leaning inward to keep their balance. Halfway to the other side they met the shape of the Arm on the ground. Lou's heart raced. She could hear the blood coursing in her head as they moved faster and faster alongside the shadow.

Insane.

And yet beyond all logic she knew the gold was there. They were getting closer to it.

They raced the clock. All she could hear now were the scatter-shot crunch of her shoes on the gritty ground and the faint whisper of the wind.

Closer.

At the end of the shadow loomed a steeper peak.

"Around it," Boonie called out, running ahead of her. The shadow of the Arm ended just above them. Out of breath, her heels slipping, Lou reached the other side of the rock only seconds behind him.

Beyond them, projecting across a dip to the hill opposite, maybe fifty yards away, lay the shadow of the "hand"—the boulder atop the Arm.

Boonie threw the nightscope against his face as though it were weightless. He held it to his eyes for a long time.

"What *is* it?" Lou demanded impatiently. "What do you see?"

"Keep going" he barked, moving again.

Lou looked at her watch—8:27. Boonie was sprinting now. When she reached him he was already lowering the scope from his face.

He handed it to her wordlessly.

The image through the lens was clear: the shadow, with the electronic enhancement, utterly distinct. The boulder atop the Arm of God cast an oblong rectangle, falling across a shallow cavity between two sharp ridges. The area enclosed was perhaps twenty yards wide and slightly longer.

Boonie stepped inside the shadow. For a moment, spellbound, he didn't move.

"It's too big," he said with a sigh of resignation. "We'll never search all of this at night." With that he began gathering rocks, piling them at the corners of the rectangle.

Lou followed him in a frenzy of disappointment. After all this work, how could they wait?

"Now, Boonie!" she cried. "Let's dig now."

He turned. "Where?" he demanded harshly. "Where the hell would you like to dig? There's no way we'll find a fucking thing in the dark. By daylight we can see what the hell is here!"

"But we have to find it now!" Lou shouted.

"I've waited seven goddamned years," he said. "And I can wait one more day." He went back to making the rock markers.

Breathless, frustrated, she watched him. Without his cooperaion she could do nothing.

"The goddamn shadow's moving," he called out. "Are you going to help mark this thing before we lose it?"

She followed his lead, gathered the rocks, and piled them in the four corners of the shadow.

▲▲▲

Ben lay in bed waiting for his mother to come home. She had not gone to the office; it had been a lie. Fifteen minutes after she left, he had called. No one had answered the phone. An hour later, there had still been no answer.

She had never lied this way before. But lately she was acting different. She'd changed. For a while Ben had thought it had something to do with Jesse, her anger at their being friends again. But no, it was something else.

It was almost ten-thirty when he heard her car chugging up the hill into the driveway. He rolled over and pretended to sleep.

Why had she lied to him? Where had she gone tonight?

CHAPTER 27

"We've got a burglar," Capper declared with annoyance as he came into Lou's office the next morning. He went on to list the items that had been found missing from the supply shed: one high-intensity search beam and battery, a ten-inch shovel, and a compass. A curious assortment, he observed, considering that many more valuable items had been there for the taking. One thing was certain: whoever had taken the stuff was not some transient or mischievous local kid.

"The lock was opened with a key, and then closed again. We wouldn't have known a thing was missing if the supply clerk hadn't spotted an open box of batteries. That started him on the inventory."

Lou nodded gravely, momentarily stuck for words. Needing the supplies, she had simply helped herself without any thought of moral consequences. Now that the act had been labeled "theft," she was mortified. What if someone else was blamed?

"Well," Capper said after a moment, "how do you want me to handle it? Let it go?"

Minor pilferage was always a problem on the sites. Lou knew it wouldn't seem unusual if she took a laissez-faire attitude. "As long as nothing really valuable was taken," she said, "just change the locks and keep closer tabs on distribution of the keys."

Capper said he would have it done today. Then he shook his head and repeated that the stolen articles were an odd assortment. "A shovel and a compass. . . . You know what I think? The men have been hearing all that Lost Russian bullshit for so long, one of them must have fallen for it. He's spending his nights looking for that gold mine." He laughed. "Can you beat it?"

They talked about the allocation of blasting crews. But all the time she was being assured that everything was on schedule, Lou could only concentrate on the fact that the mine's secret location—if there *was* anything beneath that shadow—stood just on the fringes of the area to be blasted. Under an explosive force equivalent to sixteen thousand tons of TNT, the shock to the whole mountain would be so great that every internal configuration might be altered. Although the surface entrance to the mine stood outside the blast area, the shaft itself conceivably wended a long subterranean path directly under the section being benched. Not only would any shaft tracing a route to the gold disappear, but the gold would be pulverized—literally turned to a cloud of dust.

"So you feel," Lou said when Capper finished his summation, "that we'll be ready to go on time."

"A week from today," Capper confirmed smartly.

A week!

Could she and Boonie possibly check their find in that time? She recalled his description of the difficulties involved in previous searches—mud slides, collapsed shafts, no less than several hundred square feet to be dug.

"Cap, it occurred to me . . . Ted's replacement won't be here for a couple of weeks. Maybe we should wait till—"

"Lou, are you serious?" Capper gaped at her. "This isn't some fancy black-tie ball, for Chrissakes. Ted's work on this blast was done. It can't matter a damn if his replacement is here."

"But we do have other work," Lou said. "It wouldn't matter if we delayed the blast. We could move the crews around, start the roadbeds up on the—"

"You've got to be kidding!" Capper broke in. "If we're ready to go, why delay? Who the hell wants to go through all the paperwork again?" He ticked off the procedures on his fingers: state and county permits, insurance bond, environmental-impact statements, diversion of airplanes by the FAA. "With all that in place, hon', why the hell would we want to delay?"

She noted the patronizing tone, epitomized by his use of an endearment. He wouldn't have slipped into it, ordinarily, but she understood it had been prompted by a suggestion that normally would have come only from an inexperienced apprentice.

Capper was still regarding her thoughtfully. "There's no way out of it, Lou," he said.

"What?" she responded, feeling suddenly caught, trapped.

"The cops. That's why you want to delay, isn't it? You still can't bring yourself to use strong-arm tactics to pull that vet off the mountain."

She puffed out some air, relieved that Capper had provided her with a sensible motive. Then she nodded.

Capper patted her on the shoulder. "He led you up the garden path, eh? Told you he'd move off peacefully and then went on squatting right there. After you came back that day, you said you thought it would work out."

"I thought it would."

"But you can't let it go any longer, Lou, you know that."

"I know. I'll go up there now and put him on final notice."

She rolled up the blasting plan. Capper remained by the table watching her as she walked to the rack that filled half a wall of her office and restored the roll of paper to its cubbyhole.

"You all right, Lou?" he asked finally. "I mean . . . with all that's gone on around here—Ted, Benaky, not to mention the run-of-the-mill strain of carrying the whole project on your shoulders—well, there's no one who wouldn't understand if you asked for a little time off."

She mustered a smile. "Thanks, Cap. I'm all right. Though maybe," she added, "after the blasting, I will take a vacation."

Capper left.

Sure, she thought, why not? Either way, by then she'd need some time to recover. A few days of quict relaxation—or a celebration trip around the world.

▲▲▲

When Lou arrived at Boonie's shack later in the morning, he was outside laying out the equipment they would need to continue their search. Along with the shovel and searchlight she had left, there were two pickaxes, a small spade with a folding handle, several rock hammers, two canteens, a Coleman lamp, two long coils of rope, and four heavy-duty pinions for shoring up weak timbers.

Boonie greeted her with a cursory nod and began to pack the smaller items into two knapsacks. As he knelt to buckle them closed, Lou noticed the butt of his revolver protruding from the waistband of his jeans.

The thought hit her again: What if they did find the mine today? What would he do with her? Share it all?

Gold. How quickly the promise of it poisoned the mind.

Boonie helped her into one of the two packs, and they set out across the meadow with him in the lead. At the edge, he turned in the wrong direction.

"Why this way?" Lou said. "The Arm is over there." Her eyes flitted to the gun again. To keep the secret, he could lead her to a different place—somewhere a body wouldn't be found.

Boonie answered patiently. "You've got men working all over this mountain and we're traveling in broad daylight. And there's still one or two people who might come up from town to hunt around while they can. If anyone were to spot us with all this crap on our backs, don't you think they might be curious enough to follow? Seems to me we'd be smart to meander there in a roundabout way and make sure nobody's on our tail. That is," he concluded with broad sarcasm, "assuming the plan meets with your approval."

She gestured wearily. "Lead on."

Reaching the spot they had marked took three times as long as the night before. Their route was extended by having to skirt all the way around the section being drilled. Fortunately, the crews had started on the side of the blasting area farthest from where Lou and Boonie would be searching. That, and a low ridge that stood between them and the construction site, would allow them to work undisturbed.

As soon as Boonie slipped out of his pack, he took a pad and pencil from the pocket of his denim shirt and began pacing methodically over the ground, making notations as he went.

"You take half," he called out as he traversed the width of the marked area. "Pace it off and take approximate measurements. Separate it into quadrants six by six—that's roughly the size of a shaft opening. We can save some time by digging only at the intersecting points of the quadrant. And tell me if you spot any irregularities in the surface—sinkage in the earth, a break in the rock, anything. . . ."

It was another hour, approaching noon, by the time they had completed a preliminary inspection. Neither had seen anything to indicate an opening in the mountain. Boonie untied the tools and handed Lou a pickax.

"We're down to the nitty-gritty," he said, pointing to a spot where she should start digging.

Lou took the pick but then gazed around hopelessly. "Boonie it can't work—not this way. We've got a week, then this whole face blows. If we take the time to dig deep enough, we won't cover more than a corner—"

"We've got to start somewhere," he said. "We have to hope we'll be lucky." He moved off about twenty feet, took off his shirt, and then went to work. He swung the pick back in a high arc and drove it fiercely into the ground, again and again, as if stabbing at the mountain, torturing it to force the revelation of its secret.

In a minute he glanced over at Lou, who had not yet begun. "Dig, dammit!" he bellowed. "Or are you too fucking dainty for this kind of work?"

She didn't bother to waste her temper on him. It wasn't at all a matter of hard labor—only a question of logic. She simply didn't believe that they could possibly succeed this way.

Nor should they have to. In the same way that the riddle had contained the clues to steer them to this place, there must be some other indicator, some way to pinpoint the precise location of the mine. Otherwise the riddle would be worthless. It should not be necessary to search at all: anyone in possession of the secret should be able to go straight to the entrance of the mine.

Yet all she saw around her was a barren surface of rock. She began to walk over the ground again, staring down at her feet to examine intently every square inch, every tiny detail of earth and stone.

Boonie glanced over with annoyance, but after a moment resumed swinging the pick.

For half an hour, an hour, Lou went on with her painstaking study. At this rate, it would take until nightfall to cover just half the area. Still, she was convinced it was the only way. A better way than Boonie's, certainly: by the end of two hours he had dug only two holes.

Once or twice she saw a rift in the rock, and thinking it might be the seam of an entrance, she stooped for a closer look. But each time she determined that they were only surface faults caused by the freezing of groundwater. She went on doggedly inching over the ground. Another half-hour, forty minutes, of peering at the bland grayness, and it became difficult to focus. Sweat dripped into her already strained eyes, and she began to have visions of things that didn't exist. An iron ring attached to the rock—a handle to pull up a hidden door!—proved to be, when she dropped to her knees for a closer look, a roundish conformation of orange lichen.

Her back was beginning to hurt from the constant stooping so she stayed on her knees after that.

Taking a rest break for himself, Boonie wandered over to watch her. "I could help you," he said, "if I knew what the hell you were looking for."

"Even *I* don't know," Lou replied. "All I know is there's something here to lead us . . . there's *got* to be. . . ."

Boonie returned to his digging. Lou went to one of the canteens, poured some water into one hand, and spattered her eyes with it, refreshing them. Then she picked up where she'd left off, continuing her slow snail-crawl over the ground.

She had been going for only another ten minutes when something about the rock beneath her suddenly struck her as unusual. All the rock she had seen up to now was of the igneous variety—formed by fire, thrust up out of the earth's core by volcanic action hundreds of millions of years ago, and then hardening as it cooled into these hard massive blisters on the planet's skin.

Yet the patch of rock beneath her now was sedimentary granite, inlaid with veins of quartz and feldspar. Strange. This rock was formed by a different process, the smoothing of the arctic glacier in the Ice Age; it was unlikely to find it contiguous with volcanic formations.

Lou stood and retraced her steps.

Yes. There was the change. Suddenly she was standing on the igneous surface again. She could see the sparkling highlights of crystallized acid lavas—rhiolite and dacite.

Slowly she went a few steps in the other direction.

She was back on the granite.

She got to her knees again and went slowly forward. Now she found the place where the two kinds of rock abutted. It was astounding. At a glance, it looked like one flowed into the other. They were both the same gray color, both the same texture. But two large pieces of stone formed by different earth processes could not be welded together like two pieces of metal. Lou got down closer to the ground. Now she saw that where the rock changed character, a thin line of a grayish cementlike substance had been smoothed down, colored to match the other stone. It seemed to mask a crack.

"Boonie!" Lou exploded. "Over here! Bring me one of those rock hammers."

He came running and gave her the hammer. She tapped at the line between the two kinds of rock. A piece was chipped away. Lou struck again, knocking off a few more surface chips.

"Look . . ." Boonie said in a hush.

She saw it too. A slender crack appearing beneath the camouflaging cement.

She went on working along a straight line, then saw the crack turn a corner. She moved along, chipping out the cement, and turned another corner. Soon, another.

And came around again to meet the point where she had begun. Then she stood back for a look.

Set into the volcanic rock, inlaid almost as finely as a piece of marquetry, was a stone slab measuring about five feet on each side.

"It's like a hatchway," Boonie said, excitement rising. "The entrance must be under there."

"But how do we get in? No telling what the thickness is. It could weigh a ton—or five tons."

"Well, I'm not going to stand around wondering," Boonie declared, and started to heft his pick.

"No, wait! There must be an easier way, a mechanism of some kind—"

"Mechanism! Lou, this was made by Indians, or the Spanish—hundreds of years ago."

Again she ignored him. Of course there was an easy way in, always had been. People could enter and leave at will if they knew the secret.

But how could tons of rock be moved by primitive peoples without gears, motors?

How had the pyramids been built?

Lou started pacing, looking for some kind of hidden lever. She went in ever-widening circles. Until, about thirty feet from the slab, she caught sight of a small dead root. Though vegetation was sparse on this part of the mountain, here and there a small bush had grown in the dirt that collected in crevices. Some of the plants survived, some died. There were a number of dead roots around; she had taken no notice of them before. But now, on an impulse, she crouched and pulled on the thin stump, uprooted it from the ground.

It didn't come cleanly away. A long taproot anchored it deep into the earth, and as Lou pulled harder, she realized it wasn't a taproot, but a hempen rope.

Boonie had been watching, and as soon as he saw her hauling at the strand of hemp, he came over and tugged at it with her. They pulled seven or eight feet of rope from the ground. Then they heard a soft grating noise from the slab, and when they looked over they saw it pivoting, half of it dropping away into the ground, the other half swinging up. Evidently the enormous piece of rock was balanced on a central fulcrum, as finely as two sides of a scale. When closed, it was held in place by an underground catch attached to the rope.

"Christ," Boonie murmured. "That's it . . . you found it." He edged forward and stared into the opening as if afraid to enter. In an awed whisper he added, "It's real . . . it was really here. . . ."

Almost, she thought, as if he had never expected to find it. He had been comfortable with the dream—it was an escape as much as a goal. How was it going to be for him, Lou wondered, without the impossible dream to cherish?

"C'mon," she said. She led the way, lowering herself into the chink to one side of the pivoting slab.

They dropped into a narrow low-ceilinged passage, little more than a crawl space. It seemed to tunnel down gradually into the mountain, though away from the surface, without the reference point of a horizon line, it was difficult to tell whether the incline was steep or gradual. When Lou shone the searchlight ahead, the beam traveled on into endless darkness.

They went forward for a long time. The low ceiling and narrow walls induced a sense of imprisoning claustrophobia. The air was damp, and tainted with the pungent odor of old soil and fungus and decay. Yet they could feel the hint of a draft at their backs, following them down from the surface.

Lou couldn't tell how far they had gone when the ceiling began to rise and the walls to expand—inches to start, then enough so that they could walk erect and extend their arms. Then, at the farthest limit of its beam, the searchlight picked out a wall up ahead. At first it looked like a dead end. But within a few feet of the wall, the tunnel took a sharp right angle. They turned the corner.

A chamber. Lou stopped and shone the light upward: the roof was thirty feet above. Then she began to sweep the light in a slow circle along a gently curving earthen wall.

Suddenly the images of death loomed in front of her. It was the surprise, more than any sense of danger, that brought the short scream from her throat. In fact, the human skeletons propped together in a pile looked unreal. Still, Boonie immediately threw a protective arm around her.

"I'm okay," she said after a second. He didn't let go at once, however, stood holding her. If they had been anywhere else she might have kissed him, but instead she added, "Thanks." He let go.

The skeletons were stretched out, intact, the remains of five men who had probably been left here to starve to death. Around wrist and ankle bones there were iron shackles attached by chains to large stones set into the wall. The clothes had moldered away, but on a couple, the remnants of heavy leather boots still contained the foot bones, and around the pelvic bone of another there was a rotted strip of leather and an iron belt buckle engraved with an insignia. As Boonie knelt for a closer look at the buckle, he brushed against one of the skeletons. The skull was so lightly balanced on the upper section that even the light touch caused it to topple off. It fell onto the adjacent skeleton, and then that one disintegrated. The chain reaction continued, bones clattering against each other, the remains falling like dominoes in a line. Boonie grabbed up the belt buckle.

The insignia consisted of the outline of a coronet within which was engraved P II.

"Philip the Second," Lou said, remembering what she had read in Barney Coss's brochure. "He was King of Spain during the time the Indians chased the Spanish out of here."

"So these poor bastards"—Boonie nodded at the bone

pile—"must have been Spanish soldiers who were caught in the uprising."

They went on touring the chamber, but their only other find was the corroded metal head of an old pickax. Boonie turned it over in his hands. Etched into the metal, unevenly rusted away, was a forge mark. Fragments could still be read:

OOL C TTSB YLVANI

"I doubt the Spanish were buying their tools from a company in Pittsburgh," Boonie said. "This must have belonged to the old Russian himself."

He weighed the ax head in his hand and ran one hand along the pointed end as though it was a charm that would bring him luck. Then he turned to her eagerly.

"Well, hot damn, lady! Shine that light around! It's in here somewhere."

Lou swiveled the light slowly over the walls.

In a complete circle.

She swept the light up and down, then over the floor.

Nothing but bare walls, no cracks or niches; a solid earthen floor.

No gold. Not a nugget.

"Oh, Jesus, that's beautiful," Boonie moaned. "That fuckin' Russian took it all, cleaned the place out." He smacked his forehead, driving in the realization. "Of course he did! Why the hell wouldn't he?"

"Hang on, Boonie," Lou cut in. "Whoever was clever enough to install that stone gadget up on top could have built another secret passage down here."

"Sure, Lou," Boonie said sardonically. "That makes

sense. Another trick." His voice rose. "Hell, don't you think they'd figure out that for anybody who was hard-headed enough to find their way down here it'd be pointless to hide the gold further? Nobody'd come this far and then give up."

"Well, you sure sound like *you're* thinking about it."

Boonie pursed his lips, then shrugged and surveyed the walls. "Just doesn't seem logical," he muttered.

"Seven years for you, Boonie—is that logical? Or me, copping out on my job? Isn't that a little nuts?"

Boonie didn't answer, perhaps didn't hear. He had taken up the rusted pickax head, and as Lou went in one direction, he circled in the other, stabbing the point end into the moist earth, looking for a hidden cavity.

"Why do people go so crazy for the stuff?" Lou went on nervously. "Have you figured that out? Can't eat it, as the old saying goes. You can wear it, but it won't keep you warm."

"*Lou!*"

At his shout, Lou spun around. She saw the ax head sunk deeply into the wall, and as Boonie yanked it free a huge clod of earth tumbled away.

She joined him, pulling away more dirt. Soon they had bared a hole big enough to duck into.

Even before they entered, they both knew it would be there. As they hovered at either side of the passageway, Lou and Boonie looked at each other, taking a silent vow that neither could have articulated aloud, yet both understood. For a moment they linked hands, though the opening was not wide enough to crawl through together.

She handed him the searchlight and gave him a nod to precede her—take the honor of the first sight. He smiled at her, and went into the darkness. Grabbing on to his waistband, Lou let herself be tugged through.

The tunnel was very short this time. After shuffling forward only a few feet, Boonie emerged into a second chamber, slightly smaller than the first.

As Boonie straightened up ahead of her, Lou felt him go rigid. Then she straightened up herself and saw the dazzling, paralyzing vision filling the beam of the searchlight.

BOOK IV

The Poison of Elder Brother

CHAPTER 28

There was more of it than she had ever seen in her life.

Well!—more than almost anyone had ever seen, she guessed, except perhaps for the guards at Fort Knox. An absurd amount of it. So much that she was reminded of those fanciful constructions that were put in progressively designed playgrounds, shapes to be sat on and climbed over. Rows and rows of bullion. Ingot upon ingot upon ingot upon ingot. Piles here and there that were the height and width of a picnic bench. Others that were as wide and high as tables. And at the center, one enormous rectangular mound taller than she was, taller even than Boonie—and three or four yards long!

Sinking to his knees as if before an altar, Boonie shook his head and laughed in short hysterical bursts. "Oh, God . . . I never . . . Is that the most fan-fucking-tastic thing you ever saw? Will you just *look* . . . ?"

She couldn't take her eyes from it either. The gold of the Lost Russian. The trove of Spanish bullion that had been left behind more than four hundred years ago when the Indians, enslaved to work the mine, rebelled.

Elder Brother's gold.

The personal treasure of a god who had inspired the Indians to massacre their Spanish taskmasters.

Boonie put the searchlight on the ground, setting its adjustable handle so the beam would hold on the largest stack of bullion. Walking to the gold, he slowly stretched out his hand in a gesture both timid and eager, impatient to verify the reality.

Her thoughts occupied with Elder Brother—the Indian belief that the gold was poison—Lou almost cried out: *Don't!*

But already Boonie was grasping one of the ingots, pulling it down off the top mound.

No lightning bolts were loosed upon them. No thunder pealed. No tremors to signify the anger of the god who inhabited the mountain. Of course not. Karalyevski, too, had touched this gold. He had been in and out of this secret lair many times, and no god had punished him.

Superstition. A legend.

But the gold was real

Cradling the bar of bullion in his open hands, Boonie joggled it up and down, estimating its weight.

"Feel that," he said, bringing the bar to Lou. He handed it over gently, as though it were something delicate and alive.

Holding it, Lou could feel the strain reaching up her arms into her biceps. The bar was heavy, maybe forty or fifty pounds. Muscles tiring, she dumped it back into Boonie's hands.

"What do you think it's worth?" he asked. "A hunk like this . . . ?"

She ran through the mental calculation. Forty pounds, sixteen ounces to the pound, a total of 640 ounces. The last couple of years the value of gold had been averaging around four hundred dollars per ounce. So if the bar of gold were pure, that gave you a total of . . .

"A quarter of a million dollars," she blurted. "And you can add in another six or seven thousand dollars for every pound I shorted the estimate."

Boonie let out a soft whistle. "Just four," he murmured, staring down into his hands. "Four is a million." He lifted his head and scanned the room. "There must be billions here."

She looked at the stacks of bullion. The largest mound alone was stacked twenty ingots high, three times that many in length, and almost that much in width. A single level might have between one and two thousand ingots, and there were twenty levels. That central mound alone was . . . *at least ten billion dollars in gold*. And that didn't include the other stacks, table- and bench-high.

"Might be fifteen or sixteen billion worth," she said. Her voice sounded thin and unreal to her own ears.

Boonie gawked at it all for another second. Then he slipped out of his backpack, dropped the first bar of gold inside, and went to the large mound. "Well, shit," he whooped. "Let's load up. I can handle a million in one load. You can lug a bar. In two or three trips we can . . .

He stopped. In the middle of reaching to grab another ingot from atop the stack, he jerked his hand back like a thief caught in the act, and whirled to face the tunnel connecting the two chambers.

"What's wrong?" Lou asked quickly.

Boonie kept still, frozen in the pose of a soldier alert to an enemy lurking in the jungle. "A noise, I thought . . . from out there. . . ."

Lou listened too. Nothing. Yet she was struck by panic at the notion of some ghostly thing blocking off their escape, sealing the tunnel again with dirt, entombing them.

Without thinking to grab the searchlight, she ducked into the tunnel and raced to the outer chamber. Enough light crept through the small passage to see that nothing had changed; it was still empty—except for the disarrayed skeletons. She went back to Boonie.

"Just the side effects of gold fever," she said.

Boonie kept looking into the murky shadows.

Lou moved to him, puzzled. "Boonie . . . you okay?"

"For just a second there," he said distantly, "I almost forgot. I was ready for us to take it all if we could."

"Why not? It would just sit here otherwise, not doing anybody any good."

"But I promised Joe. He'd never have told me if I hadn't made the promise: 'Not too much.' " He glanced toward the tunnel. "I guess that was him, giving me a little reminder." Boonie raised his voice, calling out to the walls, "Okay, ol' buddy. A deal's a deal. I remember." He turned again to the mound of gold. "Just one more. How's that? Two altogether." He plucked up another ingot and held it out toward the shadows.

Lou looked on in dismay. This *was* a symptom of the irrationality inspired by the gold. Confronted by riches of such enormity, the mind could not assimilate the reality. Yet it was here, to be seen, touched, its existence undeniable. So if you were forced to accept this impossibility, then nothing seemed incredible. In the realm of the gold, all reality was redefined.

And for Boonie that meant the spirit of Joe Sundown could be here keeping watch, enforcing the battlefield promise.

Boonie fit the second ingot into his pack and looked at Lou.

"Less room left than I thought," he said, "but I can carry one for you, and you take another. That'll be the limit: two apiece."

"The limit?"

"The rest stays here," he said flatly.

He didn't simply mean here for now, she realized, but here forever.

"Boonie, I'm not going to let all the rest of this be—"

"Yes, you are, Lou. I gave my word to Joe when he told me how to find this place. I agreed to respect his belief. So I'm not taking more than just enough. Two bars. Half a million bucks' worth. That'll do me nicely. Now: do you want a couple of bars or not?"

A *couple—out of thousands? And the rest to be blown away in a week's time. . . .*

When Lou hesitated, Boonie muttered "Suit yourself" and started buckling his pack shut.

"Dammit," Lou declared. "I didn't make any promises. I found this place as much as you did—and I'm not going to leave it here to be lost forever."

Boonie slipped the pack on and picked up the searchlight from the floor. "Are you coming?" he said.

He meant it. To oblige his ghosts, he was ready to walk out and leave her in darkness.

But why argue? She knew the path to the treasure now. She could come back alone.

As Boonie started out, she grabbed one of the ingots from a low stack. It was slippery, and softer than she would have imagined. Her fingers left impressions on the surface. She pulled off the kerchief she always wore against dust on the mountain, a square of red Mexican cotton, and wrapped it around the bar. Then, holding the heavy weight with both hands, she hurried to stay behind him.

▲▲▲

They made straight for the surface. Before climbing out, Boonie paused and looked carefully around the rim of the entrance. He pointed out to Lou the mechanism that held the slab hatch in place—a round stone ball set in a crude wooden chute, with hempen rope tied to the dead root attached to the rear. When pulled, the stone ball went up the chute; afterward it rolled back down to the bottom. The matching edge of the slab had a small hollow into which the ball fit—in effect acting as a catch. It was a primitive version of the little round spring catches on kitchen-cabinet doors.

They climbed up and, pushing together, pivoted the stone hatch closed. Then they smeared mud into the crack to hide it, gathered their supplies, and stowed the gold bars in the knapsacks.

By the time they had finished, Lou was exhausted. She sat on the ground resting. Boonie sat nearby.

The silence between them was long and heavy. Then, surprisingly, Boonie broke into laughter. "So *I'm* crazy?" he said. "Hell, lady, I can see it dancing in your eyes—thinking about how you'll get back here to take the rest of it!"

She turned to him slowly. "Would you stop me?"

He smiled. "No, honey, 'cause I think there's just no way you can do it. That's twenty or thirty tons down there. The Spanish army could've moved it, takin' their time about it. But what're you gonna do? You can't handle it alone. And if you show it to anyone, ask them to help you—to lift maybe just a billion or two, not bein' too greedy—they'll just as soon kill you as help you by the time you're halfway down the mountain." His voice softened. "Get a handle on yourself. You can take enough to change your life a little—but not so much you build your life around it. That's what Joe knew. That's why he made me promise—"

She couldn't tolerate his sermonizing any more. "Bullshit! There's no earthly reason to just let it stay there—and disappear. What if I do want to make my dreams come true? To have a dozen houses, and my own jet plane, and a trunkful of diamonds that make Liz Taylor's look like Cracker Jack prizes. But that isn't all, Boonie. What about feeding hungry people, building hospitals, finding a cure for cancer? Sure. I'm going to take that gold and use it. It's right *there*." She hammered a fist down on the rocky ground so hard the pain shot up to her shoulder. "Maybe it's too much for you to dare. Maybe you don't want to be a king. But I'm not afraid. I'm coming back here and somehow I'm going to get that gold before it's lost forever."

Boonie nodded passively and hauled himself to his feet. "If that's what you want, Lou, good luck. But I'm out of it. I've got as much as I need. A couple of days to pack up, and I'll be on my way." He took a deep breath, scanned the vista of desert stretching away below, then the mountain ridges, and finally the clear blue sky. His gaze held for a second on a bird that was circling high above. "Time to say good-bye to it all," he said, and started walking away.

"To me too?"

He paused for a second to give her a smile and a regretful shrug. Then he kept going in the direction of his shack.

Lou got to her feet and shouldered the second knapsack. She glanced toward the entrance of the mine, then turned to watch Boonie disappear over a ridge.

She went in a different direction, to find her own way down.

▲▲▲

Where?

Lou stood inside the door of her house and glanced from the living room, along the hall toward her bedroom, over toward her office: which offered the best hiding place? It would have to be someplace Ben was certain not to stumble into. From the way he had been affected by Jesse Silvertrees, there was little doubt that if Ben happened to find the gold he would tell the Indian.

Lou looked at her wristwatch. Ben was due home from school soon.

Her eye fell on the rug by the fireplace, and she remembered the trapdoor beneath it. The perfect place. She had never mentioned the basement to Ben. After hearing from Mercy it was caved in, she'd guessed that crawling around down there might be dangerous.

Quickly she rolled back the rug. Kneeling, she wedged her fingertips between the planking and pried up the trapdoor. A dank musty odor floated up out of the dark.

The searchlight that she and Boonie had used was still in her pack. She took it out and shone it down through the trap. Below was a small room, about nine feet square, with an earthen floor. There was just enough height to stand upright in the room. Lying across the floor was a crudely made wooden ladder that could be used to exit the trap, then tossed down again.

She dropped the knapsack carefully through the trap and let herself down into the room, holding the searchlight. In the corner was a large wooden box. Something that must have been stored decades ago, perhaps by the pioneers who used to hide here to escape Indian attacks. The top was ajar and she could see that the box was filled with papers—printed forms of some kind that had been casually tossed in together, hundreds of them. She picked one out to read.

CLAIM FORM, the paper was headed, the words printed in old-fashioned Gothic type. Lou scanned down the sheet.

> The territory of Arizona grants to the undersigned the right to work as a mining claim for a period of one year the property on Salt Wash bounded by . . .

Lou's eyes roamed away from the definition of boundaries. How old was this paper? Whose was it? She looked for a date and name and found them both handwritten in ink across the bottom, though the passage of time had faded the color to such a pale blue that she had to peer closely at the letters and numerals to make them out. "August 10, 1892" was the date. The signature was a little harder to read. One by one she deciphered the letters, the difficulty enhanced by an overly ornate script. "O-L-E-X-O-N-O-E-R" seemed to be the given name (was it Indian?) followed by "K-O-R-E-L-V-E-V . . ."

No, wait, the second V was different from the first. She raised the paper to her eyes, then saw the little tail under the letter she had read first as a V. It was a Y.

She made the connection. Some of the roundish letters she had read as O's were actually fat, curved A's. Another was a D.

ALEXANDER KARALYEVSKI!

The old Russian. Had this house belonged to him?

Did Mercy know? She had said this basement was caved in. Maybe she had never been down here. If she had, surely she would have added these old papers to her collection of memorabilia.

Lou shuffled quickly through the papers in the box. The old claim forms were all the same, certifying the right of Alexander Karalyevski to prospect for gold on hundreds of worthless claims. She wondered why he had preserved so much useless paper.

Then, glancing around, she understood.

Shrewd enough to have kept the secret of the gold throughout his life, Karalyevski had no doubt anticipated the rumors about him. So he had put this secret room here as a decoy—a hiding place empty of gold to fool those who came across it into thinking he had none. A place to store away only the reams of worthless mining claims he had collected in the years before he was given the secret by his Indian lover Yo-tee-a. It was a joke on those who came looking—these documents proving that, as a prospector, the old Russian had been a complete failure.

Lou took the gold bar from the knapsack and put it at the bottom of the box, nesting it under all the paper. As she slid the loose top back onto the box, she heard the phone ringing. Hastily she climbed up the ladder, and ran to her study.

"Lou? Where the hell you been all goddamn afternoon?" It was Capper. "I was getting ready to send the cops up to Daniels' shack."

She fought to sound cool, normal. "Sorry I didn't check in, Cap. I . . . I had to spend a lot of time with Daniels."

"He didn't force you to, did he? Didn't—?"

No," she said. "He was a perfect gentleman."

"And what's the bottom line? Is he going to make trouble?"

"No, Cap. He'll go peacefully."

"How much is he walking away with?" Capper asked.

It caught Lou off guard and it popped into her head to say "half a million"—until she realized Capper was simply assuming Daniels had accepted a payoff from the company for his cooperation.

She smiled to herself. "I didn't have to give him a thing."

Not a thing, she repeated to herself as she cradled the phone.

Elder Brother had picked up the tab.

CHAPTER 29

The middle-aged clerk blinked at her, looked down to the small chunk of gold in his hand, and blinked again. He was a barrel-chested short man with slicked-back hair and the red splotchy nose of an alcoholic.

Lou had driven to Phoenix to meet Honegger's plane. He was flying in for an afternoon with his Japanese partner to show off the project's progress and to personally negotiate with David Lohaftapowe for the Tewani's land. Lou had given herself four hours leeway, telling Capper she needed the time for personal errands. From the Yellow Pages she had located the Iron Queen Assay Office, a division of a large mining company.

"Where'd you get this?" the clerk asked, weighing the gold in his hand.

"Well, I've bought several trunks of old junk," Lou said ingenuously. "I'm on a buying trip, antiques and things, and this was at the bottom of one of the trunks. I was wondering if it was valuable." She had gone back under the trapdoor, and using a kitchen knife, sliced off a small corner of the malleable bar. There had been so much of the stuff in the cavern that she could hardly believe it was real. She wanted to know just how much it was worth.

"This is an old piece," the clerk said. "Looks to me like wet-mill smelting."

The clerk told her it was a method used before heat-refining was invented, an ore-reducing technique perfected by the Spaniards who had mined in this territory hundreds of years ago. A rare sample, this chunk, probably had as much value as an antique as it did for the gold content.

"Haven't seen one like this in years," he added. "Last time musta been . . . oh, lemme see, four or five years ago. Fella from Coopersville brought it in." The clerk scratched his head, as if to jar his memory. "Parmalee . . . that's it, a fella named Parmalee. I remember 'cause it was kind of a famous case around here. This Parmalee got hisself killed . . . couldn'ta been more'n a couple of days after he was in here. Got his head split open." He laughed merrily. "And that got people talkin' that he'd discovered one of them old gold mines, one of those Legend Mountain stories."

Lou stared at him, too frozen to respond. Her mind whirred, recalling Hal Parmalee's assurances to his wife that they were going to be rich.

The assay clerk took her silence for ignorance. "You mean you never heard of that Lost Russian malarky?"

"No, no, I haven't," Lou said, forcing a smile. "I'm not actually from around here." She was anxious to have the information she'd come for. "So can you tell me how much this is worth?"

"I can tell you right now if it's more than ten karat," the clerk said. "If you don't mind me diggin' into it."

"No, go right ahead."

The clerk went to a worktable behind the counter,

set the gold down, and picked up a tool that looked like an awl. "I'm gonna cut it just a little, just far enough down in case it's plated. And then I'll drop a bit of nitric acid on it. If it don't discolor, then we know it's higher than ten-kay. If it turns brown, you got a lot of alloy. If it turns green, you ain't got no gold at all."

Yes, yes, Lou thought, hurry up.

"Dangerous stuff, this acid," he said, slipping his hands into heavy cloth gloves and uncorking an eyedropper from a brown bottle. "Burn the skin right off you."

It took only a moment before he turned around and took off his gloves.

"No color change," he said. "Better than ten-kay, all right. In fact, you got better than fifty percent gold. But I'm gonna have to heap-leach it to find out how much better, and we're backed up with ore samples this morning. How about you come back after lunch, around two?"

Honegger's plane was due at two-thirty: it would be a rush to the airport. "One-thirty?" Lou asked. "I have to get up to Flagstaff this afternoon for an auction."

"Okay, we can push it some," the clerk answered. He pushed a form across the counter. *Name, address, phone*. With the assurance of a con man, she gave the name of a woman who cut her hair in San Francisco, filled in the address of the Transamerica Tower, and used the phone number of her dentist, which for no reason had popped into her head. The clerk initialed the form and tore off a receipt. She paid him eight dollars in cash.

"See you later, then," he said cheerily, and disappeared through a swinging door behind the counter, taking with him her better-than-ten-karat gold.

She was running across the private air terminal as Honegger's Lear jet touched the ground. The clerk at the assay office had produced his results promptly at one-thirty. The gold had looked dirty not because it was loaded with alloyed metals, but because of grit mixed in during the smelting process. And the gold was soft for precisely the reasons Lou had suspected—because gold in its purest state was naturally malleable. Lou's sample, the clerk said, was virtually pure—.995 fine, according to the report, or twenty-four karat.

But no matter how much the gold was worth, she thought, its value paled in comparison to the risk of removing more from the mountain. The last person to dream of that had been Hal Parmalee. No matter what the townspeople thought of Dora's vendetta against the Indians, someone had indeed slammed an ax into her husband's skull—someone who knew he had found the mine.

Didn't Parmalee's death point to someone else knowing the location of the mine? The Tewani, perhaps, who would kill rather than see their god's home defiled.

Whoever it was, sooner or later they would notice the evidence of Lou's discovery: chips in the stone door that lifted to reveal the shaft, and maybe even the absence of a few bars of gold.

As Lou stepped onto the tarmac toward Honegger's plane, her mind arrived at the most chilling possibility. She and Boonie might already be marked for the same fate as Hal Parmalee and all the others who had accidentally come too close to the secret of the mountain.

▲▲▲

Honegger made fast work of David Lohaftapowe, cutting the price for the Tewani land by two and a half million dollars. Lou took the doctor aside to apologize, but he merely grinned and pulled a piece of paper from his wallet. He had jotted the result he expected before the meeting, and on the paper had listed a price of six and a half million, along with several concessions: free rent on prime retail space in Legend City's downtown and an Indian museum to be built and paid for by the Honegger Corporation. Honegger, assuming he held the upper hand with the price, had agreed down the line.

At the site Honegger toured the east face of the mountain with his partner, Y. E. Katsumoya. The Japanese developer, who wore a plain gray suit and a yellow golf hat, smiled at everything Honegger said. Lou, sunk into her own thoughts, could only gaze away toward the ridge where she had gone with Boonie the day before—the shallow cavity hiding the secret entrance to the mine.

"Oh, yes, he was a wonderful old character, Karalyevski," Honegger was saying to Katsumoya. "The kind American history is full of."

Lou snapped from her reverie. He was talking about the mine.

"We'll get a lot of public-relations mileage out of it," Honegger went on, "the Royal Russian mine."

Lou turned. What had Honegger said? The *Royal* Russian mine?

"You mean the Lost Russian," she corrected him.

"Ah, yes," Honegger said, smiling. "A linguistic slip. Of course I meant the *Lost* Russian. Sometimes I shift languages in my head without even thinking."

Lou persisted. "Shift languages? I don't understand."

"Well, because of the character's name—the Russian who found it—Karalyevski."

"Sorry, I'm still missing the point," Lou said, and the Japanese partner nodded in agreement.

"Karalyevski," Honegger repeated. "That's what it means in Russian. It's the word for 'royal.' "

Lou nodded mutely as the two men continued walking toward the end of the road, where the last holes had been drilled. She lagged behind them, her mind turning cartwheels. The pieces began shifting and fitting together into neat designs, like shapes of a kaleidoscope setting at last into a pattern.

Royal . . . Karalyevski.

An account in the name of A. Royal.

A vast fortune in a Boston bank.

Alexander Karalyevski was A. Royal.

Lou thought back to the story of the Russian's life, the colorful yarn she had read so long ago in a tourist brochure. He had been in love with an Indian girl, Yo-tee-a, who had betrayed the riddle of the shadows and led him to the mine. And they had cut out her tongue and left her to die.

Or *had* she died? In the story, Karalyevski had found her near death and taken her back to his cabin. Perhaps then he had been able to save her.

Lou took a step forward. Honegger and Katsumoya were engaged in laughing banter, gesturing their arms over the valley they owned.

Roy to Royal. She had changed her name to hide the identity.

Lou thought of her first meeting with Mercy Roy that afternoon at the ranch. Mercy had grown angrily passionate on only one subject.

They just don't get treated right around here, they get the worst of everything.

Half-breeds.

And now, beyond doubt, the root of that angry passion came clear. Mercy Roy was herself a half-breed, the child of the Tewani girl Yo-tee-a and the fabled Russian, Alexander Karalyevski.

The tumblers clicked and the lock opened. And Lou understood. Yo-tee-a had survived, been sent to live far from the danger of retribution. And she had passed on the secret of the mine to her daughter.

Later Mercy Roy had come west. Now Lou knew why Mercy had been such a generous benefactor to the Tewani; the Indians could not touch their own gold, but she could use it for them. Could that have been her role—as perhaps it had been her father's—middleman to Elder Brother? As long as only she handled the gold, didn't plunder it greedily, and used it for the Indians' benefit, there would be no "poisonous" effect—as the Indians saw it—no danger of the wrath of Elder Brother. That could explain why she had remained alone, unmarried—frightened that anyone she wed could demand ownership of the gold. She, too, must have known of the Arizona inheritance laws that David Lohaftapowe had bitterly cited, laws that deprived anyone with Indian blood of his property.

Again Lou recalled her first visit to the Double Diamond Ranch—and the burial bowl on the mantel. It had not been purchased by Mercy—it was a religious reliquary, a symbol used in the ceremony of death for her own mother.

For sixty years she had protected her secret, Lou thought. By any means necessary.

Did that include murder?

"I was going to call it Honegger City," the thickly accented voice was saying. Honegger and his partner were returning along the drilling road. "But I'm not *that* vain, and I thought it would be so much better to exploit the local history, the legends. It gives people something to believe in and makes a good story for the advertising, when we're ready." They stopped at her side. "Don't you think so, Lou?"

Yes, Lou agreed, Honegger was right. It made a good story.

CHAPTER 30

At the top of the great bowl in which the Double Diamond ranch was nestled, Lou stopped. She wondered if Mercy could hear a car approaching. Below, the lights of the main house glowed, and Lou could just make out horses in the corral. She hesitated a second longer, then started down.

Maybe you'd better take it on a month-to-month basis.

Now Lou understood why.

She parked at the base of the driveway and stepped out. She couldn't help noticing the emptiness of the country around her. She felt isolated, alone. Perhaps it was dangerous coming here, but she had to have the answers. And she couldn't really believe Mercy was a murderer.

She heard a pounding noise behind her, the crack of metal on wood, and caught a glimpse of a lone slender figure behind the barn. A shot of anxiety pulsed through her and brought her to a halt.

At the fence rimming the barn, Peter White Lightning worked at repairing a post, hammering a crossbeam into place. The handyman's surliness—on that first day and then, later, in town—ballooned with new meaning: if Mercy Roy were guilty of any crime, it would have been the handyman who carried out her orders.

Still, Lou continued up the stone path to the front door. She touched the bell panel in the adobe frame.

Mercy answered, dressed in riding clothes misted by fine dust. "Lou! What an unexpected pleasure," she said, beaming. "What brings you out this way? Come on in."

"I was . . . just, uh, on my way home . . . from Phoenix," Lou fumbled for innocent words.

"Good timing," Mercy boomed heartily. "Dinner's on the stove for me and Peter. Why don't you join us?"

Exuberant as always, Mercy gestured toward the dining area at the rear of the house.

"No . . . no, thank you," Lou said uneasily. "I have to get home to Ben."

"You'll have a drink then, won't you, sit a bit?" Mercy said, and when Lou hesitated, looked at her peculiarly, puzzled that Lou should have dropped in if she didn't want a friendly visit.

Lou followed her into the large beamed-ceiling living room.

"Gin and tonic?" Mercy called out from the sideboard.

"Fine," Lou said, her eyes drifting over to the pictures of the old Russian, the tintypes and newspaper clips. A collection of local memorabilia, Mercy had elaborately explained. Except that now Lou could see the resemblance, the high forehead and broad chin shared by father and daughter alike.

Mercy returned with the two drinks. "I heard the great Mr. Honegger himself paid a visit to our town today. You must be pretty excited, what with all the activity and the blasting this week."

"Yes . . . it's been quite a day," Lou said. She sat on the couch next to Mercy and sipped her drink.

She could put off the confrontation no longer.

"Mercy, there's something that's been nagging at me." She gave the old woman a very direct look. "Why did you change your name before you came out west?"

"Change?" Mercy asked blithely.

"It was Royal before you got here, wasn't it?"

Mercy registered nothing more than bemusement. "Goodness, did you drive all the way out here just to ask me that?"

"Well, I *am* curious. Didn't your name used to be Royal?"

"Yes, indeed it was," Mercy said. "How did you happen to come across it?"

Lou stared down into her drink. "One of our rent checks to you ended up in Boston somehow," she said, and gave a laugh. "Our computers go haywire if all the dollars and cents don't add up to the penny. So we had to track it down. It turned up in an old trust account in the name of Royal."

Mercy chuckled. "Banks! You'd think with all their electronic marvels they could deposit a check without making a mistake."

"But it was your account," Lou said. "Why *did* you change your name?"

"Well, Lou, can't you guess?" Mercy said lightly. "Imagine coming to a place like this sixty-two years ago with a name like Royal. There are nice plain folks here, and I wanted to settle among them. I didn't want anyone thinking I was some fancy high-hat from the east putting on airs. And changed my name. I wanted to be accepted."

Lou couldn't let the lie rest. "No, Mercy," she said,

"that's not the reason. You know it isn't. It's because Royal was your father's name, too. And that was just a little too close for comfort."

Mercy's gaze flickered for an instant and the friendly sparkle in her eyes faded. Setting down her drink, she stood and crossed the room to her collection of photographs. Her hands chose the largest one, a rotogravure print of the old prospector in a heavy gilded frame. It was a long moment before she answered.

"How did you find out?" she murmured finally, her eyes still averted from Lou.

Lou explained the irony—a mere slip of the tongue, Honegger's facility with languages—that had led her to the truth.

"I suppose it was inevitable," Mercy sighed at last. "No secret keeps forever, maybe. It's true, Lou—exactly the way you spelled it out. And now I'll answer the question you really wanted to ask. Yes, I know where it is. I've known since I was a child, ever since my mother told me."

She settled onto the couch and went on. "I was fifteen. My father came to Boston for my birthday. He didn't show up very often, I guess because he was afraid of being followed. They were always trailing him, the ones who thought they could somehow steal his secret. And even in the tribe there were a few who knew my mother was alive, and they wanted to kill her. You see, she wasn't supposed to know the secret herself, but she believed it had been given to her for a reason, that it was Elder Brother's desire for her to find someone to help the Tewani use the poisonous gold. And from the moment I was told, I understood my mission—to come west and live near the mine and guard its secret."

"You've done that for sixty years," Lou said. "And

have you protected that secret—no matter what you had to do?"

Mercy shook her head. "The secret kept itself. Just as it always has. Even my father didn't *find* the mine. He was told where it was. By my mother."

The confession had come so matter-of-factly, Lou thought, without hesitation. "You aren't worried that I know," she said.

"Not at all, dear. Why would I worry?"

Lou wondered how Mercy would respond if she thought she was being threatened. "What if I told someone?"

"Lou, you can tell my secret to everyone, if you like." Mercy smiled faintly. "But I don't think you will."

An implied threat? Or did Mercy already know that Lou had found the gold, too, and would protect the secret? "Mercy, you seem so relaxed about all this. . . ."

"Yes," Mercy said simply.

"But someone has been killing people—dozens of people over the years—to protect that secret."

Mercy leaned sharply forward. "Are you saying *I* harmed those people? No, Lou, it wasn't me. Only greed killed them, the greed of prospectors or the greed of developers who wanted to change this place into something it was never meant to be. Nothing else hurt them. Only greed, and the spirit of the mountain."

"And Hal Parmalee?" Lou said. "Did a spirit kill him, too?"

The singling out of Parmalee among all the mountain's victims stunned the indignant expression from Mercy's face. "He was different. Hal Parmalee was different."

"How?"

Mercy leaned closer, putting her hand on Lou's. "I

knew Hal well. He was a fine man, raised two fine boys, worked his ranch." She shook her head. "But this gold fever took ahold of him, I don't know how it started, but it was terrible. He stopped minding the ranch and spent his every spare minute up there looking for the gold." She stopped and put a hand to her forehead, squeezing her temples as if the memory itself pained her. "Peter used to watch a lot . . . he'd watch to see if anyone was climbing around up there. And he was there the day Hal found the entrance to the mine. But he didn't hurt him, just came back and told me. And I said keep an eye on him, that's all, don't do anything." She paused and turned a sincere gaze on Lou. "I figured Hal would take no more than a bar or two, and that was fine. And because I believed that Hal had been allowed to find the gold—not steered away like everyone else—I never interfered."

Something in Mercy's confession had snagged Lou's attention. *Allowed*. Hal Parmalee had been *allowed* to find the gold.

Allowed by whom?

Mercy continued: "But Hal had gone over the edge, down into that snake pit of greed where gold turns people's minds inside out. It broke my heart when Peter told me about it, Hal hitching up a string of mules to clear out the mine. Peter caught him. He argued with Hal then, and warned him to pack up only a few bars and move far away, sell the ranch and build himself a nice spread somewhere and forget about the mine. That's when Hal attacked him, started swinging his ax and shovel. And Peter had to defend himself. . . ."

The anguish in Mercy's voice was not lost on Lou. It pained her that a man had been slain, and Lou found herself sympathizing. Was Parmalee any less guilty than the handyman who had killed him in self-defense? And how could she judge anyone—when her own fever was drawing her to the same dream?

"Mercy," Lou observed, "the gold took you over, too. You've stayed here just to be near it, watch it—when the world could have been yours. . . ."

Mercy reached out and put a hand on Lou's. "Dear child, can you still not understand? Even before I was born, my fate was written. You know the legend—the gold is poison to the Indians. It was in Elder Brother's plan to save his people from corruption. But he didn't want to deny them the benefits. So it cannot be touched by the Indians. But when my mother told my father the secret, he saw his duty. And as his offspring, I've seen mine."

"But . . . your mother was punished by the tribe."

"No," Mercy said sadly. "That wasn't true. My mother was mutilated by some white prospectors who abducted her and tried to get her to tell them the secret. After it happened, though, and people assumed it was the vengeance of her own tribe, the story was allowed to spread. Another deterrent to anyone who might deal carelessly with the Tewani."

Lou could feel no more condemnation of Mercy. The old woman had sacrificed her life to the legacy of her birth, and Lou's heart went out to her. But in two days the gold would be blasted to kingdom come, gone forever. Unless they made plans to retrieve it now. Should she tell Mercy of her discovery? Wouldn't Mercy sooner divide the gold, let Lou keep her share, than forsake it all?

"You must be devastated by what's going to happen."

"Happen . . . ?"

"Mercy, I can't stop the blasting from going ahead,

not unless I tell Honegger why, and either way, the mine is going to be lost to you. Before that happens, don't you want to start moving the gold out, get Peter up there . . . ?"

Mercy shook her head calmly. "No, Lou, I don't have to do anything."

"For God's sake, Mercy, you don't know how powerful those blasting charges are. We're benching that mountain, we're going to lift thousands of tons of rock and shake that damn thing to its core. Wherever that gold is—"

"Is where it'll stay," Mercy interrupted with utter certainty. "The gold, like the mountain, is Elder Brother's. He will keep it safe."

Lou gaped at the old woman. Mercy was actually going to entrust the fate of the mine to her mountain god. But Lou had seen the effects of powerful explosives—and she had never seen them stopped by a god.

"Go home, Lou," Mercy said then, "go home and don't worry. Everything will work out all right."

Lou rose automatically, and Mercy, maternally draping an arm around her shoulders, escorted her to the door.

"I promise you," Mercy said as she saw Lou out, "things will happen as they must."

▲▲▲

She drove home in the unquiet darkness. To the left, beyond the desert expanse, was the mountain. Ever-present. Eternal. It almost seemed to be moving alongside her, like an escort.

Of all Mercy had said, one word edged like a splinter into Lou's consciousness.

Allowed.

Those who found the mine, Mercy said, had been allowed to do so by the spirit of the mountain.

So why had she and Boonie been led to the hidden door?

Why had they been allowed?

CHAPTER 31

On his way from English to social studies, Ben saw the crowd of kids by the bulletin board and went over.

OFFICIAL NOTICE said the words stamped in bold red letters across the top of a printed sheet. Underneath was a warning issued by county authorities that this Friday, the day after tomorrow, at some time after seven A.M., high explosives were to be detonated on Legend Mountain and all persons were accordingly informed hereby that entering the area was strictly forbidden.

To the other kids it was an opportunity for a party. The younger kids were planning bicycle caravans. The juniors and seniors were all talking about cutting school, climbing into their four-wheel-drive pickups, buying a bunch of sixpacks, and heading out to a nice safe spot in the desert to watch the fireworks.

But Ben brooded about it the rest of the day in school, and then on the bus ride home. He regretted that Jesse had been absent from school today; he would have liked to say something to show he was sympathetic—though what could you say? "I'm sorry your god's home is gonna be blown up." Great. The only thing that would count with Jesse was action; that was the Indian way. It occurred to Ben now that Jesse's not showing up at school was probably tied into the blasting—maybe a gesture of repudiation against all those who could plan and permit the sacrilege.

Arriving home, Ben clumped through into his room, tossed down his book bag, and threw himself on the bed. Shit! What could he do to help Jesse? He'd sworn an oath to do anything. Some kind of sabotage, maybe, threatening notes to the construction company signed "Elder Brother." Or running away, leaving word that he would never reappear if the blasting was not abandoned.

Though at moments Ben wondered why he should care so much. Was Jesse *really* his friend? Hadn't everything he'd done been to serve his own ends? To save a mountain.

Only a mountain.

But Ben couldn't shake the feeling that if he didn't prevent the mountain from being destroyed, terrible things were going to happen.

His mother might die—as Jesse had warned.

The longer Ben was alone in the house, the more the feeling grew. It was as if a bomb was planted right here, ticking away.

More out of a need for distraction than out of hunger, he went to the kitchen and started making a BLT. Then he heard the noise from the yard, a sound like a sheet flapping in the wind. Moving along the counter, he scanned the yard through the window. Nothing to see but the silhouette of the mountain, faintly outlined against the evening sky. The yard was empty. He started to pull away . . .

. . . and heard the flapping again just as his eye was

drawn to the fluttering blur of white in the corner of the yard. Something on the fence. A towel, maybe, that had blown off the laundry line and snagged on a fencepost. Leaning across the counter, Ben pressed his face closer to the glass, trying to see past the reflection of the kitchen lights.

The fluttering stopped.

He could see the outline of the fence, but now there was nothing . . .

No, wait. Nothing, my ass. Now he had a fix on it, and as it slowly flexed its wings, spreading them out to their full span, he wondered how it was possible that, even for a second, he could have missed seeing it.

The white eagle.

The same one he had seen the very day he had arrived in Coopersville.

Holy shit. It was the biggest goddamn bird he had ever seen. The span of those wings looked as wide as the door on a two-car garage.

The bird folded its wings again and for the next couple of minutes held its perch without moving, not a single feather. Ben stayed at the window, transfixed by the sight. He stared so intently that his eyes began to feel strained. And along with the deepening of the twilight, and the reflection on the inside of the window, this strain produced an odd illusion. At moments, the whole image of the bird seemed to shimmer and flicker, even to fade away. But when he pressed his face up to the glass, the bird was right there—though its stark whiteness cut only intermittently through the dark, like a torch flame in a high wind, flaring brighter with some gusts, then nearly dying away with others before being revived.

After five minutes, the eagle was still on the fence,

and Ben decided to try going outside. Chances were, of course, that as soon as he did, the eagle would fly away. But being a passive observer from behind the window had lost its kick. The challenge now would be to see how close he could get. He turned off the gas under the bacon pan, moved slowly across the kitchen, and eased out the back door. It closed softly behind him, the noise as it met the frame almost imperceptible—

But the eagle's head darted around instantly. Small as the movement was, it startled Ben. Having that beak arched toward him felt a bit like being threatened with a sword. Each of the talons gripping the fence rail looked as big and as sharp as a stevedore's loading hook.

For a minute Ben stood still and stared at the eagle. The eagle looked back—so perfectly still, Ben thought, that it looked stuffed.

Finally Ben dared a slow half-step forward.

The bird allowed it. Not a move.

Ben took another step, and a third. And then continued steadily across the yard.

The scream froze him, a shrill sustained note that rose out of the bird's throat like an alarm going off.

Ben stood stark still, listening until the faint echo of the eagle's cry had died somewhere out in the desert.

It occurred to him now how remarkable it was that the bird hadn't flown away. Wouldn't its most natural reflex of defense be to escape?

This one had not only come down right beside the house, it was lingering.

As Ben went closer, the eyes of the eagle glittered through the gathering dark with the reflected light from the kitchen window. No more than sparkling pinpoints at first, but as Ben reached the halfway point between the house and the fence, he could see details in the eyes, the golden coronas around their black centers, and a tiny silhouette—the reflection of his own outline.

The closer he got, the more Ben's attention was locked onto the eyes. The huge snowy body of the bird melted out of consciousness. He saw only the two polished black orbs within the golden rings—and the reflected silhouette, growing larger as Ben advanced. In a corner of his mind, he was half-aware of slipping into a kind of hypnotic state. He tried then to look away, but couldn't. He walked toward the shadowy silhouette in the eagle's eyes as though down a dark tunnel to meet a waiting friend.

And then he saw the feathers jutting up from the head of the figure reflected in the bird's eye. Like the badge of feathers worn on the headband of an Indian brave.

Suddenly he realized it couldn't be his own silhouette mirrored in the eye. There must be someone behind him.

Jesse!

Ben spun around.

No one. He was alone in the yard.

But he was sure he had seen . . .

He whirled back again to face the eagle.

There was nothing on the fence.

Without a sound, it was gone. No cry, no flapping of wings.

Frantically backtracking across the yard, he bumped into the door behind him, slipped inside, and slumped into a chair, trying to catch his breath. There wasn't a doubt in his mind about what he had seen. That eagle had been some kind of Indian spirit—a messenger from Elder Brother with a final warning.

Oh, God, what could he do to convince his mother to leave the mountain alone?

flap

The noise again. Wings. Ben sat bolt upright in his chair. The eagle was in the house with him.

He turned slowly around, expecting to see it perched on the refrigerator, like those birds lined up on the jungle gym in that old Hitchcock movie they showed on television. But the only thing atop the refrigerator was the huge Dutch oven his mother had lugged from San Francisco.

He heard it again, the snapping rustle of wings. And then the realization came: it wanted *him*.

"Please!" Ben cried out. "It's not my fault! I tried to stop it!"

The moment he heard his own loud call, the spell was broken. He was flipping out, for Chrissakes. Actually begging for mercy from an Indian spirit he imagined to be flying around inside an eagle . . . ?"

C'mon! Cool it, he commanded himself, and took some slow deep breaths.

Better.

He thought back over everything that had happened since he had first seen the eagle fifteen minutes ago. Had he really witnessed anything impossible? Okay, the eagle had come down right outside on the fence; that was pretty stupendous, not your everyday event. But from there on he'd simply psyched himself. Who could say what kind of shadow he'd seen reflected in the tiny mirror of a bird's eye?

The flapping noise broke the silence again. It was coming from the living room, Ben thought. It didn't frighten him this time. He knew it had to be something real, explainable.

He left the kitchen table and walked into the living room. In the dark he scurried to the first table where he knew there was a lamp. Switching on the light, he scanned the room, seeking the cause of the noise. The logical explanation.

Of course, there it was. In front of the fireplace. The rug was turned back at one corner, and one of the glass patio sliders nearby was ajar. A breeze coming through must have flipped back the rug. Or it could have been a small animal that had gotten into the house, a desert mouse or a lizard.

Guessing the animal would still be near, Ben approached the rug warily, and with the toe of one sneaker poked gingerly at the folded corner. When he saw no sign of an animal, he bent to straighten the rug again.

Where the floor had been bared, he noticed a crack cutting across the wooden planking. Shoving the rug back farther, he saw the whole outline of the trapdoor. He gaped at it. It might be the entrance to a hidden tunnel. Or maybe some past inhabitant of the house had been a murderer who used this place to bury his victims.

From beneath the floor came a burst of the flapping sound.

The same animal that had flipped the rug must have nudged up the trapdoor and crawled beneath it.

Logical. Explainable.

But he couldn't help it now: the fear was rising again. Yet with it came a need to find out what was down there. Reaching over to the set of fire tools by the hearth, Ben armed himself with the poker. Then, wedging the fingers of his free hand into the crack that framed the trap, he lifted the door.

Light slanted through the square opening into the

small room below. Ben saw a fallen ladder lying on the earthen floor, and a box stuffed with papers against a wall. Nothing moving, though, nothing that could have caused a noise. Unless an animal was burrowing in the box of papers.

Hanging on to the cut edge of the planks, Ben let himself down through the hole and jumped the last few feet to the ground below. Immediately he moved to the box and grabbed up a handful of papers to examine. Within seconds he realized what they were—a bunch of old claim forms belonging to the old Russian himself! If they were here . . . then this must have been the prospector's house. And if he had saved these claim documents, there could be only one reason: one of them must be the claim that turned out to contain the lost mine. . . .

Rummaging some more in the box, he saw there were hundreds and hundreds of forms. How would he ever find the one . . . ?

Suddenly he saw a flash of color through the white. Shoving the paper aside, he came to a red Mexican scarf wrapped around some rectangular object. He grabbed the bundle to lift it out, but the weight resisted him more than he had anticipated. His clutching fingers succeeded only in pulling the piece of fabric away.

He stared at the material in his hand. His mother's scarf? Just a couple of days ago he'd seen her wearing it tied around her neck.

So the existence of this room wasn't going to be his secret, after all. In fact, it was *hers*. So she had known about this room and never told him.

Ben glanced back into the box to see what the scarf had been wrapped around.

The sight of the gold stunned him. Slowly he put out his hand, needing to make sure it wasn't an illusion that would vanish as mysteriously as the eagle. His fingers slid over the smooth yellow metal, tingled with the thrill of touching it.

Where? Where had she . . . ?

Then abruptly he jerked his hand back. Poison, the legend called it—and the legend, Ben knew now, was true. The gold was Elder Brother's, and it was the spirit of the god that had appeared tonight to lead the way to the treasure that had been stolen from him.

The realization crushed down upon Ben. His mother had found the gold and kept it a secret. But Elder Brother knew, and would destroy her.

He was torn apart by anger at her deception—and his need to save her. What could he do? Would it make any difference if he warned her again, told her that the Indian spirit had come to reclaim his gold?

There was only one person he could go to for help. But he would have to arrange it without his mother knowing, or she would try to stop him. It would have to wait until tomorrow at school.

Jesse would know what to do. Jesse had the *diyi*, didn't he?

CHAPTER 32

Lou stood in the doorway watching, saving the images for souvenirs. Boonie had let his guard down, hadn't even heard her approach. It wasn't until she shifted her feet that he caught the movement from the corner of his eye and turned from the table.

"I came to say good-bye."

"We already said it, didn't we?"

His bluntness didn't hurt anymore, it was so much a part of him. She had walked up to his cabin, seen the open door, and assumed he was gone. The disappointment had been so strong that she was physically weakened by it. Now she wanted to run in and embrace him, but that kind of emotion was far outside the boundaries they had established.

"Then I'll . . . I'll say good-bye again," she said. "I had to be up here this morning anyway, to check the blasting circuits."

He turned back to the pine table, where he was roping together his old pots and pans, hobo-style. "So it blows on schedule, huh? You couldn't manage to put it off until all your gold was tucked away safe?"

"Not yet," she said.

"But that's only because you're still sittin' on the secret, I suppose. I mean, if you just told somebody—the *right* somebody—that it was there, you could do it. Like the big boss, Honegger. He'd wait for it, wouldn't he? Only then you'd have to pay for the favor. He might even want most of it for himself, and you can't bear to let it go. . . ."

"Boonie," she said softly, to get him to look at her again. To make him stop cudgeling her with reminders of her greed. To make him be gentle again. Oddly, she recognized that her feelings for Boonie ran deeper and were more engulfing than any of those ever aroused by Matt—for that matter, by any man. Love? Of a kind, yes. Though in the language she and Boonie spoke together, the word seemed not to exist.

He went on berating her. "And, Christ, if *he* had it, can you just imagine what he'd do? Ten, twelve billion. Shit, that's just about enough to build himself another five or six of these cities. Wouldn't you say that's just what he'd do—fuck up another half-dozen beautiful places on God's earth?"

"Boonie!"

He turned his eyes to her again, and she could no longer deny her feelings. She bolted from the doorway and threw herself against him.

He caught her and gathered her in, brought her close.

"I wish there was something else," she whispered. "Don't you understand? I wish there was something else to want besides that gold, something that meant more. I wish . . ."

She was unable to bring forth the words, though they were in her mind. Finally she simply pressed her lips to his. She felt the welling of a warm dampness between her thighs. Any moment she expected him to lift her up as he had before, and carry her to the bed. She longed for it.

She clutched at him, pleading softly. "Stay, Boonie. Be with me."

He regarded her passively. "Is that the choice? Me or the gold?" He gave her his slow smile, the one with all the charm. "Or since it's too late to get the rest, have you decided to marry me for my money?"

She tried to laugh, and failed. "No, Boonie, it's more, honestly. . . ."

He gave her a long measuring glance. "Lou, you're looking for something, but it isn't me. Maybe it's not your job anymore either, but I can't fill what's missing."

"But you could, dammit!" she cried. "We could help each other. I'd give you back something you lost, too!"

"How? With the power of love? That's for kids, Lou. Not us."

He turned away from her then. With a quick glance at a jumble of tools spread out on the table, he snatched up a screwdriver and walked out of the cabin. She knew it was a pretext to stop her from talking, but she couldn't let him go so easily.

She followed him outside, where he was unfastening a rusted thermometer from the side of the shack. "Boonie, I can't help it, I know it seems impossible, but I care for you, I really do, I think I'm in—"

"Don't," he cut in quickly, his teeth clenched as he spoke. "Don't say it."

"You'd rather be alone," she said mockingly.

"Right," he said.

"Then why is it whenever we touch I can feel something under all your toughness and anger coming back to life?"

He pressed the blade of his screwdriver hard into the notch of a rusty screw, his whole face contorting as he tried to twist it. "Shit, Lou," he whispered. "Stop."

"Why deny it, Boonie? When two people felt what we did . . ."

He pulled the screwdriver away from the side of the shack. "I don't know what we felt." His voice was low. " 'Least I don't know what I did."

"But if you let yourself—"

"No," he said quietly. "It's not there. Forget it." There was a silence as he looked down at the ground, and when he looked up it was the first time that his eyes carried no warnings, no threats, no secrets—the first time he looked completely vulnerable. "Nobody realizes," he said, "and they still don't. But how do you explain? Everybody wants to believe good things can't die, love conquers all. You want to believe it, don't you, Lou?"

He waited for an answer, and she had to nod.

He gave her a thin smile before he looked down again. "I believed it, too. Once."

He turned and stared into the middle distance.

"Boonie?"

"I even remember the day I stopped believing." He paused and let out a short laugh. "A Thursday. The reason I remember is that we had a captain who was crazy about softball, and he'd gotten a league together from a bunch of different squads. We played every Monday and Thursday, and since I was starting pitcher for my squad—and there were two of us—we switched off. I always started on Mondays. Except this one day. Kinberg, the other pitcher, had gotten killed in a search-and-destroy the Tuesday after the last game." He shot her a glance again. "Do you get it? In the morning, softball on the playing field. Then after lunch you climb into the chopper and they ferry you to the zone and you kill a few VC—or maybe they kill you—and if they don't, then it's back to the camp to think about why you lost, not the battle sometimes, but the game, because it all happens so fast you don't know where you are." He looked away to the meadow as if, just beyond the edge of the mountain, he could see the other side of the world. "My arm was still sore because I'd just pitched a few days before—and we used to play hard because if we won the captain felt good and he'd give us extra leave. But that day . . . well, I didn't have the stuff, so the other team was belting me all over the place. The captain was steaming. But he wouldn't take me out—like he just wanted to rub it in, make me realize that if Kinberg hadn't . . ." Boonie stopped and shook his head, as though reminding himself that none of this mattered. "Anyway, by the end of the game the captain was in a bad mood, I mean really black. Maybe that sounds strange, too—if you weren't there. But in Nam if there was anything that meant something to you—anything that wasn't mixed up with the death and blood—then it became everything. For some guys it was a woman, often as not just some whore up in Saigon they'd turned into a Madonna in their heads. For others it was dope, or poker, or books, or their guitar. And for the captain it was his fuckin' softball, and when he lost, it was like he hated the world. So that's how he was when we got ordered out on another S-and-D. There were supposed to be some VC harassing traffic on one of the roads, and we were told to smoke 'em out."

Boonie's gaze was very distant. He was looking toward a place that seemed even farther than the other side of the world. "We'd been out about an hour when we got raked by small-arms fire. We ran about a hundred yards up the road and saw a bunch of women and kids squatting by the side, cooking soup or something in metal pots over fires. The captain brought up the translator and started interrogating these poor people, really going at 'em because this was about where the shooting had come from and he was sure they were VC. The women said they were refugees from a village the VC had taken over, but the captain wasn't getting the answers he wanted, and he was already pissed off about the goddamn softball game, so he kicked over their pots with all the food these people had. Then the kids got scared and scattered, and the women started running after them."

Boonie was talking rapidly. "For about ten seconds the captain stood watching them, and we thought he was gonna leave it at that, let 'em all go—what the hell, some women and kids. But then he ordered us to stop them. They had such a head start that we all thought he had to be kidding; we couldn't run fast enough to bring 'em back. But some of the men started to dash forward and then the captain screamed, 'I didn't say *catch* them, I said *stop* them. And that's an order!' For a second nobody moved, and maybe nobody would have . . . but then across the paddy the small arms started rattling again, and that threw the switch. All of us went down and started firing back . . . only there was nothing to shoot at but these women and kids running away across the paddy. And within thirty, forty seconds they were all down, they'd all . . . been hit."

Boonie halted again, and the silence lasted so long that Lou guessed he must be waiting for some response from her. She tried to assemble some thoughts about the nature of war, some comforting assurance about responsibility having to be redefined in the heat of battle—all right, clichés, but better than nothing—but when she took the first step closer to touch him, he resumed sharply:

"Finally we were able to walk out into the paddy and look at the women and kids. Fifteen of 'em altogether. I found one body myself, practically stumbled over it when we spread out into the paddy. A woman it was, lying on her back. The bullets had . . . had ripped her open across the middle, but her face was okay, and she was staring straight up. When I stood over her, I could look into those eyes and it was like they were staring at me. I'd already killed a couple of guerrillas—shooting back at enemies that shot at me— but none of 'em were women, none of 'em stared back so . . . so *alive*. The longer I stood there—and I couldn't tear myself away—the more I knew that she'd have been alive, and the kids too, if the captain hadn't been pissed already by losing a stupid softball game, and the more I realized how insane the whole thing was. I could feel the woman telling me about it, how she knew it was all crazy. Then I went nuts myself. I couldn't stand looking at her anymore, but I didn't want anyone else to see her because she might tell them it was all my fault. So I unclipped one of my grenades, and I set it down on her face like she was kissing it, and then I pulled the pin and ran like hell, shouting 'Booby trap! Booby trap!' so all the other guys would hit the earth, and because that was really how I saw her—those eyes were the booby trap that blew away any belief in goodness that was left in me, all of it, forever."

Once more the silence was almost interminable. But this time Lou realized she should wait for him, and at last he looked at her and spoke. "I live with it, Lou. Okay? I think I've got a handle on it. But I can only manage it by being alone." He swept his eyes around the mountain once more. "It was good here. I even had one dream I still allowed myself to chase." He laughed softly to himself. "Who would've thought it'd come true? I guess I wasn't expecting that." Abruptly he strode back inside the cabin, another escape.

Finally she knew that none of her arguments, none of her pleas, would make any difference.

But the rejection—his cynical demolition of the value of love—infected her with his bitterness. She went to the cabin door. Boonie was gathering up more of his meager belongings, tossing them into a footlocker.

"So you won't stay forever. But you're my only chance to delay the blasting now. Hold out here and some media sympathy will develop. They'd have to put it off, reschedule. There might be another week or two—"

"For you to get the gold," he said.

"You want me to see things your way, Boonie? All right, there it is. I can't ask you to stay for me, so I'm asking you to stay for the gold."

He fixed her in the sort of steady penetrating gaze that adults give children to inspire shame.

Lou cracked under the scrutiny. "Well, don't you owe it to me?" she cried. "I gave you the answer to your riddle, didn't I? I got you *your* gold!"

Boonie nodded slowly. Then he waved his hand toward the bed, where the knapsack lay, the canvas squarely outlining the brick of bullion.

"You want gold?" he said. "Then take that. Two bars to go with your third. That's close enough to a million bucks' worth."

"There's billions more in—"

"No!" Boonie erupted. "I'm not staying! You want more fuckin' gold, then take mine. Go ahead. Take it!" He grabbed up the knapsack and thrust it at her savagely. "Go ahead. *Take it!*"

"But it's everything you—"

"You still don't get it, do you? I wasn't here for the gold. I was here just because it was something good to believe in. Because every other thing I tried to put some faith in turned out to be nothing. But this one turned out to be real, and it doesn't matter if I've got a couple of lumps of gold or not. Because in a way, the way that matters most, I get to take away all of it." He was still pushing, urging the gold on her.

"But if you've got that—if you've had one dream come true—why not believe in others, give yourself a chance to . . . be with someone?"

At last he eased the pressure on her, giving her a half-smile. "There's dreams," he said quietly, "and there's fairy tales. Some things are always gonna be too hard for me to believe."

She shook her head. After a moment she said, "Goodbye, Boonie," and headed for the door.

She heard his footsteps following, but she didn't turn. She kept going out of the shack and across the meadow. From the voice that called to her, she could tell he had stopped in the doorway.

" 'Bye, Lou. I'll be leaving tomorrow at the last minute. Before you start to blow it up. Good luck with the mountain—either way."

Only when she reached the far side of the meadow did she pause for a backward look. Today, for the first time, he hadn't remained there watching to see which direction she took.

CHAPTER 33

Lou walked across the east face of the mountain with Capper, checking the blast holes. Thirty-two had been drilled—sixty-five feet apart and covering almost a half-mile of mountainside. Each hole was sixty feet deep and eight inches across, and when every one was filled with a slurried mix of ammonium nitrate and fuel oil, the greasy combination would detonate with the explosive force of 200,000 pounds of dynamite. The extraordinary destructive power of this mixture—more efficient than TNT—had been discovered on a complete fluke at a small Southern port in 1947. Hundreds of gallons of diesel oil had accidentally flooded the hold of a ship filled with ammonium-nitrate fertilizer. Somehow—perhaps a careless crewman flipping away a cigarette—a fire had started, and the result had made headlines around the world as the "Texas City Disaster." An entire harbor town had been blown away.

If today's blast were properly engineered, a whole section of the mountainside would be lifted up, pulverized, and then set down again—each particle where it had been before. Afterward the mountain would look veritably the same, except that thousands of tons of rock and dirt could be shoveled away to leave the huge flat "bench" where the towers would be built. There was a phrase used to describe the ideal blast: maximum fraction, minimum motion. The best engineers could perform the trick so that spectators could stand no farther away than the length of two football fields and barely feel a puff of dust.

By early afternoon Lou and Capper had checked the charges of the first twenty-nine holes on the blasting line. The last three holes were still being filled with ANFO from the mix-and-pump truck. Once these were done, all that remained was to wire the radio-timing devices that would allow the charges to be set off in sequence.

"No need hanging around," Capper told Lou. "I'll make sure the last three are topped right."

"You know the rules," Lou said. Even though Capper was far more experienced in blasting, for a job of this magnitude the person of highest authority on the site had to review all arrangements.

But in fact, while she lingered, Lou thought less about the installation of the charges than what she could do to sabotage them. Especially these three holes—for they were at the end of the line nearest the ridge that separated the blast site from the mine. If these charges could be kept from detonating, the shock might be reduced just enough to keep the subterranean tunnels from caving in. That would gain many weeks during which it would be possible to travel in and out of the mine. Once the tunnels collapsed, however, relocating the trove of bullion deep in the heart of the mountain would be no simpler than finding a needle in a haystack.

But Lou could think of no way to abort the process.

"The radioman'll come up this afternoon to wire in the remote units," Capper said, "and we'll be set to go." He took a few steps away, then stopped to wait for Lou. He hadn't yet taken his lunch break and was obviously anxious to leave. The whole slope was emptying of workers.

"Go ahead, Cap," Lou said. "I'll make it down on my own."

He studied her curiously. "Something wrong, Lou?"

"I'm just taking a last look at this place, the way it was."

He came the few steps back to her. "Got under your skin, huh—an attack of conscience about what we're doing here?"

She shrugged. "It's been like this a few million years. I just thought somebody should take a moment to mark the fact that it's changing, say good-bye."

Capper smiled. "Nothing's going anywhere, Lou. It's a mountain, that's all, it'll stay right here. We're just gonna put a new face on it." He said he'd see her down at the depot and started away.

The other workers had all left. Lou watched Capper go, waiting for him to disappear over the rim. Then she'd have her chance to tamper with the charges.

But would she? She couldn't be sure until the moment came.

She saw Capper, halfway across the stretch of open ground, stoop down to pick up his windbreaker and a clipboard. Abruptly he straightened up and she expected him to hurry away. For a moment he stood rigidly erect, and only then Lou saw that his body was still arching slowly backward, as though he was recoiling from something in front of him.

Suddenly a garbled cry rose from his throat and he

started to spin and stomp around in a wild dance, shaking his right arm vigorously. It looked like he was having some sort of fit.

Lou broke into a run. What was wrong with him? As she dashed across the deserted slope, she saw Capper's solitary figure reeling in haphazard circles, waving one arm around in jerky pumping movements.

She was twenty yards away when he spotted her coming. He stopped moving and gave out a thin whimpering cry, incongruous in such a large man.

"Help me, Lou! For God's sake, help me!" He held out the arm he'd been waving and grabbed hold of something that was dangling from his wrist, a dark flicking wedge that looked like a piece of fabric torn from his sleeve. He yanked at it as if trying to tear it off, perhaps to get at some wound underneath. A *snakebite*, that must be it.

"Hang on, Cap, I'm coming!"

He went on whirling and tugging at the dangling piece of his workshirt.

Suddenly Lou realized that the dark wedge flapping at his wrist wasn't a piece of fabric at all. It was the scaly striped torso of a gila monster. It must have crawled into the folds of the windbreaker on the ground, and when Capper reached to pick up the jacket, the reptile had clamped its vicious teeth into his wrist. Thick as Capper's wrist was, the jaws of the gila monster virtually encircled it, the head like a grotesque bracelet studded with two tiny glittering stones, the garnetlike eyes. The lizard had a short stumpy body, but its head was huge. The rows of razorlike teeth through which the gila injected its venom could have sunk directly into the main artery at Capper's wrist . . . .

The engineer's meaty hand had a firm grasp on the

animal, yet with all his strength he was unable to tear it loose.

"Your knife, Cap," Lou shouted, and pointed to the sheathed hunting blade he always wore on his belt.

He strained to grab for the blade with his free hand, but couldn't reach the leather sheath hanging from his belt on his right hip. He tried, kept trying, but each desperate effort also turned his body, so that he was spinning pathetically like an addled dog chasing its own tail.

Lou tried to grab the knife herself, but Capper's lurching movements kept her away. "Use your right hand!" she screamed.

Capper stopped spinning. But when his right arm flailed around his hip, his fingers ineffectually grazed the knife's bone handle. The venom, Lou thought—already numbing Capper's limbs, working its way through the artery toward his heart. She could see tiny movements of the reptile's jaws as it continued to gnash down into the skin and sinew. The tiny beady eyes seemed to glitter with malevolent pleasure as the teeth pumped in more and more poison, working it into the increasingly raw wound by chewing and chewing. . . .

Capper flailed helplessly. "Oh, Christ, Lou," he murmured, his voice a hoarse croak. "I can't." Weakened by the venom, he wavered dizzily on his feet and then dropped to his knees. "Jesus, Lou, help me. . . ."

Lou stared at his hands, flopped over in his lap, the free one clutching so feebly at the reptile that he almost seemed to be petting it rather than trying to pull it away. The eyes of the lizard shone like beads in a bizarre rosary. She darted around, unsheathed the knife, and crouched beside Capper. His arm was resting in his lap so that the neck and tail of the lizard lay directly over his crotch. Lou was afraid to stab at it, and there was nothing solid to press against while she cut through the body.

"Move your arm, Cap. Onto the rock. Quickly."

His head bobbed languidly, but his arm remained resting in his lap. The numbing effect of the venom had evidently crept up to his shoulder. His eyelids were drooping, Lou saw. The poison was being carried through his blood to his brain.

Fighting down her repulsion, she swung Capper's arm away from his body and put it down on the ground. It took her a few seconds to get the blade of the knife centered over the lizard's neck. Then, with one consummate thrust, she pushed down hard on the blade. Blood spurted out as the scaly body separated from the head. Tail still thrashing, the torso went flipping away across the ground.

But the head was still vised firmly onto Capper's wrist—and the steel-trap jaws went on moving, gnashing, the razor teeth kneading back and forth over the raw wound so that Lou could see flashes of white muscle and bone through the blood.

Capper made pitiful murmuring sounds as his body slumped over and his arm automatically retracted.

She had to get the head off. The gila was dead, chewing only by reflex, but the venom sacs were still being emptied. She worked the tip of the knife into the lizard's mouth just under the snout and tried levering the jaws apart. Impossible. There was no choice but to cut the head away bit by bit. It was like trying to open a tin can with a chisel. Scraping, chipping, hacking, prying. The flesh came away and still the bony jaw was clamped to Capper's wrist. She cut where she thought the muscle hinges might be, but that did no good. Slipping the whole blade into the mouth might also slice into Capper's arm, but she forced the edge of the blade between the jaws, twisting and wrenching upward with all her strength. The dead mouth opened a bit wider, then popped open, and the severed head plopped off onto the ground. The eyes were still wide and glittering brightly—as if the gila were still alive.

Lou turned back to Capper. He was still slumped over, balanced on his knees. "Okay, Cap," she said, laying a comforting hand on his shoulder. "I'll get help. Lie back and . . ."

His body slid from under her hand and started to roll down the grade. Blocking him with her legs, Lou pushed him over onto his back.

He stared up sightlessly, his eyes filmy and dull. Lou let out a stifled cry. "Oh, God," she muttered, "oh, God . . . oh, God. . . ."

Was it a prayer or a condemnation? And to whom, against what? As she stood over Capper's dead body, the legend came suddenly clear—the part that said the gila monster was the spiritual embodiment of the poisonous gold.

Lou looked down at the head and torso of the dead lizard, scattered in pieces on the ground. The spirit had killed the man directly responsible for preparing the mountain to be blasted.

As Mercy had predicted, Elder Brother was protecting his home.

CHAPTER 34

It was nearly five o'clock by the time Lou unlocked the door of the office in Coopersville. The secretaries had all left early, concluding for themselves that the death of the construction superintendent would merit a cessation of business. Pausing at Capper's desk, Lou glanced at the framed eight-by-ten photo he had recently received from his daughter, the only child of a marriage that had ended fifteen years ago, showing her happily receiving her license as a real-estate broker.

Capper had beamed when he showed her the picture. "Great, huh?" he'd said. "We're going into business. I'll build 'em, she'll sell 'em."

The memory of his voice raised a lump in Lou's throat. She sighed. The daughter should be told personally—one more telephone call to make. After hesitating a moment, Lou reached down to the bottom drawer, where she recalled Capper kept a bottle of Johnnie Walker. He hadn't been a hard drinker, but at the end of the day he liked to mix a little Scotch with some water from the cooler and put his feet up. Lou remembered a time a couple of weeks after she'd come on the job when Capper had given her a drink after work, too, and she'd sat for an hour listening to him talk about the year he'd spent in Saudi Arabia putting up palaces for a few sheikhs. She liked his stories.

Christ. He was dead. How much was she to blame? Had the gila struck to express the anger of a mountain god?

Then why wouldn't it strike at her?

Because it was nonsense. Capper was the victim of carelessness.

And so was Hump Davis.

And Jack Benaky.

And Ted.

Lou pulled out the lower desk drawer. The bottle was still there, more than half-full.

She didn't bother going to the cooler for water, nor even for a paper cup. She took a long swig straight from the bottle.

It wasn't like her. But a drink was supposed to help after a day like this. Having her heart shut down by Boonie. Seeing a decent and gentle man like Capper die in front of her. A grueling session with the police and the medical examiner that had been stretched out by the coroner's refusal to believe that Capper could have died so quickly from the gila's bite—complete paralysis of the nervous system might take hours, he said, and fatalities were extremely rare.

She carried the bottle back to her own office. One swig hadn't helped, but the object was to start somewhere—and keep drinking until you were smashed.

She got to her own cubicle, stood in the middle of the floor, and started to lift the bottle to her lips.

And then the memory of her mother went off in her brain like a flare: the shell of a woman bunched into the corner of her sofa like a thin throw pillow with half its stuffing gone.

Lou lowered the bottle and put it aside on a bookshelf. A close one. Under pressure, ladies? Reach for everybody's favorite remedy. What would she turn into if she really did get her hands on all that gold?

She sat in her chair, waiting for the phone to ring.

By radio patch-through on a CB in one of the Jeeps, Lou had called the company's coast headquarters while she was still on the mountain. After getting through to Peter Knapp, head of the Western Division, she had reported Capper's death and made a request to delay the blasting until a new superintendent could be brought in. It was understood, too, that she expected the postponement as a matter of simple respect. The crews Capper Tate had commanded, she pointed out, could not be ordered to go on with "business as usual." The passing of a man like Capper ought to be marked by some sign of respect, some time to mourn. Knapp had agreed, but added that the decision would first have to be cleared through Honegger.

Now Lou waited to hear what Honegger had said—waited for the delay that would make her rich.

Much as she grieved at Capper's death, she was fully aware that it was her reprieve. A few days. Perhaps a week. During that time she could make two or three trips a day into the mine, bring out four, five bars at a time. More with the proper planning, using dollies and ropes. Even more if she could find an ally to trust. But who was there besides Ben?

Not Ben, no. He was friends with the Indian boy who believed in the mountain god.

The god to whom the gold belonged.

Who had killed to protect it.

Lou glanced over at the bottle on the shelf. She felt sick with herself, with her own greed, the way it had dulled her other emotions. She couldn't fully cry for Capper, nor could she fully regret her failure to reach Boonie. Her heart had been broken twice, in two different ways, and yet she was unmoved.

As if it had been blasted by the best engineers: maximum fraction, minimum motion.

She yearned to wipe all knowledge of the gold out of her mind. Forget she'd seen it. Forget the answer to the riddle.

Instead, knowing it was there, she could only hunger for it. The obsession gripped her and wouldn't let go. It was as if one of those venomous lizards had clamped its jaws into her very soul and the poison was working its way in deeper and deeper—

The jangling bell of the phone broke into her thoughts. She snatched it up. It was Peter Knapp calling from San Francisco.

"I've spoken to Honegger, Lou. His plane just landed in New York. You know, he flew in from abroad just to be at the Legend site tomorrow. He was planning to take off for Phoenix late today, then come up from there by helicopter."

"It's a good thing you reached him before he made the trip," Lou said.

There was a momentary pause at the other end of the line. Then Knapp said, "Lou, Honegger's coming anyway."

"He doesn't want to wait until we blast?"

"We are, Lou. Tomorrow. On schedule."

Lou groped for words. "But . . . but we need a specialist on the site, and no one—"

Knapp quickly explained that Jack Yeager had been

pulled off a job in Texas. Another of the company's crackerjack blasting men, he would be heading out to the mountain in a chartered jet in time to arrive at the site, check the lines once more, and oversee demolition.

"Goddammit!" Lou blurted. "You can't do this, Peter."

Can't destroy my last chance, she was thinking. Can't bury all that untouched wealth forever.

But she clung to an appearance of the nobler motive.

"Capper Tate meant a lot to the people here," she went on, "to me, the company. You can't lose a man like that and just pretend it didn't happen, that nothing's—"

"Cap would've been the first to understand, Lou, and so should you. We're construction people. The business is dangerous, death is always a possibility. But what we build is part of the memorial to the good men we lose. We still have to get the job done. The mountain blows. Tomorrow morning."

She couldn't argue. That *was* the game. And anyway, it wasn't really out of respect for Capper's memory that she'd been protesting.

She assured Knapp she would cooperate fully with Yeager and said good-bye.

For a minute after hanging up, she sat wondering if there might yet be some way to save it.

If she told Honegger, perhaps, as Boonie had sarcastically suggested.

Of course he would lay claim to all the gold. After all, it had been found on *his* property.

And, yes, he might build more cities. If he did not dream with such imperial grandeur, he would never have conceived Legend City in the first place.

It had to be hers, Lou resolved. Hers . . . or no one's.

Or would it always belong to no one but Elder Brother?

CHAPTER 35

Where was Jesse?

Ben paced back and forth at the foot of the hill by the bus stop, anxiously waiting for the pinto's appearance on the horizon. Was Jesse going to be absent two days in a row? Was he planning somehow to stop the blasting? In the pauses between his short strides, Ben thought he saw streaks of brown far off in the distance, puffs of dust raised by the hooves of Jesse's horse.

But when he looked closer, they turned out to be balls of tumbleweed whipped by the morning wind. Jesse was never late, which probably meant he wasn't coming at all.

Ben was in a state of high panic when he heard the bus approaching. He *had* to warn Jesse about the gold, get his advice. Invading Elder Brother's mine would surely incite his wrath even more than trying to build a city on the mountain. And Jesse had already rendered his judgment on what would happen:

Elder Brother will destroy us all.

There was no sign of Jesse as the bus coasted toward Ben and the yellow "Stop" flap flew out on the driver's side when the doors opened inward. It was too late to run. Dammit, he should have split before the bus got here.

▲▲▲

By the end of third period Jesse still hadn't come.

Ben was desperate to get to the reservation, find Jesse. Until now Ben had considered himself an expert at sneaking away from school; at Chadwick you could always find a senior with a car who would cut classes with you, or you could tell a teacher you had to be at a yearbook meeting, there was a printer's deadline and you absolutely had to be there. You could race off to Burnett's, the hamburger joint, and no one was the wiser. But what did you do out here? Pioneer Valley Regional was three miles from the main road.

He decided he would have to take a chance and hope nobody spotted him. The one good thing about this place was that the attendance records were computerized and the computers never seemed to work. It would take them days to discover he had cut a few classes.

And by then it wouldn't matter.

After fourth period he walked straight through the cafeteria, out onto the volleyball fields, and past the main quadrangle. No one called out, no one snitched to a teacher.

But when Ben reached Route 63 he realized how stupid the whole maneuver was. How the hell would he get *anywhere* from here? He had seen county buses on this road; one of them had to go to Coopersville. But that would take forever, stopping at every dinkhole little town on the way. Or he could hitch, couldn't he? In the city it was dangerous, you never knew what kind of nut would pick you up, but here it might be okay.

There wasn't much traffic, but Ben stuck his thumb out anyway, praying silently: *No cops, please, no cops.*

He waited fifteen minutes, twenty, half an hour, ambling slowly backward with his wrist cocked toward the road. The frustration welled up in him. Stop, for Chrissakes, we're all going to die if you don't stop.

A huge black car, one of those ancient tanks with big tail fins, zoomed by, and then—as though the driver had heard his silent call—slowed and pulled over. Ben raced up to it.

"Howdy, son, where you goin'?"

The man behind the wheel was real old, with shrubby white hair sticking out of his ears. He wore a baseball hat with a mesh top and a blue-and-red *International Harvester* patch above the visor.

"I got to get to the Tewani reservation right away," Ben said. "My mom's sick."

"Shouldn't you be in school?" the driver asked skeptically.

"I had to leave," Ben said, improvising, " 'cause they called . . . they called from the reservation, that's where she works, but they didn't have time to come and get me, and there wasn't anybody at school who could leave . . . please, I have to get there in a hurry."

The man behind the wheel gave him a dubious smile. "Okay, sonny, climb in."

Ben got in, slammed the door.

"So your mom's sick, huh?" the man said as he pulled back out onto the road. "Out at the reservation, huh?"

"Yes, sir, she is, she's real sick," Ben said, getting into the part, starting to feel pleased at the way he was putting it over on the old guy.

"Well, now, I guess we ought to get you out to the reservation, then."

"You know where it is?"

"Oh, sure, been there a couple of times, makin' deliveries."

"What do you deliver?" Ben asked, anxious to keep the man answering questions instead of asking them.

"My wife and me, and her dumb brother, we run a little machine-parts depot over in Hackberry, and we make deliveries, which nobody much does these days, so we got a pretty good business. You go to the Regional, huh?"

"Yessir, I do."

"Went there m'self," the man said. "Back when it weren't much more than an outhouse and a couple of desks in a shack. The name is Quint, son, Norman Quint. What's yours?"

"Ben Palmer, sir. My mom works for the Tewani, she's a social worker."

Ben wondered how the old guy was taking this. Jesus, what the hell did a social worker do, anyway? Did the Tewani need them?

Norman Quint glanced over appreciatively. "When I went to school," he said, "I'd get an itch sometimes, just to get away and go fishin', play hooky with a friend, maybe, who'd stayed home pretendin' he was sick. You ever do anything like that, Ben?"

"No, sir," Ben answered seriously. "I'd never do anything like that. I really like school."

"Do you, now?" Norman Quint said. "Well, that's good." He turned off Route 63 onto the two-lane road that went to the reservation. "Now, let's see if we can't make a little time here and get you to your sick mother."

With that, he floored the old car into the left lane, with a squeal of tires that left a tread of rubber on the entrance ramp. It scared Ben a little, an old man driving so fast, but they were making time, like he said.

"What do you want to be when you grow up, Ben?"

"I . . . I don't know," Ben said nervously as the car swerved a little and shimmied. "A doctor, maybe."

Norman Quint chuckled. "Well, that's damn fine, Ben, but if you change your mind, I'll tell you what you ought to do."

"What's that, sir?"

"You ought to become a storyteller, son, because you're already pretty damn good at it."

▲▲▲

Ben hurried into the village and straight onto the mall. Except for the three-story building with the ambulance parked under a shelter, the reservation looked like a toy town. He had been expecting . . . What? Tepees?

He stopped the first Indian he saw, a girl who looked like Cher, and asked where Jesse Silvertrees lived.

"Friend of yours?" the girl asked nicely.

"Yes, from school," Ben said quickly.

She pointed to a path leading down a hill, saying that Ben should turn right at the bottom. "But don't go inside any of the buildings. Jesse is . . . well, he's busy today. So you wait outside, all right?"

"Okay," Ben called over his shoulder, already on his way.

But when he reached the camp of hogans, he saw Jesse immediately, sitting on a low stool in a circle of old men. They were gathered around a kind of stretcher, like a beach chair spread out flat, except it was on wooden sawhorse legs. An old man with pillows propped under his head lay on the stretcher, dressed in the same kind of costume Jesse had worn on the mountain. All of them had costumes on, leather vests and pants streaked with paint.

One of the old men noticed Ben and touched Jesse's

shoulder. Jesse leaned over, the man whispered, and Jesse turned around.

Instinctively Ben understood he was an intruder. He wasn't welcome here because something important was happening. He stopped walking.

Jesse stood and went to the old man on the stretcher, said a few words, and then leaned over so his ear was directly over the man's mouth. The old man's lips quivered. He lifted a trembling arm and tugged Jesse closer.

Ben's whole body strained forward, tense with his message for Jesse. But he held himself in check, stayed rooted to the ground. More than ever he felt the threat of the gold and the evil his mother had unleashed by finding the mine. The evil was like a cloud in the air that had hovered around him since last night. This morning he had avoided going anywhere near the trapdoor, partly to avoid raising his mother's suspicions and partly because the gold itself seemed to warn him away. The eagle had showed him the gold, but it was evil nonetheless.

Jesse rose from the old man's stretcher and came up the path from the hogans. There was a solemn cast to his face that Ben had never seen before. Ben suddenly realized what was happening: the old Indian was dying. Ben glanced over at the stretcher. The old man looked as if he were dead already, so thin the bones in his cheeks were sticking right out.

Jesse caught Ben's glance.

"His spirit is weak," Jesse said, looking toward the old man. "He is feeling the pain of the mountain." He faced Ben directly. "You have come to tell me something."

Ben started babbling about the eagle, how it was sitting on the fence just staring at him, and then it was underneath the house and then inside the trapdoor under the rug, and it was down there, his mother took it, stole it and hid it there, and now they were all going to die, Jesse had to do something, save them. . . .

Jesse hushed him with a raised hand. "She stole what?"

"I told you, she took Elder Brother's gold, there's a big bar of it, and now . . . now . . ." His voice cracked.

Jesse's eyes narrowed. "We must give it back to Elder Brother," he said quietly.

"But how? They're blasting tomorrow!"

"We must trust Elder Brother," said Jesse plainly. "He will protect his home."

"But we've got to do something about the gold."

"Wait," Jesse said, and turned back down the path.

He stopped at the side of the stretcher, leaned over and whispered again to the dying old man. They spoke for barely a minute before Jesse returned. "You must meet me tonight. Bring the gold."

"But it's heavy, Jesse, and how will I get it out of the house? If I touch it I'll be poisoned."

But Jesse had no time for complaints. The gold would not be poisonous to Ben if it was being returned to Elder Brother. Rapidly he spelled out the terms of their rendezvous for Ben. One of the men who served the elders would drive him home to get the gold.

"Go now," Jesse said. He started away, leaving Ben feeling stranded, but stopped and turned for a final encouragement. "This, my brother, is your destiny."

▲▲▲

As the tribe's Jeep climbed the hill to his house, Ben had a thumping headache, and when he saw Lou's

BMW in the driveway, his heart belly-flopped in his chest. There was no way to get the gold immediately.

Ben sent the Jeep away, giving the Indian driver a message for Jesse: I'll be late, wait for me.

The evening passed slowly. The hands of the clock seemed frozen. Ben pretended to do his homework on the living-room couch, keeping an eye on the rug near the fireplace, but the notes he made were scribbles, and once he discovered himself holding his algebra textbook upside down. He was even afraid to risk a trip to the bathroom. What if she moved the gold?

Or had already moved it?

At ten-fifteen he closed his eyes, rolled over on the couch, and feigned sleep. He knew his mother wouldn't bother to wake him. She'd wait until she was ready for bed herself, and only then nudge him gently to his own room. The fabric of the couch cut into his face and he itched terribly. But he stirred only a few times.

He sneaked a peek at the kitchen clock as she rolled him over and whispered, "Ben, into bed now. Come on."

He produced a huge yawn. "Okay," he said, covering his mouth.

It was ten past eleven.

▲▲▲

Jesse waited at the appointed spot near the bottom of the hill. He held the backpack open as Ben loaded the gold bar into it. There had been no problem retrieving it from the musty cellar; his mother had been snoring lightly. Twice on the way down the hill he had stumbled under the bar's weight, but otherwise all had gone smoothly.

They made the ride to the mountain in what seemed

to be minutes. Ben was a mute witness as Jesse checked his watch and they followed the shadow of the Arm of God cast by the moon. It was an ancient secret, Jesse cautioned, one Ben must never speak of again. Never, Ben agreed. He would die under torture before betraying Jesse and the secret of the tribe.

They reached a spot where Jesse said the mine could be found. But he ordered Ben to sit on the ground facing into the desert, with his hands over his eyes. Ben protested: he had already sworn his undying loyalty. Jesse silenced him with a warning; even now, he said, Ben was privy to greater secrets than any white man had a right to know.

Ben fell silent and obeyed.

He heard Jesse groaning behind him, as if struggling under a heavy weight, and then the scraping of stones.

"Come," Jesse said, and Ben uncovered his eyes.

The earth had opened. The moonlight picked out the edges of the shaft and illuminated the enormous stone slab slanting into the hole.

"Jeeezus," Ben whispered, his voice an astounded croak.

Until then, despite the bar of gold and his faith in Elder Brother, there had been only a picture in his mind, an idea of the Lost Russian mine. Not in his heart and soul had he ever dreamed he would ever set foot here.

Jesse slung the backpack over his shoulder and motioned Ben to follow.

They slithered past the stone door, Jesse leading the way, into the tunnel's mouth. Jesse lit a torch—a clump of wadded cloth soaked in kerosene and set in a cup at the end of a long pole. Cautiously they edged forward.

At the sight of the skeletons Ben jumped, skittered

back, and smacked his head against the wall. He thought he was going to throw up.

"These men enslaved my tribe," Jesse said, remarkably unfazed. "They used my people as animals to dig for Elder Brother's gold."

Ben was awed. "Have you . . . ever been here before?"

"In spirit I have been here," Jesse said. "Today, when you came, our wise men decided it was time for me to be told."

Unfrightened, Jesse led Ben down the long corridor. It seemed to end directly ahead.

"It goes nowhere," Ben said shakily.

"Follow," Jesse answered firmly. "I have been instructed."

They took the right turn at the end of the long shaft and reached the crudely opened hole made by Lou and Boonie. But when they crawled through into the cavern filled with gold, even Jesse was struck dumb by the sight. It was the legend made real, the heritage of his tribe. For Ben, the stacked bars flickering in the light cast by Jesse's torch were something out of an adventure story, those paperbacks ordered by mail in grade school, or a treasure Indiana Jones would hunt for in *Raiders of the Lost Ark*. With trepidation and a superstitious terror that everything might vanish in a second, Ben walked over and stroked his fingers down the nearest pyramid of gold.

He felt the cool smooth surface of the metal.

Real.

Jesse held the backpack out to Ben. "You must replace the gold," he said. "I cannot touch it."

Ben opened the backpack, slid out the bar of gold, and transferred it to the top of a stack.

At that moment he heard a noise reverberating from

the mouth of the tunnel, like the rushing of the tide against a beach. Ben spun toward the sound—

He recognized it—the rapid whirring of wings he had heard in the backyard.

The eagle.

Quickly Jesse ducked through the hole in the cavern wall into the long tunnel.

Grabbing up the torch, Ben chased after him. "Wait!" he screamed. "Wait for me!"

But Jesse was already far away. Ben heard his footsteps pounding on the dirt. Holding the torch higher, he raced after him.

"Jesse, please, wait!"

His own cry boomed back at him from the stone-and-dirt walls. Tripping on the floor of the shaft, Ben caromed into the wall and back again, nearly upending the torch. Fraught now with claustrophobia, a primeval fear of the underground, he pursued Jesse faster, until he could finally see the light from outside—the twinkle of moonlight.

Safe. Almost there.

But hurrying to reach the tunnel's mouth he lost his balance and tumbled, frantically attempting to cushion himself by flinging an arm toward a beam extending from the ceiling.

He came to rest against the wall.

A near-miss. He could have rolled head over heels and broken his leg.

But in the moment while he stood and thanked his luck, the beam he had grabbed began separating from the packed dirt. It had been wedged into the wall for four hundred years, but now it was weak.

Ben let the wood go. Too late. The earth above him cracked, raining clumps of mud and rock, and before he could move, the entire tunnel gave way, throwing him to the ground as the timbers collapsed inward and the path to the entrance filled up before his eyes. What little he could see of the entrance was abruptly cut off by blackness.

He was sealed in.

He tried to sit up, bracing himself on his left arm. But before he could move the pain seared through him and an involuntary yelp burst from his throat.

His wrist was swelling. His arm throbbed from his shoulder to his fingertips.

Pulling himself up by his right hand, he scrambled on his stomach to the top of the heap of rocks and dirt. *There!* A pinpoint of light still showed somewhere beyond the gap in the rubble. No more than a few inches wide. But there *was* light.

Ben screamed into the tiny opening with all his strength: "Jesse! Get me out of here!

There was no reply. Ben strained to hear. No answer.

How much of the tunnel had collapsed?

Frantic, he began clawing toward the little hole. He ripped away hunks of dirt, small rocks, and pieces of smashed timber. Deeper and deeper he dug into the gritty earth.

"Jesse! Jesse!" he screamed all the while, mindless of the pain as he scraped his fingers raw. "Can you hear me?"

CHAPTER 36

Waking as the sunlight touched her face through the open window, Lou sat up in bed and saw the mountain. A mute shadow on the skin of the earth, it seemed to be waiting stoically for whatever was to come. Today it looked not so much like an animal half-buried in the earth as a meditating figure seated and bent forward in genuflection, like those Oriental monks who kissed the ground before the statue of the Buddha. An image of tranquillity and acceptance.

Surprisingly, she felt at peace, too. She had slept soundly, the best night in months. The result, she thought, of her own acceptance. The blasting could not be delayed. The gold was to be put out of reach forever. Very well.

She glanced at the clock. A few minutes before eight. She had set the alarm for eight-thirty, later than her usual rising time, but today seemed a bit of a holiday. The pressure was off, there could be no more turmoil as she schemed to have the gold; she had shaken off the demon of greed.

She couldn't laze about in bed, however. There were still several things to do before the big boom went off at ten. Make sure she was at the site to meet Honegger's helicopter. Meet Jack Yeager and double-check the security arrangements around the blast area to be extra certain there were no inadvertent casualties.

She dressed quickly and went to the kitchen. "Ben?" she called as she started the coffee. "Time to get up!"

She had decided to play down the blasting, get him off to school as usual. She knew of course that a lot of local people were planning to come out to the mountain to see the fireworks, plenty of kids among them. The mayor had asked her to designate a safe place to accommodate the expected crowd of spectators, and for the sake of good community relations Lou had obliged by having a small viewing stand erected at the designated spot. But with all the friction between herself and Ben about the mountain, the last thing she wanted him to see was the demolition. She would not have made an issue of it by refusing if he asked to come, but she was relieved that he hadn't. Perhaps he preferred to avoid witnessing the moment of defeat in his personal battle.

"Ben!" she called louder when she heard no movement from his room. She poured his glass of orange juice, set out some boxes of cold cereal on the table, and went to prod him out of bed.

She was halfway along the hall when she caught the flash of red on the floor near the front door. Her Mexican kerchief. For a moment she was puzzled. When had she dropped it? Couldn't remember even wearing it in the last day or . . .

Then it struck her. The scarf hadn't been worn at all. Not since . . .

She spun around and dashed into the living room. At once she saw that the rug over the trapdoor was slightly askew. When she lifted the hatch, she saw papers from the box where the gold had been hidden scattered all over the ground below. The bullion was gone.

To the mountain. An act of friendship for Jesse. Lou had no doubt that was the motive. He had warned her so many times about offending the Indians' god. Having stumbled (how? sheer chance that he had looked under the rug, found the trapdoor?) onto the hidden bar of gold, he must have determined to return it to Jesse.

Lou raced for her bedroom to dress. Maybe she could catch up, find Ben on the road. It was early enough in the morning—he might have left only a few minutes before she woke.

Or had he again sneaked out in the middle of the night? The gold might already be in Jesse's hands.

And then what would the Indian do with it—the gold that was poison to touch?

She finished dressing in jeans, workshirt, and her heavy-treaded boots.

Yet she still wasn't sure where to hunt for Ben. The reservation? The mountain?

She checked his room, found no clue, and ran out to the car, still wishing that some magic impulse would steer her in the right direction. Then it came to her: there was only one answer—though at first it seemed impossible.

The boys would want to return the gold to its rightful owner: Elder Brother. They would try to put it back in the mine. But Jesse couldn't know the way there. It was a sacred secret of the tribe, unused by them because the gold was taboo.

But of course someone in the tribe must still know the secret. If other traditions were kept alive, legends passed down, why not this one, the most precious one of all?

Now, if Jesse showed the bullion to the elders, telling them his intention to return it to Elder Brother, wouldn't the *hati'i* give him the secret?

Or would Jesse even *touch* the gold, since he believed in the legend? He would need Ben to carry it for him.

She had to get to the mountain. In less than two hours the section near the mine would be blasted—blown to bits by a colossal explosion that would collapse every underground tunnel. Anyone who was down there would be entombed forever.

▲▲▲

Lou scrambled over the rough face of the mountain on the approach to the ridge where the mine was located. She couldn't squander the time to assess her next move, or look for the most solid niche to place a foot. All she could do was keep moving as fast as possible. Her hiking shoes slipped from footholds too hastily chosen. Repeatedly she fell, slipped, bruising herself again and again. Yet she kept pushing forward.

Every few minutes she checked herself with a backward look to the foot of the mountain. She could see, far below, the striped awning of the viewing stand, and around it the growing cluster of cars and people. The day had been boosted into quite an occasion. At one point she looked down and her eye was dazzled by a flash from a huge clump of gold. She thought it must be her mind playing tricks, but as she stared harder she realized the effect came from the sun bouncing off a tuba—a band was assembling, from one of the schools in the area.

Lou looked at her watch. A quarter to nine. Plenty of

time. Almost an hour and a half to get Ben and bring him off the mountain.

Or had she gone about it all wrong? So hell-bent on getting to Ben—to the mine—she had neglected to take the vital steps first: get to Jack Yeager, explain what had happened, ask for help, and give orders to stop the blast. She had done none of it. Though it was not merely an oversight.

It was greed, she knew, that had again made the choices for her. Once she asked for the blasting to be stopped, there would be no way to help Ben without sooner or later revealing a connection to the mine. Ben himself would have to explain his presence on the mountain. In fact, it all might end with the news being broadcast to the world: the famous Lost Russian mine had finally been found. Then the mountain would be ravaged by fortune hunters, picked clean.

Hers, or no one's.

Even knowing that she was moving farther and farther beyond the safe option of going back, asking for postponement, she kept climbing.

Cresting the ridge, Lou saw at once the vertical line of stone projecting from the gentle curve of the smooth rock surface. The entrance to the mine was open.

Open. Ben was inside.

Though already winded from her rapid climb, she dragged still more air into her lungs and started to run the last two hundred yards to the mine entrance.

Suddenly the darkness fluttered over her. One moment the sun was stabbing down from a clear morning sky; in the next she was in the cool cover of shade, as though sheltered under a tree. Glancing up as she ran, she saw nothing at first but the hovering black shape interposed between herself and the sky. She tilted her head slightly, trying to define its size, its limits.

She tripped over a small spur of rock and went sprawling. She landed hard, her splayed hands catching the weight so that her palms were left stinging and grated bloody by the rough surface. But she barely noticed the pain. Looking up from the ground, she was finally able to determine what had been floating over her. While she ran she had been keeping pace with it—or it with her—but as soon as she stumbled it had glided on ahead. Now, held by the sight of the moving form, Lou stayed on the ground watching until it fluttered down to perch on the open door to the mine.

The white eagle.

For the first few moments she could only marvel at the sight of the majestic creature, an animal that even in motionless repose projected an awesome authority.

Here? Now?

Where had it come from?

Then the memory of the other time she had seen the eagle struck her—that first day when she and Ben were driving into Coopersville. She knew now that it was not just a mere creature that had flown in to confront her. Swooping in with it, seizing her consciousness like the eagle itself sinking its talons into some unwary prey, came the stunning revelation of what the bird represented—the evidence for a whole system of belief that she, and too many others, had discarded as mere folklore.

The legend—the spirit of Elder Brother.

The earthly form of the deity had always been recognized in the name given to the spiritual leader of the Tewani, the man designated to lead the *hati'i na'antan*: White Eagle.

Slowly Lou raised herself and advanced. Not running anymore, but proceeding a step at a time.

The golden eyes of the white eagle followed her every inch of the way. There was no doubt in her mind: the force of something more than an animal intelligence shone out at her from those eyes. The eagle roosted on the piece of stone guarding the way to the gold—*his* gold—like a king mounted on a throne.

It sat motionless until Lou was ten yards away. Then, as she dared the next step, it came abruptly to life, flapping its enormous wings and giving out a loud shrill caw.

Lou stepped back instantly. The bird settled again.

The spirit was not going to let her get near the tunnel. She couldn't go after her son.

The *spirit?*

The belief that a moment ago had filled her mind broke up and dispersed like a reflection on the surface of water rippled by a pebble. A god? Here in front of her in animal form?

It must be the sun, the stress—the cumulative effect of months of dealing with problems that were too big for her—that had made her so vulnerable to irrational ideas. This eagle was no more than a thing of nature, impressive but not supernatural. In her panic she was surrendering too easily to the legend, letting it overwhelm her. An eagle, an albino eagle. Perhaps descended from a mutant strain that had lived for decades on the mountain; that alone could explain the name adopted by the leader of the *hati'i*. . . .

But how did she get past it? Weren't eagles supposed to be capable of carrying whole sheep off in their talons? Or was that folklore too?

But what had made this one put itself between her and her son?

The will of a god? Or the whim of nature?

She had to bet on what was easiest to believe. Lou scanned the ridge, looking for something that might be used as a stave. There was nothing of sufficient size, only a few roots.

Rocks? She didn't think she could defend herself for long by throwing them at the eagle, but they might hold it off while she made a dash for the entrance. That was the only way she could get into the mine—hope that before the bird could stop her, she'd manage to slip down through the opening, where it would be unable to follow.

Retreating several yards, Lou scavenged the ground until she found two egg-sized rocks light enough to throw with some speed. Clutching one in each hand, she edged up toward the eagle again. As if aping her, showing it could move delicately too, the bird made small fluttering movements of its wings. But it let Lou come within eleven or twelve feet, much closer than she'd been before. From here, she thought, if she made a quick dash for the entrance, shielding herself with her arms waved overhead, or hurling a stone to drive the bird off, she ought to be able to get into the shaft.

She hauled in a deep breath and launched herself into the run.

The white eagle exploded simultaneously in a blur of movement, wings flapping furiously, stirring up a small tornado of air that, by itself, seemed to press Lou back. She took a second to poise herself, and tried to dash again.

Once more the bird flapped and squawked, but this time Lou kept going forward. Head down, tented under her arms, she could see that she was approaching the opening in the ground. Another second and she'd get through. . . .

The bird let out a terrible screech and flailed one of its claws. Something raked comblike through the strands of hair that had fallen down over Lou's face, and a pointed and shiny shape flashed within an inch of her eye. Startled, she leapt back, and only then realized how close she had come to being flayed by the eagle's talons. She backtracked rapidly, stopping when she had again put several yards between herself and the entrance to the mine.

Would she ever get in?

Or did she have to? The underground tunnels leading to the mine were so long that she had assumed Ben wouldn't hear her calling from the surface—and that even if he did, he might not respond. But she might as well try.

"Ben!" she called out, her voice tempered by fear of a loud noise agitating the eagle.

No sound came back, but at least the bird had remained at rest.

Lou called louder. "Ben . . ." Still the eagle watched her passively, utterly certain of its strength.

She hollered at the top of her lungs. "Ben, can you hear me? You've got to come out . . . they're going to blast. Ben!"

No sound came back at her but the soft whisper of the drafts curling down off the higher ridges of the mountain.

Like a cold wind of the soul, the despair cut through her. My God, she couldn't even be sure that Ben was really in there. Perhaps he was safe on the reservation with Jesse, and she was risking her own life for nothing.

No. Instinct told her this was where he had come. But down in the bowels of the mountain, it was simply impossible for him to hear.

She fixed the eagle once more in a determined gaze. "Damn you," she said aloud. "You're not going to stop me!"

Before she could think any more about it, she sprang forward again.

Now, like any bird roused by a sudden movement, the eagle flew up off its perch.

Thank God, Lou thought. Only a bird, it had given up. She made for the entrance.

But the eagle had lifted only twenty or thirty feet into the air before it wheeled in a tight circle. While Lou ran for the stone hatch, the bird came zooming in from behind. Just in time she felt the rush of air at her back and whirled around. The eagle was bearing down, a dark projectile homing in like a rocket. Somehow Lou managed to raise a hand and launch one of the stones, heaving it like a shotput.

With a raucous caw, the eagle peeled off to one side and escaped being struck. With the way still clear, Lou continued toward the mine.

But then the beating of wings was behind her again, getting louder. She started to turn, saw the dark shape bearing down, almost on top of her, and could only avert her face and throw up her hands.

As it flew by, the bird pecked her savagely on the shoulder. For a fraction of a second after the piercing impact of the beak, Lou felt nothing, just a sudden numbness. Then she was hit by a searing bolt of agony that seemed to electrify her whole body. She staggered, and was kept from falling only by clinging to the knowledge that if she gave up now Ben might die. The bird had flown past, still had to circle back, and if only she could keep on her feet, she could get into the tunnel.

Just a few feet to go.

She lurched forward, reached out to touch the piece of stone guarding the entrance, and steadied herself, about to descend—

Knives. Four or five of them, plunged suddenly into her arms, her shoulders, her back, with a force that knocked her forward. She would have pitched onto the ground, but the stone hatch was in front of her and when her arms came up by reflex, she caught the top edge. She gave a wordless scream of pain, though in her mind there were words wanting to be said.

Ohpleasenopleasenopleaseno

The pain was so terrible she wanted to die if that was the only way to stop it.

And the sheer fright was worse—as she felt the weight on her back and saw the huge wings flapping at either side and realized that the eagle had its talons sunk into her. My God, was it going to fly with her? She had visions of being carried high into the air and then dropped to her death.

But the ground stayed close beneath her, and the huge weight kept bearing down, even though the wings went on beating the air. She felt herself being dragged backward, away from the mine, until the distance to the entrance was again five or six yards.

Then the knives were plucked out of her. The eagle fluttered upward to a height of thirty or forty feet, gliding in a lazy circle.

Released, she felt too weak to stand. Dropping to her knees, she watched the bird circling and wondered for a moment how quickly it could dive from that height. Wondered *only* a moment—before deciding it had proved its supremacy. If it had given her more leeway, it was only to taunt her.

The white eagle—the spirit of the mountain—would never let her get into the mine. She could only hope that Ben and Jesse would replace the gold and get out in time.

At that moment she heard a faint raspy noise. It sounded like the shuffle of feet over the earth, but there was no one else on the slope. Had Elder Brother assumed another form, an invisible ghost? She glanced up. The eagle was still gliding in a circle overhead.

Then she heard it again—and realized it was echoing up from the tunnel. She swung her gaze to the slit in the earth. Dear Lord, could it be Ben? All her pain seemed to vanish, soothed by the surge of joyful relief as the sounds echoed louder from the tunnel, and Lou realized that someone was about to climb out. Unable to wait, she pulled herself to her feet and started to move closer—then stopped at the sight of the feathers rising from the ground.

The Indian boy was wearing a headband from which a handful of large white feathers protruded. Grabbing the edge of the hole, he hoisted himself up with one quick flex of his strong arms and stood erect before Lou, his expression grimly challenging. Lou looked past him, waiting for Ben to emerge.

The Indian read her anxious look. "He will not come, Mrs. Palmer."

"Not . . . ?" Now it struck her: the Indian's arrival at this moment was not just coincidence. He had been *waiting* inside the mine until the eagle was finished with her. He had also wanted her weakened, punished. And if he was capable of such cruelty for the sake of protecting his mountain . . .

"My God!" The cry burst from her. "What have you done to Ben?"

"I have done nothing. It is Elder Brother who keeps him here."

In the past, she would have scoffed at his dramatics. No longer. She felt a growing hopelessness, fueled partly by the pain that was coming back, accompanied by nausea and dizziness. "What do you mean? *How* is he being kept—?"

"As a hostage," Jesse replied.

She understood: Ben's life in exchange for the mountain. "Jesse, for God's sake, you've got to understand. . . ."

She meant to shout, but her voice was weak. She felt a sticky wetness running down the back of her arms, curling around her wrists, and when she looked down she saw parallel trickles of blood. All she could muster now was a pleading whimper. "Please, Jesse, if you don't let Ben out, there won't be time to get down to—"

"Let him out? But I have told you, Mrs. Palmer. I am not keeping your son."

"Then why isn't he out here?" Lou pleaded.

The Indian boy's eyes sparkled as he said, "The tunnel has caved in."

"Oh no," she gasped, shocked not only by the news but also by the callousness inherent in the boy's placid delivery.

Jesse went on coolly, "There is no danger—except from your people. Ben has air enough to breathe until he can be rescued. But the digging will take time . . . several hours. So you see, if he is to survive, you have no choice but to stop your blasting. The mountain has taken Ben prisoner, only the mountain. And if it dies, if it is harmed in any way, your son will die with it."

She stared at Jesse, and then opened her mouth, trying to summon some brilliant argument, some strategy of emotion that could make a difference. But finally she knew it was pointless. The decisions were not Jesse's to make; they had been made for him, for Ben, her, for all of them.

The only way to save Ben was to get down to the base of the mountain and order the blasting stopped.

But was there still time?

For one more prayerful moment she stood glancing around wildly, looking for a savior, a miracle. Nothing around her moved, nothing but the eagle circling slowly above.

There were miracles, perhaps, but none that would help her.

She turned from Jesse and ran.

CHAPTER 37

She tore across the slope, gasping for breath. Streams of bright red trickled down her arms, baked dry in seconds by the wind and sun. She tried not to think of how much blood she was losing, and struggled on.

She had to go east, and then down, until maybe they could see her. Someone half a mile away would scan the terrain with binoculars, the townspeople awaiting a kick, a thrill. They would catch sight of her—of course they would—before the charges were set off, and alert the engineers. *There's a woman up there!* Someone would shout. A woman, and a boy they had no way of knowing about.

Oh, Ben, I'm sorry. I'm sorry I didn't listen.

She would wave her arms, she thought as she tripped blindly forward. She could tear off her shirt and wave it as a flag. They would have to see her.

Barely slowing her pace, she raised her hand and tried to read her wristwatch, saw hands angled to form a mountain turned on its side.

Twenty to ten!

But how could it be? When she approached the mine, there had been more than an hour. Had she lost all conception of time? Or had the eagle, the spirit, with the beat of its wings, blown away the minutes?

Twenty minutes until a single toggle switch was thrown, a circuit completed, and Ben was crushed to death.

Time, dear God give me time, she shouted soundlessly in her own mind.

Cutting across the mountain was taking too long. Better to aim straight down, try to reach the viewing stand.

She fled stumblingly. Off in the distance, on the two-lane blacktop leading to the site, she could see cars crawling in a steady line toward the viewing area.

Blindly she forged on. Her legs ached from where she had fallen when the eagle attacked. Now she sensed rather than felt the rocks shifting beneath her feet. Arms pinwheeling she tried to steady herself, but slipped to the ground, tumbled, and rolled over, splayed on the dirt like a pinned butterfly.

Wincing in pain, weaving drunkenly, she crawled onto her knees and used her arm as a fulcrum to boost herself into a crouch. Spasms wracked her muscles; her back felt as if it might be broken. She was bleeding all over now, her entire body streaked with bloody dust.

But she had to keep going.

The other shape on the mountain registered in the corner of her eye, disappeared in a burst of sunlight, then flashed again among the rocks. Lou paused, shielded her eyes with her palm. Someone was over there, moving.

The eagle was tracking her. . . .

No!

It was Boonie.

The miracle she needed. True to his sentimental

plan, he had stayed on the mountain until the last possible moment.

Cupping her hands, she called out. There was hardly enough air in her lungs to expel the words. Her consciousness wavered and the dry tan surface of the mountain shimmered before her eyes, flattened into a disk. . . .

She was passing out.

But then her breath returned. She had never imagined that the sound of her own voice would sound so sweet, ringing out like a warning bell.

The scream reached Boonie. He stopped, turned, then broke into a run.

He had barely reached her before the terror spewed out of her mouth: "Ben . . . trapped in mine." She took deep breaths, coughing. "Eagle . . . attacked me . . . blasting now . . ."

"I'll go for Ben," he said quickly. "You get down there and tell them to wait."

"No time, ten minutes . . . sequence can't be stopped."

"We gotta get out of here," Boonie answered breathlessly, and seized her arm.

"*Ben!*" she screamed. "We can't leave Ben! He'll die in there!"

"But they'll wait for you, Lou, won't they? They'll wait! They won't set it off unless you're there."

Lou's strength ebbed. "No, Boonie, it's all scheduled . . . nobody can stop it . . . all electronically timed."

Boonie straightened, dropped the bundle he'd been carrying and pulled her toward the road.

"Let's go," he said. "We've only got one choice: disarm the detonators."

It was the old axiom she had heard a million times and never believed: her whole life passing before her eyes. In a split second fragments of scenes erupted like dreams: wedding, birthday party, Ben dangling from the doctor's hands. They had barely ten minutes to reach each of the thirty-two charges.

She ran at full steam, oblivious to the pain in her side and the bruises on her arms and the blood still oozing from the gashes everywhere.

Boonie reached the first charge—the closest to them, at the edge of the asphalt road that had been built for the drill. He was bending down to undo the fuse when she screamed:

"Boonie, don't! It's spring-loaded!"

He waited till she sprinted to his side. She showed him how to remove the fuse without setting off the charge.

"Where are the wires?" Boonie asked. "We can cut 'em."

"Buried," Lou said. "A trough they dug with the holes."

"Shit," he said through clenched teeth, and loped toward the next charge.

She passed him in a jerky run, the wind burning through her lungs. She defused the third charge as Boonie burst by in a blur on his way to the fourth.

They each did another one.

And then another.

She kept thinking she was going to black out. But she kept going, a burst of new strength coming from deeper down in the reservoir, nearer and nearer the bottom. . . .

Five down. Then seven.

Eight.

Nine.

"We can make it," Boone boosted her on his way to number ten. "Just keep moving, and we can make it."

Only simple commands issued from her brain: run, unscrew, hold spring, drop cap. Run, unscrew, hold *spring, drop cap, run, run, unscrew, hold cap, drop cap, run, run, unscrew, hold spring, drop . . .*

It fell from her fingers, the fuse from the thirteenth charge. She heard Boonie clump past her, and was halfway into her runner's crouch when at last her body rebelled. The ache in her side cramped, encircling her stomach in a wide band and tightening like choking hands. Not supposed to happen this way, she thought; adrenaline should carry you through, superhuman strength in emergency.

She slumped to her knees.

"Lou?"

The shout reached her from a million miles away.

"Lou?"

She struggled to her feet, turning.

"Lou, come on."

Arms outstretched, as though she could paddle her way through the air, she headed for the next charge, swaying like a broken marionette.

She managed somehow to fall next to the fifteenth charge. By feel instead of sight she worked her fingernails under the cap, held the spring, twisted the fuse free. She dropped the cap. The machine in her head went on with a will of its own.

Halfway there.

Boonie's arms were around her, propping her head against his knees. "Lou. Don't stop! Not now. I can't do it all."

Her throat hurt. Every word singed her vocal cords

with fire—the hot desert air. "Boonie, I can't . . . enough . . ."

He yanked her to her feet, slung her up and over his shoulder, and carried her past the next charge.

"Do it," he said, setting her down.

She arched her back and lifted her head. He was running back to the one—no, two—they had gone by. Dirt and sweat stung her eyes.

Hand on cap. Hold spring. Fuse off.

He was scooping her up again, carrying her. Past two charges, and then she was on the ground again. There was the sun above her. She was on the beach, with no cares *take me down to the water, Daddy. . . .*

"Do it, dammit!" Boonie called. His voice had brought her back.

Hand on cap, spring . . . where's the damn spring? . . . Fuse off.

The warm ground soothed her, and she realized she was staring at the sky. Time was running out.

Up, came the order from her brain. *Stand*, went the message to her legs. Simple as that. *Go away, pain.*

She made it to the next charge, but whatever had carried her this far deserted her at last. Her body convulsed and she slid down, a snow angel in the dust.

Boonie came running. He picked up her hand; she thought he must be checking her pulse, but it was her watch he wanted.

"We've got four minutes. I'll do as many as I can. Stay here."

And where else would I go? I'm dying here.

Her left hand stuck to the softening asphalt. She tugged it away, made a motion to wipe the sludge on her dress.

He seemed to return almost as quickly as he had left. Hauling her into his arms, he started to run.

"Why . . . ?" she murmured. "All done. Why run?"

He panted as he ran. "Still three left. We're out of time."

She flailed, accidentally striking him in the face and sending them both into a rag-doll sprawl.

"Have to finish," Lou said, clumsily getting to her feet. "Big charges . . . Ben . . ."

She leapt toward the road, dragging her weak leg. She hopped a short way and then collapsed. Boonie chased after her, grabbing her foot to hold her back.

"Ben'll be all right!" he shouted. "It's far enough away now."

Could he be right? How far to the mine? She hesitated, then tried to tear herself from his grip.

"Dammit," Boonie muttered, and swept her up again.

The smell of tar and dust flooded into her nostrils as Boonie ran. Her head flopped on his shoulder and she saw the ridge ahead, the outcropping just beneath the mine. It masked the sun, covered them in shadow.

The roar suddenly split the air.

The shock pounded into her eardrums. The earth shook, shifted, clods of earth rained down.

The first one had blown.

Boonie didn't stop. He ran on to the ridge and laid Lou down behind it. Then he fell on her, sheltering her with his own body.

There was a moment of settling, and echo.

The second charge blew with even greater force, timed both to finish the job of the first and level the next plateau of the bench. Above Lou and Boonie more rubble was shaken free. Dust clogged Lou's nose and mouth.

We'll suffocate, she thought. We'll be smothered.

Another air-battering roar.

The third charge rang through the mountain as a thousand batons beating on a thousand drums, a deep bass boom unleashing an avalanche of boulders from high on the jagged peaks, a sea of pounding stone. Lou, lying on her side, opened her eyes and saw them bounce over her head, smashing shards from the shielding ridge above.

Thunderous, it seemed neverending. The aftershock continued for two minutes, raining an incessant shower of debris. Then it slowed and Lou tried to raise herself. But Boonie's weight pinned her down. He had taken the brunt of the avalanche, she realized, might be crushed, dead on top of her.

But as she pushed upward, he moaned and began scrabbling through the dirt around them.

"Boonie?"

"You okay, Lou?"

"I . . . I think so."

"Don't move."

He patted himself, checked for broken bones, then heaved the weight of the rubble from his back. Lou sat up creakily as he checked her too. Her vision clouded. She thought she had gone blind. But it was only the effect of blinking away the dust.

They went on their knees when the tremor began, a low rumble underneath the mountain. They turned to each other, catching their breath, and reached out.

For a moment Lou assumed they had missed a charge. There was no other explanation, but there was no explosion.

The earth continued to shake, the sound far away. It was like the echo of the drumbeats, but muffled. Unthinkingly Lou stood up, and immediately she understood. Down at the base of the mountain a crack had opened in the desert floor, spreading in fits and starts, opening wider until a chasm had appeared. Another distant rumble echoed. Lou saw bushes ripped from their roots and then slide into the crack, widening and deepening as it crept north like a slithering snake.

"Earthquake," she mumbled.

Boonie gaped and reflexively wrapped his arms around her.

The Hurricane Fault.

They had known from when the first surveys were done that Legend Mountain was at the far southern end of the fault, which extended up the Colorado Valley north the whole way to the Grand Canyon. But all the industrial geologists had rendered the same opinion: the fault was deep in the earth and stable, hadn't budged in half a century. It was safe to blast.

But the charges had set off a shift in the subterranean fissure, a gouge in the earth's very crust.

The charges, Lou thought, the explosions . . . or Elder Brother?

In one more vibration the gargantuan snake slithered out beyond the desert to the highway, and then it stopped. Lou could see people running, cars flooding the road away from the mountain.

This was truly the end, she thought. There would be no Legend City. No one would ever again think of building on Legend Mountain.

But in the awful desolate silence following the final tremor, consciousness of where she had been and where she was now came back to her.

She turned to Boonie, empty but for one thought: "Ben . . . oh Ben . . ."

CHAPTER 38

She turned to scramble toward the mine, up the cliff and over the ridge behind them. But her swelling leg dragged her back. Boonie boosted her up, and using his shoulders as a ladder she threw herself over the ledge of rock, flat onto her stomach. Silent prayers kept running through her mind: don't let him die . . . please, God, don't let him die. She gave no thought to the gold. Who cared if the mine was lost? If only Ben hadn't been buried!

As Boonie climbed over and lifted her to her feet, she felt faint and slumped against his chest. He held her and was guiding her forward when without warning he froze in his tracks and thrust out an arm.

"Lou, look!"

It took her a moment to focus in the bright sunlight, and then, like a vision, she saw Ben and Jesse standing together near the open entrance to the tunnel, both mottled with dust. Her heart leapt to her throat and tears welled in her eyes. Alive! Thank God. Jesse had helped dig him free, after all. She tore away from Boonie, but her legs refused to carry her and she could only hobble toward the two boys. It was not until Ben was racing toward her that Lou saw there was something else that had caught Boonie's attention. Ben, in mid-step, halted at her change of expression, and turned.

Ascending over the ridge, advancing in a stately march toward the center of the slope, were the *hati'i na'natan*, all dressed in their ceremonial costumes. The man leading the procession cradled a bowl in his hands. Near the end of the line, four of the men carried the animal-hide cot, its occupant the pale emaciated form of the tribal leader.

And at the end of the line marched Mercy Roy, also clothed in the traditional Tewani garb and tenderly clasping the limp hand of the old man on the cot as she trudged wearily up the slope. What were they doing here? Lou wondered. And how had they arrived so quickly? The relief that had surged through her when she saw Ben gave way to an altogether mysterious sense of completion, as if she had somehow known they would both survive.

The feeling disconcerted her as the procession crested the slope and continued across the plateau. From the far side Jesse moved to join it, and Ben followed him. Magnetized by the sight, she and Boonie fell in alongside the march on the flank opposite Ben.

Allowed. Lou remembered Mercy's confession, the puzzling word. They had been allowed to find the mine—as it had been ordained that they would be here, part of this moment.

When the old men had stopped and laid the stretcher on the dirt, Ben threaded around them to stand with her. He looked so small, his face pale, his hair windblown and layered with grime. She pulled him to her, hugged him tightly, and an understanding passed wordlessly between them: the rift was over.

Mercy separated herself from the old men and approached, her gray eyes liquid and rimmed red from tears. "Are you badly hurt?" she asked. Her gaze held no other questions, as if she needed no explanations for what had happened.

"I'll be all right" Lou murmured "What are you—?"

Mercy raised a hand and touched Lou's face. Her curious half-smile seemed to mix sadness—for the old man, Lou assumed—and an odd mirth, a kind of happiness.

"You see now, don't you?" Mercy said. "You see why it never could have been yours?"

But before Lou could answer, the voices of the *hati'i na'antan* rose in a chant, a repetitive mournful dirge. The words were unintelligible, but the music swelled with the grandeur of a muezzin summoning the faithful to prayer. The song belonged to the ages, Lou thought, had been composed no doubt by the ancestors of these men on this desert plain thousands of years ago. She followed with Ben as Mercy led them closer to the old men, now circling the figure lying in the center—White Eagle, the elder who had led the ceremony in the hogan when she asked for help in building Legend City.

"He's leaving us now," Mercy whispered, "and this is the place his soul must depart."

Thinking the old man was dead, Lou was stunned now to see the old man's arm, thin and gnarled as a stick, rise from the rawhide stretcher. His eyes flickered open as he made a feeble beckoning gesture. To Mercy, Lou guessed, but from the other side of the circle Jesse stepped forward. He made his way to the stretcher, knelt down, and pressed the old man's hands between his own. Then White Eagle whispered, slipped his hands free, and placed them on Jesse's head in benediction.

The eleven remaining elders raised their withered, veined arms to the sky and intensified their chant. Their bodies shook in their grieving furor. The song rose to a wail as Jesse slipped something from under the old man's leather cloak. When Jesse started drawing in the dust, Lou recognized the scepterlike tool—the yarn-wrapped "talking prayerstick."

Deftly Jesse etched a series of figures: a thunderbird form, the mountain, and double diamonds with a dot in the center. Around them he quickly stroked a circle and a vast spray of rays, evidently representing the sun, then once more took up his kneeling position at the old man's side.

The chant grew louder, became a heartrending cry full of the men's inconsolable grief. The mountain seemed to pick up the song, and the elders' moaning was lifted higher and higher until the chant surrounded them like the wind itself.

The men lifted their eyes to the sky as they intoned the words, and then abruptly the chant died to a whisper, first as the men stilled their voices and again when the mountain let go of the echo. No one moved. The silence and the heat enveloped them.

Now the sudden quiet was broken by the beating of wings. From out of nowhere the enormous white bird glided into view. It flew in a narrowing spiral of circles, closing in to a single column of turns above the old man. Lou tugged Ben to her side.

The eagle descended gently to the stretcher's edge and perched, its enormous claws hooked over the wooden dowel holding the canvas to the frame, only inches from the old man.

The dying Indian made a motion to lift his head, but the exertion proved too much for him, and he lay back. His arms drifted up from his sides to touch the majestic bird, as if to draw it closer. Lou shrank back, but behind her she felt Mercy's soft touch on her shoulders and heard the old woman whisper soothingly, "There's nothing to fear, Lou."

The bird spread it wings wide now and opened its hooked white beak. From the throat a shrill cry issued, a pure high note. The cry of the eagle, like the chant of the elders, echoed across the mountain. But instead of fading, it returned with renewed strength.

It was no longer the warning caw of an eagle, but the cry of the mountain itself, of the whole earth. It rose higher and higher, louder and louder, until Lou had to clamp her hands over her ears. Even then it penetrated to her brain, an arrow of sound.

And now something was happening to the sun, the light changing.

All the others craned their heads to the sky as the eagle took flight.

The sun seemed to concentrate on the hovering bird. All around them it was as though the night had come quickly down, as though storm clouds had drifted across the face of the sun, leaving only one keyhole through which every ray was focused. Lou squinted and shaded her eyes from the shimmering light that coalesced and took shape around the bird. The vast floating yellow pool cast a golden shadow over the dying man, encompassing everything below, and the eagle and the old man were suspended together, motes of dust caught in the beam of a single spotlight, the very eye of the heavens.

The eagle's cry rose in one final caw and the corona

of golden white seemed to thicken into a nearly solid screen. Sparkling pinpoints of light melded together, so bright they blocked the view. The dying Indian had vanished in darkness, and the eagle itself shone as no more a blurry mass of movement.

And then, in one blinding explosive flash, the light was gone. The darkness was whisked away and it was day again.

On the stretcher the old man lay still as a stone.

"His soul has departed," Mercy said to Lou, a catch in her throat.

Lou saw Jesse rise from his knees. There was a new aspect to his bearing, a self-possession and confidence that had a kind of nobility, something . . . regal. It could have been in the grace of his stance as the eleven elders gathered around him, or his serenity in the presence of death. But mostly, Lou thought, the change came from inside him. Her fear of the boy, indeed her contempt for and near-hatred of him evaporated, supplanted by a feeling of respect, even awe.

She saw Jesse glance at Ben and smile, and in the smile was a hint of the boy again—the boy who had sat astride his horse not far from her door.

Above them now the bird hovered for another long moment, and then it took wing. It soared ever upward, first in a grand sweep over the entire plateau and then into the decreasing circles of its spiral.

Lou felt a warm hand clasp hers. It was Mercy. "Now?" the old woman asked again. "Do you understand now?"

Lou held Mercy's hand tighter, a signal of acceptance as she awaited an unfolding she knew would certainly come.

The eagle circled higher, now directly above Mercy and Lou.

Then Lou felt Boonie stir beside her, and she realized he was moving away. She turned quickly, saw him retreating.

"Boonie," she called softly.

He stopped and glanced around.

She tried to think of what to say, and decided they'd said it all.

He kept looking at her, though, and came near again. "I won't forget you, Lou," he said. "But I suppose you know that."

"No," she said quietly. "I didn't."

For an instant his sentiment made her wonder again if it wasn't possible that she could have a life with him—not merely live in his memory. But she knew now that he had to go, as surely as she had to stay.

"Good luck," she said.

He grinned, the soft smile she'd seen only once or twice before. "Don't worry about my luck," he said, and reached across one shoulder to slap the pack on his back. "From now on, I'm carrying mine with me." He winked, spun away, and started toward the ridge. She watched him for just a second, not wanting to see him actually vanish over the horizon.

She tilted her head back again and watched the eagle float higher. It was impossible to tell now the distance between them and the white bird, but the soaring shape still seemed as large as the sun itself. There was no gliding motion, no flapping of wings. The bird floated straight up, until one moment it was there and the next moment it was gone, merged into a cloud of purest white—the single cloud in an otherwise unbroken expanse of blue.

EPILOGUE

The Woman of Many Families

Lou propped the back door open with her foot as she edged into the kitchen carrying the two bags of groceries. She wanted to have Ben's favorites on hand. Real food now—he had at last outgrown his junk-food appetites. At the same time, she had surprised herself by learning how to cook—to *really* cook, not heat-in-the-oven dinners from packages but entire meals from scratch. No more store-bought bread, either; she baked her own. Who would have guessed that Lou Palmer, former construction executive, would develop such reverence for hearth and home?

Hefting a bag of flour onto the kitchen counter, she glanced up at the clock, wondering what time Ben would arrive. There were two buses each day from Phoenix, one at three in the afternoon, another at ten o'clock. She had wanted to be at the stop to meet Ben, but he'd said his plans were indefinite—depending on which flight he caught out of Boston. She was disappointed only because the welcome-home present she'd bought him would have made an especially nice surprise, waiting right there when he got off the bus. But it would keep. . . .

She finished shelving the groceries, scrawled a note to herself to check on her order for new saddles, and went to the front hall for the mail that had arrived while she was at the store. Quickly she flipped through the envelopes: a few bills, a subscription renewal for Rodale's gardening service, a notice of the lab charges for Ben's pre-med courses. Then, tucked in among the envelopes, she caught a flash of color: a postcard picturing a line of hula girls with HAWAII spelled out in a long flowery lei. Already guessing at the message she would find on the other side, she turned it over.

There it was, scribbled in pencil: "Happy Anniversary."

There was no signature, but she needed none. In all this time, there had been just two other cards, each bearing the same salutation. The first had come from Nova Scotia, of all places. And then the second, last year, from Hawaii as well. So it seemed that he had finally settled down.

Lou stood for a moment musing over the card, the coincidence of its arrival today while she was waiting for Ben. Had it been just five years to the day that they had found the gold? And had the woman obsessed with immeasurable riches really been her?

Sometimes she liked to think of that Lou Palmer as another person, an impostor who had worn her clothes and used her name, but who was only a distant and unpleasant cousin to the Lou Palmer she was now. If she had been different, she wondered, would Ted Lundberg and Capper Tate still be alive?

No, in the end she couldn't hold herself responsible. Elder Brother had been protecting his mountain. She gave herself the same explanation for the airplane crash that had killed Lawrence Honegger on the very day he departed from Legend Mountain.

Lou turned to the fireplace, her eyes grazing over the tintypes of the old Russian propped on the mantel, where they had been since Mercy moved them before she died. There, too, sat the burial bowl Mercy had willed to her, one of the old woman's final acts in those last days when she was too ill to do much of anything but lie on the couch and reminisce. Lou remembered how Mercy would sometimes pause, concerned that Lou had lost interest in her stories.

But Lou never did.

The clip-clop of a horse trotting up near the back of the house pulled Lou out of her reverie. She went outside and saw her horse trotting toward the barn to be groomed. It always returned alone, as its sire had for Mercy, and Lou moved down to the barn as it came in.

With long brush strokes she had begun to curry the horse when she heard a car pull up and a voice calling from near the house:

"Mom? Where are you?"

Lou stepped around the barn and saw the taxi pulling away. "Over here!" she called.

In loping strides, Ben came toward her, arms outstretched. The wariness and unease between them was long gone. If Lou held him back a second at arm's length, it was only to take in the changes that were always so noticeable after he'd been away for a few months. On every trip home he seemed to have grown more manly and self-assured. Matt's strong features had come to dominate his face along with those of her own father.

"Good trip?" she asked after they had embraced.

"Fine. I slept all the way out on the plane." He looped an arm around her waist and they began to move back toward the house. Looking around, he inhaled deeply and added, "God, it's good to be back here. I miss this place more each time I leave it."

Lou smiled, recalling the time when Ben had resented her bringing him here. "I'm glad you feel that way."

They were nearing the front of the house now, and Ben glanced to the shiny Mustang convertible standing in the driveway behind the old Jeep Renegade. "Who's visiting?" he said.

"Nobody," she answered.

"Mercy's old wagon finally giving out?"

"Nope. Solid as ever."

"But then . . . ?" The question faded as he caught Lou's broad smile.

"I know it's a month before your birthday," she said, "but I figured with your working out at the clinic this summer, I didn't want to be stranded here without my own car, so . . ."

"You're terrific!" Ben said. He swooped her into a quick hug and then broke away toward his new car. But after a couple of strides he stopped dead and looked back. "Hey, you *can* afford it, can't you? I mean, it's *your* money, not from . . . ?"

Lou laughed. "Ben! Of course it's my money."

He continued toward the car and had just opened the door when they were startled by a clattering gallop racing around the barn. They turned.

Jesse sat commandingly astride the animal, riding bareback as always. Lou could remember when he was just a sullen withdrawn boy, angry at the world and impatient with the members of his tribe who refused to live in the old ways. But in only a few years his new responsibilities had mellowed him. He bore clearly the stamp of a leader—though Lou still had difficulty imagining him sitting among the old men, being addressed reverently as White Eagle.

"How are you, Jesse?"

"Da-go-ta," Jesse replied warmly as he dismounted. "I'm fine. It's good to see you." He turned to Ben. "Someone in the tribe said he'd seen you get off the bus in town. He said you were even taller now than I am. But I told him it couldn't be so . . . and came to make sure." He put his arms straight out on Ben's shoulders as if measuring him, and for a moment his face remained a solemn mask. Then he broke into a laugh, and the two friends embraced.

"Now," Jesse said, "I want you to see the new eye-care wing we've built at the clinic and—"

"Hold on," Ben protested, laughing. "I got here five minutes ago. I haven't even had a chance to talk to Mom."

"It's all right, Ben. We'll talk later. Go with Jesse."

Ben kissed her and turned to the Indian. "Okay, but today, for a change"—he pointed to his new car—"we're taking *my* 'horse.' "

Lou stood by as the boys climbed into the car, and overheard Ben start to tell Jesse about his studies, and what he'd learned about new equipment that ought to be acquired for the clinic. "We should have some of that laser equipment for cataract surgery," he said. "It works miracles."

Miracles, Lou thought as the car went down the driveway. The Indians ought to have anything that worked miracles. She turned to look at the mountain. Later in the week, perhaps, it would be time for a trip out to the mine for a bar or two. Aside from equipment for the clinic, the reservation's roads needed paving again this summer, and the scholarship funds could stand replenishing.

The mountain held her attention for another moment, and she bowed her head slightly. Then, hearing a car approach, she wondered why Ben was coming back. As she turned, an enormous black Lincoln was pulling into the driveway. The driver parked, stepped out, and hailed her.

"Mrs. Palmer?" he called.

She ambled up the driveway to meet him. "Yes, I'm Lou Palmer," she said, extending a hand. The man was in his late twenties, tall and slender, wearing a summer-weight tan suit.

"Well, hi, good to meet you. I'm Don Cafferty." He glanced around. "Nice spread you have here."

"Thanks," Lou said genially. "What can I do for you?"

"I've just been in town, and everybody says you're the woman to see. I understand you own quite a bit of property hereabouts, and I'm looking to rent a house."

"I do have a few vacant places," Lou said.

"Well, I need something for about a year, maybe longer. A couple of bedrooms, since I'll be bringing my family out. I work for the Bartlett Corporation. Ever heard of us?"

"Oh, I think I have," Lou said, smiling wryly and pretending to think. "Construction business, isn't it?"

"Gee, that's right. You're pretty well-informed, Mrs. Palmer. I didn't think we had much of a name in Arizona."

"Seems I've read about you in the papers," Lou said. "Are you planning to build somewhere nearby?"

"Yes, we bought that big Legend Mountain tract

after the Honegger Corporation went into bankruptcy, and we're going to develop it."

"That right?" Lou said, aware that her aw-shucks manner was coming on a little thick. "What're you planning?"

"A big resort complex," said Cafferty proudly. "I think you'll be mighty impressed, Mrs. Palmer, when you see the plans."

"Call me Lou. Out here we don't hold so much with all the Mrs.-and-Mr. stuff. How big a resort will it be?"

"We're going to put half a dozen hotels right on the side of the mountain—tennis courts, pools, golf courses, the whole shebang."

"Well, that's interesting," Lou said. "I didn't imagine anyone would ever try that again. I mean, after what happened when we . . . when they tried to blast the last time."

Cafferty looked properly confident. "We've had some new studies done," he said. "And the reports all tell us that with the new vibration-proof foundations, and since we're only on the edge of the fault, we'll be able to build safely. I'm heading up the survey team, so I guess I ought to be here quite awhile."

Lou hesitated a moment, then hooked her arm through Cafferty's and started walking him toward his car. "You know," she said, "I've got a house I'll bet you'll like. A beautiful place, completely restored. Two bedrooms, big fireplace in the living room, and the backyard faces right out onto a glorious view of the mountain."

"Perfect," Cafferty said, beaming brightly with enthusiasm. "Sounds ideal, just the kind of place I'd like to spend a year or so."

"It's ideal, all right," Lou said with a pleasant smile. "But I tell you, I think maybe you'd be wise to rent on a month-to-month basis. . . ."

About the Author

NICHOLAS CONDÉ has been a journalist, a charter sailboat captain, and a farmer. He has lived in London, the Caribbean, New England, and now makes his home in New York. He is the author of *The Religion*, also available in a Signet edition.